Graham Greene and the Politics of Popular Fiction
and Film

Graham Greene and the Politics of Popular Fiction and Film

Brian Lindsay Thomson

First published 2009 by
PALGRAVE MACMILLAN

Palgrave Macmillan in the UK is an imprint of Macmillan Publishers Limited, registered in England, company number 785998, of Houndmills, Basingstoke, Hampshire RG21 6XS.

Palgrave Macmillan in the US is a division of St Martin's Press LLC, 175 Fifth Avenue, New York, NY 10010.

Palgrave Macmillan is the global academic imprint of the above companies and has companies and representatives throughout the world.

Palgrave® and Macmillan® are registered trademarks in the United States, the United Kingdom, Europe and other countries.

ISBN-13: 978–0–230–22854–2 hardback

This book is printed on paper suitable for recycling and made from fully managed and sustained forest sources. Logging, pulping and manufacturing processes are expected to conform to the environmental regulations of the country of origin.

A catalogue record for this book is available from the British Library.

Library of Congress Cataloging-in-Publication Data
Thomson, Brian Lindsay, 1976–
    Graham Greene and the politics of popular fiction and film /
    Brian Lindsay Thomson.
        p.   cm.
    Includes bibliographical references and index.
    ISBN 978–0–230–22854–2 (alk. paper)
    1. Greene, Graham, 1904–1991—Criticism and interpretation.   I. Title.
    PR6013.R44Z893 2009
    823′.912—dc22   2009013632

10   9   8   7   6   5   4   3   2   1
18   17   16   15   14   13   12   11   10   09

Printed and bound in Great Britain by
CPI Antony Rowe, Chippenham and Eastbourne

Contents

Acknowledgments

My deepest thanks to Dr. John Brannigan of University College Dublin (UCD), the best mentor I could have asked for and a good friend. Very special thanks also to Dr. Ron Callan, the first friendly face I encountered when I arrived in Ireland (though certainly not the last). Without their unflagging support, I probably would have collapsed well before reaching the finish line. I also owe many thanks to Professor Neil Sinyard of the University of Hull, whose passion for Greene and enthusiastic response to the manuscript helped convince me that I had perhaps written something that other people might want to read.

Thanks to Wm. Thomas Hill, who generously gave me a platform from which to offer my somewhat idiosyncratic views on Greene, and to Robert Murray Davis, whose kind words suggested that I might not be talking nonsense after all.

I would also like to thank Palgrave Macmillan, particularly Paula Kennedy, who was willing to gamble that a b-movie director could be capable of making an original contribution to the literature, and both Steven Hall and Priya Venkat, the unfortunate souls charged with the task of shepherding this book (and its rather sluggish author) to print.

The unsung heroes of the book are naturally the librarians and archivists who assisted me from first to last. Special thanks to the stewards of the collections at UCD, Trinity College Dublin, New York University, the University of Texas (UT) at Austin, the British Library, the National Library in Dublin, and especially the Harry Ransom Center (HRC) at UT. The HRC generously awarded me a research fellowship that enabled me to access material with a profound bearing on the political economy of creativity. Last but not least, I would like to thank the staff of the Bethpage Public Library, a small community library on Long Island that played a major role during the planning stages of this study.

While I offer no thanks to Micheál Martin, whose philistine public health agenda helped evict my colleague Dr. Malcolm Sen and I from our comfortable (albeit highly carcinogenic) offices amidst the rafters of Bewley's on Grafton Street, I do want to thank the barmen of Dublin's Northside, who helped ease the transition to a smoke-free Dublin while pouring the thousands of pints my comrades and I consumed while I was gradually hashing out a Marxist theory of reader response (and they were doing actual work). My thanks, solidarity, and love to

Dr. Enrico Terrinoni, Dr. Chiara Lucarelli, Dr. Ciara Hogan, Dr. Andrea Comincini, Dr. Andrea Binelli, Dr. Mirko Zilahy De'Gyurgyokai, Dr. Fergal Casey, Liam and Rita Kelly, Dr. Kate O'Malley, Dan O'Grady, Dr. John Gibney, Dr. Christopher Farrington, and Dr. Michelle O'Connell. *Venceremos*!

My final thanks go to my family: to my mother and father, who have continued to support me despite the demonstrable fact that their money would have been better invested in Lehman Brothers stock; to my Aunt Di, who cultivated both my curiosity and my sense of social justice during long discussions and many cigarettes over the holiday table; and to the love of my life, Dr. Tara Keenan-Thomson, the sexiest scourge of fascism ever to walk the earth.

Introduction: The Politics of Reading Greene

Toward the end of the first wave of critical interest in the fiction of Graham Greene, David Lodge observed that:

> The reception and reputation of Graham Greene's fiction is, indeed, a subject in itself. Briefly, he enjoys the admiration of reviewers, fellow novelists, and 'general readers,' who praise particularly his 'craftsmanship,' his ability 'to tell a story'; and of some critics with a vested interest in Christian or specifically Catholic literature. But in the mainstream of Anglo-American literary criticism his reputation does not ride so high.[1]

Lodge commented that even Greene's defenders had often succumbed to the temptation 'to abstract from the fiction the author's version of reality, measuring this against a supposedly normative version, rather than assessing the persuasiveness with which the novelist realized his vision'.[2] The method leaves much to be desired, particularly in its treatment (or non-treatment) of the writer's readers.[3] Greene's 'version of reality' is neither fully communicated in any of his novels, nor consistent over the course of his career. Conversely, distinguishing a normative version of reality from the opinion of a particular critic becomes more difficult the further one moves from broad generalizations. If, however, the reception and reputation of Greene's fiction can be considered as 'a subject in itself', then scholars' preference of this method above other, more persuasive critical modalities furnishes one of its central questions. The present study, 'Graham Greene and the Politics of Popular Fiction and Film', answers three questions that Greene's critics have often posed at a rhetorical level but only rarely addressed in more substantive terms: how did the writer become as popular as he did in the middle years of

1

the twentieth century, why have scholars (save those with 'vested interests') tended to neglect Greene and downplay the significance of his contribution to and influence upon twentieth-century fiction, and how have these two phenomena converged to influence the critical record on the subject of Greene's work?

The present study is thus by no means intended to serve as a survey of the work that Greene produced over the course of his very long career. During the early stages of my research I considered adhering to a more rigidly chronological framework that would have demanded close examination of a much broader cross-section of Greene's oeuvre than one will find on offer here. Ultimately, however, the critical record determined the texts included and omitted here, rather than personal preference or an inevitably inadequate desire to be comprehensive. In particular, the final third of Greene's career is considered here less for the responses the works themselves elicited from either the public or scholars than because their publication more often served as a staging area for retrospective analyses of Greene's career aimed at supporting or contesting his claim to the status of a 'Grand Old Man of English Letters'. Thus, for example, Bruce Bawer's venomous response to *The Captain and the Enemy* in the pages of *The New Criterion* seemed more pertinent to a discussion of Greene's reputation than the novel that occasioned it. The same can be said of films derived from Greene's work during this period. One will search in vain for filmmakers influenced by Otto Preminger's *The Human Factor*, and James Mason's performance as Doctor Fischer of Geneva has largely disappeared without a trace. If Maggie Smith's turn as Aunt Augusta in *Travels With My Aunt* was more widely revered than Orson Welles's Harry Lime, then the shape of the present study would certainly have reflected it—but this is simply not the case. These works arguably deserve consideration, but the goal of the present study was to understand and to communicate the significance of gaps in the critical record, rather than to fill those that I encountered with my own commentary.

For a writer regularly praised as 'the most distinguished English novelist writing today'[4] during his lifetime and as 'a major figure in 20th-century literature'[5] after his death, the critical record reveals an astonishing lack of curiosity on the part of scholars toward aspects of Greene's work that do not bear directly on the writer's life. A recent overview of Greene's work went so far as to explicitly locate the significance of the novels in the intersections between the 'author embodied in the works and the man whose personal life inevitably exerted a profound influence over those works'.[6] Mudford's 1996 pamphlet on

Greene charted a similar course and offered valid but ultimately irrelevant insights, such as: 'Without Catherine Walston, *The Heart of the Matter* would not have been completed, *The End of the Affair* would never have been written, and [Greene's] subsequent writing would have been very different.'[7] While a method like Mudford's may shed light on the personal significance of a given novel to its writer, it fails to illuminate how the work came to signify x to the publics for whom it was produced and packaged and by whom it was consumed and realized. Despite these crippling limitations the method has nonetheless dominated Greene studies.

Given the symbolism that characterizes several of Greene's most consistently valorized novels it is perhaps not surprising that this sort of interest has coalesced around the question of Greene's religious and quasi-religious beliefs. Was he an orthodox Catholic?[8] If not, then what was the substance of his heterodoxy?[9] Was Greene's early Catholicism later displaced by existentialist and/or Marxist convictions?[10] Were these later convictions held with the same sincerity (or lack thereof) as the earlier adherence to Catholic dogma?[11] Scholars tend to examine Greene's life more closely than his work to formulate their answers, and then interpret the work along whatever lines their biographical sketches suggest. In light of recent postgraduate work, there seems to be little enthusiasm for pursuing alternate approaches to Greene's fiction.[12]

Only rarely does one encounter scholarly work that attempts to situate Greene's work in a wider matrix of cultural negotiations. In the past 15 years, Diemert and Malamet have examined the uses Greene made of generic conventions that prevailed during different stages of his career (particularly those associated with 'the thriller').[13] Neither study succumbs to the scholarly penchant for identifying serious writers as 'those whom one could never suspect of writing with their reader in mind', to use Wayne Booth's apt formulation of academe's modernist and postmodernist bias.[14] Brian Diemert in particular seeks to grasp how Greene's texts operate through 'a complex series of relationships between readers and texts and among texts themselves'.[15] In what one may read as a retort to Diemert, Damon Marcel DeCoste argues that Greene was deeply influenced by literary modernism, but that literary modernism itself has been unjustly aligned with the forces of reaction: 'The masterworks of high modernism...convey a dread of the historical present, not as it fails to sustain past grandeur but as it tiresomely re-enacts past enormity.'[16] Thus, in DeCoste's view, Greene liquidates history in *The Ministry of Fear*, leaving behind only the liberal self doomed to heroically repeat the failure of self-creation amidst the ruins of a wilfully forgotten past—a reading that neatly dodges the need to historicize the ideology underpinning the concept of the masterwork, the alleged 'dreadfulness' of the modernist's present, and the implicit valorization of the liberal conception of the self. John Coates, by contrast, attempts less to focus on the writer's attitude toward history than to historicize the public's association with its syntactic features in his study of *The Confidential Agent*.[17] In a reading indebted to Northrop Frye, Brian Thomas has argued that *The Third Man* heralded Greene's (re)discovery of the romance.[18] Thomas Wendorf attempts something similar by examining Greene's and Tolkien's respective appropriations of quest-romance structures, although his neglect of the reader's role in generic processes renders his conclusion concerning the relationship between realism and fantasy more speculative than it might have been.[19] Nonetheless, each of these studies takes the student of Greene some distance from the grim rehearsal of the writer's idiosyncrasies that characterizes such a formidable part of the scholarly record.

These more conventional responses to Greene reflect in the field of aesthetics what John Kenneth Galbraith once referred to as the near-fetishization of production in contemporary economic thought: it is as an author or auteur, a producer of meaning (rather than a producer of texts) that Greene is considered when he is considered at all, rather than as someone who wrote texts that were also read by large sections of diverse populations.[20] Norman Sherry's authorized biography of Greene is a particularly clear demonstration of this tendency: his explicitly stated aim of 'resurrecting' the writer and those close to him led him to attempt to undergo the same experiences that Greene himself had undergone: travelling through Liberia, visiting the whorehouses of Vienna, and even—perhaps unintentionally—growing alienated from his wife.[21] The result is a project as ambitious and as futile as that of Pierre Menard, the Borges character who attempts to (re)write Cervantes's *Don Quixote*, verbatim and in the original Castilian, as a work of twentieth-century French modernism. Reading Sherry, one learns less about Greene than one does about contemporary tastes, interpretive priorities, and ideology as they are deployed in the contemporary practice of literary biography. On the one hand, Sherry represents the state of the art in Greene scholarship; on the other, he seems woefully out of step with the methodologies favored by contemporary intellectuals.

Despite the near-universal consensus that Sherry's third volume had fallen spectacularly short of its mark, consideration of the project (and speculation concerning the project's effect on Sherry's sanity) nonetheless occupied the front pages of literary magazines and newspaper supplements.[22] Whatever its status as an intellectual orthodoxy, the death of the author has not yet been recognized by the public at large. The writerly cult of personality remains an effective force in publishing houses and in universities, perhaps because it furnishes an easily comprehended and pedagogically amenable answer to the vexed question of how books come to mean something: they mean something because an author intends them to mean something.

From the very beginning of Greene's career, critics have paid little heed to the dialectical quality of literary meaning and have subsequently ignored consumption on the part of the reader or readers. Few literary critics today would agree that the production and consumption of fiction are mutually exclusive pursuits. Most would suggest that the answer lies somewhere between, that reading and writing become meaningful activities only as an act of collaboration (or, perhaps, confrontation) between readers and writers. Greene's critics, however, rarely take this view. Janice Radway could have been describing the general tenor of a huge proportion of Greene criticism when she characterized the attitude of romance readers to the fiction they read in her study *Reading the Romance*:

> They believe that meaning is *in* the words only waiting to be found. Reading is not a self-conscious, productive process in which they collaborate with the author, but an act of discovery during which they glean from her information about people, places, and events not themselves *in* the book. The women assume that the information about these events was placed in the book by the author when she selected certain words in favour of others. Because they believe words are *themselves already meaningful* before they are read, [they] accept without question the accuracy of all statements about a character's personality or the implications of an event.[23]

Rather than engage the fiction at a linguistic or rhetorical level, Radway's readers engage the fiction at the level of myth (the 'ideal romance') and end up reproducing ideological conditions conducive to the gender regime that encourages romance reading as a coping mechanism. The method of many Greene critics is strikingly similar: rather than engage the texts Greene produced, they engage the author and end up reproducing an intellectual regime that valorizes the peculiar concept of literature enunciated by Booth above and, alongside it, a solipsistic critical practice. John Spurling's fitfully insightful survey of Greene serves

as a case in point. The proposition that 'a writer can no more disguise…his distinctive voice, the pattern of his mind, than he can alter
his fingerprints' implies a clear methodology (isolating the distinctive
qualities of the voice, unravelling the pattern of the mind, and so on)
but also signals a clear bias toward the unique, the individual, and the
exceptional (all of which can only be located within the artist) at the
expense of the communal, the shared, and the conventional that serves
as the interface between writer and reader.[24] In one stroke Spurling
attempts to devalue *all* of Greene's comedies on the grounds that
the characters are 'dummies', that the 'conclusions are foregone', and
most significantly that the tone is 'derisive, if not actually vengeful'.[25]
Spurling suggests here that by revealing his contempt for his characters, Greene reveals himself, and thus contravenes the modernist—and
Leavisite/New Critical—prohibition on authorial intrusion.[26] Of course,
in order to recognize authorial intrusion in the comedies, Spurling must
have already formulated an idea of Greene (which he has done over
the course of his critique) that renders his own readings of those novels
he finds successful 'foregone conclusions' in the sense that these novels can be made to demonstrate the critic's own impression of Greene's
literary 'fingerprint'. Both Radway's romance readers and Greene's critics tend to read in order to discover meanings that have already been
placed there: in the former instance by the romance writer, and in the
latter by the critic himself.

To a large extent, Spurling's appropriation of the figure of Greene is
merely representative of the dominant critical practice in Greene studies, and not necessarily of broader theoretical or interpretive trends.
When scholars address Greene's work, they often do so through a discourse that is author-centric in Foucault's sense of the term ('the basis
for explaining not only the presence of certain events in a work, but also
their transformations, distortions, and diverse modifications'[27]), and
that consequently helps cultivate and maintain a number of myths that
the institutions which orchestrate contemporary society find useful: the
writer imagined as an essentially autonomous being, limited only by his
imagination and willingness to place his energies in the service of productive work; as a being who does not require communities in order to
realize his full potential; and consequently as one whose only struggle is
a fundamentally private, internal one.[28] For example, V.V.B. Rama Rao's
epic struggle to prove the thesis that 'Saintly sympathy is the characteristic feature of Greene's outlook' leads him to the unlikely observations
that in *The End of the Affair*, 'Parkis's boy…is really a Gothic element
which raises a good laugh', that 'the spirit of comedy' is enhanced by

'the deliberate introduction of God as an unseen but omnipresent character, making fools of everyone for His is the power and the glory for all that happens', and that 'the heroine's death also makes for comedy'.[29] Whether Rao could demonstrate such conclusions with reference to the rules and conventions that structure any existing interpretive community seems doubtful; the direct appeal to the writer's authoritative 'vision' conveniently sidesteps the need to substantiate such a reading by recourse to the way people actually read.

The principal aim of this study is to furnish students of Greene with some sense of how readers have participated in the development of Greene's reputation. They purchased and read his books *en masse*, making him a popular publishing phenomenon—a status which itself conferred upon the writer's future commentators an intriguing set of interpretive difficulties. Miriam Allott, for instance, has observed that because so many critics have believed that 'No really good or serious writer... could possibly be as popular as [Greene]' they have devoted themselves to resolving 'the paradoxical question of his enormous success'.[30] Greene's popularity as a writer (though not as a subject for scholarly inquiry) has lasted from 1932 until the present—a fact that seems to indicate that on some level readers have not only purchased the books and seen the films adapted from them, but that they have also responded to the techniques, tropes, interpretive clues, and narrative devices that Greene has presented in his work. In other words, for nearly 75 years readers have encountered in Greene's fiction ideas and themes that have engaged those tastes, biases, and prejudices which criticism in its most nostalgic mode has sometimes reduced to 'the spirit of the age'. Some of these tastes and biases have no doubt evolved from prior exposure to works of art, whether of the 'high' or 'low' variety, from the cinema palaces and the popular tradition of *film noir* as well as the rarefied traditions of modernist poetics. Other tastes and biases no doubt have evolved from the world beyond film and literature: from experience on the factory floor, from gazing up through the glass ceiling, or from sitting in a university chair. Not even Greene's critics doubt that there is a political dimension to all writing; few of them, however, have considered the political implications of reading his work, much less questioned how these political implications have shaped the range of things it is possible or desirable to write or say about Greene's fiction.

Psycho-biographical approaches may indeed help resolve the mystery of why Greene turned his attention to particular themes, or why he chose to develop those themes through particular tropes and narratives. At their best, surveys like Spurling's, polemics like those of John Atkins and Michael Shelden,[31] and other varieties of literary biography that aim to trace 'the trajectory and characteristics of the literary career: the kind of writer [Greene] became and why' may persuade readers to approach the fiction with a set of expectations that may prove productive in their textual encounters.[32] But these studies do not begin to explain—or generally *attempt* to explain—why the tropes and narratives in Greene's novels proved satisfying to a large enough section of the reading public to demand polemic or other scholarly appraisal.

In order to study these problems it is necessary to study the history of Greene's readerships. Naturally this presents its own set of problems: how does one gauge the way a readership responds to a work of literature, particularly when so many sections of the public leave few traces of their reading behind? After all, the 'common reader' is virtually by definition a reader who has no interest in communicating his or her experience of reading through journal articles, reviews, or classroom teaching. Thus 'uncommon readers'—readers whose thoughts and opinions on literature are valorized by the institutions with which they are affiliated: the university, the popular press, the cinema, and so on—tend to produce the material that the student of literature has at his or her disposal. A considerable part of the present study therefore concerns how the evolution of different institutions over the twentieth century helped shape the priorities of the readers associated with them, how the readings offered through these institutions constituted what Fredric Jameson has referred to as symbolic moves in the strategic and polemical confrontation between the classes, and how, specifically, these readings have helped produce a particular vision of Greene and his work.[33] Fortunately, many uncommon readers—particularly reviewers and film producers—have addressed their polemics to common readers, so that if it is not possible to 'know' common readers, it is at least possible to understand how different institutions imagine (or construct) them and make use of the tastes, biases, and prejudices they attribute to them.

This study offers a detailed analysis of five of Greene's novels: *Stamboul Train* (1932), *The Third Man* (1949), *The End of the Affair* (1951), *The Quiet American* (1954), and *Our Man in Havana* (1958). While these analyses may suggest new avenues of interpretation for the texts in question, they do not aim at suggesting that Greene's work should rightfully occupy a different place amidst the ethno-spatial-temporal tangle of contemporary canons, but rather question why, as Elliott Malamet has observed, the problem of Greene's canonicity has had such a profound effect on shaping critical responses to the work.[34] By applying the methods of reader-response to both Greene's texts and the polemical responses they have occasioned one can grasp the difference between the range of interpretations texts might reasonably sustain and the range of interpretations that scholars working under different professional regimes have required those texts to sustain. What artistic conventions have Greene's novels drawn upon and deployed? What sort of 'stock responses' have these conventions demanded from those who had previously been exposed to them, and how did the novels sometimes transform their readers' horizons of expectations? What extra-artistic conventions, biases, and prejudices did the novels exploit? What were the political ramifications of engaging with Greene's novels: did they unsettle readers' convictions, reassure them of their convictions' propriety, or encourage them to pass over the novels in respectful or indifferent silence? To be certain, these questions do not dismiss the question of 'authorial intention' as an irrelevance; nor, however, do they propose that the meaning of the work is an extension of the author's personality as in some of the more extreme strains of *auteur* theory. Instead, following Booth, the intention of the author is considered in the light of a reader-oriented rhetoric, as a strategy for configuring one's expectations and interpretations over the course of a novel.

By coming to terms with the decisions readers are called upon to make as they read Greene's novels—rather than with the meanings which, from the vantage of psycho-biographical approaches, Greene has already placed in the novels *before* reading—the study will help show what sorts of interpretive strategies have been privileged (and which marginalized or ignored) in Greene criticism. In this respect, the study applies Peter Rabinowitz's elaboration of the potential for political critique implied by Booth's methods. He views the author not primarily as a static entity that vouchsafes textual meaning but rather as an element of the dynamic process by which readers distance themselves from their immediate concerns and circumstances in order to participate in the realization of a text's meaning. Readers attempt to read as an author intends them to read, not because they necessarily believe that an all-powerful author has invested a text with significance but because fiction deploys rhetorical devices, generic conventions, and meta-textual cues to signal how it desires a reader to react.[35] (One does not, for instance, need to plumb the depths of Greene's allegedly Jansenist theology in order to grasp the fact that he 'intends' for readers to see *Brighton Rock's* Pinkie as a youth with unwholesome proclivities.) On the basis of this sort of authorial reading it becomes possible to explore both the political and ideological demands a text makes on its readers and the fashion in which these demands support or come into conflict with prevailing ideology. Rabinowitz illustrates this point with reference to *War and Peace*, noting that if one does not acknowledge that the narrative encourages the reader to construe Natasha's victimization as a reward, 'Tolstoy's misogynist text is indistinguishable from feminist irony.'[36] By focusing principally on Greene's personal stances instead of on the stances the texts he produced encourage their readers to adopt, a large portion of Greene criticism has at best neglected the political dimension of his work and, at worst, actively attempted to render it invisible.

Grasping the significance of these critical choices, omissions, and evasions is the second aim of this study, and demands a historical analysis of the ideologies and institutions which have cultivated particular methods of inquiry at different times and in different places, and which have indirectly furnished critical practitioners with material suited to their methods. Greene's critical star was in the ascendant for a relatively brief time—roughly the two decades following the Second World War—when a generation of scholars trained in Leavisite and New Critical methodologies found themselves part of an institution undergoing profound professional change in order to accommodate the beneficiaries of both the nascent welfare state and, in Britain and America, the long boom that Eric Hobsbawm (among others) has identified as the Golden Years of western capitalism.[37] As the profession grew, and the need for accreditation grew alongside it, the range of material that constituted 'suitable literature' for study broadened to an extent that a 'popular but serious' writer like Greene could be incorporated into scholarly discourse, often through the nascent auteurist sensibility. This period thus witnessed the first attempts at providing sustained accounts of Greene's achievement.

The rhetoric and content of these analyses bore the imprint of their time, particularly in terms of the institutional pressures brought to bear on the act of reading *as* an intellectual. As E.M. Forster had predicted in the late 1920s and the Leavises had lamented in the 1930s and 1940s, the function of the university in general and the humanities in particular changed as the societies that sustained them changed.[38] Resenting the commercialization of the study of literature (a by-product of the commercialization, or pragmaticization, of the university), intellectuals tended to favor reading strategies that, in Terry Eagleton's words, reflected the conviction that English represented 'the very spirit of the social formation'.[39] But as institutions changed, so too did the theoretical frameworks that supported them. Thus mastery of I.A. Richards's 'psychological theory of value'—a method of reading, rather than a body of knowledge—gradually gave way to mastery of an esoteric body of auteurist knowledge as an emblem of one's intellectual credentials.[40] Needless to say, this development had a considerable impact on what it was possible or desirable to say about Greene's work, and influenced the way that future scholars felt comfortable assessing that work. (When a large number of intellectuals agree to recognize a writer as a 'Catholic author', for instance, analysis along different lines becomes less likely.) By even the early 1970s Greene had become merely 'the largest living novelist in English' (as the front page of a *New York Times* review heralded him), a status that implied appreciation rather than analysis.[41] In short, two decades before Greene's death critical interest had already begun to settle within its present boundaries: a reserve for evangelicals, eccentrics, and enthusiasts—but not for serious scholars.

For understanding the institutional significance of responses to Greene's work the methods of cultural materialism complement the methodologies of reader response, particularly as the latter have been formulated by Booth and developed by Rabinowitz. Although numerous intellectuals appropriated Greene in order to make symbolic moves in the polemical and strategic confrontation between the classes, the broader intellectual community was hardly obliged to validate them. It is one thing to grasp why a critic like David Pryce-Jones might have responded ambiguously to Greene's work in the early 1960s and then venomously upon a reassessment published in the late 1980s; it is quite another to grasp why an organ like the *New Republic* would choose to publish Pryce-Jones's response and inject it into the fields of intellectual and public discourse.[42] In other words, it is not enough to suggest that Greene is in some way significant because his work provokes a response from intellectuals; if he is significant, it is because institutions have invested these responses with some measure of authority. As Louis Althusser has argued, the primary responsibility of all institutions must be to reproduce the conditions of their existence, and Greene's significance (or insignificance) to intellectual institutions can therefore be gauged by the extent to which responses to his work have aimed at reproducing the ideology of the prevailing relations of production.[43] If, as Robert Murray Davis and Alan Warren Friedman have argued, Greene's work no longer appears particularly productive of scholarly analysis, then the reason would appear to lie partly with Greene's work (which sustains a large but limited variety of interpretations) and partly amidst the difficulties scholars confront in reconciling their own responses to Greene's work with the sort of responses privileged at any given time by academic discourse.[44]

The first half of this study thus considers the transformation of Greene's reputation from that of a minor failed novelist to that of a popular writer and finally to that of a cinematic author (or auteur); the second, the transformation from cinematic author to quasi-canonical curiosity. The study explores the discursive qualities of these transformations, rather than their personal or psychological significance for Greene: how and why have critics 'spoken' Greene in different ways over the course of his career? What institutional priorities have made these discursive transformations possible or desirable? *Stamboul Train*, the focus of the first section, constituted an abrupt and permanent departure from the mannerisms (and commercial failure) of Greene's three prior novels. Although these early novels seemingly represent a sort of blind alley for the scholar interested in the development of Greene's technique, they arguably had an impact on contemporary critics' assessments of Greene's more popular work and the subsequent development of his reputation. Even more importantly, however, *Stamboul Train* arrived at a time when Leavisite priorities and methodologies were assuming the hegemonic position in the humanities that they would maintain throughout the most prominent period of scholarly interest in Greene. Specifically, the study examines how and why Greene's critics insisted on labeling his work cinematic, and how this designation shaped the sort of critiques it was possible to make of Greene. The label, after all, implied many of the stylistic features and techniques associated with high modernism—manipulation of point-of-view, the use of free indirect discourse and interior monologue, and so forth—without necessarily implying that the writer had deployed these techniques to worthy ends.

The second section focuses on *The Third Man*, the most spectacular of Greene's (literally) cinematic successes. Its producers released the film at a moment when critical antagonism toward the cinema had begun to wane in the face of a surge of self-consciously 'art-house' films from continental Europe. The stench emanating from the 'cinematic writer' label had begun to lose its pungency partly on aesthetic grounds, but also on professional ones. The institutional legitimization of the auteurist sensibility can also be traced to a historical development of this period: the divestment of the Hollywood theatrical distribution apparatus from its major studio owners as the result of a Supreme Court antitrust decision. Ironically, the studio's 'bigger, brasher, better' approach to limiting the potentially damaging effects of market forces led to a generally favorable revaluation of extant cinema and helped create a market for riskier (and often less profitable) independent productions, of which *The Third Man* continues to be held up as an example.[45] All of these developments helped pave the way for the first wave of scholarly appraisals of Greene's work by altering the standards by which academics could judge it. Thus while critics were powerless to make Greene an unpopular writer, they could at least appropriate work like *The Third Man* as an anti-popular polemic and situate Greene among the auteurs.

With *Our Man in Havana*, Greene began to double back over some of the themes he had explored in his previous novels, although his treatment of these themes was far less sympathetic and less capable of sustaining the sort of earnest critiques that had recently begun to crystallize around his earlier work. A novel that could be read as dismantling political agency as a valid concept, illustrating the futility of nationalism, and suggesting that family was the only possible medium for the expression of commitment sat uneasily in proximity to a novel like *The Quiet American*, whose rapturous reviews had rushed to announce a new Sartre preaching the gospel of existential engagement. In a political environment dominated by the growth of transnational corporations and the needs of an internationally financed, permanent war economy, and in a social environment producing human beings capable of transforming uncertainty and paranoia into the professional virtue of adaptability, such a *volte-face* was not necessarily problematic; but in an intellectual environment reacting to those political and social disturbances with musty Leavisite and New Critical axioms and avant-garde theories of meaning as the direct expression of an artist's personality, this same *volte-face* appeared intolerable: it demonstrated for many intellectuals (like Bawer and Pryce-Jones) that Greene could never have been serious in the first place, and forced those intellectuals who believed that he had been serious to pursue increasingly abstruse, sometimes mystical, methods of reconciling the writer to the work he had produced.[46]

The final section considers *The End of the Affair* and *The Quiet American*, two novels that Greene produced at the height of his public fame, to which reviewers responded kindly, that have sustained criticism in one form or another since their publication, and that have been deemed suitable for cinematic adaptations in recent years. The handsomely produced, big-budget film adaptations unsurprisingly sparked a brief flowering of comment in the popular and scholarly presses, and so help the student of Greene to gauge with some precision how the things different institutions permit one to say about Greene have altered over time. Specifically, the chapter considers how both *The Quiet American*'s metamorphosis into a travel guide for well-heeled expatriates and international venture capitalists, and the straight-faced fixation of reviewers on the question of whether Neil Jordan's version of *The End of the Affair* had been 'faithful' to Greene's novel demonstrate how the anxiety of the postwar settlement has gradually become the conventional wisdom. Intellectual responses to this anxiety—particularly the development of new methodologies and shifting fields of institutional legitimacy—have come to pose a perhaps insoluble problem for the modern student of Greene: to take his work seriously in the context of postmodern discourses is to be confronted with decisions that demand to be made, but which postmodern discourses insist cannot be made. Scholars, however, cannot flout postmodern discourses without running the risk of compromising their claims to institutional validation.

For a brief period in the 1970s and the early 1980s cultural studies seemed likely to furnish an exit strategy for those trapped in this particular manifestation of the professional/hermeneutic circle. Early efforts to theorize an 'organic' conception of culture and later emphases on signifying practices vigorously included both manifestations of popular culture and a reception-oriented critique of the ideological structures bound up with those manifestations. In his essay on 'The Rediscovery of Ideology' Stuart Hall formulated the cultural studies project in terms quite similar to those of the present study:

> First, how did a dominant discourse warrant itself as *the* account, and sustain a limit, ban, or proscription over alternative or competing definitions? Second, how did the institutions which were responsible for describing and explaining the events of the world . . . succeed in maintaining a preferred or delimited range of meanings in the dominant system of communications? How was this active work of privileging or giving preference practically accomplished?[47]

But as Robert Scholes and Robert Young have pointed out, the impact of Reagan's and Thatcher's educational policies forced the fledgling discipline into a corner. Young observed that 'When theorists found themselves wanting to defend their disciplines against successive government cuts they discovered that the only view with which they could vindicate themselves was the very one which, in intellectual terms, they wanted to attack.'[48] The practical necessity of resolving this difficulty arguably pushed cultural studies toward the pluralist strategy of inclusion on the grounds of 'race, class, and gender' that has gained ground in the field since the late 1980s. On none of these grounds, of course, does Greene resemble a figure in need of rescuing.

That Greene will continue to be read for the foreseeable future seems likely—but by whom? To what ends? In the past, when Greene's work has been read at all, it has been read as the work of a great, good, or (occasionally) bad author: that is, as texts that do not require readers to realize their significance. As such, the critical work Greene's fiction has occasioned has tended to conceptualize writing as an activity that in any ideological sense lacks 'values'; a symbolic move ostensibly aimed at maintaining the myth that both critical activity and the institutions that sponsor it are somehow neutral. By analyzing how critical responses to Greene have indeed communicated very particular schemes of value the present study offers a means of grasping the readers' significance in the production of meaning vis-à-vis both Greene's work and the productive institutions of literature at large.

Part I

From Failed Novelist to Popular Writer

1

Institutional and Critical Priorities at the Beginning of Graham Greene's Career

Neither the great authors of the twentieth century nor the great authors of any other century ever sat down and wrote 'literature'. They wrote texts that became books (i.e., physical objects: manuscripts set by printing houses and published in hardcover or paperback, usually with financial backing from an investor). People read them for pleasure and enlightenment. Some books disappeared quickly because people decided that not reading them made them feel more pleased and enlightened than reading them did. Other books remained in print for years because people never tired of reading them—or at the very least never tired of buying them.

Only books that appealed to a very particular type of reader became 'literature'. Publishers, for instance, desired to know what sort of books people bought and rarely troubled themselves with the question of whether the fiction that filled their lists was literature. Stanley Unwin went so far as to suggest that publishers spent their time far more profitably in conversation with booksellers than with writers.[1] Many intellectuals, on the other hand, would have found conversation with a bookseller entirely beside the point—unless, of course, they desired to document the decay of public tastes, as Q.D. Leavis did in her 1932 study, *Fiction and the Reading Public*.[2] They preferred the conversation of the artist, who 'is concerned with the record and perpetuation of the experiences which seem to him most worth having [and who] is also the man who is most likely to have experiences of value to record'.[3] Both publishers and intellectuals could claim knowledge of a kind of truth, even if it was only a partial one: the publishers saw reading as principally a social phenomenon, since they could hardly expect to continue making a comfortable living without appealing to a relatively broad cross-section of the public. The intellectuals (who primarily worked for universities, or else did not have to work at all) saw reading as an individual endeavor, since they could hardly maintain their social eminence without fiction that suggested, in one way or another, the inadequacy of their society's tastes. In intellectual circles, then, the publisher's opinion would not have carried much weight (and vice versa) because the institutions that fostered both sorts of readers had different priorities and worked toward conflicting ends.

Few phenomena illuminate the different positions of the intellectuals and the publishers as clearly as the development of popular literacy. The Education Act of 1870 had made it possible for local authorities to frame by-laws rendering attendance at elementary schools compulsory, while Disraeli's Act of 1876 required children to complete their elementary education and obtain a certificate before they could join the workforce.[4] In 1881, the Education Act consolidated these gains and made provision for the finance of free, compulsory education on the US model. Within two generations, urban illiteracy had nearly disappeared. More importantly—from the perspective of publishers and intellectuals—a new kind of reader had appeared.

As the market for reading matter expanded entrepreneurs quickly stepped in to meet the increased demand for books and newspapers. As Chomsky and Herman document in *Manufacturing Consent*, exponentially increasing demand compelled newspaper publishers to adopt economies of scale. They required more capital for investment, more machinery, and larger distribution networks in order to reach the growing reading public. Chomsky and Herman observe that 'the total cost of establishing a national weekly on a profitable basis in 1837 was under a thousand pounds, with a break-even circulation of 6,200 copies.... *The Sunday Express*, launched in 1918, spent £2,000,000 before it broke even with a circulation of over 250,000.'[5] The number of entrepreneurs with access to the necessary resources plummeted as the nineteenth century wore on, and the media became concentrated in fewer, more genteel hands. The cost of the newspapers themselves declined as clever owners discovered that the real profits in the business came from advertising revenue rather than from sales, and that a growing circulation provided the best means of ensuring the growth of that revenue source.[6] The boom in popular literacy had no real 'down side' for the entrepreneur who could access enough capital to exploit it.

Critics like Q.D. Leavis, F.R. Leavis, I.A. Richards, and T.S. Eliot saw the matter from a different vantage point: for them, popular literacy had led inexorably to a decline in cultural standards. When only the educated aristocracy and a small cadre of self-educated men had read fiction, they had read fiction composed by writers who were, de facto, their intellectual equals. Q.D. Leavis argues:

> It could never occur to a novelist of Scott's day that there could be any other public to address than one's peers, and Scott exhibits accordingly the dignity of a well-bred man who is sure of himself and his audience, he has none of Thackeray's uneasiness. For all his yawns and indolence and stiffness Scott has a splendid self-assurance which Lytton in the next generation woefully lacks, but then Lytton had discovered how to exploit the market.[7]

She objects less to the competitive aspect of the literary market than to the growth of the successful 'firm' (poor fiction) and its efforts to secure itself against market forces through the cultivation of easily satisfied consumer demand (i.e., the debasement of popular taste). For Leavis, popular literacy makes the production of good literature unfeasible by allowing 'mass man' to supplant the natural aristocrat as the predominant participant in the literary economy.

> Whereas in George Eliot's time literature had paid, that is to say, a serious novelist could make a handsome living without surrendering anything, by Conrad's it had ceased to do so. Novelists of the stamp of Gissing and Henry James…cannot in any case hope to make a living from their novels.[8]

As publishers adapted to economies of scale, they began to make their profits through wide distribution rather than from expensive but limited editions. In order to secure wide distribution, publishers needed to select material that would appeal to readers with diverse backgrounds, interests, and tastes. Had the reading public remained smaller, or had the state remained content to treat literacy as a problem better suited to individual initiative than to public provision, then the publishers would have had no choice but to continue those commercial practices which Leavis and others believed had proved conducive to literary achievement in the past.

Leavis's verdict was perhaps more prophetic than indicative of existing conditions since the process of corporate consolidation took far longer in the book trade than in the newspaper industry, partly because of the dynastic character of the major houses, and partly because many firms' overheads did not demand economies of scale until the Second World War paper-rationing crisis and the postwar spread of television forced the industry into a crisis. Nonetheless, as early as 1880, 55 years before Penguin inaugurated the paperback revolution, George Hutchinson began publishing 'sixpenny Blacks', inexpensive paperbacks that catered to an expanding working-class audience.[9] The commercial imperative continued to assume a larger role in the trade as audiences grew until, by 1950:

> ... only the smallest firms, content to remain small, could continue to float a list by bringing out a book or two, issuing review copies, subscribing titles to the trade through shared travellers, and distributing the resulting orders, hand-packed, perhaps by the directors. For the medium or large-sized firm, a network of experts came to seem essential.[10]

This network of experts increased the costs of production and gradually pushed the book trade in the same direction the newspaper magnates had taken earlier.

For Leavis and the critics of her generation, the growth of the reading public implied a plunge into the murky waters of commercialism, emotionalism, and anti-intellectualism first charted by Lord Northcliffe, proprietor of the *Daily Mail*. Graves and Hodge suggest that Northcliffe had effectively invented the modern newspaper by adopting the policy of 'giving the people what they want' and by expanding the definition of 'news' to include not only 'what men talked about in clubs. [Northcliffe] knew it to be also what people talked about in kitchen, parlour, drawing-room, and over the garden wall; namely other people.'[11] Leavis and her fellow critics, however, did not admit the possibility that 'the people' could want anything worth having and so excised them from 'society':

> 'Society' was to be interpreted in the eighteenth-century sense in which, like 'the world,' it meant a select, cultured element of the community that set the standards of behaviour and judgment, in direct opposition to the common people ... [The] individual has a better chance of obtaining access to the fullest (because finest) life in a community dominated by 'society' than in one protesting the superiority of the herd.[12]

No responsible newspaperman or publisher could have endorsed such a sentiment through corresponding actions—not because they could not agree in principle, but because the institutions that supported them could no longer function in isolation from 'the common people'. By contrast, intellectuals could hardly reject such sentiments since the institutions that supported them—particularly the universities—existed precisely to allow some people to distinguish themselves *from* 'the herd'. In 1931, only four children out of every thousand who received an elementary education managed to progress to the university; far fewer than one in every thousand managed to get a place at Oxford or Cambridge[13]—which, along with Trinity College Dublin, constituted 'one grade' with other universities lumped together as 'the rest'.[14] As Leavis and others noted, however, the university could not survive for long as a mechanism for natural selection of the fittest minds in an era of profound—often democratic—social transformation.

In his Clark Lectures to the students of Cambridge E.M. Forster remarked on the novel phenomenon of 'the pseudo-student' who undertook a course of study not to attain mastery over his chosen field but rather to increase his ability to climb the social ladder.

> A paper on *King Lear* may lead somewhere, unlike the rather far-fetched play of the same name.... As long as learning is connected with earning... so long must we take the examination system seriously. If another ladder to employment was contrived much so-called learning would disappear, and no one be a penny stupider.[15]

By the time Forster delivered his lecture, employers had ceased to consider simple literacy much of an accomplishment; it no longer served to distinguish the deserving from the undeserving, or to identify from a crowd of working-class children the handful who had taken their first steps toward becoming 'self-made men'. That work had passed to the exam system, and required institutional participation rather than individual achievement (through self-tuition, for example, as Leavis preferred). Although Forster clearly resented earning's connection with learning, he also clearly felt that the pseudo-scholar who attended university to pass his exams did not learn anything truly worth knowing anyway: the system reserved 'true' knowledge only for those students who could free themselves from worldly concerns. In a sense, education had become more valuable but less valued—a situation that Richards and the Leavises attempted to overturn.

The fact that few people could hope to free themselves from commerce presented a serious obstacle to Leavisite ambitions. Taxes on the wealthy had increased from 8 percent prior to the First World War to nearly a third of one's income after it, thus contributing to the reintegration of the rich into the world of business throughout the inter-war period. His future no longer a foregone conclusion at birth, the aristocratic scion could no longer consider the diploma on his wall simply a handsome adornment. Commercial society could not afford the arbitrary genetic niceties underlying the sort of quasi-feudal society eulogized by the likes of Ford Madox Ford in his novel *The Good Soldier* or agitated for by Q.D. Leavis in her *Fiction and the Reading Public*. A talent for making money was not, after all, one that could be easily passed along a bloodline.

In addition, the modest redistribution of wealth through public services, unemployment insurance for select industries, and the temporary production boom manufactured by the war created new opportunities for members of the working class to improve their social position, particularly through higher education and the examination system disparaged by Forster. The First World War helped in this respect by nurturing conditions that demanded the development of a primitive meritocratic system. A.J.P. Taylor observes that while the state was nearly invisible before the war, during the war 'The Englishman's food was limited, and its quality changed by government order. His freedom of movement was restricted; his condition of work prescribed. Some industries were reduced or closed, others artificially fostered.'[16] An increase in the number of regulations necessitated an increase in the number of regulators, thus contributing to the growth of the civil service. The same changes that signaled the beginning of downward mobility for the hereditary aristocracy signaled upward mobility for the working classes, for whom an education no longer implacably signified the certificate required to work in a munitions factory: there were not, after all, enough Oxbridge graduates to sufficiently man the whole ship of state.

The growth of the state not only absorbed a larger portion of the body politic than it ever had before: with increased prosperity the 'common people' began to play a different role in the nation's economic life. Feudalism and early industrialism had theorized the working classes primarily as producers or, at best, as the middle-men of distribution networks. Following the war, industry began to see them as Northcliffe had seen them: through the pound-colored lens of consumerism. Working-class purchasing power was a necessary component of the overall success (or failure) of the British economy—an insight J.M. Keynes developed throughout the Great Slump and synthesized in his *General Theory of Employment, Interest and Money* (1936). By 1930 Keynes had already suggested turning away from the orthodox economic policies relentlessly advocated by Philip Snowden, the Chancellor of the Exchequer in Macdonald's second Labour government, who had believed that 'a balanced budget was the greatest contribution which a government could make to overcoming the Depression'.[17] Keynes revealed the paradox Snowden had resolutely ignored:

> It is the characteristic of a boom that [businesses'] sale-proceeds exceed their costs; and it is the characteristic of a slump that their costs exceed their sales-proceeds. Moreover, it is a delusion to suppose that they can necessarily restore equilibrium by reducing their total costs, whether it be by restricting their output or cutting the rates of remuneration; for the reduction of their outgoings may, by reducing the purchasing power of the earners who are also their customers, diminish their sale-proceeds by a nearly equal amount.[18]

Instead, market instability necessitated that somebody—presumably the state—guide the 'invisible hand' of neoclassical theory by injecting money into the economy in order to increase the purchasing power of the earners without forcing businesses to cut output. The steps that governing and private interests had taken in this direction—unemployment insurance , the nascent meritocracy, experimental schemes of consumer credit, and so forth—had two effects: they lay the groundwork for the explicitly interventionist policies undertaken during the Second World War and they pragmatically served to reduce the threat of social unrest (a major concern after the General Strike of 1926) by reformulating the central questions of class struggle in terms of individual gain rather than collective achievement. The consumer society to which Keynesian economics gave rise gently prompted the worker to forget alienation from his labor and to concentrate on alienation from his neighbor, since the business of 'keeping up with the Joneses' literally fuelled the economic recovery while contributing to a widespread (though hardly universal) rise in material standards of living.

As with the 'problem' of popular literacy, members of different institutions grappled with the 'problem' of a more equitable distribution of wealth, opportunity, and leisure in different ways. Commercial interests, like the publishers and newspapermen before them, took the opportunity to begin adapting their operations to take advantage of the benefits accruing to economies of scale—not only greater profits but also greater security from the sort of 'market forces' that had decimated Britain in the wake of Wall Street's collapse. The intellectuals unsurprisingly protested against the commercialization of culture. Q.D. Leavis suggested that 'commercial and economic machinery' that had 'assumed such a monstrous impersonality that individual effort towards controlling or checking them seems ridiculously futile' had exacerbated the cultural decline prompted by the spread of popular literacy.[19] Here, however, the Leavisites encountered a tactical conundrum: despite the futility of individual resistance, contempt for 'the common people' made wide-scale resistance untenable. After all, in F.R. Leavis's *Mass Civilization and Minority Culture* the leading intellectual of the day had unambiguously declared his belief in the aristocracy of talent:

> In any period it is upon a very small minority that the discerning appreciation of art and literature depends: it is (apart from cases of the simple and familiar) only a few who are capable of unprompted, first-hand judgment. They are still a minority, though a larger one, who are capable of endorsing such first-hand judgment by genuine personal response. The accepted valuations are a kind of paper currency based upon a very small proportion of gold. To the state of such a currency the possibilities of fine living at any time bear a close relation.[20]

The problem provoked various responses. Leavis himself eventually wrote *The Great Tradition*, which furnished the second-class minority with judgments to which they could assent: 'The great English novelists are Jane Austen, George Eliot, Henry James, and Joseph Conrad—to stop for the moment at that comparatively safe point in history.'[21] Q.D. Leavis advocated—in pristine Leninist prose—'resistance by an armed and conscious minority' whose missionary zeal would find an outlet in 'pamphlets and publications by a private Press with a conscious critical policy'.[22] Richards articulated a less ambitious but more practicable plan in *Principles of Literary Criticism*:

> To habilitate the critic, to defend accepted standards against Tolstoyan attacks, to narrow the interval between these standards and popular taste, to protect the arts against the crude moralities of Puritans and perverts, a general theory of value, which will not leave the statement 'This is good, that bad,' either vague or arbitrary, must be provided.[23]

Although the Leavisites did not manage to stop the commercialization of culture in the 1930s, they did manage to transform the study of literature. Terry Eagleton observes that:

> In the early 1920s it was desperately unclear why English was worth studying at all; by the early 1930s it had become a question of why it

was worth wasting your time studying anything else. English was not only a subject worth studying, but *the* supremely civilizing pursuit, the spiritual essence of the social formation.[24]

Richards might have failed to produce a theory capable of explaining in absolute terms why a poem was 'good' or 'bad', but his theories of poetry nonetheless gave rise to a pedagogical practice uniquely suited to the political and ideological demands of the times. He took the first steps toward transforming the distinguishing characteristic of the intellectual from *what* he read to *how* he read—arguably a necessary step in the professionalization of literature but also one that would later endanger the Leavisite project. As Jonathan Culler remarks of the American New Criticism that evolved partly from Richards:

> Those old enough to have experienced the transition, its emergence from an earlier mode of study, speak of the sense of release, the new excitement breathed into literary education by the assumption that even the meanest student who lacked the scholarly information of his betters could make valid comments on the language and structure of the text. No longer was discussion and evaluation of a work something which had to wait upon acquisition of a respectable store of literary, historical, and biographical information.[25]

Students from poor and working-class backgrounds could meet the children of privilege on an infinitely more level playing field than had previously been available: they had only to recognize the autonomy of the text, and apply themselves to showing 'how [a poem's] various parts contribute to a thematic unity' while doing so 'without reference to possible external contexts, whether biographical, historical, psychoanalytic or sociological'.[26] The method struck a neat balance between equipping students with a practical skill, enabling them to appreciate the superior judgment of their betters (who chose the texts they studied and suggested the themes to whose unity the various parts of the poem contributed), and instilling a 'natural' contempt for the producers, products and consumers of 'mass culture' which privileged 'crude, elementary prose, carefully constructed in phrases and simple sentences so as to read with the maximum ease'.[27]

In this respect the Leavisite program built on the recommendations that Sir Henry Newbolt published in his government-sponsored report on the teaching of English in England in 1921. Newbolt recognized that classics could no longer form the basis of a scholarly curriculum for an institution that needed to produce not only scholars and intellectuals, but also the new administrative class. For these purposes Newbolt deemed the study of English both as language and as literature more appropriate, since 'it would have a unifying tendency'.[28] Although Newbolt explicitly frames his argument in terms of 'class', his use of the word 'class' carries few of the economic connotations conventionally associated with the term:

> Two causes, both accidental and conventional rather than national, at present divide one class from another in England. The first of these is a marked difference in their modes of speech. If the teaching of the language were properly and universally provided for, the difference between educated and uneducated speech, which at present causes so much prejudice and difficulty of intercourse on both sides, would gradually disappear. Good speech and great literature would not be regarded as too fine for use by the majority, nor, on the other hand, would natural gifts for self-expression be rendered ineffective by embarrassing faults of diction or composition. The second cause of division amongst us is the undue narrowness of the ground on which we meet for the true purposes of social life. The associations of sport and games are widely shared by all classes in England, but with mental pleasure and mental exercises the case is very different.[29]

Newbolt refrained from suggesting that an inequitable distribution of wealth divided one class from another, presumably because he could see as well anybody that the study of English would do nothing to remedy the 'national' cause of class divisions. Like Richards, the Leavises, and the American New Critics, Newbolt adopted a fatalistic perspective on economic and political matters. Since class divisions could not be eliminated without considerable danger to the liberal ethos, the best that one could hope for was for both parties to come to a gradual accommodation: the working classes could learn to speak like the middle-classes (an injunction with few discernible benefits for the working class *as* a class), and the Professors of Literature could 'learn to call nothing common or unclean—not even the local dialect, the clatter of the factory, of the smoky pall of our industrial centres' (an injunction that studiously avoids condemnation of the factory system which lay at the root of both England's prosperity and its class divisions).[30] As John Guillory points out, however, while one may acknowledge 'the existence of admirable and even heroic elements of working-class culture, the *affirmation* of lower-class identity is hardly compatible with a program for the abolition of want'.[31] Newbolt's program sought this sort of affirmation, and the Leavisite program in large measure delivered it. Newbolt's and the Leavisites' emphasis on language and on literature as first and foremost a manifestation of linguistic coherence (or 'unity') sidestepped the various historical and political problems thrown up by literature. Raymond Williams helpfully asked several of the questions the new mode of institutional criticism neglected in *Culture and Society*:

Is the deliberate exploitation [of popular institutions] a deliberate pursuit of profit, to the neglect or contempt of other considerations? Why, if this is so, should cheapness of expression and response be profitable? If our civilization is a 'mass-civilization', without discernible respect for quality and seriousness, by what means has it become so? What, in fact, do we mean by 'mass'? Do we mean a democracy dependent on universal suffrage, or a culture dependent on universal education, or a reading-public dependent on universal literacy? If we find the products of mass-civilization so repugnant, are we to identify the suffrage or the education or the literacy as the agents of decay? Or, alternatively, do we mean by mass-civilization an industrial civilization, dependent on machine-production and the factory system? Do we find institutions like the popular press and advertising to be the necessary consequences of such a system of production? Or again, do we find both the machine-civilization and the institutions to be products of some great change and decline in human minds?[32]

Critics could hardly answer such questions without arriving at the conclusion that 'the best that has been known and thought' (in Matthew Arnold's famous formulation) had actually been thought by particular persons, at particular times, and in particular places and that value could only be assigned to such knowledge and thought as the result of an equally particular psychological–temporal–geographical conjuncture. Propagating universal and eternal truths—the aim of the measures recommended by Newbolt[33] and put into practice by the Leavisites— therefore demanded a further methodological refinement: the exclusion of the reader from the process of realizing textual meaning. As Peter Rabinowitz has noted, Leavisite and New Critical methodologies tended to privilege a text's 'theme' as the basis for its unity (and hence, for its success or failure) without ever providing a theoretical framework capable of explaining how the critic arrived at his or her vision of the text's theme; thus 'by equating the positions of the critic and the reader,

New Criticism offered no perspective from which the act of reading itself could be critically examined.'[34] Without a dynamic theory of reading criticism could not hope to recognize the legitimacy of Williams's questions, much less provide answers to them.

This critical blind-spot had a massive impact on the sort of texts that critics deemed suitable for study. Richards proposed that work which appealed to 'stock responses' be excluded on the grounds of 'fixing immature and actually inapplicable attitudes to most things... Against these stock responses the artist's internal and external conflicts are fought, and with them the popular writer's triumphs are made.'[35] Unfortunately, without a theory of reading one could not say what these stock responses were, or how texts made use of them. Even the identification of 'stock responses' relied on intuition, rather than logic. At an intuitive level critics could not conceive that work capable of attracting a popular audience could possibly be worth reading, since the existence of a large reading public implied that the artist had made concessions to immature attitudes or had ceased to fight his internal or external conflicts. Thus a critic like F.R. Leavis could justifiably dismiss a writer like Dickens on the grounds of mass appeal despite the latter's 'great genius'. Likewise, neither Richards nor the Leavises felt that the cinema could constitute an 'art' in any legitimate sense of the word since technological and entrepreneurial innovators had developed the medium as a method of communicating with a relatively undifferentiated (or 'mass') audience—particularly before the introduction of synchronized sound. For the Leavisite, *all* cinema therefore performed the same work as *bad* literature: '[Films] involve surrender, under conditions of hypnotic receptivity, to the cheapest emotional appeals, appeals the more insidious because they are associated with a compellingly vivid illusion of actual life.'[36]

Great literature, by contrast, did not attract a large audience. It expressed its own vivid illusion of actual life by making an appeal to the intellect, rather than to the emotions. A reader might sympathize with a character in literature, but he would never empathize with him: he would remain outside the text peering in, like a scientist overseeing an experiment in an age prior to the advent of Heisenberg's uncertainty principle. Texts like Joyce's *Ulysses*, however, left Leavis feeling disoriented because they declined to present him with an easily comprehensible theme: '... there is no organic principle determining, informing, and controlling into a vital whole, the elaborate analogical structure, the extraordinary variety of technical devices, the attempts at an exhaustive rendering of consciousness.'[37] Leavis obliged great works of literature to announce their themes, but to do so obliquely—or, as Eliot put it, the individual talent responsible for a great work of literature marked himself out as such by 'a continual self-sacrifice, a continual extinction of personality' in the interest of maintaining continuity with the (thematic) tradition that furnished him with material in the first place.[38] For the Leavisites and the New Critics, then, great literature affirmed conventional liberal-humanist wisdom through unconventional means, while work that functioned through conventional means, or that somehow communicated unconventional wisdom, fell short of classification as great literature. Despite the rhetorical praise of unity and coherence, what critics like Richards, Leavis, and Eliot truly valued in literature was the text as a site for *imposing* unity and coherence. Rabinowitz has observed that in the wake of generations of New Critical hegemony 'the academy puts high value not on coherence per se, but rather on the activity of applying rules of coherence on works that are not evidently unified, but that can be made so through critical manipulation'.[39] Without a dynamic theory of reading, popular fiction struck the Leavisite reader as far too coherent, too overdetermined by the useful fiction of 'stock response', to warrant close study.

2
The Failed Novelist

Graham Greene helped launch his lengthy career as 'the most distinguished English novelist writing today' by writing several novels that the public did not like, and to which numerous reviewers responded with pronounced ambivalence.[1] The early novels—*The Man Within*, *The Name of Action*, and *Rumour at Nightfall*—nonetheless had the effect of communicating an idea of Greene's vocation and techniques that a generation of intellectuals enthralled by Leavisite and New Critical principles might not have found objectionable. These novels furnished critics with texts vague enough to require the application of institutionally sanctioned rules of coherence. With several impeccably intellectual novels under his belt, however, Greene then produced *Stamboul Train*, a novel that won enough popular acclaim to prompt Twentieth Century-Fox to purchase the rights and adapt into a film. In terms of contemporary critical discourse, Greene's popular success suggested that the writer himself had in some way curtailed his talent as an artist in order to exploit 'stock responses', although both the technical innovations he deployed and the themes his work suggested muddied the critical waters. How could an intellectual conceptualize Greene's achievement, which was at once both popular and intellectual?

The problem, however, only emerged over time. Shortly after the publication of *The Man Within* in 1929 it must have appeared to Charles Evans of the publishing firm William Heinemann that in Graham Greene he had discovered a diamond in the rough: a novice writer who produced critically acclaimed fiction that did not lose money. He did not sell as well as the two great workhorses in the Heinemann stable, J.B. Priestley and John Galsworthy—but then Greene was only 25 and he had already published a volume of poetry (*Babbling April*) as well as several articles for journals like the *Weekly Westminster Gazette*. He had worked as an editor on the *Oxford Outlook* and as a sub-editor for the *Times*, and—perhaps most importantly—he had weathered the rejection of two still-unpublished novels by nearly every publisher in England and had still retained enough patience and ambition to write a third. *The Man Within* received notices that even more established writers would have found enviable. *The Saturday Review of Literature* ran Bartlet Brebner's review under the title 'Promise Almost Fulfilled', although the implied qualification barely materialized over the course of the article:

> British critics have somewhat diminished their stock of superlatives over the flawless artistry which they find in this book. They have a good deal of provocation for it is an assured and competent piece of work. It is remarkable, too, that its author, a twenty-three year old London journalist, should have in his first novel forged a literary weapon sharp and sure enough to cut through the many layers of public indifference. I suspect that the strength of his Excalibur is literary integrity.[2]

Florence Codman of *The Nation* wrote that:

> as a study of a man of inherent moral weakness, of a coward and an unredeemed sinner whose one noble gesture occurs too late to be chastened of its futility, the interpretation is flawless...and it is expressed in language of rare purity, fluency, and richness in a manner that is strikingly original, forceful, and graceful.[3]

Doubleday's advertising copy reflected the critics' enthusiasm for the young writer's style and unorthodox approach to narrative:

> With the surety of true genius *The Man Within* is making itself known in both America and England, as the great literary discovery of the year. Drums of critical acclaim are steadily beating on both sides of the Atlantic to welcome this new star on the literary horizon. No synopsis can convey anything of the exciting art of its narration. Read it—and its vise-like grip and strange, indelible beauty will hold you as few modern novels can.[4]

The Man Within sold a respectable total of 8000 copies before going out of print.[5]

Several commentators mentioned that in addition to the linguistic fireworks, Greene had also managed to produce a novel with a plot so engaging that readers would not be surprised to learn that 'Mr. Greene has a family relation to Stevenson'.[6] The *Times Literary Supplement* (*TLS*) reviewer who noted this, however, did so principally in order to illuminate the gulf that separated the two writers:

> ... they will quickly find that what interests Mr. Greene is very much less the outward adventures of [the protagonist] Andrews than the spiritual adventures of 'the man within.' Tantalized by the thrill of a pursuit in the fog, they have to stand still while Mr. Greene analyzes every drop in the shifting current of Andrews's frightened mind. In fact, the whole action is enveloped—in fog we were on the point of saying, but the word would be unjust to the delicate, translucent mist of psychologizing with which Mr. Greene enhaloes his characters.[7]

The *TLS*, the *Spectator*, and even to a lesser extent the Doubleday advertising writers all came close to suggesting that if *The Man Within* had succeeded in finding a modestly popular audience it had done so either through guile on the part of the author or through carelessness on the part of common readers in Britain and abroad.

Greene's next two novels demonstrated both to the public and to Greene's own publisher that their boy genius had in fact swindled them. *The Name of Action* told the story of Oliver Chant, an idealistic upper-middle-class Briton who goes to a foreign country he knows nothing about in order to foment a revolution. Its story explicitly foreshadows *The Quiet American*, although the absence of Fowler's ironic commentary forces the narrator to squeeze what tragedy he may from material better suited to an adventure story or a bedroom farce. Once again, however, Greene subordinated elaboration of the plot to the work of illuminating the protagonist's tortuous psychology—generally through equally tortuous grammar. Chant falls madly in love with Anne-Marie Demassener, wife of the sexually dysfunctional, puritanical dictator Chant has traveled to Trier to help overthrow by means of revolutionary poetry printed on a jury-rigged press hidden away in the basement flat of a bilious Jew named Kapper. The narrative establishes this premise in about 20 pages; thereafter, the bulk of the long novel charts Chant's romantic entanglements in scenes such as the following, in which the two lovers try to express their feelings to one another:

> 'It has made me hate you,' she said, and angered, perhaps, by the consciousness of how excuse and belief must compare in any final judgment, 'now I can only pity you.'

He took the blow painfully. 'There is nothing pitiful about me,' he said, with an absolute lack of conviction. 'Unless,' he added, without dubiety, 'that I love you.' The statement called for something with greater integrity than taunts. 'God alone knows,' she said, with no real belief in a Divinity less puzzled than herself, 'whether I love you or not.'

The two assertions had been made and the ground was clear, if not for reconciliation, at least for a mutual cutting of the bond that held them still with pain together.[8]

The manner of the telling slows the progress of the story to a crawl. The constant qualifications of speech and action suggest either an absurd level of self-awareness on the part of the characters, the narrator's mistrust of the reader (who may fail to grasp the significance of the details he chooses to reveal), or even the writer's mistrust of his own narrator's selection of details to reveal.

Numerous reviewers, however, did not feel quite as cheated by the novel as the public: Katherine Tomlinson of *The Nation and Athenaeum*, for instance, so loved *The Name of Action* that she depleted the remaining stock of superlatives that British critics had neglected to hurl at *The Man Within*:

> *The Name of Action* is a notable book; the writing, sculptural in character, resembles the warm chastity of pure Gothic with a little Byzantine to add wonder to our delight. It is enriched by similes that only a poet could tender: 'Through the black Roman gate, which stood away from the street lights like an old elephant fascinated but afraid of the camp fires lit in its familiar jungle, Chant passed into an Easter peace.'[9]

She described the sexually dysfunctional dictator as 'Rodinesque', compared two of Greene's characterizations to Shakespeare's Caliban, and expressed 'relief' for the presence of Frau Weber in the story, whom Tomlinson felt possessed 'the serene beauty of an eighteenth century ship's figure-head'.[10] Edith Walton of the *New York Times* concurred, and responded with a review that Doubleday could have proudly cribbed. 'To summarize the book... is to give no hint of its quality, to convey nothing of its magic... [Greene] is one of those people who seem to be born with a knowledge of good writing. His prose is not mannered, or precious, or self-conscious. It is merely remarkably good.'[11] Audiences, however, seemed less inclined to gape at the sculpture garden Greene had assembled than Evans might have hoped, and more resistant to the magical powers invested in the aristocracy of talent than Doubleday had expected. The novel sold 2000 copies according to Greene.[12] *Rumour at Nightfall* made its predecessor look like a runaway success by comparison. Reacting to such observations as 'Nothing was almost like a sound perceptible to the senses' and (announcing dusk) 'The rocks, which had been lit by the sun into masses of warm fruit, became no more than depositories of metallic ore',[13] the *Spectator* issued a terse review: 'Mr. Greene is one of those authors who have something to say but whose turgidity prevents them from saying it. The theme is the interplay of one Spanish and two English characters in the Spain of the Carlist Wars.'[14] Likewise, *The New Republic* felt that 'the characters stagger under the overwhelming weight of their own mental questionings and probings.'[15] A complicated courtship scene reminiscent of Chant's unsatisfactory rendezvous with the dictator's wife ends with one of the English characters attempting 'with heavy steps to climb [Euleilia's] mood of laughter, but he [Crane] found the ledge insecure, the foothold treacherous, the fall too terrifying'.[16] The public, however, did not consider Euleilia's mood worth the climb, and the novel sold only 1200 copies.[17] Neither *The Name of Action* nor *Rumour at Nightfall* ever returned to print, and are among the very select number of Greene's novels to which the film rights remain free.

In the first scholarly study of Greene in English, Allott and Farris had likened the early novels to the work of an obsessed brick-maker 'desperately trying to make bricks with very little straw; and sounding therefore at times like a writer for the glossier women's magazines'.[18] Greene himself described his short period of creative and financial solvency after *The Man Within* as 'the brief promise of a dud rocket on Guy Fawkes night'.[19] Still, the work that Greene produced between 1929 and 1931 had two profound effects: it illustrated that he could no longer hope to earn money as a novelist by writing the same sort of novels he had in the past, and it showed critics and reviewers that, despite his failures, Greene took the work of writing novels very seriously indeed. For the student or critic committed to the Leavisite or New Critical dispensations, the failure of Greene's Byzantine fictions to find an audience would not necessarily have counted as a mark against their quality, and may well have appeared in some quarters to vouchsafe the young writer's promise. *The Nation*, for instance, felt that Greene depended too much on 'strangeness' to achieve the effect of beauty, but did not condemn *Rumour at Nightfall* on the grounds of ugliness. 'Fortunately', the reviewer wrote, '[Greene's] rhetoric is excellent and this in part makes up in subtlety of style for what it lacks in wisdom.'[20] The *TLS* (which F.R. Leavis admittedly believed only a vulgarian could consider a 'critical organ'[21]) described Greene's work in *Rumour at Nightfall* as 'a thing which is at once valuable and difficult' before concluding that while the ending strained credulity the rest of the novel 'contrived a subtle and elaborate interweaving of brute facts and the reaction to them of tortuous and sensitive minds'.[22] Although Greene may not have written a novel bearing the stamp of Gissing or James, neither had he produced a fiction that any contemporary readers believed had made use of stock responses.

According to Q.D. Leavis, when nineteenth-century sentimental writers like Lytton and Dickens had discovered 'how to exploit the market' they had discovered not only a commercial method of producing books that sold well in the form of serials but also a principle of composition:

> The difference between the popular novels of the eighteenth century and of the nineteenth is that the new fiction instead of requiring its readers to co-operate in a sophisticated entertainment discovers 'the great heart of the public'... [Dickens] discovered, for instance, the formula 'laughter and tears' that has been the foundation of practically every popular success ever since (Hollywood's as well as the bestseller's). Far from requiring an intellectual stimulus, these are tears that rise in the heart and gather to the eyes involuntarily or even in spite of the reader, though an alert critical mind may cut them off at the source in a revulsion to disgust.[23]

Whatever faults reviewers might have discerned in Greene's novels, none suggested that his narratives aimed at wrenching an emotional response from their readers. His convoluted elaboration of motivation served to distance readers from the characters rather than vice versa. His novels worked more through 'plot' (as defined by E.M. Forster in his Clark Lecture series) than through 'story', the latter of which Forster felt could only suit the tastes of 'cave-men or... a tyrannical sultan or... their modern descendant the movie-public'.[24] Although superior to 'story', plotting carried its own risks:

> ... the plot, instead of finding human beings more or less cut to its requirements, as they are in the drama, finds them enormous, shadowy and intractable, and three-quarters hidden like an iceberg. In vain it points out to these unwieldy creatures the advantages of the triple process of complication, crisis and solution so persuasively

expounded by Aristotle. A few of them rise and comply, and a novel which ought to have been a play is the result. But there is no general response. They want to sit and brood or something, and the plot (whom I here visualize as a sort of high government official) is concerned at their lack of public spirit: 'This will not do,' it seems to say. 'Individualism is a most valuable quality; indeed my own position depends upon individuals; I have always admitted as much freely. Nevertheless there are certain limits, and those limits are being overstepped. Characters must not brood too long, they must not waste time running up and down ladders in their own insides, they must contribute, or higher interests will be jeopardized.'[25]

Forster's higher sort of government official would certainly have found that Andrews, Chant, Chase, and Crane had overstepped their limits, and that the last's mood-climbing activities constituted a serious dereliction from the character's duty to contribute to the plot—a transgression that Forster himself would almost certainly have condoned. By writing characters who spent far more time brooding than acting, Greene had aligned himself with the sort of writing hailed by Forster and Leavis for privileging inner conflict over the interpersonal or social interaction of more overtly dramatic—and popular—forms. The very conventionality of the settings he used—smugglers and pirates on the Cornish coast, Continental revolutions—underlined for 'high-brow' and 'low-brow' reviewers alike how little the novels resembled conventional appropriations of such settings in popular fiction, and this discrepancy in turn revealed the extent to which the narratives demanded an intellectual, analytical response, rather than an emotional one.

From this perspective, the principle merit of Greene's early novels for the 1930s intellectual becomes clear: they drew attention to the fact that the writer had at least attempted to organize his experience in a meaningful way. Even those criticisms leveled against his work reflected I.A. Richards's proposition that '[an artist's] *failures* to bring order out of chaos are often more conspicuous than those of other men...it is a penalty of ambition and a consequence of his greater plasticity'.[26] In short, then, Greene's failures signaled his ambition and plasticity and set him in many ways above 'the masses' whose experience of art the dominant critical practice sought to de-legitimize.

To his publishers, however, Greene's failures signaled that his ambition and plasticity had cost them a substantial amount of money that they could have better spent promoting the ostensibly less ambitious and plastic works of Priestley and Galsworthy (two writers with large, adoring publics and, consequently, two writers that the Leavisites held in contempt). In his autobiography Greene himself offered a fable of *Stamboul Train*'s genesis that cited economic pressure as the foremost influence on his fourth published novel:

> [In 1931], for the first and last time in my life I deliberately set out to write a book to please, one which with luck might be made into a film. The devil looks after his own and in *Stamboul Train* I succeeded in both aims, though the film rights seemed at the time an unlikely dream...I suppose the popular success of the film *Grand Hotel* gave me the idea of how to set about winning the jackpot.[27]

Greene's explanation could not have been better calculated to disqualify himself from entry into the lists of great literature by offending the sort of high-brow opinion that dominated intellectual discourse during the 1930s. Had she taken an interest in Greene, Q.D. Leavis might have observed that at this stage in his career Greene discovered the 'great heart of the public', decided like Lytton before him to exploit the market, and plumped for the formula of 'laughter and tears'.

Greene himself seems to have been quite aware of how perceptions of his works' contexts could influence their reception. Greene offered his fable of *Stamboul Train* in 1980, at the dawn of the Thatcher era, by which time many intellectuals, perhaps most, had accepted in principle the artistic potential of popular forms like the cinema and genre fictions. Just prior to *Stamboul Train*'s publication, however, Greene had published a review whose conclusion implied an alternate, explicitly high-brow account of *Stamboul Train*'s genesis: 'A technical device is practiced by the novelist half-consciously a long while before the critic analyses it. Henry James did not invent the "point of view", but his prefaces gave the method a general importance it lacked as long as it was practiced unconsciously.'[28] In his earlier novels, Greene had used a very limited point of view in order to dig deep—arguably too deep—into his protagonists' psyches; in *Stamboul Train* he used the device both to limn his characters (albeit at lesser length) *and* to propel the action of the story forward. To numerous reviewers, this novel appropriation of the technique appeared 'cinematic', while intellectuals enamored of Greene found its association with James—one of Leavis's great English novelists—a means of justifying their interest in the popular writer's work.[29]

What neither of the Leavises could have said—and what Greene had no reason to say—was that a writer could no more *write* a 'popular' novel than he could a 'literary' one: social forces alone could accomplish the transformation of story into either cultural capital or hard currency, and the Leavisite aversion to social forces meant that literary value assumed a mystical quality, irreducible to the institutions that in fact fostered it, which the critic could consequently only accept or reject as a matter of faith. Thus John Atkins, writing in the Leavisite mode many years after Greene had become a 'major'/'popular' writer, ascribed the cause of *Stamboul Train*'s popularity to an inscrutable personal transformation in the writer himself: 'The fact is, Greene can only write well in one way, and this is the first novel in which he finds his personal style.'[30]

There is undoubtedly some truth in what Atkins suggests, just as there is probably a kernel of truth in Greene's account of how he came to write *Stamboul Train*. In 1931 Greene stopped doing a number of the things he had done in the early novels: he began to abbreviate his extended metaphors; his characters brooded far less and acted a bit more; and the narrator set out the concrete details of the scene as often as he filtered them through the consciousness of his characters. In *Stamboul Train* Greene chose to focus the reader's attention on the narrative's status as a story, rather than on its status as a psychological or moral inquiry into 'the divided mind'. The new novel did not abandon psychology or philosophy; nor, however, did it demand that its reader approach the text with a 'horizon of expectations' derived from a primarily psychological or philosophical set of interests, beliefs, and biases.[31] With *Stamboul Train*, then, it appears that Greene began to address his narratives to a different sort of reader than his earlier work had addressed. In Peter Rabinowitz's terms, he began to write for a different 'authorial audience':

> An author has, in most cases, no firm knowledge of the actual readers who will pick up his or her book. Yet he or she cannot begin to fill up a blank page without making assumptions about the readers' beliefs, knowledge, and familiarity with conventions. As a result, authors are forced to guess; they design some more or less specific *hypothetical* audience, which I call the *authorial audience*. Artistic choices are based upon these assumptions—conscious or unconscious—about readers, and to a certain extent, artistic success depends on their shrewdness, on the degree to which actual and authorial audience overlap.[32]

The Man Within, *The Name of Action*, and *Rumour at Nightfall* had all made use of a more or less specific authorial audience—an audience that considered a characters' impression of a thing or an action more important than the thing or action itself; an audience more interested in psychological ambiguity than clarity of purpose; an audience prepared to accept linguistic complexity as signifying that ambiguity rather than signifying a writer with a shaky hold on his craft; an audience that, with any luck, had just put down Woolf's latest and would turn to the latest Lawrence after finishing 'the new Greene': an audience, in short, among whom the average Leavisite would feel quite at home.

Stamboul Train clearly postulated its audience in a different but no less specific fashion. Its audience would not sit still while characters brooded at length. It would welcome a clever turn of phrase, but not a metaphor that dragged on for three pages. It would relish ambiguity—provided that the ambiguity contributed to the story's suspense. It would not feel disappointed if something improbable happened to a character so long as the narrative related the ramifications of the event with strict plausibility. And in order to extract the maximum amount of suspense from the plot, it preferred to have characters that it could relate to on something beyond an intellectual level. Equipped with this hypothetical audience, Greene produced a novel that many 'actual' audiences agreed was in large measure a successful adventure story.

In 1931, however, a writer could not produce a novel that intellectuals would consider an adventure story without making 'a symbolic move in an essentially polemic and strategic ideological confrontation between the classes'.[33] To do so implied accepting the tastes, values, and judgments of the same popular audience that the dominant ideology disseminated through intellectual discourse sought to exclude from participation in the work of cultural production. The Leavisites, after all, had elaborated their program along the same lines as Walter Lippmann, a prominent American sociologist who had successfully propagated a model of democracy that limited the role of the public to offering assent to the opinion of experts. 'One mind, or a few', Lippmann had written, 'can pursue a train of thought, but a group trying to think in concert can as a group do little more than assent or dissent'.[34] The Leavisite program held that since no ordinary person could figure out how literature worked, an expert had to tell them how it worked, how it could be made to work better, and what measures to implement in order to make it work better. Armed with this expert opinion, the 'man on the street' either assented or dissented. Assent ('Lawrence is a great author', for instance) demonstrated the enlightenment of the man on the street while dissent ('I prefer the cinema to Austen') simply re-validated the rationale for the existence of the elite so long as the institution that conferred power on the members of the elite retained its legitimacy in the eyes of the public.

John Carey has observed that in the specific context of intellectual literary discourse, novels like Joyce's *Ulysses* constituted a symbolic move quite in keeping with the ideological demands of Lippmann's model of democracy.

> One effect of *Ulysses* is to show mass man matters, that he has an inner life as complex as an intellectual's, that it is worthwhile to record his personal details on a prodigious scale. And yet it is also true that Bloom himself would never and could never have read *Ulysses* or a book like *Ulysses*. The complexity of the novel, its avant-garde technique, its obscurity, rigorously excludes people like Bloom from its readership.... Mass man—Bloom—is expelled from the circle of the intelligentsia, who are incited to contemplate him, and judge him, in a fictional manifestation.[35]

For slightly different reasons, Greene's early work also invited appropriation by readers interested in expelling mass man from the circle of the intelligentsia. They presupposed an audience interested in the sort of things that interested elite opinion: the psychology of 'the divided mind', linguistic complexity, and so on. For instance, the reader who grows irritated by Oliver Chant's fickle psychological posturings in *The Name of Action* has arguably not understood the book; he has, at the very least, imposed on the narrative a set of expectations that the narrative itself has done little to foster. In this respect, Greene's novel seems less duplicitous than Joyce's: one can easily imagine Chant (or Andrews, or Chase, or Crane) glorying in the ambiguity (or turgidity) with which their respective narratives relate their stories. But then none of these characters would have considered themselves representative of social norms, and so the reader who successfully applied rules of coherence to their narratives would necessarily have found himself contemplating the text from the same distant, ironized position as the characters themselves. Like *Ulysses*, then, Greene's early work was ripe for appropriation by conservative intellectual polemicists.

Stamboul Train's authorial audience, on the other hand, made it difficult (but not impossible) for intellectuals to appropriate the novel for use in Leavisite polemic. The story dealt for the most part with doggedly average characters caught up in extraordinary circumstances: a businessman lusts after a young woman; a chorus girl searches for security; a 'has-been' tries to reclaim his faded glory while a 'would-be' embraces criminality in the name of ambition; a journalist pursues her quarry while a gold-digger finds a new mark; a novelist researches a new novel. None of them seem likely to agonize over the implications of *Mass Civilization and Minority Culture*, and all of them might conceivably read an adventure story for no better reason than to pass the time of day. Thus when a reader applies rules of coherence to the narrative he does not necessarily end up considering the characters from a distant or ironized position. And because the narrative requires its readers to apply these rules as much to the characters' actions as to their intentions or motivations, the end result is something Rabinowitz describes as an 'ethical effect':

> A New Critic would view neither a paraphrase nor the act of sitting in at a lunch counter a verification of the proper understanding of Chester Himes's *If He Hollers Let Him Go*. One is a different text altogether; the other is irrelevant to literature considered 'as literature.' Indeed, one of the most persistent residues of our New Critical heritage is our readiness to assume that when we speak of ethical effects, we are speaking of something extraliterary.[36]

By declining to draw attention to itself 'as literature' *Stamboul Train* (like many of Greene's later novels) demands the reader's participation as a socially constituted subject—a vastly different proposition than the undifferentiated mass of mindless consumers imagined by the Leavisites to comprise the bulk of the reading public.

The Leavises and the New Critics may have held the 'mass' in contempt, but they could hardly do without it, since the dangers of 'mass civilization' served to legitimize their claim to superior understanding. Those forms they chose to deride—the popular novel, genre fictions, the cinema—blurred the distinction between the mass and the intellectual precisely because those forms gave 'the man in the street' the chance to participate in an ethical debate that contemporary intellectuals insisted on carrying out in isolation behind the closed doors of academe. Their fundamental errors stemmed from the conviction that popular fiction actually functioned as easily as intellectuals believed it read: that popular narratives never used irony or subtlety; that readers experienced generic conventions passively; and that 'stock responses' could not be deployed in provocative ways (despite the fact that all linguistic expression in narrative or poetry demands a vast store of shared responses). Umberto Eco takes up a number of these assumptions in an essay on Ian Fleming's (hugely popular) James Bond novels, and argues that Fleming's use of stock characters 'is always dogmatic and intolerant—in short, reactionary—whereas he who avoids set figures, who recognizes nuances and distinctions and who admits contradictions is democratic... If Fleming is a "Fascist" he is so because of his inability to pass from mythology to reason'.[37] But for Eco it is Fleming's *use* of stock characters that signals dogmatism, and not simply their presence. Fredric Jameson offers a further refinement of this idea when he makes the point that genres themselves are not necessarily stable because readers experience them as a generic process rather than as a discrete set of characteristics: '... *all* generic categories, even the most time-hallowed and traditional, are ultimately to be understood... as mere ad hoc, experimental constructs, devised for a specific textual occasion and abandoned like so much scaffolding when the analysis has done its work.'[38] Fleming does little to estrange the reader's perceptions of his generic villains, and so they remain the same stock characters at the end of the novel as they were at the beginning (save that they are universally dead by the end); by contrast, Greene begins *Stamboul Train* with stock figures trapped in what was even by 1932 a stock situation[39] but thereafter plays on his readers' awareness of the genre, on their biases and prejudices, hopes and aspirations, in order to dismantle the generic scaffolding and, along with it, the fiction of the popular reader as passive consumer.

3
Readers and Generic Processes in *Stamboul Train*

Stamboul Train requires its readers to participate in the realization of the text's meaning by performing different operations than the earlier novels had required them to perform. *The Name of Action* and *Rumour at Nightfall* did not emphasize plot: Chant and Chase found themselves in the midst of exciting historical events, but the narratives presented casual relationships between those events and the characters. They served as occasions for thought and reflection, rather than as subjects of thought or the immediate causes of action. The reader who elected to read these novels as a member of the authorial audience did not need to pay much attention to the intricacies of the Carlist wars; instead he measured the success of a character like Chant by the extent to which the character managed to alleviate the boredom that first set him on the path to Trier. (Unfortunately for Greene and his publishers, many readers found Chant's excitement rather dull and inconsequential.) John Buchan used a similar opening gambit in *The Thirty-Nine Steps* but ended the sequence by placing an actual corpse in Richard Hannay's smoking room, thus furnishing the protagonist with a set of realizable goals: staying alive, eluding both the police and the killers, and saving England and the world from a vast Jewish conspiracy.[1] While Hannay confronted obstacles from without, Chant drew most of the obstacles that stood in his way from within. The reader must wilfully look beyond the plot for the text's meaning, accept the legitimacy of Chant's inner obstacles (or Chase's), and accept as satisfactory a resolution presented in terms of these inner obstacles. *Stamboul Train* prompts the reader to engage the plot more rigorously since the narrative limns its characters principally through their actions; thus as the reader attempts to read as a member of the authorial audience he or she invests in the characters whatever psychology the plausibility of a given set of circumstances demands.

On the one hand, the method opens the novel to the charge of psychological implausibility, generally leveled by the sort of reader who prefers writers to explicitly elaborate the psychological states of his or her characters. On the other hand, it clears a space for the narrative and readers to cooperate in producing nonpsychological, extraliterary (or 'ethical') effects.

Mabel Warren, *Stamboul Train*'s drunken sadomasochistic lesbian journalist, sets many of *Stamboul Train*'s events in motion, and it is through Mabel that the narrative configures many of the reader's generic expectations. Although a successful career woman, the modern reader would hardly recognize Mabel as a spokeswoman for the emancipation of her sex from the conventions of gender; rather, she has carved herself a niche in the very system that assigns sex and gender to their 'natural' positions in the social hierarchy. With her tie, her stiff collar, her tweed 'sporting' suit, her rough hands and dark hair worn 'like a man's', Mabel cuts a very masculine figure, though not merely because she resembles a 'butch' caricature; more importantly, she has internalized capitalism's value structure, particularly insofar as it touches the media. Mabel's ambition—and, subsequently, her willingness to distort the facts as she understands them in the interests of self-aggrandizement—plays a more significant role in maintaining the story's suspense than what another character refers to as her 'unhealthy' sexual habits. Instead, Mabel's sexuality constitutes an excessive gesture, and reflects for the reader both the sensationalism to which Mabel has devoted herself as a reporter of 'human interest' stories and the sensationalism associated with the story of adventure.

The narrative communicates Mabel to the reader less as an individual than as an assemblage of surfaces that Mabel precariously presents to the outside world. Her drunkenness, like her lesbianism, momentarily obscures the instability of her character by overshadowing it, particularly during a scene that relates one of the 'regular rites of Mabel Warren's journalistic career . . . the visible shedding of her drunkenness':

> First a hand put the hair into order, then a powdered handkerchief, her compromise with femininity, disguised the redness of her cheeks and lids. All the while she was focusing her eyes, using whatever lay before her, cups, waiter, glasses and so on to the distant mirrors and her own image, as a kind of optician's alphabetic scroll.[2]

Mabel becomes 'herself' by relating to a range of objects outside herself that ironically includes her own image. The narrative carefully communicates the passivity of Mabel's participation in the process: her hair is put into order not by her own hand, but by *a* hand, just as the task of disguising her drink-savaged face is delegated to the handkerchief itself, rather than to the human agent who presumably manipulates the powdered cloth. By highlighting Mabel's instability, however, the narrative suggests a more powerful force at work in Mabel: the single-minded determination necessary both to visibly shed her drunkenness, and to accept the legitimacy and necessity of such a ritual in the first place. Mabel refers to this force as 'professionalism' and describes its impact on her life as follows:

> [There] wasn't a town of any size between Cologne and Mainze where she hadn't sought out human interest, forcing dramatic phrases onto the lips of sullen men, pathos into the mouths of women too overcome with grief to speak at all. There wasn't a suicide, a murdered woman, a raped child who had stirred her to the smallest emotion; she was an artist to examine critically, to watch, to listen; the tears were for paper.[3]

Mabel's devotion to a professional ideal enables her to force the disparate aspects of her personality into a functional unity, just as it enables her to transform events into stories. By contrast, the presentation of Mabel's professionalism in the story illuminates the cracks in her own façade, reveals how arbitrarily facts can be invested with meaning by someone with the will to do so, and prepares the reader for the role Mabel will play in the story, assembling facts and hunches, manufacturing narrative, reciting it with the relish and false emotion of a ventriloquist.

The narrative uses Mabel to complicate the reader's relationship to the story. The journalist suspects that Richard John, an old man travelling aboard the Orient Express, may in fact be Dr. Czinner, a revolutionary long since exiled from his native Belgrade. While ransacking John's room Mabel discovers a Baedeker guide with strange marking that she believes contains the plans for an uprising in the slums of Belgrade: 'The map was loose, the paper in a Baedeker she remembered was thin and insufficiently opaque; if one fitted the map against the pen drawing on the earlier page, the lines would show through. My God, she thought, it's not everyone who would think of that.'[4] Although the reader does not know for certain whether John is Czinner, Mabel has seeded the possibility so extensively that the question propelling the story forward has become whether or not the Baedeker will confirm her suspicions, and how John will react when confronted with 'proof' of his identity. When Mabel seizes the opportunity to compare the map and the Baedeker, it seems clear that she has discovered something— but what exactly has she discovered? The reader has not been given the information to make a valid hypothesis, and so the narrative reveals as so much wishful thinking the process by which Mabel has arrived at the premise that the Baedeker contains the plans for a slum uprising. Which forces, after all, create the revolution Mabel sniffs out: the oppression of the Belgrade poor or the *Clarion*'s need for newsworthy events to narrate for the public? Mabel's desire for such a story arguably drives her to find one, whether or not the facts as such will support it. The reader's position is more dubious: he must suppress his misgivings concerning Mabel in order to let her find the 'something' that will enable the plot to continue developing and in this sense he must align himself with the very readership Mabel herself simultaneously cherishes for the quantitative legitimacy it offers her and holds in contempt for being so easily duped by her false tears.

When Mabel finally confronts John with her suspicions, the narrative has prepared the reader for one of two outcomes. John will either confirm that he is Czinner and that he plans to go to Belgrade and launch a revolution or else he will deny it all. In this sense, the reader is aligned with both Mabel and the *Clarion* readership. The narrative, however, abruptly shifts gears: after confirming that he is indeed Czinner, the older man refuses to confirm or deny Mabel's speculations about the revolt in Belgrade. Instead he hands her another narrative in the form of an article from a German newspaper: 'What she read was more extraordinary, a failure which put [Czinner] completely out of her power. She had been many times bullied by the successful, never before by anyone who had failed.'[5] Although her surmise of the Baedeker's contents has proved accurate, her timing has not. The uprising has already taken place and it has already been crushed by Colonel Hartep, Belgrade's Chief of Police. The revolution's failure has conferred upon Czinner a negative freedom similar to that which the departure of Janet Pardoe, Mabel's mistress, confers upon the journalist: freedom from the social and personal ties that have hitherto made both of their actions meaningful. They can both now act as they choose, but with the qualification that whatever actions they choose will lack personal or social significance. For the reader, this reversal creates a similar problem: the direction in which the narrative has progressed for a third of the novel's length has unexpectedly run into a blind alley. Suspense culminates in surprise, and peters out into bathos as Mabel places her call to the *Clarion* offices from Vienna.

The sequence forces the reader's 'horizon of expectation' onto a conscious plane. If he has been reading an adventure story, then the adventure has apparently come to an abrupt end. If he has been reading a tale of espionage, then at this moment he learns that the spies have all had their covers blown by Colonel Hartep and his cronies. As for Mabel and Czinner, so too for the reader: he finds himself freed from the conventions which the narrative had seemed to suggest, but he also finds that he has lost his bearings in a text that now taunts him with the threat of meaninglessness. Mabel's call to the newspaper office underscores how tenuous the situation has become. She paraphrases the story from the German paper, then concocts a story in which Czinner learns about the revolution's failure while travelling through Würzburg and then leaves the train in Vienna, heartbroken and muttering, 'If only they had waited'. After relating this story she continues:

> Got that? Now listen carefully. If you don't get the rest of the dope in half an hour cancel everything after '[Czinner] reached Würzburg' and continue as follows: And after long and painful hesitation decided to continue his journey to Belgrade. He was heartbroken and could only murmur: 'Those fine brave fellows. How can I desert them?' When he had a little recovered he explained to our special correspondent that he had decided to stand trial with the survivors...[6]

Mabel posits two versions of the story, neither of which seems derived from available facts. Her desperate, cynical hope reflects the reader's own: that *something* will happen to propel the story forward. At this point, Mabel disappears from the narrative: in the Vienna station she loses her luggage, her reporter's pass, and her money; with the loss of sexual identity, professional identity, and the medium for expressing both of them, she consequently loses the interest of the reader whom the narrative forces to look elsewhere for the sensation she has failed to deliver.

Mabel does several things in the story: she encourages the reader to participate in *Stamboul Train* as though it were an espionage narrative, but she simultaneously debunks the espionage narrative and reveals the luridly voyeuristic impulses to which such a narrative appeals for its success. In her role in the story Mabel embodies all that the Leavisites despised about the popular press: like Northcliffe, she believes she knows 'what the people want' and she determines to give them as much of it as she possibly can. Her role in the narrative, however, exploits both the reader's awareness of the journalist stereotype and his ambivalence toward it. Mabel excites the reader but ultimately fails him—not because she uncovers a failed plot, but because she justifies herself by calling attention to a commercial scale of values incommensurable with the scale of values the reader applies to the story of which she is a part. For the critic who adheres to I.A. Richards's formula of psychological value ('the organization which is least wasteful of human possibilities is best'[7]) *Stamboul Train* does not necessarily pose a problem: it does so only if the critic insists on the author as the sole architect of textual organization. From this perspective, a critic can only find Mabel wanting: she is too flat, and her characteristics too pat, too clearly elaborated in order to meet the demands of the plot. If, however, the critic considers Mabel as a meeting point between reader and author, he begins to grasp how the narrative plays on the reader's stereotype, reveals it as such, and opens the way to the reader's realization of a fuller range of human possibilities.

Mabel is not the only character the novel utilizes in this fashion. The male protagonist, Carleton Myatt, begins as a stock figure as well: the Jewish merchant. The narrative presents him first through the eyes of the purser collecting the landing cards at Ostend. 'I can't get away from their damned faces, the purser thought, recalling the young Jew in the heavy fur coat who had complained because he had been allotted a two-berth cabin; for two God-forsaken hours, that's all.'[8] The purser views Myatt as a stock character: the heavy coat symbolizes a fondness for the display of luxury; when he complains about his berth, Myatt signals to the purser both his material success (since he is clearly accustomed to better) and his lack of breeding (since a better-bred man would have accepted without complaint). By calling Myatt 'the Jew' he gives a name to this alien presence. The purser resents Myatt as clearly as he likes Coral Musker, the English chorus girl whom he helps aboard the train. When he forgets her half an hour later, it is on account of her familiarity: he remembers only the 'others', the Jew and the schoolteacher who makes him wonder 'whether something dramatic had passed close by him, something weary and hunted and the stuff of stories'.[9] Because he occupies a privileged place in the narrative—as the first eyes through whom we see the story—the purser's observations carry a special weight: they constitute the only details of the novel's world available to the reader, and they raise particular questions. He spends the most time with Coral, suggesting her importance, but only the man who turns out to be

Czinner and 'the Jew' make an impression, also signaling their importance. When the narrative picks up the story with Myatt, the reader pays close attention to whether or not the purser's observations were correct. As soon as the reader hears Myatt think, he grasps the inadequacy of the purser's resentment, since Myatt himself recognizes both the causes and the effects of that resentment. The burden of this knowledge wearies him. As he passes through a cloud of smoke on the platform he reflects that, 'for a moment he was at home and required no longer the knowledge of his suit from Savile-Row, his money or his position in the firm to hearten him'.[10]

Later on, the narrative allows Myatt an indirect soliloquy that resonates with the troubling influence of Shylock:

> Forty years in the wilderness, away from the flesh-pots of Egypt, had entailed harsh habits, the counted date and the hoarded water; nor had a thousand years in the wilderness of a Christian world, where only the secret treasure was safe, encouraged display; but the world was altering, the desert was flowering; in stray corners here and there, in western Europe, the Jew could show that other quality he shared with the Arab, the quality of the princely host, who would wash the feet of beggars and feed them from his own dish; sometimes he could cease to be the enemy of the rich to become the friend of any poor man who sought a roof in the name of God.[11]

The modern reader joins the authorial audience only after considerable—and considerably distasteful—effort, particularly as he grasps that Myatt is offering not to wash the feet of a beggar but rather to lend an attractive woman (Coral Musker) his berth after she faints. Myatt's bombast may appear insufferable, but it clearly attempts to demonstrate the sort of self-awareness and humanity that the purser automatically denies him. Michael Shelden has dismissed the novel as anti-Semitic, and some of its implications are indeed troubling: Myatt's biblical rhetoric sits uneasily with his almost purely secular obsessions; placed side by side they suggest a writer grappling with the difficulties of presenting the Jew as a human figure in the 1930s. Nonetheless, the use the narrative makes of Myatt hinges on both the reader's awareness of the stereotype of the Jew and his willingness not to judge Myatt on the basis of his ethnic background.

Through Myatt, the narrative dramatizes the same concern that prompts the Leavisite critics to offer their judgments and aesthetic programs: the rather embarrassing dichotomy of class and taste. Myatt himself has no recourse to the mythological resolution propounded by Richards and the Leavises: the idea of a 'natural' aristocracy of talent and discrimination that transcends class. Myatt grasps too firmly the unnaturalness of his situation, and the narrative presents the man whose fur coat conceals someone who feels unworthy of the opulence he has attained in language reminiscent of *Macbeth*. When Myatt meets Coral, her gaze causes him to reflect on his gratitude 'that she had shown no distaste, no knowledge of his uneasiness in the best clothes that money could buy'.[12] As an outsider cognizant of the mistrust and contempt he excites among his adopted countrymen his sense of self has become contingent upon the only system of relations available to him: the commercial sphere, the universe of 'figures'. Because the reader approaches Myatt through a narrative that insists upon retaining the outward trappings of romance, his tendency to quantify and calculate seems idiosyncratic at best and, at worst, mercenary and slightly obscene. The dream sequence that closes the first section of the novel illustrates how commerce blends with sexuality in Myatt's imagination. As he drives along a road with his business associates, Myatt encounters Coral walking alone:

> . . . he jumped from the car and offered her a cigarette and after that a drink and after that a ride. That was one advantage with these girls, Myatt thought; they all knew what a ride meant, and if they didn't care for the look of you, they just said that they had to be going home now. But Coral Musker wanted a ride; she would take him for her companion in the dark of the car, with the lamps and the inns and the houses left behind and trees springing up like paper silhouettes in the green light of the head-lamps, and then the bushes with the scent of wet leaves holding the morning's rain and a short barbarous enjoyment in the stubble.[13]

As the dream draws to a close, Coral mutates into Stein, Myatt's competitor in the currant business. Unlike the Jew-anarchists in *The Thirty-Nine Steps*, the narrative forces the reader to engage Myatt through competing, often contradictory codes: commerce versus romance, lust versus calculation, class versus sexuality, and acumen as discrimination. Myatt's contradictions force the reader to reconcile the tensions his character implies, to interpret—an activity not consistent with the role assigned by Richards to the sort of 'stock responses' characteristic of popular literature.

The reader does not experience Myatt in isolation, but rather as one actor in an evolving relationship. The other actor, Coral Musker, is herself no stranger to calculation. Myatt's gift to her of his ten-pound sleeping car provokes the following reflection:

> Chocolates and a ride, even in the dark, after a theatre, entailed no more than kisses on the mouth and neck, a little tearing of a dress. A girl was expected to repay, that was the point of all advice; one never got anything for nothing. Novelists like Ruby M. Ayres might say chastity was worth more than rubies but the truth was it was priced at a fur coat or thereabouts. One couldn't accept a fur coat without sleeping with a man. If you did, all the older women would tell you the man had a grievance. And the Jew had paid ten pounds.[14]

In this passage Coral becomes Myatt's double: the train of thought that eventually brings her to Myatt's bed is the same that leads Myatt to invite her to share it. Calculation, the cool summarization of pros and cons, and even the appeal to tradition distinguish both characters' deliberations. As Coral ponders her situation, Myatt ceases to be the man who has lent her his fur coat, or who has offered her his sleeper car; instead Coral, like the purser before her, abstracts Myatt into 'the Jew', an impersonal 'figure' to be valued alongside other figures: the cost of the sleeper car, the inconvenience caused by accepting a fur coat, and so on. Where Myatt is caught between the vicissitudes of commerce and the quasi-biblical sensibility that he applies to his own *causa-sui* narrative, Coral finds herself caught between novelistic tradition (in the figure of Ruby M. Ayres) and the received wisdom of 'the old women'.

Neither character 'automatically' wins the reader's sympathy (or enmity) as a 'stock character' like James Bond or Dr. No ostensibly would. Their love affair occupies the bulk of the second third of the novel, and they carry it out amidst an atmosphere of approbation and mistrust which communicates the sense of their mutual struggle for imaginative priority over the story they share. In this sense, their story reflects the story of Mabel and Czinner, to an equally ambiguous end. Myatt desires to transform his commercial acumen into social respectability, although this is the one quality that he knows to be incommensurable with commerce. At the same time Coral desires to translate her sexuality into wealth and comfort, although her willingness to do so cheapens her in the eyes of potential buyers. Both characters project their frustration at the paradoxes which rule their lives onto their fraught relationship, as in a brief scene in which Myatt offers Coral a currant and asks her what she thinks of it:

> [Coral said,] 'Juicy.'
>   'No, no, that one's not juicy.'
>   'Have I said the wrong thing?'
>   'That was one of Stein's. A cheap, inferior currant. The vine-yards are on the wrong side of the hills. It makes them dry. Have another. Can't you see the difference?'

For Myatt, commercial ideology determines sense perception, or would in an ideal world. Like Mabel (whose single-minded devotion to her profession commercial ideology also naturalizes) he knows the result beforehand and asks only for confirmation. Dissent simply confirms his suspicion that the person he has asked is unqualified to judge.

By presenting Coral as a character well-adapted to the role Myatt requires her to perform (i.e., the Pavlovian consumer who quickly learns which answers serve her own interests) the narrative keeps both characters in play, and defers the reader's judgment until the end of the novel. Where Myatt attempts to fit lived experience into a pre-ordained order, Coral continually attempts to recast the events that befall her into an evolving narrative. Waking from the night in which they have slept together, Coral approaches Myatt and tries 'gently to arrange his hair into some semblance of her lover's'.[15] She makes an imaginative distinction between 'Myatt' and 'her lover' which the reader cannot entirely accept. Given the choice between the reality at her fingertips and a fictional narrative, Coral chooses the fiction, while the reader must negotiate between the two. When the police in Belgrade later arrest her along with Dr. Czinner and another passenger, she harbors dreams of escape that center less on her relationship with Myatt than on an idealized and highly conventional story of their affair:

> ... she dreamed that she was very old and was looking back over life and she knew everything and she knew what was right and wrong, and why this and that happened and everything was very simple and had a moral. But this second dream was not like the first one [in which she had been a child], for she was nearly awake and she ruled the dream to suit herself ... In this dream she began to

remember from the safety of age the events of the night and the day and how everything turned out for the best and how Myatt had come back for her from Belgrade.[16]

The mechanism of the dream illustrates for the reader not only how Coral responds to her circumstances, but the practical inadequacy of that response. If the reader has yielded his experience of the story to the conventions of romance or, more broadly, the thriller, then this moment reveals those conventions as a mere contrivance or, in Fredric Jameson's words, an ad hoc experimental construct designed for a specific textual occasion. The reader cannot naturalize these conventions (as Coral attempts to do) because the narrative itself has prompted the reader to demythologize the very conventions it invokes. The reader knows, for instance, that Myatt has left the train in pursuit of Coral, but that he has also hampered his efforts by compromising with his commercial acumen, wasting time negotiating with the cab driver who brings him to the station where the police have detained Coral and the others, and by his desire to preserve his own life whatever the cost to Coral, as he demonstrates by telling the cab driver to slow down. The point on which the suspense appears to be hanging—whether or not Myatt will arrive in time to rescue Coral—is thus complicated by questions hardly typical of a 'stock' suspense narrative. Which Myatt does Coral desire to be rescued by: the lover of her dreams, or the Myatt with messy hair? Since the reader knows the Myatt who exists bears little resemblance to the lover of Coral's dream, does he anticipate a happy resolution for Coral even if Myatt does manage to arrive at the station in time? Since the reader knows that Coral loves her dream rather more than she loves the Myatt she will end up with if he does rescue her, does he anticipate a satisfactory conclusion for Myatt if he arrives in time? The reader recognizes that the resolutions each character anticipates cannot be reconciled save through myths that have already had their legitimacy revoked.

Generic processes in *Stamboul Train* prevent the reader from arriving at a moment in the narrative which demands a definitive judgment. He may despise Myatt, or he may sympathize with the contradictions Myatt proves incapable of surmounting in the story; but because his position as a reader has so often reflected Myatt's own situation he can never simply dismiss him. *Stamboul Train* thus becomes not an adventure story, or a tale of international intrigue, or a tragicomedy; realized through the agency of the reader, the narrative becomes an experience that requires active engagement in the interpretive process rather than stock responses to the stale recital of fixed and stable generic conventions. The novel acquires significance as a symbolic move in the polemic and strategic confrontation of the classes by revealing the arbitrariness of the myths invoked in defence of the status quo and by demanding of the reader neither assent or dissent but rather an answer to the questions 'Why?' and 'On whose authority'?

4
Cinema as a Strategy of Containment

For critics of the Leavisite and New Critical dispensations, a popular fiction like *Stamboul Train* should not have raised the sort of questions it did. Likewise, if a novel did raise difficult questions, then the public should logically have responded to it with lumpenproletarian indifference and boredom. An adventure story—particularly one written by someone less exalted than a Leavis-authorized genius—should have been an adventure story: identifiable, predictable, and easily dismissed; it should not have prompted its readers to question the nature of their involvement in the story, or forced them to make interpretive choices. In the prevailing intellectual discourse, a novel could not appeal to someone who read 'for the plot' and someone who read 'for the deeper meaning'. As Ben Ray Redman noted in his review of *Stamboul Train*, 'Nothing is more elusive than the line across which we step when we pass from merely good current fiction into the realm of genuine literature'; Redman, however, did not dare suggest that Greene's novel was anything more than *very* good current fiction.[1]

Anne Armstrong of the *Saturday Review* trotted out an adjective to describe *Stamboul Train* that *Nation and Athenaeum* had used as a mild pejorative several years earlier:

> *Stamboul Train* is a modern novel for modern people and if you are a modern person and if you like modern novels and your fiction in snippets, why then you are in luck—but if you are none of these things I doubt very much that you will approve or appreciate Mr. Greene's novel.[2]

While Armstrong seemed constantly on the brink of placing Greene's novel in the same 'modern' tradition as the novels of Joyce, Woolf, and others experimenting with the application of James's point-of-view techniques she did not continue her argument along literary lines at all: 'It is *Grand Hotel* all over again, only in this case Mr. Greene has used a train instead of a hotel.'[3] Although she commended the novel, she also seemed uncertain that modernity was a particularly good thing, an ambiguity that became a Villon-esque lament in Redman's review:

> Whatever the reason, whether or not it is the fretful, shifting move-ment of modern life, which makes continued concentration upon a single subject more difficult for us than it was for our fathers, there has recently developed a kind of fiction . . . calculated to please minds that are darting, impatient, and ever avid of variety.[4]

For Armstrong, the writer had crafted a novel that reflected public tastes; for Redman, the public had created the conditions that made the novel's success possible; neither of them, however, considered the rela-tionship between the writer and the public a particularly desirable one. Both reviewers struggled to preserve both the myth of the artist's autonomy and the Leavisite dichotomy between writer and audience; consequently, each reviewer ended up investing supreme interpretive authority in one or the other, leading each to offer odd rationales for their favorable opinions. Since they deemed the public incapable of demanding a good novel, and since they deemed a good author inca-pable of producing a bad one, they focused on what they referred to as Greene's 'motion picture' or 'cinematic' technique.

The cinematic label enabled the reviewers to recognize Greene's formal innovations—and even to acknowledge his popular success—without necessarily forcing them to affix their 'seal of approval' to the novel. *Stamboul Train* provoked the sort of reader response gener-ally associated with 'high-brow' novels but did so through what one might term a vernacular narrative grammar. The doubling of Czinner and Myatt, for instance, does not qualitatively differ from the doubling of Septimus and Clarissa in *Mrs. Dalloway*: the two characters com-ment on one another and the narrative asks the reader to consider the actions of each from the perspective of the other. *Stamboul Train*'s climax even ironizes both perspectives: Czinner delivers the grand ora-tion he has dreamt of delivering (save that nobody bothers to listen to him) while Myatt abandons Coral to an uncertain fate and ends up engaged to his competitor's niece—the beginning of a relation-ship whose future prospects horrify even the least shrewd reader. But reviewers like Armstrong did not conclude that *Stamboul Train* was

Mrs. Dalloway all over again; it was *Grand Hotel* all over again, presumably because its popularity implied some quality that a writer could easily reproduce. By contrast, an intellectual would not even know how to apply the category of reproducibility to a genuine work of art whose meaning was itself, and whose claim to greatness rested on the author's facility for psychological organization. A critic, however, could easily apply the *New York Times*'s analysis of Greene's style to many of the 'great' works of literary modernism: 'Something of the motion-picture technique is used, with brief glimpses of the actions and thoughts now of one character, now of another, interspersed with longer stretches of narrative. These glimpses enable the reader to reconstruct the past of each, and often they help point the irony.'[5] The reviewer offers a reasonable analysis of how Greene's novel works (i.e., by involving the reader in the creation of suspense)—but why does he insist on attributing the technique to the cinema rather than to James's 'point-of-view' (as Greene himself suggested), or to Dos Passos's and Joyce's use of ostensibly 'literary' montage? Redman implies an answer of sorts in his review:

> The authors who cater to [readers' impatient minds] weave, telescope, or jumble, according to their skill, six or a dozen stories into one. Instead of dogging the steps of a hero or heroine from birth to death, after the fashion of yesterday, they establish momentary contact with a group of characters, fortuitously or forcefully gathered together on some spot of the earth's surface, and reveal them to our dancing eyes in a series of quick flashes. Whether it be from room to room of a grand hotel, from house to house of a city block, from cabin to cabin of a luxury liner, or from one guest to another invited to the same dinner party, our attention is shuttled back and forth as the author turns swiftly from tale to tale.[6]

Presumably neither James, nor Dos Passos, nor Joyce catered to anybody: they wrote in order to express themselves and their chosen themes without regard for the public who might have eventually read what they had written. From this vantage point, in Wayne Booth's terms, the author himself ideally comprised the sole member of the audience for whom he wrote—a mode of production better suited to a schizophrenia ward than to a publishing house. The cinematic label recognizes the experimental qualities of *Stamboul Train* but squarely situates the novel with other 'mass' phenomena that intellectuals believed had contributed to cultural decline: jazz, the music hall, the popular press, and, of course, the cinema itself. Since *Stamboul Train*'s commercial success suggested that it had failed to perform the ideological work of literature—that is, since the novel failed to filter intellectuals capable of grasping it from the 'mass'—and since many critics nonetheless recognized that the novel performed a good deal of the aesthetic work associated with literature, the reviewers' decision to impose the cinematic label constituted an evasive, somewhat reactionary polemical move. By so doing critics sought to prevent the novel and the 'mass' readership implicated in the production of its effects from revealing the arbitrariness of the standard by which intellectuals measured the greatness of literature, and the political interests of those committed to maintaining such a standard in nominally democratic societies.

The designation of Greene's work as cinematic has had consequences that his contemporaries could hardly have foreseen. The Leavisite orthodoxy privileged what present-day screenwriting guru Robert McKee refers to as 'literary purity': ' "Literary purity" does not mean literary achievement. Purity of novel means a telling located exclusively at the level of inner conflict, employing linguistic complexities to incite, advance, and climax the story with relative independence of personal, social, and environmental forces: Joyce's *Ulysses*.'[7] For I.A. Richards and the Leavises, 'literary purity' (in McKee's sense of the term) was *the* benchmark for measuring literary achievement and they naturally could not attribute that quality to a 'cinematic' novel. Nor, however, could they admit that novels like *Ulysses* and *Mrs. Dalloway* told their stories partially through the elaboration of personal, social, and environmental conflict. Filling this void has furnished several generations of Marxist, feminist, and historicist scholars with lifelong projects. The student of Greene, however, has long confronted a different sort of challenge: from the environmental, social, and personal conflicts elaborated in Greene's novels critical orthodoxy has obliged them to distil a unique, all-powerful authorial voice.

In response to this obligation a considerable proportion of Greene criticism—perhaps the vast majority of it—has attempted to present the writer in the conventional guise of a genius writing for an authorial audience of one, a writer who only became popular by mistake. When John Atkins, for instance, suggests that 'Greene can only write well in one way, and this is the first novel in which finds his personal voice' he fails to consider how the effectiveness of 'Greene's voice' in *Stamboul Train* depends on the conventions the narrative invokes and manipulates with the assistance of the reader.[8] Allott and Farris marvel at 'the vast amount of information we seem to have acquired about the

lives and background, not only of the principle figures, but of everyone who makes even a fleeting appearance in the action' of *Stamboul
Train*.[9] They do not pause to reflect on the extent to which the reader
supplies much of this information from his store of literary and social
conventions; instead, they present Greene as a kind of magician who
creates the effect 'partly by following interior monologues, partly by
the use of the appropriate image, partly by means of the packed station interludes, and partly by the exact disposition of broken fragments
of dialogue in which Greene reveals his excellent ear....'[10] In a more
recent analysis, Brian Diemert dissected the representation of popular
culture within the narrative (focusing particularly on the cockney novelist Quin Savory) but did so principally in order to demonstrate that
'while Greene may have denigrated certain aspects of popular culture,
the structures of popular fiction could be valuable so long as they did not
become a trap for the writer'[11]: once again, the emphasis falls on writing
the popular, rather than the popular as a mode of understanding the
relations between writer and reader. No longer subject to the same prejudices as the Leavisite critic, Diemert views Greene's gradual absorption
of popular structures in positive terms but nonetheless incorporates his
reading into precisely the sort of *Bildungsroman* narrative suited to the
valorization of the 'individual talent' at the expense of the public that
enables the individual to communicate his or her talent.

By designating Greene's novel as cinematic, critics attempted to recognize the writer's technical innovations, retain an author-centric scheme
of textual meaning, and account for the book's popularity without
suggesting that the popular audience itself had much to do with the
novel's success. The actual institution of the cinema had little to do
with the designation: instead it functioned as an evasive metaphor
to describe what V.S. Pritchett characterized as the feature that distinguished Greene's writing from that of his contemporaries. In his review
of *It's a Battlefield* (1934) Pritchett wrote:

> ... it is hard to find any novel of quality which presents the social
> problem of today or even draws men and women as they are condi-
> tioned by our industrialized life. There is almost a literary convention
> that the significance of the conditions under which our heroes and
> heroines earn the leisure for their psychological worryings shall never
> be mentioned. We have, of course, our 'modern' novels about 'mod-
> ern' people, with 'modern' talk and even 'modern' morals, but the
> books which present them, however chic, photographic, or daring,
> make little attempt to relate these people to the community....[12]

Although *Stamboul Train* and *It's a Battlefield* certainly attempted to relate their characters to their environments, they achieved an effect of documentary realism not by exhaustively (or 'photographically') presenting reality as such, but rather by allowing readers to round out the novel's presentation of reality through their perceptions of their own reality. While the novel shared this strategy with many examples of the popular cinema—particularly those executed and distributed within the framework of an institutionally propagated set of generic conventions—the strategy itself did not 'belong' to the film medium any more than it did to popular fiction. Pritchett insists otherwise: 'Each character is a cameraman and the shot taken reveals not only what he sees, but how it mingles with the thoughts ticking by in his own life.'[13] As film theorists like Seymour Chatman have observed, however, this is precisely the sort of effect that the cinema can only produce by recourse to specifically literary means (through voice-overs, for instance).[14] By reducing Greene's technique to a cinematic phenomenon and, furthermore, by excluding the actual cinema from the 'cinema technique' Pritchett manages to avoid the difficult question of the audience—the very 'industrialized society' he applauds Greene for at last delivering to readers—and instead concludes his review with a conventional Leavisite portrait of the genius at work, citing '[Greene's] integrity as a writer, his humanity, his subtle moral sense and his patient, supple and startling intuition of human character' in order to demonstrate that '[he] is far more than a merely visual artist.'[15] By appropriating the cinema as a means of communicating sophisticated truths to an elite audience capable of appreciating them, Pritchett prophetically suggested the direction that scholarly understanding of both the film medium and Greene's work would take.

Part II
From Popular Writer to Author

5
Cinematic Evasions After *Stamboul Train*

The cinematic evasion characterized critical approaches to Greene's work for nearly two decades. Between the publication of *Stamboul Train* and the release of *The Third Man* (1949) Greene wrote seven novels that reviewers insisted achieved their effects through the writer's use of the 'cinema technique'. Some of these novels—*A Gun for Sale* (1936), *The Confidential Agent* (1939), and *The Ministry of Fear* (1943)—deployed explicitly conventional characterizations and plot devices in order to achieve unconventional effects after the fashion of *Stamboul Train*. Others, like *It's a Battlefield* and *England Made Me* (1935), seemed to distance themselves from conventional generic processes, and relied more heavily on linguistic variety in order to achieve their effects. Critics like V.S. Pritchett nonetheless affirmed that they worked because in them Greene demonstrated mastery of 'the cinema technique'.[1] Still others—*Brighton Rock* (1938), *The Power and the Glory* (1940), and *The Heart of the Matter* (1948)—deployed symbolic codes that did not sit 'naturally' with their respective generic processes. Neither gangster stories, nor chase thrillers, nor tales of espionage necessarily required their readers to realize the significance of the narratives with reference to Catholic symbolism or ideology, although the rhetorical strategies of each of these novels suggested the legitimacy of such avenues of interpretation. Each of the above novels solicited the participation of its readership in a different way: by deploying different sorts of characters, some recognizable as types and others less so; by emphasizing different elements of the narrative, the actions of some characters, the reflections of others; by using environments concretely or abstractly, and so forth. By characterizing Greene's achievement in these diverse novels as 'cinematic' critics sought to impose a conceptual unity on the oeuvre as a whole, thus helping to create the conditions necessary for future generations to explore 'Greeneland', a term encompassing the imaginative territory ostensibly created solely through an act of Greene's will.

In his study of Greene's fiction the critic John Atkins claimed that *A Gun for Sale* was one of Greene's worst fictions because it succumbed to 'the curse of the film':

> The filmic quality of Greene's fiction has frequently been pointed out and as often praised. In fact, it is his worst work which invites the film comparison. Novels like *A Gun For Sale* could easily be filmed (and were) and remain second-rate literature. Later Greene was to learn that excellence in one particular art depends on an adherence to the rules of that art. It cannot be approached through another.[2]

Atkins strenuously objected to the action in *A Gun for Sale* because he felt that it did not arise from properly motivated characters. He preferred *England Made Me*, one of Greene's least commercially successful novels, and one in which the narrative largely eschews action in favor of presenting a psychological portrait of its ne'er-do-well protagonist through stream-of-consciousness passages and other conventionally literary means. *A Gun for Sale*, by contrast, offers only a few details of its protagonist, the professional assassin Raven: he has a harelip, and he grew up in an institutional home after the state executed his father and his mother cut off her own head with a bread knife. Raven does not 'lack' psychology; even the reader without a knowledge of Freud or Jung can grasp that Raven's childhood trauma has determined his present. In the context of the story, however, Raven reveals these details at a moment in the story when the reader's sympathy is torn between Raven himself and the woman he has kidnapped in order to evade capture by the police, Anne Chowder. Although Raven serves as the novel's protagonist, the narrative does not present Raven as a typical hero: in the opening pages of the novel he assassinates a socialist minister who has worked to keep Europe from descending into war and then compounds his crime—particularly in the eyes of the reader—by murdering the minister's elderly secretary in cold blood in order to eliminate any potential witnesses. For the reader, as well as for Anne, the revelation of Raven's childhood has troubling ramifications. While these details may make Raven comprehensible, they do not necessarily make him sympathetic and they certainly fail to justify the actions he has undertaken throughout the novel (particularly in the opening sequence). Instead, they illuminate the gulf separating understanding and reparation and demonstrate psychology's shortcomings when it comes to explaining or rationalizing actions that have consequences that reach beyond the individual. When Atkins condemns *A Gun for Sale* for having 'nothing fine, nothing noble, nothing attractive in it' he suggests an equivalence between the characters and situations within the narrative (which admittedly seem neither fine nor noble nor attractive) and the reader's perception and interaction with the various elements of the narrative.[3] From his perspective, the only position available to the reader vis-à-vis the narrative is passive acceptance of the novel's ugly portrait of a society in which 'everyone will be prepared to betray you.'[4] F.R. Leavis identified this same attitude with the modern cinemagoer, whom he accused of sitting before the screen in a state of hypnotic receptivity. But it seems a strange 'moral' to divine from a narrative that persistently requires the reader to carefully gauge the extent of Raven's culpability, and to weigh it against Anne's prejudice and the unfettered greed of his employers in the steel and armaments trade. As in *Stamboul Train*, the narrative suspends a final, definitive judgment; but this hardly implies that the reader must take the characters and the world they inhabit at face value, as Atkins and other commentators have been content to do.[5]

Atkins's response to *A Gun for Sale* helps illustrate one of the aspects of Greene's writing that the cinematic label has helped to obscure: namely, that it is no more visual than work executed in other, more literary genres—the *Bildungsroman*, the *nouveau roman*, or, indeed, the psychological novel. *To The Lighthouse* begins with the image of a mouth saying, 'Yes of course, if it's fine tomorrow'; the 'camera' then pulls back to reveal that the mouth belongs to a woman, who continues, 'But you'll have to be up with the lark'. The 'camera' continues to pull back and reveals that she is an older woman, with a smiling young child, and so on.[6] Where *A Gun for Sale* differs from *To The Lighthouse* is not in its representation of a photographic reality—both suggest one, though neither produces one—but rather in its relation of physical actions undertaken by the principle characters. *A Gun for Sale* narrates far more 'action' than Woolf's novel, and asks its readers to assess the characters on the basis of these actions. But just as a text can never produce a photographic image of the world, nor can it perfectly capture the action of a character. When a character does something in a book, it is both a textual event and something else: a happening on a different plane than language, an event in the 'deep structure' of the story. Film represents action quite easily, but has far more difficulty commenting on the actions it presents; novels tend to work the other way around. Both media, however, rely on their respective audiences in order to realize the significance of the action. Since the action communicates itself to the audience structurally, however, it does not necessarily demand a linguistic response. This presents a serious problem for the critic or the intellectual, whose only legitimate medium is language—at least according to institutional conventions that have dominated study since literature in the vernacular languages emerged as a subject worth studying. Thus when Atkins suggests that it is only Greene's 'worst work' that lends itself to cinematic adaptation he reveals on the one hand an awareness that the cinema's strength lies in the depiction of action and, on the other, the common bias that action cannot communicate anything worthy of the critic's attention. (Part IV considers why the erosion of this bias in contemporary scholarship has not yielded more or better results in the field of Greene studies.)

Pritchett's analysis of *It's a Battlefield* is interesting in this regard for precisely the opposite reason: the novel does not seem cinematic at all. Nothing much happens. The central event takes place prior to the opening when the Communist bus driver Jim Drover kills a policeman during a riot in Hyde Park and is sentenced to death. The novel gives the reader only a short glimpse of Drover in his cell, sleeping upright in his chair and presumably dreaming of better days. The central character, Conrad Drover, is—if anything—more a stock figure of ironic modernism than of any popular genre: the intelligent failure who broods incessantly on his own inadequacies. Jim's widow, a rich Fabian improbably named Mr. Surrogate, a factory girl, a widow, an Assistant Commissioner of the police, and a self-deluding journalist round out the cast. Each, in their own unique way, tries and fails to save Jim Drover from the death house. A reprieve arrives at the last moment in the fashion of a *deus ex machina*. For its own inscrutable reasons the Home Office has decided that Jim Drover should not be executed. Of course, each of the characters has by this time concluded that their lives will be much easier when Jim dies. The characters do not grow or progress, and the ending of the novel largely reiterates the status quo of the beginning; what changes over the course of the novel is the reader's relationship to the status quo. To accomplish this transformation *It's a Battlefield* does not rely on action to achieve its effects; in fact, along with *England Made Me*, the novel seems almost like a reversion to the technique of the early novels: insignificant, inconsequential action, followed by reflection. Unlike *The Name of Action* or *Rumour at Nightfall*, however, *It's a Battlefield* does not invoke generic structures (such as the adventure story) only to subsequently abandon them, and its contemporary setting helped make its satire sharper and more accessible than would likely have been the case amidst the psychologizing fog of Greene's Carlist battles. After

all, it contains several scenes that would be nearly impossible to produce cinematically—particularly by the monolithic commercial entities
responsible for producing most films of the time. One such scene paints
the picture of a prison. The chief warder points out several cubes of
stone:

> 'That's Block A. The new prisoners all go there. If they behave them-
> selves they get shifted to that one there, that's Block B. Block C, the
> one we passed, that's the highest grade. Of course if there's any com-
> plaint against them, they get shifted down. It's just like a school,' the
> warder said, raising his old kind eyes with an expression of reverence
> towards Block A.[7]

The filmmaker would have two choices: either show the great cubes of
stone in order to illustrate the irony of the prisoners' progress through
the 'school' or else show the prisoners themselves in order to show the
prisoners performing their appointed tasks. The first would sacrifice the
passage's clarity, the second its irony. A bit later, however, the narrative
uses the passage in an anti-cinematic fashion by repeating it, this time in
the context of a factory:

> In the courtyard the manager pointed. 'That's Block A. The new
> employees go there for the simplest processes. Then if they work well
> they move to Block B, and so to Block C. Everyone in Block C is a
> skilled employee. Any serious mistake and they are moved back to
> Block B.'
> 'I suppose they have more pay,' the visitor said.
> 'And other privileges. A quarter of an hour longer at lunch time.
> The use of the concert-room.'[8]

The specificity of the visual image would, of course, work against the
grain of the passage's irony, which the narrative communicates rhetor-
ically rather than visually. It is not, after all, a visual identity that links
the two locations in the novel, but rather a functional one.

Why then does Pritchett insist on the novel's cinematic qualities
when the very qualities he ascribes to the cinema are in fact rhetorical and literary rather than structural or visual? Allott and Farris seem
much closer to the mark when they suggest that in *It's a Battlefield*
'mood blurs the edges of visual impressions in a manner sometimes
reminiscent of Virginia Woolf's *Mrs. Dalloway*',[9] although the popular
success of *Stamboul Train*—particularly its status as the Book Society's

official selection for December 1932—may have made it difficult for a critic to offer a similar appraisal in 1934 without risking the charge of catering to the sort of middle-brow tastes that had thrust Greene's fourth novel onto the public stage.

When, decades later, Norman Sherry discussed *It's a Battlefield* in the first volume of his *Life of Graham Greene*, he followed Pritchett in attempting to situate the passages above in the context of documentary realism. He did not speak of the cinema, but rather of Greene's research while composing the novel:

> Two areas of the novel required deliberate seeking out of information: the prison scenes and the match factory scenes. On 7 October 1932 when he was in London to learn of the Book Society Award, Greene recorded in his diary: 'Went to Wormwood Scrubs and saw over the prison. In great white letters on the walls, staring out over a flat common ringed with railway lines, the words "Youth Fight or Starve" & the Communist hammer and sickle.'
>
> On 3 December he visited a second prison for copy: 'Took a bus out to Wandsworth Prison to inspect the terrain for Opus V.' He also visited a match factory: 'V[ivien] went up to town for the day. I went into Gloucester & saw over Moreland's Match factory for use in Opus V. The noise of engines, too loud for anyone to speak, gave me a headache after one hour: the employees work from 7.30 to 5 for a five day week, on a minimum of 30/- for girls. Wormwood Scrubs was infinitely preferable.'[10]

Through his selection of details, Sherry suggests that Greene aimed at producing the effect of verisimilitude through the use of the repeated passages; given how clearly the narrative abstracts both environments in order to play the one off the other, this reading seems extraordinary even by the biased standards of literary biography. Priorities had changed since Pritchett's day: with *Mrs. Dalloway* itself a fixture of reading group culture, the cinema widely hailed as a legitimate artistic medium, and Greene still a marginal figure in literary studies, the biographer attempts to reinvent Greene as a gritty realist, a chronicler of his time whose technique complements Sherry's own: the dogged pursuit of people Greene had known, travel to the locations the writer had visited, even the contraction of the same tropical diseases his subject had contracted half a century earlier.[11] The 'definitive' biographer produces a writer who values the definite and concrete, and consequently situates *It's a Battlefield* amidst interpretive codes that seem alien to it.

All of these critics align *It's a Battlefield* with a particular genre, and the genre they each select reflects the time in which they offer their criticisms as well as the priorities of the institutions that valorize their critiques. Pritchett praised Greene's cinematic technique to an audience who presumably had little or no knowledge of the cinema, but who may well have recognized the modernist overtones of his critique. Allott and Farris specifically invoke modernism and high-brow precursors in order to produce an author worthy of study in the academy of F.R. Leavis, T.S. Eliot, and Cleanth Brooks. Sherry addresses a different audience again, one whose aesthetic sensibilities had been shaped to an even greater extent by the immediacy and depth of 'cool' television than by the 'hot' and distant medium of cinema, and for whom Greene's greatest achievements lay in the distant past.[12]

The post-publication fates of *A Gun for Sale* and *It's a Battlefield* illustrate how critics attempted to fit some of Greene's work into accepted generic categories. But during this period Greene also produced several novels that posed a different sort of problem. *Brighton Rock*, *The Power and the Glory*, and *The Heart of the Matter* related highly conventional stories: in the first, a gangster attempts to secure his power; in the second, a fugitive attempts to evade the law; and in the third, an unhappily married man has an affair with disastrous consequences. Like *A Gun for Sale*, each of these novels could be read according to generic norms: the gangster story, the chase thriller, and the melodrama. In these novels, however, Greene deployed typical generic elements—gangsters with scars, dutiful policemen, wise-fool wives—along with strong suggestions that the novels be interpreted according to Catholic doctrine. Thus *Brighton Rock*'s 17-year-old gangster speaks impeccable Latin, 'Credo in unum Satanum', and splits his time evenly between liquidating members of his gang and pursuing eternal damnation.[13] As one contemporary reviewer noted, these two pursuits are in a deep sense mutually exclusive, the one resulting in action, the other in absurdly erudite dialogues between Pinkie, the members of his gang, and his wife, Rose: 'There is plenty of horror and even a degree of pathos in these events, but we have only Mr. Greene's word that the sense of mortal sin has much to do with it.'[14]

The story of *Brighton Rock* takes the reader along a familiar path, whether he recognizes it from Shakespeare's *Macbeth* or from William Wellman's gangster film *Public Enemy* (1931). Having reached the pinnacle of the social order that is familiar to him, Pinkie must now assert the legitimacy of his claim to leadership and destroy anybody who threatens his position. Judith Hess observes that 'This pyramid is a microcosm of the capitalist structure', and that the hero's journey (or the anti-hero's) has various ambiguous ramifications for the member of the audience who must continue to live among capitalist structures when the story ends:

> ...the gangster film implicitly upholds capitalism by making the gangster an essentially tragic figure. The insolubility of his problem is not traced to its social cause; rather the problem is presented as growing out of the gangster's character. His tragic flaw is ambition; his stature is determined by the degree to which he rises in the hierarchy. We are led to believe that he makes choices, not that he is victimized by the world in which he finds himself.[15]

Brighton Rock complicates this reading in several ways. Pinkie's antagonist, Ida Arnold, attacks him from outside the pyramidal gangland structure and manifestly does not aim at supplanting the Boy as leader of the racecourse gang. The narrative uses the very incommensurability of Ida's cheerful vision of a just society and Pinkie's Darwinian machinations to invest the problem of damnation with dramatic force. If Ida's vision was adequate or at all accurate, after all, then people like Pinkie would not exist. Thus even readers indifferent or hostile to Pinkie's ultra-doctrinaire conception of Catholicism or skeptical of what *New Yorker* reviewer Louis Kronenberger referred to as 'some mystical fudge about the Boy's being the Spirit of Evil' can grasp the significance of, say, Rose's decision to 'damn' herself through suicide as alignment with a realistic rather than idealistic vision of her environment.[16]

Contemporary reviewers largely ignored or marginalized the significance of *Brighton Rock*'s explicitly Catholic symbolism. Many, like Kronenberger, noted the novel's affinity with *Macbeth* and observed that Greene had dealt well with the problem of maintaining suspense after starting off 'with a murder which is not a mystery'.[17] Other reviewers simply situated Greene in the thriller tradition. Basil Davenport wrote that Pinkie Brown reminded him of one of the cold-blooded killers 'out of Dashiell Hammett'.[18] *The New Republic* emphatically concurred: 'The author may be own cousin to Robert Louis Stevenson, but his literary father is Dashiell Hammett and nobody else.'[19] Although most critics noted Greene's keen nose for the smells of gutter life, several actually reviewed the novel as an explicitly political critique of the class system. William Plomer felt that Greene accomplished this despite the theological symbolism, rather than because of it, and that the novel showed how 'Catholic writers are quite as sensitive as Marxists to social corruption.'[20]

Jane Southron believed the novel continued the critique Greene had begun in his Liberian travel book *Journey Without Maps*, in which Greene had attempted:

> ...to discover the evolutionary cause of our peculiar susceptibility today, to brutality, to find out not only 'from what we have come' but also 'recall at which point we went astray.' Here the probing is carried further in a brilliant and uncompromising indictment of some of the worst aspects of modern civilization, showing us the hard-boiled criminal mind not as a return to savagery but as a horrible perversion of cerebration.[21]

From Southron's perspective, the Catholic element of the novel (whose elucidation has sustained the bulk of commentary on the novel since the late 1950s[22]) becomes symptomatic of cerebration, and indeed within the novel the elaborate rituals and formulae for salvation and damnation constitute *for the characters* a persuasive justification of the status quo which neither Pinkie nor Rose can imagine escaping. Ida's meddling, Pinkie's horrific end, and the 'worst horror of all' that awaits Rose when she returns from confession coalesce into a comprehensive critique of Pinkie's ambition and character flaws, of the environment that produces him, of middle-class neutrality and its indifference to slums like Nelson Place, of the uses and abuses of faith, and of liberal reformism that refuses to dismantle the micro- and macro-cosmic pyramids erected at Brighton and elsewhere.

Brighton Rock functions rather differently than Hess suggests it should, principally because the gangster genre is not nearly as fixed as she desires it to be. The suspense at the end of the novel focuses not on Pinkie but on Rose. Will she go through with the suicide pact, even though the reader knows that Pinkie has no intention of carrying through with it? He wants to eliminate her in order to prevent her from ever testifying against him, but his desire to destroy her alienates him from the remaining members of his gang. By the time he arrives at Peacehaven with Rose, Pinkie has already fallen to the base of the pyramid although he has not realized it yet. Unlike Hess's gangster-hero, Pinkie no longer has any choices to make: he has lost his legitimacy and the gang itself has dispersed. When the final blow falls, it resounds with bathos:

> 'Come on, Dallow,' he said, 'you bloody squealer,' and put his hand up. Then she couldn't tell what happened: glass—somewhere—broke, he screamed and she saw his face—steam. He screamed and screamed,

with his hand up to his eyes; he turned and ran; she saw a police baton at his feet and broken glass. He looked half his size, doubled up in appalling agony: it was as if the flames had literally got him and he shrank—shrank into a schoolboy flying in a panic and pain, scrambling over a fence, running on.

'Stop him,' Dallow cried: it wasn't any good: he was at the edge, he was over: they couldn't even hear a splash. It was as if he'd been withdrawn suddenly by a hand out of any existence—past or present, whipped away into zero—nothing.[23]

By relating Pinkie's death through the eyes of Rose and Dallow, the narrative suggests the 'hand' of providence at work, although the reader who has followed the story thus far may reasonably question the validity—or, indeed, the desirability—of the characters' reading. Although on one level *Brighton Rock* relates the conventional gangster story of ambition punished, it does so against a backdrop of competing ideologies—Ida's liberal humanism and Pinkie's Catholic Manichaeism—that persistently fail either to normalize the social relations that make life in Brighton so cheap, or to offer the prospect of redress to a situation the reader can only deem intolerable.

Novels like *Stamboul Train* and *A Gun for Sale* played fast and loose with generic conventions in order to work out problems that intellectuals did not normally associate with the genres to which they assigned them. Greene's thrillers (*A Gun for Sale*, *The Confidential Agent*, and *The Ministry of Fear*) made an alarmingly democratic appeal to their readers. They neither required nor produced passive observers of stable genres presented in photographic images, but rather active participants willing to take a hand in dismantling stereotypes and myths. *Brighton Rock*, *The Power and the Glory*, and *The Heart of the Matter* also played fast and loose with generic conventions and required their readers to think carefully about the myths that legitimized the unequal society of the late 1930s and 1940s. But by giving the characters in these novels religious interests, predilections, and obsessions, the novels also posed interesting questions about the relationship between mind and body, ideas and action.

Reviewing *The Heart of the Matter* for *Commonweal*, Evelyn Waugh suggested that 'It is a novel which only a Catholic could write and only a Catholic can understand. I mean that only a Catholic can understand the nature of the problem.'[24] Waugh views faith as a central component of the reader's horizon of expectations—which it arguably is, presuming one wants to be able to read the story as an illustration of doctrine. However, the Catholic beliefs of Henry Scobie, the novel's protagonist, do not matter much in the generic framework of the story: that is, they matter more *as* beliefs than as specifically Catholic beliefs. Whether Scobie's suicide at the end of the novel seems tragic or bathetic depends largely on whether one believes that commitment to ideas is more important than commitment to other people or vice versa. The crucial decision Scobie must make is whether or not to tell his wife that he has been having an affair; the question of mortal sin that stems from Louise's insistence on taking communion together amplifies this problem for the faithful reader but does not alter its dramatic dynamic. Scobie wants his cake, he wants to eat it, and in the end he decides that he prefers death to choosing between the two. The specificity of Scobie's beliefs matters little. For most readers (save perhaps for Waugh) the drama of Scobie's decision to take communion in a state of mortal sin climaxes in the decision to abdicate his responsibility to both wife and lover and to henceforth inhabit a universe divested of beings but filled with systematic and systematizing ideals. The 50-page anticlimax assists believers to confirm their suspicion that Scobie is a saint, and grants unbelievers incontrovertible proof of Scobie's monstrous self-absorption, selfishness, and immaturity.

Once again, however, the novel suspends definitive judgments and leaves the reader free to determine the merits and flaws of Scobie's decision—a freedom numerous critics declared heretical:

> The suggestion of Scobie's salvation in spite of his suicide is a classic instance of Greene's use of grace to attain ends which would be impossible if he were presenting authentic doctrines… Such endings look pious or orthodox, whichever term is correct, but they actually violate Christian ethics (and hence challenge his claim to be a Christian writer) as well as represent an inconsistency in characterization.[25]

In the passage above, Sister Houle's eagerness to demonstrate Greene's heterodoxy prompts her to ignore a number of questions relating to the reader: does the reader have any reason to expect that Scobie has been the recipient of grace? Would the reader find this a desirable outcome? Has Scobie's story even progressed in a fashion that makes the question of grace an important one? Once he decides not to leave Helen but to prevent Louise from learning the truth, Scobie wrenches the question of grace from its theological moorings: only the most devout and literal reader can insist that Scobie's 'damnation' constitutes something qualitatively different than the psychological displacement of guilt it functions as in the story.

In stark contrast to Sister Houle, George Orwell judged the novel inconsistent from this very psychological perspective:

> Scobie is incredible because the two halves of him do not fit together. If he were capable of getting into the kind of mess that is described, he would have got into it years earlier. If he really felt that adultery is a mortal sin, he would stop committing it; if he persisted in it, his sense of sin would weaken. If he believed in Hell, he would not risk going there merely to spare the feelings of a couple of neurotic women. And one might add that if he were the kind of man we are told he is—that is, a man whose chief characteristic is a horror of causing pain—he would not be an officer in a colonial police force.[26]

While Orwell judges Scobie's actions and Houle judges Greene's intentions, both seem as content as Waugh to read *The Heart of the Matter* as an illustration of Catholic doctrine, albeit an inadequate or misleading one; consequently, both view Scobie as an irreducibly tragic figure, a perspective the narrative does not unequivocally endorse.

This last grouping of novels—*Brighton Rock, The Power and the Glory,* and *The Heart of the Matter*—furnished prospective critics of Greene with (quite literally) some 'thing' to talk about: theology, philosophy, ideas— phenomena that could be most easily and most exhaustively explored through the medium of language. For the lover of cinema, the fact that he or she had 'only Mr. Greene's word that the sense of mortal sin has anything to do with [*Brighton Rock*]' might have counted against the book (and indeed, the film scripted by Greene and Terrence Rattigan played down the Catholic element of the novel[27]); for the scholar, the fact that Mr. Greene had said something—rather than 'shown it' or implied it through action at the level of deep structure—signified an active mind mulling over problems that were not alien to the critical discourse of the time. Published shortly before the appearance of the first book-length study of Greene in English, Waugh's review of *The Heart of the Matter* even implied that several of Greene's novels could be made to filter the cognoscenti from the 'mass'. If scholars were loathe to dig deeper into Greene's work, however, it was perhaps because he continued to produce narratives that also functioned through action and deep structure, that performed phenomenally well in the marketplace and successfully appealed to the 'mass', and that could be—and often were—adapted into films. During the 1940s, Greene stories constantly appeared in the cinema: *Went the Day Well* in 1940; *This Gun for Hire* in 1942; *The Ministry of Fear* in 1943; *The Confidential Agent* in 1945; *The Man Within* and *Brighton Rock* in 1947; and *The Fallen Idol* in 1948. Quentin Falk relates that Paramount purchased the rights to *The Ministry of Fear* for £2250 on the basis of the title alone—a happy circumstance for Greene but one that could hardly have endeared him to the era's Leavisite intellectuals.[28]

In this respect, *The Third Man* proved a turning point when British Lion and London Films released it in 1949. Connoisseurs of the cinema took it seriously, awarding it the Grand Prix at the first Cannes Film Festival, but it also set critics on the path of reconsidering the aesthetic potential of a medium they had long derided—as well as the work of a writer who had long been consigned to the ghetto of the 'cinema technique'.[29] Prior to *The Third Man* Greene's novels had been shunted off to various genres: the adventure story, the thriller, the shocker, the gangster story, and even (after *Brighton Rock*) the Catholic novel; after *The Third Man* it became possible to speak of the Greene novel.

6
Greene and Genre

The novels Greene wrote during the 1930s and 1940s produced a discursive field that enabled interested critics to make various statements concerning his work within the institutional contexts that supported them. Greene's continuing popularity and his association with the cinema—not only as a novelist whose work adapted easily to the screen, but also as a writer for hire and as the *Spectator*'s official film critic—prevented him from entering the pantheon of contemporary 'serious' novelists, but did not prevent critics like V.S. Pritchett and Evelyn Waugh from noting that Greene was attempting to do strange, intelligent, often serious things within genres that did not themselves constitute 'serious' literature. Still, his supporters, and even later critics like John Atkins, considered many of the genres in which Greene ostensibly worked somewhat déclassé, unable to sustain the sort of transformations he seemingly wrought upon them. As Ben Ray Redman had suggested apropos of *Stamboul Train*, Greene's best efforts could only amount to very good current fiction because the writer's perception of the genres' strengths prompted him to introduce elements—contemporaneity, action, and suspense—that did not fit the mould of the timeless literary classic.

When the Leavises derided popular fiction for catering to public tastes, their critique was at least consistent with their conception of literature: by appealing to the tastes, biases, and prejudices of readers in the present, writers often produced literature that would not likely withstand 'the test of time'. Peter Rabinowitz, for instance, notes how differently the member of Thomas Dixon Jr.'s *The Leopard's Spots*'s authorial audience appears from the contemporary reader. At the novel's climactic moment the hero makes a speech that ends up unifying the

Democratic party and winning him the nomination for the governorship. Rabinowitz observes that 'Few of the readers who pick up this text have trouble recognizing that, for the authorial audience, this is an inspiring speech—especially since Dixon gives clear signals as to how we should react':

> Two thousand men went mad. With one common impulse they sprang to their feet, screaming, shouting, cheering, shaking each other's hands, crying and laughing. With the sullen roar of crashing thunder another whirlwind of cheers swept the crowd, shook the earth, and pierced the sky with its challenge. Wave after wave of applause swept the building and flung their rumbling echoes among the stars.

'But,' Rabinowitz continues, 'should the actual reader respond emotionally, as the author intended, to the *content* of the speech?' He then quotes the speech as follows:

> ... The African has held one fourth of the globe for 3000 years. He has never taken one step in progress or rescued one jungle from the ape and the adder, except as the slave of a superior race ... and he has not produced one man who has added a feather's weight to the progress of humanity.[1]

Rabinowitz makes the point that the ability to join the authorial audience does not necessarily imply that one passively endorses the hypothetical distortions that enable the writer to produce a narrative for that audience. On the contrary, the reader always enjoys a degree of autonomy from the demands a text makes upon him. As a proponent of literature as temporally and spatially transcendent communication, F.R. Leavis necessarily denied the reader this measure of autonomy, just as generations of theorists approaching the problem of genre have accepted the stability of generic conventions over time and thus denied readers a role in producing meaning through the manipulation of generic structures. Leavis's 'Great Tradition' is, after all, little more than a genre: a set of texts that a particular community agrees perform a similar function. The Leavisites adopted I.A. Richards's definition of this function as the optimal organization of personal experience. Fiction that they believed was based on stock responses—melodramas, thrillers, science fiction, etc.—was debarred from inclusion because it appealed to structures that existed apart from the writer's personal experience.

Of course the optimal organization of personal experience was no less determined by time and place than the association of pinstripe suits and Thompson machine guns with narratives about American gangsters—it simply seemed that way to the scholars doing the determining.

Greene's work throughout the 1930s and 1940s played heavily on his audience's awareness of generic conventions, even to the extent that Myatt's characterization makes joining *Stamboul Train*'s authorial audience in the twenty-first century nearly as problematic as joining the authorial audience of *The Leopard's Spots*. But different audiences used these conventions in different ways. Some critics used the conventions in *Stamboul Train* to read a story celebrating modernity, others a story glancing sideways at it. The producers at Fox used the narrative's affinity with the thriller tradition in order to appropriate and paraphrase the story as 'two youthful hearts fleeing from life, crashing across Europe on the wheels of fate'.[2] Some of the most influential scholars of the day clearly used these conventions in order to justify not reading the novel at all. The later 'Catholic novels' were not always read by Catholics, although even non-Catholics seemed able to grasp the significance of those conventions which other readers felt only Catholic readers could understand.[3] Semantic *and* syntactic conventions that worked well on the page did not always work so well on the screen: thus Mabel Warren's lesbianism failed to make the final cut of *Orient Express*, and the need for maintaining wartime morale meant that the villains of 1942's *This Gun for Hire* had to work for a fifth-column chemical plant, and not for a British steel firm doing its patriotic duty by producing armaments by the ton. The very adaptability of Greene's work counted against it because it demonstrated only too clearly that while his texts could conceivably 'mean what they were' in sound Leavisite fashion they could also mean what somebody else needed them to mean or desired them to mean. Even those critics like Pritchett and Waugh who defended Greene did so by imposing categorizations that sought to limit the ways his work could be appropriated. By asserting a claim to superior understanding of the work they attempted to rule out contemporary scholars (through the cinematic designation), Greene's vast non-Catholic readership (through the Catholic novelist designation), traditionalists (through the 'modern' designation), the squeamish (through the hard-boiled, thriller, and 'seedy' designations), and others as legitimate readers.

As Rick Altman has noted, 'Genres were always—and continue to be— treated as if they spring full-blown from the head of Zeus.'[4] All the generic designations applied to Greene's work implied fixed categories with precisely the sort of stable characteristics that so much of the fiction encouraged its readers to oppose, reconsider, and redefine. The alleged fixity of these conventions made the various designations interchangeable with 'the popular' in scholarly discourse since intellectuals like Richards specifically theorized the 'mass man' as one incapable of sufficiently organizing his experience to undergo valuable change. From the Leavisite point of view, genres were fixed in large part because the people who produced and consumed generic literature did not change. In *Fiction and the Reading Public*, Q.D. Leavis pined for a lost era in which this had not been the case, when the people who might have produced and consumed what she considered generic literature (had such a designation been discernible in the eighteenth century) were too illiterate, poor, and overworked to do so. Altman addresses this bias, taking care to illustrate the explicitly political significance Leavis preferred to treat aesthetically:

> Just as city planners once thought that people would automatically inhabit their city as designed, so genre theorists once believed that readers and viewers would automatically follow the lead of textual producers. In fact, there was once a time when both expectations were to a great extent correct—not because use-as-planned is built into cities and texts, but because the economic and social support structures surrounding cities and texts silently and effectively exhorted populations and audiences to play their expected role.[5]

The Leavisite program actively propagandized the idea that 'use-as-planned' was in fact built into texts—a proposition contested by Greene's fiction and that of other successful writers (from Wells and Bennett through John le Carré and Len Deighton)—if not always thematically, then by the sheer range of readers who helped realize their texts through horizons of expectation cultivated across class, ethnic, geographical, and educational boundaries. The Leavisites could not abide the popular-but-serious genre since it threatened to erase the boundary between discrimination and popular taste over which they had appointed themselves stewards. Leavis himself unsurprisingly saved some of his most bitter rhetoric for Arnold Bennett, whom he accused of manufacturing geniuses from Philistines: 'How is it that [Bennett] can go on exposing himself in this way without becoming a by-word and a laughing stock? (For the author of *The Old Wives' Tale* is a public figure, and differs in this from the minor pontiffs who compete with him in the Sunday papers).'[6] No institutionally sanctioned intellectual of the 1930s—save, perhaps, for Empson—could have subscribed to the manifesto against universality and timelessness Antonin Artaud issued (from a very different kind of institution) in 1938:

> It is idiotic to reproach the masses for having no sense of the sublime, when the sublime is confused with one or another of its formal manifestations, which are moreover always defunct manifestations. And if for example a contemporary public does not understand *Oedipus Rex*, I shall make bold to say that it is the fault of *Oedipus Rex* and not of the public.[7]

The public did understand Greene—a fact that made it difficult to understand his work in terms of the timeless and universal. *Stamboul Train* had manifestly not sprung from the head of Zeus. And to make matters worse (for a certain type of reader) the work itself seemed somehow free of formal constraints, hopping lightly between the page and the screen, and disconcertingly clouding the generic lens through which more sympathetic readers attempted to apprehend it.

For intellectuals the problem of Greene had always been the problem of genre, just as the problem of literature in general had always been the problem of genre: how could one identify literature and distinguish it from that which was not literature? Most scholars could not conceptualize Greene's accomplishment because they were ill-equipped to recognize the collection of texts he had produced over 20 years *as* an accomplishment. The novels he produced could be adequately explained with reference to the generic categories that seemed to delimit the extent of their signifying power (as in Judith Hess's model of the gangster film, which cannot help but endlessly reiterate the punishment of ambition).[8] But the absence of a dynamic theory of genre was only one side of the problem; on the other lay the vast, under-theorized audience split into the cognoscenti and the mass whose members lacked the ability to organize the impressions of their own experiences sufficiently to transcend the need for stock responses. The only 'accomplishment' discernible in Greene's career from such a perspective would have been the marshalling together of a broad range of stock responses: nothing to distinguish Greene from the most junior writer on the staff of *John Bull* or *Tit-bits*. Generic processes, as theorized by Jameson and Altman, could not be identified (much less valorized) because on the one hand intellectuals failed to recognize the generic qualities of the literature they read, while on the other they vigorously resisted the idea that the bookish activity non-intellectuals engaged in could be considered reading in any legitimate sense of the term.

In short, Greene's work in the 1930s and 1940s furnished critics and reviewers with a broad discursive field, capable of sustaining a wide range of generic operations—save, of course, for the generic operation most valued by intellectuals: the imposition of rules of coherence predicated on the grounds of the unique authorial personality. Even Eliot's injunction to artists, to extinguish themselves in the service of the tradition, could only be applied to writers whom intellectuals recognized as being in some sense larger than life to begin with, and whose efforts at self-immolation on the altar of art were therefore all the more visible. The Leavisite 'great artist' was himself a genre: a collection of choices and limitations and of semantic and syntactic relationships embodied in various texts that enabled a critic to suggest that the writer composed his work for an audience of one. Greene's work, by contrast, was too heterogeneous, his appeal too broad, and his use of conventions too pronounced to sustain under protracted scrutiny the idea of a 'Greene' genre.

The Third Man did very little to alter the status quo insofar as it touched the relationship between intellectuals and popular culture. No single book or film could have: the political values of the intelligentsia had to change before such a transformation could become conceivable, and institutions themselves had to adapt before critics and teachers could put the ideas into practice. For Greene's own critical fortunes, however, *The Third Man* marked a significant turning point. Prior to the film's release he had produced fiction whose significance could easily be assigned to various genres and whose technique could be characterized (and implicitly dismissed) as cinematic; with *The Third Man* he succeeded in producing popular cinema that encouraged intellectuals to apprehend and formulate its significance in literary terms. The film worked in the same way that many of his fictions worked: deploying the semantic vocabulary of ostensibly stable genres, but doing so in a fashion that invited audiences to dismantle for themselves the generic structures that, in Richards's and Hess's view, *contained* meaning. From this perspective, the writer producing a 'genre' fiction simply dipped his hands into the generic well, plucked out a selection of readymade meanings, and splashed them across his or her text—as Atkins and others have argued Greene did in composing the entertainments that performed so well as films. Destabilizing genre in an avowedly popular medium cleared room for critics to apply a new kind of discourse to Greene's work: the 'cinematic technique', redolent of high modernist practices but effectively dispersed across prohibitively popular genres, could afterward be appropriated by interested parties and discussed as 'Greene's technique'.

7
Strategic Moves: Genres, Brands, Authors and *The Third Man*

The Third Man helped turn the tide of Greene's critical reputation. Between the treatment, screenplay, and film of his original story, Greene produced a set of texts that enabled intellectuals to valorize him in an institutionally useful way: as an 'author' or, as the young generation of critics and filmmakers at *Cahiers de Cinema* and the *Village Voice* might have called him, as an 'auteur'.

Carol Reed's film of Greene's script did many of the things Greene's earlier novels had done: it mixed genres and constantly set the viewer at odds with the allegedly fixed rules of generic convention. It ended on an ambiguous, half-comic and half-tragic note for its protagonist, and failed to deliver the tidy resolution that even progressive intellectuals associated with the medium in general and with Hollywood films in particular.[1] It relied heavily on the signifying power of action—save that it did so in a medium far better suited to achieving effects through action than the printed word. It deployed identifiable character 'types' in situations that seemed a step ahead of viewers' horizons of expectation, playing upon stock responses in order to transform them into something else. In short, *The Third Man* performed all the work that Greene's 'cinematic' novels had performed, but in a medium that elite prejudice had hitherto rejected on the grounds that its commercial status precluded legitimate aesthetic effects (i.e., non-stock responses).

But although *The Third Man* worked the way many of Greene's novels had worked, it belonged to an entirely different world: to Hollywood—then as now a byword for commercial values and debased art. Several features distinguished this film from others that had been adapted from his work. Firstly, some of these films, like *The Ministry of Fear* and *The Confidential Agent*, had been produced by major Hollywood studios. Others, like *Brighton Rock* and *The Fallen Idol*, had been produced on a much smaller scale in Britain but had employed Greene as a screenwriter. With *The Third Man* Greene finally pressed his talents into the service of a Hollywood film. From an intellectual perspective, the film should have simply exploited stock responses and done little to wake viewers from the semi-conscious state of hypnotic receptivity F.R. Leavis attributed to them; critics, however, took a rather different view when Selznick and Korda released the picture in 1949. William Whitebait, writing in the *New Statesman and Nation* (one of the few contemporary journals to win Q.D. Leavis's approval), observed that 'Karas's improvisations, Graham Greene's characters and dialogue, and Carol Reed's narrative skill with camera, actors, and background form a collaboration of genius and provide tensions that lift this film high out of its thriller class.'[2] Whitebait attributes to the film an imaginative agency that intellectuals had long denied to the medium in general. But he goes further than this: by suggesting that the contributions of Greene, Reed, and Karas (the Viennese street musician who composed the film's zither score) lifted the film 'high out of its thriller class' he implies that stories which deploy generic codes do not thereby surrender all claim to the status of art or literature. Seventeen years earlier, Redman and Armstrong had retreated from making precisely this sort of statement of principle, suggesting instead that, at best, one could consider *Stamboul Train* 'very good current fiction'.

Secondly, *The Third Man* performed better than most responsible Hollywood producers dared to dream their productions would perform—better, in fact, than any subsequent Greene adaptation has performed. David O. Selznick himself had written that he hoped *The Third Man* would blaze a new trail for international film finance and production, allowing producers on both sides of the Atlantic to turn currency restrictions and investment regulations on their heads to the mutual benefit of companies in both the United States and Britain. In his memos to Korda and Reed, Selznick constantly stressed that such cross-fertilization would not be possible unless they could produce a film that American audiences would find palatable:

> It is all well and good for a film to be a great hit in the West End of London, or with the critics of the London Daily Press, but it is quite another thing when the film reaches Main Street, Kansas City ... Carol should bear in mind that unless THE THIRD MAN is successful on both sides of the ocean, deals of this kind will be impossible in future, and his own work will be tremendously affected, since obviously neither Alex [Korda] nor [Arthur] Rank nor anyone else will be able to tolerate such schedules, or to permit such costs, as those

involved in recent films. Further, neither American freelance stars, nor those under contract to studios, will be available for future British films if the films are unsuccessful for the American producers who are affiliated in them and damaging to the following of the stars because American audiences find them too British in basic material, and/or in dialogue and treatment, and/or in understandability.[3]

One can scarcely imagine a mission statement better geared to confirm the contemporary intellectual in his or her prejudice against film. Selznick's vision of international cooperation implied subordinating the British flavor of the film to American tastes—a sensible financial policy considering box office demographics, but one hardly geared to endear him (or the filmmakers who listened to him) to scholars enamored of the myth of the artist's autonomy.

Peter Rabinowitz stresses that 'once he or she has made certain initial decisions, any writer who wishes to communicate—even if he or she wishes to communicate ambiguity—has limited the range of subsequent choices';[4] Selznick's memo helps illustrate how the economic realities of the film industry further limited the range of choices Greene and Reed could make in putting together *The Third Man*. Selznick based his scarcely veiled threat to Reed—fall into line or else—on a sound analysis of the problems confronting the British film industry in the late 1940s. ABC and the Rank Organization owned 1000 of Britain's 4500 cinemas—generally the best, in terms of location and admissions— and regularly received three-fifths of the country's box office receipts.[5] Through arrangements with American corporations (i.e., Warner Brothers, 20th Century Fox, etc.) they could avail themselves of the more inexpensive rental fees exacted by Hollywood films that had generally recouped their costs through American box office receipts alone:

> In 1946 British cinemas paid £26 millions to hire the films they showed. After the deduction of expenses connected with distribution, £8 1/2 millions was the amount left for the film companies, of which less than £2 millions went to British companies... The position of the independent producer in these conditions has been made almost impossible.[6]

If Korda wanted to continue producing films on the same ambitious scale as those he produced and directed during the 1930s (e.g., *The Private Life of Henry VIII*, *Rembrandt*, etc.), then he had to discover a method of financing them that did not rely entirely on British receipts. In the silent era, it might have been easier to produce films that could succeed elsewhere—on the continent, or even in the Far East—but in the age of the talkie, a common language made the United States the most obvious target for penetration, despite the latter's inestimable material advantages. Succeeding in the United States meant taking American tastes, attitudes, biases, and prejudices on board while developing a property for the cinema. Selznick, for instance, harped on the difficulty American audiences experienced in understanding British accents—a valid point, but one whose proposed solution no British filmmaker could possibly have countenanced without a deep shudder: 'It has been my experience that British actors are capable of two or three degrees of "Englishness" in their speech. If they would only sound like Churchill everything would be all right.'[7] Success only required the canny producer to eliminate most of Britain, its social divisions, and the class system as viable subjects: what could be more straightforward?

British, continental, and international economic policy likewise pushed producers like Korda into a corner. When businesses made profits on international investments they often found it impossible to convert those profits from the local currency in order to repatriate them for reinvestment. For writers like Greene, currency restrictions had sometimes been a boon: since the profits from international translations of his work tended to get 'trapped' in local banks across Europe and Asia he always had a reserve waiting to be withdrawn when he chose to visit different countries.[8] In light of the stringent controls placed on currency during and after the Second World War, producers began seeing their trapped funds in the same way: as capital for investment on foreign productions, capable of paying for local crews and (albeit less frequently on account of accents) local casts. Korda's decision to film *The Third Man* in Vienna or Rome—rather than in London, the location for which Greene had initially conceived the story—stemmed from these considerations.

In March 1948, the British government pushed through additional reforms that they hoped would stimulate the domestic film industry. They imposed a quota, allowing American companies to export a fixed number of films for every British film that it distributed. American companies were to be allowed no more than £4.25 million in sterling remittances of profits made by US films in the United Kingdom. The money, they hoped, would be used 'partly on approved commercial undertakings and partly on "film purposes" ', and would help keep British artists and technicians employed.[9] This gave rise to the 'quota quickie', nominally British productions slapped together as quickly as possible in order to secure slots for more profitable Hollywood fare—a result that surprised many contemporary commentators. In the *New Statesman*, for instance, Woodrow Wyatt had predicted that American companies would swarm Britain in order to exploit their sterling reserves, and that 'the swollen resources of American-sponsored British companies will enable them to bid higher for personnel, for film rights of books, and to outdo their genuine British counterparts in every direction'.[10] As Selznick's memo suggests, this appears to have been Korda's business plan as well and the steps he took in assembling *The Third Man* suggest that he was quite comfortable with whatever compromises and concessions success in the American market might necessitate.

As *The Third Man* moved into production Korda issued a public statement in reply to criticisms leveled at him by Paul Rotha (a leading British documentary filmmaker and critic), acknowledging the interrelatedness of aesthetic and commercial interests in the contemporary film industry: '... while the avant-garde should be a carefully fostered and important part of the nation's film industry, it should not be forgotten that it is the garde itself which has to carry the day.'[11] Korda, like Selznick, was sensibly averse to risk and desired, wherever possible, to make films capable of appealing to as wide an audience as possible— an attribute for which Greene, in his capacity as film reviewer for *The Spectator* from 1935 to 1940, often took him to task. In one of the most xenophobic reviews of his career, for instance, Greene lamented that 'There are times when one cannot help brooding with acute distress on the cheap silly international pictures exported under [the label 'English film']:

> England, of course, has always been the home of the exiled; but one may at least expect a wish [*sic*] that *émigrés* would set up trades in which ignorance of our language and culture was less of a handicap: it would not grieve me to see Mr. Alexander Korda seated before a cottage loom in an Eastern country, following an older and better tradition. The Quota Act has played into foreign hands, and as far as I know, there is nothing to prevent an English film unit being completely staffed by technicians of foreign blood.[12]

Thirteen years later, with *The Third Man*, Greene helped produce just such an international picture for the same 'alien' producer hoping to exploit the sterling reserves of an American firm and employ primarily foreign (i.e., British) talent while shooting on-location in an Eastern country.

Greene matched his outspoken contempt for Korda's crass (even 'alien') commercialism with an equally outspoken profession of avant-gardist aspirations. He publicly mocked Selznick's role in the production of *The Third Man*. In an article for the 1958 *International Film Annual*, he had related the story of a production meeting with 'DOS':

> The conference began as usual about 10.30 p.m. and finished after 4 a.m. Always by the time we reached Santa Monica dawn would be touching the Pacific.
>
> 'There's something I don't understand in this script, Graham. Why the hell does Harry Lime...?' He described some extraordinary action on Lime's part.
>
> 'But he doesn't,' I said.
>
> Selznick looked at me for a moment in silent amazement.
>
> 'Christ, boys,' he said, 'I'm thinking of a different script.'
>
> He lay down on his sofa and crunched a benzedrine. In ten minutes he was as fresh as ever, unlike ourselves.
>
> I look back on David Selznick now with affection. The forty pages of notes remained unopened in Reed's files, and since the film proved a success, I suspect Selznick forgot that the criticisms had ever been made.[13]

In the *Film Annual* article, he mentions that he continued to review Korda poorly even after he began to write films for him—but Greene also gives Korda credit for 'neglecting' to contractually stipulate that either he or Reed needed to take any of Selznick's criticisms seriously. He works hard to give the impression that Korda conspired to allow Reed and himself free rein in creating an experimental film that sought to explore Cocteau's thesis that mistakes in continuity constitute the unconscious poetry of a film.[14] But few contemporary reviewers mistook *The Third Man* for *Blood of a Poet*, and scholarship has since uncovered evidence that Reed took many of Selznick's suggestions on board.[15] As Whitebait observed, the film looked like a thriller, had characters that behaved like characters in a thriller, sounded like a thriller (albeit an unusual one), and worked like a thriller (the very genre that enabled Hitchcock to move easily from Britain to Hollywood)—a situation that could not have come about without substantive agreement between the creative and financial teams as to who constituted the authorial audience for the picture. If Greene had written *Blood of a Poet*, or if Reed had somehow managed to shoot it from Greene's script, then Selznick (and probably Korda as well) simply would have pulled out his financing and/or his stars and there would have been no film whatsoever.[16]

The financial constrictions and industrial regulations Korda confronted furnished the filmmakers with one set of problems to solve; but the American film industry had also undergone a profound transformation during the development of the film. Several months before production on *The Third Man* began the United States Supreme Court issued its decision in the long-standing case against Paramount Pictures and the eight major Hollywood studios. The verdict demolished the vertical integration of the industry: the possession of both the means of film production and the means of distribution and exhibition by a common owner. Paramount and the other major studios made films, but they also owned or controlled the distributors responsible for leasing the prints of finished films to the theatres, and even, in many cases, the theatres and theatrical chains that exhibited the films. When one of the major studios decided to produce a film they knew in advance that the film would be distributed and that it would find an audience thanks to the geographical distribution of the studios' theatrical chains. The Supreme Court determined that this situation constituted a restraint of trade:

> In 92 cities of the country with populations over 100,000 at least 70 per cent of all the first-run theatres are affiliated with one or more of the five majors. In 4 of those cities the five majors have no theatres. In 38 of those cities there are no independent first-run theatres.[17]

The decision ordered the studios to divest themselves of their distribution interests and altered the entire dynamic of Hollywood film production: it reintroduced an element of competition into what interested observers had long viewed as a monopoly, but in doing so it eliminated the cushion provided by the studio's theatre chains and undermined the security that enabled the studios to periodically take risks in terms of subject matter, casting, promotion, and so on. For different commercial interests, divestment meant different things: for the majors, it meant trying to ensure that their films would still succeed in finding audiences, generally by throwing money at the screen in the form of sprawling narratives, lavish sets, and increasingly expensive stars; for the independents it meant that for the first time since the rise of the majors they had a chance to compete on a more even footing— provided, of course, they could produce the sort of films exhibitors believed their audiences wanted to see. Selznick was an independent but he was a major independent, with a studio pedigree (MGM, Paramount, RKO, MGM again), films like *Gone with the Wind* and *Duel in the Sun* in the can, and an agent brother, Myron, who had wooed Hitchcock to Selznick International Pictures for the proverbial song.[18]

Selznick's status as a Hollywood insider/outsider undoubtedly shaped his view of genre, particularly in terms of how it could be used to exploit a given property. For the major producer, generic identification was a double-edged sword that most of the studios had avoided whenever possible during Hollywood's 'golden age' (usually assigned to the period from the beginning of synchronized sound through the Second World War).[19] On the one hand, marketing a film as an adventure story or a horror film or a western could ensure that fans of that particular genre would flock to the theatre. On the other hand, however, it meant that fans who did not appreciate the genre might very well stay away. John Kenneth Galbraith has persuasively argued that large businesses tend to prefer security to profit, and Hollywood during the studio system's golden age was just about as secure a business as any.[20] Rick Altman has shown how the studios' financial security led them to market their films in a way that de-emphasized generic identification, citing as one example the publicity poster for *Only Angels Have Wings*:

> Hollywood has no interest, as this poster clearly suggests, in explicitly identifying a film with a single genre. On the contrary, the industry's publicity purposes are much better served by implying that a film offers 'Everything the Screen can give you'. During Hollywood's golden years, this usually meant offering something for the men ('EACH DAY a rendezvous with Peril!'), something for the women ('EACH NIGHT a Meeting with Romance!'), and an added something for that *tertium quid* audience that prefers travel to adventure or romance ('the mighty tapestry of the FOG-SHROUDED ANDES').[21]

Smaller studios like Universal (as well as those that faced financial difficulties) played it safer by marketing their films under generic labels: Universal Western, Universal Gibson Productions (westerns starring Hoot Gibbons), Universal Sci-Fi, etc.[22]

At first, Selznick marketed *The Third Man* the way that Columbia had marketed *Only Angels Have Wings*; that is, he attempted to appeal to the generic expectations of several different groups. The US trailer for the film began with a prestige-oriented title 'Announcing the FIRST GREAT PICTURE OF 1950'. The designation 'great' could signify nothing (to a critic like Leavis, for instance, who would not have felt that any film could be 'great') or it could signify everything. It would mean something different, of course, to people who had enjoyed *Stagecoach* and to those who had preferred *How Green Was My Valley*, but its seeming neutrality was its greatest strength as a marketing tool and might even have appealed to people who did not often attend the cinema but who adopted a less narrow perspective on its artistic potential than the Leavises.[23] In contemporary terms, it might have appealed to the Merchant-Ivory audience, the predominately middle-aged and middle-class 'prestige-picture' audience. After the trailer's opening title a virile male voice said, 'The third man—hated by a thousand men...', and was immediately answered by a sultry female voice, '...desired by one woman'. The male voice cut in again with 'The third man—hanging is too good for him', followed once more by the female voice: 'Nothing is too good for the third man.' The male voice speaks over shots of action—a shadow dashing down an alley, the police invading the sewers—while the woman's voice speaks over shots of Alida Valli emoting in various poses. The second half of the trailer addresses the *tertium quid* audience for whom neither sewer chases nor tears work any magic, and instead focuses their attention on Vienna, 'a city fearful of its present, uncertain of its future. The once-gay capital of a light-hearted people. Here in the shadows of its palaces and ruins is all the tenderness, drama and suspense of the story of the third man.'[24] Initially, then, the producers determined to pursue a multi-genre approach to selling the film and shaping audience expectations.

As the film progressed from the Cannes Film Festival and into the theatres, the producers began to realize that they had a film that they could exploit much more comprehensively than they had at first believed possible. Anton Karas's score for *The Third Man* galvanized all of the audiences that were exposed to it. Nearly every review of the film contained a paragraph devoted exclusively to the curiously apropos twang that accompanied nearly every shot. Whitebait enthused in the *New Statesman*:

> What sort of music it is, whether jaunty or sad, fierce or provoking, it would be hard to reckon; but under its enthrallment the camera comes into play, looking here and there and at close range springing surprises.... [The tune] will see us through the whole adventure. At moments the plucked chords will instil a plangent horror. The unseen zither player...is made to employ his instrument much as the Homeric bard did his lyre.[25]

Cyril Ray thanked Karas's 'neurotic nerve-wracking zither' for helpfully drowning out Bing Crosby's 'terribly Oirish' performance as a 'Californian leprechaun' in *Top o' the Morning*.[26] An unusually reserved piece in *Sight and Sound* described Karas's music as 'trite and commonplace' but commended Reed for recognizing that 'the zither, as sheer sound, was something fresh enough and new enough to excite the listener's interest and attention whatever the quality of the music it played'.[27] In 1950, *Billboard* announced that Guy Lombardo's orchestrated version of the song was the fourth best-selling album in America. Karas's version was number three.[28] Nobody involved in the production of the film had any idea that the music would be successful. A British Lion executive who had just seen the finished film for the first time wrote to Reed: 'Dear Carol, saw *The Third Man* last night. Love it. I think you've got a big success there. But please take off the banjo.'[29] Selznick appeared inclined to agree with him until the London premier. He immediately cabled his office:

> Cannot commence to tell you sensation caused by Karas's zither music in 'Third Man'. It is rage of England and has already sold more record copies than any other record in entire history of the record business in England...and ads here use 'Hear Harry lime theme,' etc., in type dwarfing all other billing...Inevitably this success will be repeated America if we are prepared for it. We should be able to make a fortune out of this music.[30]

The Third Man became one of the first nonmusical films to be marketed on the basis of its score as Selznick began to plan 'a unique distribution of *The Third Man* to tie in with anticipated popularity of its background music'.[31] The success of the film in London, and particularly of its unconventional musical soundtrack, enabled its producers to turn the generic process on its head: rather than limiting *The Third Man*'s potential buyers (that is, its audience members) by associating it with a genre, or even appealing to a broad cross-section of the public by associating with multiple genres (tenderness, romance, *and* suspense), they begin cultivating the '*Third Man*' brand itself, which possessed one major advantage over conventional generic designations: it was proprietary. Altman writes: 'Besides films as such, studios also create labels, characters, plots, theme songs, techniques, processes and devices that may in the long run have greater value than the films in which they were first deployed.'[32] Over the next decade Selznick and Korda exploited their proprietary rights to the fullest.

After the soundtrack came the radio. Material related to *The Third Man* was first broadcast in April 1951. As the program began, the show's producer gave the home audience a flat summary of the action:

> Greetings from Hollywood, ladies and gentlemen. In tonight's play, *The Third Man*, we have a perfect setting for a murder mystery—post-war Europe: filled with spies, intrigue, and black markets. Into this atmosphere of cunning and subterfuge comes an American, only to take up the trail of the unknown murderer of his friend. A trail that leads him into hazardous and chilling adventure....[33]

A commercial cuts in and advises young ladies to use Lux facial products in order to find husbands by the summer. Then the play starts with Karas's theme song and Joseph Cotten, reprising his role as the hapless Holly Martins, asks Colonel Calloway for a drink. This abridged version of the film simplifies Martins's character: he is rarely drunk and does not swing at Calloway in the bar. The abridgement drops the problem of Martins's poverty and thus loses any reason to include the embarrassing sequence at the literary lecture the hero delivers under false pretences. Far from the starry-eyed romantic of Reed's film, the Lux Radio Theatre's Holly Martins is a clear-thinking and thoroughly conventional hero who happens to have bad information on account of European duplicity. Lime dies screaming 'Suckers and mugs!' repeatedly, until a gunshot cuts him off at 'Suckers'. The play ends with no suggestion that Martins fired the shot.

The Lux Radio Theatre play was only the beginning of *The Third Man*'s metastasis. According to Charles Drazin the BBC approached Orson Welles in 1950 with an idea for a project:

> It was an irresistible concept, its very premise contained those opening disembodied lines of the film. 'I never knew the old Vienna before the war, with its Strauss music, its glamour and easy charm—Constantinople suited me better.'...Here was someone who could have been Harry Lime, in *Sunset Boulevard* fashion, recalling an episode that ended with the death of Harry Lime.[34]

By 1951, Welles had started writing and performing *The Lives of Harry Lime* for BBC radio. The series recounted the adventures that Harry Lime had lived through prior to the events of *The Third Man*. In the episode 'A Ticket to Tangier' (broadcast on 24 August 1951) Lime becomes involved with a plot to sell off a huge store of heroin that had come into the possession of a woman after her husband died in mysterious circumstances. When he discovers that the woman murdered her husband to get her hands on the dope he immediately alerts the authorities, then relates the end of the adventure: 'I had no trouble in getting a good price in Marseilles the next week. But honestly, I don't approve of drugs. That's why I threw the original stuff into the Bay of Tangier and delivered several nicely wrapped packages of confectioner's sugar. So my conscience is clear.'[35] Drazin notes that 'There were also comic strips, and a 1959 TV spin-off starring Michael Rennie (although the producers had originally wanted James Mason), playing Harry Lime as an international art dealer cum amateur detective.'[36]

If the film of *The Third Man* could support multiple configurations of generic expectations, then the proprietary genre (or 'brand') that the film's producers created from the raw material of the film was polymorphous. Patriotic Americans could experience Holly Martins as Boy Scout on Lux Radio Theatre. David Thomson once remarked that *The Third Man* suffered from Welles's prodigious charisma: 'There is a struggle between Greene's bleak attitude (poisoned penicillin for children) and the film's urge to give people a lift (not just Welles, but the comedy and the zither)'; on the BBC, however, listeners could have their lift without the poisoned children.[37] And for the vast *tertium quid* audience there remained the theme song, disembodied from the poisoned children, the foolish American hero, and the charming gangster, but still redolent of some imaginative and handily non-specific milieu, neatly packaged and ready to fill the home with all the tenderness, romance, and suspense of the story of 'the third man'—whoever one decided he was.

The Third Man generated a perfect storm. It provided the producers with a quasi-discursive space (i.e., the brand) vague enough to sustain contradictions as well as correspondences and similarities. To a certain extent the film-brand operated along the lines suggested by Foucault:

> To take a very simple example, one could say that Ann Radcliffe not only wrote *The Castles of Athlin and Dunbayne* and several other novels, but also made possible the appearance of the Gothic horror novel at the beginning of the nineteenth century; in that respect her author-function exceeds her own work ... Ann Radcliffe's texts opened the way for a certain number of resemblances and analogies which have their model or principle in her work. The latter contains signs, figures, relationships, and structures which could be reused by others.[38]

The Third Man indeed made possible a number of resemblances and analogies that other producers could recycle. In *Rear Window* and *Vertigo* Hitchcock used Jimmy Stewart's characters in a fashion strikingly reminiscent of the way Reed had used Cotten's. Hitchcock's *North by Northwest* involved an innocent character attempting to solve a mystery he repeatedly fails to comprehend.[39] Numerous commentators have remarked that Albert Broccoli and Harry Saltzman's Bond films all bear the imprimatur of *North by Northwest*,[40] although Drazin has observed that Ian Fleming began writing Bond's character shortly after the BBC began broadcasting the lives of the resurrected, reformed, 'cool', and jet-setting Harry Lime.[41] The intertextual web only gets thicker the longer one struggles with it. But the branding of *The Third Man* did more than make possible a number of resemblances and analogies; it created a new field of legitimacy: the official product to be preferred in the face of mere imitators. In this sense, it emptied *The Third Man* of anything that intellectuals would have recognized as significant: what, after all, could an art dealer cum amateur detective have to do with Greene's story of a hack writer gradually realizing that his best friend poisons children for profit? Nothing of course—save that audiences were, for a time, prepared to accept that it did have something to do with it. The exploitation of the film created a proprietary genre in which the producers of content could 'fill out' the brand, but it simultaneously generated a complex system of legal relationships that conferred on those producers a level of control that probably would have left Radcliffe's publishers speechless.

In a sense the brand represents an author-function without identifiable authors but nonetheless granted all the authority available via legal protections to writers under the modern copyright regime. Like the modern corporation that cultivates it, the brand can go on forever provided only that it offers some sort of product or service that people have both the desire and means to procure. In a very real sense, Greene was and remains the 'author' of the phenomenon, since without the story he wrote for Korda there could have been no comic books, record pressings, or television programs. At the same time, however, there comes a definite point at which Greene stops authoring the phenomenon: that is, when he no longer contributes to the process of expanding the boundaries of the proprietary genre.

Gene Roddenberry, the 'author' of the *Star Trek* phenomenon, did not stop growing his proprietary genre until he died; George Lucas continues to expand the boundaries of the *Star Wars* phenomenon today and may well do so until he dies. Greene did not wait so long to remove himself from *The Third Man*. He wrote the treatment, later published as the novella *The Third Man* in an edition that paired the story with a reprint of 'The Basement Room' (re-titled to confirm that it was the story that had served as the origin of Reed's film, *The Fallen Idol*); he then wrote the screenplay purchased by British Lion and produced by Korda and Selznick. After completing the screenplay, however, he put an end to his active involvement. He declined to become involved with Alvarez Fernandez's proposed Spanish stage adaptation.[42] When Harry Alan Towers asked for permission to use the character of Harry Lime in the BBC series Greene consented and was compensated with £1000 advance on 5 percent of the program's royalties—but only on the condition that his name never be used in advertising to promote the program nor upon the program itself.[43] When the Amalgamated Press began publishing its illustrated novellas based on the BBC series (*Harry Lime Joins the Circus* and *Two Many Crooks*), it did so through Towers's right to the character Lime rather than Greene's; nonetheless he continued to anonymously collect his 5 percent.[44] When British Lion approached him for the rights to the characters' identities for the television series in 1958 he gave his permission once again (this time for £2000, but with no percentage) on the condition that his name never be associated with the program, that he never be required to consult with anyone on the series, and that the stories from the program never appear in print.[45]

In addition to actively distancing himself from others' use of *The Third Man*, Greene took a keen interest in those uses that necessarily involved him. In 1952 the manager of Jugoslavija Films surprisingly announced that in order to publicize the first showing of the film in Yugoslavia his firm would be publishing their own translation of the novella. When Greene's literary agent, David Higham, registered his client's strenuous objection to an unauthorized edition of the novel, he received the astonishing reply that the novel had already been translated, printed, and distributed.[46] Confronted by a *fait accompli*, Greene consented and took his usual scaled percentage of the gross. When Pearn, Pollinger & Higham learned that the Greek publisher Pigassos was threatening to do the same in July 1953, however, they appointed an agent with power of attorney to enforce Greene's copyright.[47] Greene personally wrote several irate letters in which he expressed his desire for putative damages to be assigned by the courts.[48] After 2 years of trying to settle with Pigassos, PPH's Greek representative died having collected 1000 of the 12,000,000 drachmae in compensation Greene had demanded. Pigassos published the book anyway, but, alas!, furnished no sales figures.[49]

Greene made an obscene amount of money from *The Third Man*, although the amount Selznick and Korda made would have made it look merely vulgar by comparison.[50] But while Selznick and Korda made their money quite visibly, Greene severed his ties to the brand just as visibly, save that he did so in writing that did not constitute a legal separation from his rights as author. In his preface to the novella of *The Third Man*—actually the treatment for the film he originally prepared for Korda—he clearly delimited the terms of his involvement:

> To the novelist, of course, his novel is the best he can do with a particular subject; he cannot help resenting many of the changes necessary for turning it into a film or a play; but *The Third Man* was never intended to be more than the raw material for a picture. The reader will notice many differences between the story and the film, and he should not imagine these changes were forced on an unwilling author: as likely as not they were suggested by the author. The film in fact, is better than the story because it is in this case the finished state of the story.[51]

Here Greene echoes John Atkins's admonition that excellence in one art form demands that one obey the rules governing that art form. Korda and Selznick expanded the brand by whatever means they could manage; Greene himself, however, appears to contract: in the introduction to his most popular story—the one that even his authorized biographer identifies as the story most often associated with Greene—he declares himself an artist first and foremost and communicates a subtle disdain for the medium that enriched him.[52] In his introduction to *The Fallen Idol* (also printed for the first time in the 1950 edition) he wrote that '*The Fallen Idol* unlike *The Third Man* was not written for the films. That is only one of many reasons why I prefer it.'[53] In this way, Greene managed to turn *The Third Man*'s popularity into a platform from which he could assert his autonomy from the cinema, distinguish himself from the phenomena which had crystallized around the book, and press his claim to be accorded the status of a literary figure. In a sense, he appropriated the brand's popularity *as* a text that enabled him to make a conservative polemical and strategic move (if also an indirect one) in the confrontation then being fought on the battlefield of postwar cultural politics.

8
Amateurs and Professionals, Auteurs and Intellectuals

Although *The Third Man*'s popularity enabled Greene to make symbolic moves geared toward transforming his name into a proprietary genre, such a move did not necessarily mean that people would line up around the block in order to buy the products bearing its imprint. (This is not merely a metaphor: in 1950 Greene set up Graham Greene Productions Ltd., which for many years served as the corporate entity to which Greene's rights in novels, films, and stories were assigned for tax purposes.[1]) Greene's strategy as a professional, however, was distinctly at odds with his strategy as a writer, for in *The Third Man* he produced a story that worked on several levels and could solicit the participation of vastly different authorial audiences. He produced a story that viewers and readers could appreciate as an unusually artful thriller produced by 'Hollywood', or as an unusually thrilling work of art by an author (in Foucault's sense of the term) named Graham Greene.

Greene had begun writing the story shortly after the United States announced its intention to provide funding for the reconstruction of war-torn Europe through the Marshall Plan. Responses to the plan differed substantially on either side of the Atlantic, but they help illustrate the different attitudes to which *The Third Man* could appeal. The film producer Walter Wanger argued strenuously that Hollywood films were an essential counterpart to the plan (which he felt posed a 'positive, imaginative challenge' to Soviet communism) because they were 'the most important medium we have for spreading enlightenment abroad'.[2] After all, he observed, 'electrically-heated blankets and automatic washing machines and all the gold in Fort Knox are not enough to bring security to this nation. The security of any nation lies not in its material strength alone but in its strength of character, ideals and standards.'[3] From a perspective such as Wanger's, Martins's journey in *The Third Man* could be described as the story of a man holding true to his ideals (e.g., friendship and loyalty) and proving the strength of his character by helping the police pursue Lime once he discovers that his friend has, in fact, stepped far beyond an acceptable standard of conduct (i.e., by poisoning children for profit). The British response to the Marshall Plan was in many quarters less enthusiastic. Richard Strout wrote in *The New Statesman*:

America wants peace and security, and will pay a big price for them. There are plenty of other motives mixed in, from simple idealism to hatred of Russia, and nobody can strike an exact balance. But...the real driving force is a national yearning for a peaceable, stable world—a world in which all the little Main Streets can get on with their particular American dream of lots of cars, high schools, television sets, no universal military training, and nice long foreign vacation trips, from Ann Hathaway's cottage to the delightful sense of proximity to sin in wicked Paris.[4]

In Strout's article, American 'character, ideals, and standards' serve only to obscure the fundamental purpose of the Marshall Plan: to rebuild the European markets according to an American ideological blueprint and ensure continued American dominance of the postwar business world. Reading *The Third Man* from this perspective practically forces one to adopt an attitude ironically not unlike David O. Selznick's—namely, that Martins is an 'utter damn fool' hopelessly out of his depth in an environment that only the European characters (and perhaps those Americans like Lime who consort with them and assimilate their materialist scale of values) seem capable of navigating with any success.

Selznick's response to Greene's script illustrates just how challenging negotiating the story's ironies proved for some readers, but also suggests why many readers found the story so satisfying. His main complaint, for instance, was that the American characters in the script were too foolish and unsympathetic. Greene, of course, had not written the characters as Americans: for all their haplessness and villainy, Martins and Lime had initially been conceived as old friends whose relationship had been forged in the furnace of the British public school system. When Selznick came on board and donated the services of Joseph Cotten to help defray costs and (with any luck) win a larger share of the American audience, the change necessitated a re-write. After Carol Reed cast Orson Welles as Harry Lime, the balance of sympathy shifted decidedly toward the British, represented by the cool and calculating Trevor Howard as

Colonel Calloway and the tough, loyal, and decent Sergeant Paine. Selznick felt the situation would damage the film's appeal to American audiences and recommended several changes:

> There is Lime, one of the blackest scoundrels ever written. There is Martins who is an utter damn fool; who is completely unmotivated, at best, in his determination to risk his life and to cause trouble for everyone in order to clear the reputation of a dead man whom he has not seen for many years... It is an absolute *must* as far as I am concerned that this situation be corrected through straightening out Martins's motivations, and proving Martins's character and charm and courage; and introducing a major authority who is presented in a light comparable to that in which every single Britisher in the picture is presented; and through the introduction of some minor American characters, soldiers who perform in some fashion comparable to that in which every single Britisher is presented.[5]

By furnishing the film with American stars, of course, Selznick had created precisely the imbalanced situation he now sought to remedy. Had all of Selznick's proposed changes been implemented (demonizing the Russians, kidnapping Anna, etc.), the story probably would not have resembled the one Greene had constructed.

Still, in the finished film Tyler becomes the Romanian Popescu, a helpful American soldier waves Martins through customs, and Welles invests Lime with considerable charm—although Martins's 'motive' in pursuing Anna remained as muddled as ever. Selznick himself tinkered with the introductory monologue on the black market, originally spoken by Reed but re-voiced almost verbatim by Cotten for the American release. What Selznick seems to have missed is the way that the film might have appealed to both audiences even if it had remained untouched. Martins's motivations might have been muddled, but apart from the very minor figure of Sergeant Paine he was also the only perfectly sincere and honest character in the story. When Lux Radio Theatre eliminated his drunkenness and violence, they merely threw into high relief the quality that carried many audiences along with Martins throughout both versions of the film: his unshakable conviction in his friend, a quality that becomes more charming and sympathetic the more clearly the narrative reveals it to be based on false assumptions.

In the 'Lux Radio' reading of the story, the individual triumphs over his environment, as he had in countless Western novels and films modelled on precisely the sort of fiction Martins himself writes. In Selznick's, the environment overwhelms the individual, as it so often did in post-war European fiction and cinema (in Beckett, Rossellini's *Roma, Città Aperta*, de Sica's *Ladri di Biciclette*, and so forth). The story does not force its readers and viewers to choose between these possibilities, but rather presents characters capable of appealing to the different sets of generic expectations fostered by different social and institutional contexts.

The success of Greene's strategy in presenting his name as a proprietary brand rests partly in the contradictions *The Third Man* smoothly negotiated in this fashion. The film was as professionally executed as any that had ever been made, and was as ruthlessly exploited and marketed to a popular audience as any of the films that gave the Leavisite heart palpitations. But while it could sustain commercial designations and generic readings—as a thriller, a romance, or even a travelogue—it could also sustain ostensibly 'deeper' readings: as a critique of capitalism, of American 'innocence' and ideology, of the relative merits of amateurs and professionals, and of popular culture's simplifications. Mary McCarthy, for instance, had risen to Greene's defence shortly after the American publication of *The Ministry of Fear*, observing that 'For the last twenty years the detective story has been the official bedside book of the tired brain worker':

> But the detective-story reader, insofar as he is an intellectual, has always been uneasy; he is ashamed of his predilection (or is it a vice?) and seeks to justify it, not only by precedent, but, at length, on esthetic grounds; he makes a virtue of necessity, a literary cult of what is really a pastime, praises Hammett for his realism, Dorothy Sayers for her bluestocking wit and learning, Margery Allingham for her neoromantic sensibility, so that you would have thought, to hear people talk a few years ago, that these detective story writers were being read exclusively for their style.
>
> Graham Greene is God's gift to this group of readers. He has silenced forever the embarrassing question: But is it art?[6]

With *The Third Man* Greene produced a story that became popular in what had always been a popular medium but that, for 'tired brain workers' participating in the story with a set of expectations fed by intellectual preconceptions, could constitute a scathing critique of the popular itself, both in its representation of professionalism and in its complex use of genre.

For the intellectual reader, the film's treatment of the psychology of its central characters, the professional writer Holly Martins and the professional criminal Harry Lime, could reasonably align *The Third Man* in direct opposition to those market forces that deeply influenced the producers' intensive (and often deliberately misleading) marketing campaigns.[7] The black market, capitalism shorn of its legitimacy and consequently 'purified' or 'refined' is, after all, the only social structure that appears to function properly in the Vienna of *The Third Man*. Other avenues for procuring life's necessities may exist, but they function haphazardly and fail to meet the needs of the population. Apart from the police, the viewer encounters only two ostensibly legitimate social structures: the Cultural Re-education Section of General Headquarters (CRS of GHQ) and the medical charity administered by Harry Lime. The former proves incapable of deciding what exactly constitutes culture—Sergeant Paine and the head of CRS, Mr. Crabbit, argue about whether a group of performers were Hindu dancers or strip-teasers—and in any event has no direct interest in maintaining the physiological needs of the impoverished public. The medical charity operates exclusively as a front for Lime's penicillin racket. Baron Kurtz, a member of Vienna's faded aristocracy, explains to Martins the ubiquity of the black market:

> Everyone in Vienna is [mixed up in some racket]—we all sell cigarettes and that kind of thing. Why, I have done things that would have seemed unthinkable before the war. Once when I was hard up, I sold some tyres on the black market. I wonder what my father would have said.[8]

Later on, Anna offers Martins a whiskey when they first meet in her dressing room. He declines and she expresses her relief: 'Good. I wanted to sell it.'[9] Shortly afterward, the viewer learns that Anna's presence in Vienna has been facilitated by yet another black-market transaction, through which Lime secured a set of forged papers for her. Lime may personally embody the black market, but no character lives outside the long shadow it casts.

The film's opening montage (suggested by Selznick in order to clarify the mechanics of the occupation) underlines the volatility of Vienna's social climate: it shows ornate statues that hint at the glorious but inaccessible past of the city, followed by scenes of the black market at work: money in one's purse for the professional and anonymous death for the amateur. Then the camera pulls back and shows the viewer these statues against the backdrop of the rubble to which the war has reduced the city, underscoring the extent to which the old regime has failed to maintain continuity with its shattered golden age. The black market shows the dynamic new order: movement, cash and goods changing hands, and all the violent paroxysms of unrestricted capitalism; the old Vienna, by contrast, seems rooted in place, fixed in marble monuments to its 'Strauss music and easy charm' but unable to keep pace with the forces of novelty unleashed by the war. The montage then cuts to the four-power police force assembled to patrol Vienna and rein in the black market. They stand at attention in front of the vehicles that will shortly whisk them around the city to establish order—but they are themselves askew, their lines uneven, their gazes unable to fix on a common point. The narrator refers to this period in the city's history as 'the classic period of the black market', suggesting that the city's corruption had attained a sort of formal perfection. 'We'd run anything if people wanted it enough—mmm—had money to pay. Of course a situation like that does tempt amateurs. But well, you know, they can't steer the course like a professional.'[10] The film juxtaposes the last line with the image of a bloated corpse floating in the Danube. When the black market functions at optimal capacity it continues to produce victims: both the amateurs and, presumably, those without the money to pay. The conventional trappings of a 'classical' culture—Strauss music, perhaps, or in Q.D. Leavis's phrase 'a code of manners, wit, and polite intercourse'—no longer retain their value; culture no longer serves as capital and the manners of the well-born are at best a debased currency and at worst (as in the case of Kurtz) an impediment to procuring life's essentials. All of the characters save Martins and the comical Crabbit of the CRS recognize money as the sole measure of one's place in society, and life, naked existence, is the only viable distinction between the professional and the amateur. For the *tertium quid* audience, this montage might suggest the excitement of the postwar society; for another kind of audience, however, the juxtaposition of the jaunty narrator and the grim images of a wasted city might suggest a troubling status quo in which values skew toward the commercial: a society dangerously out of touch with 'the best has been thought and written'.

The narrative presents Martins as both a professional and an amateur. He is a professional writer who composes western romances like *The Lone Rider of Santa Fe* and *Death at Double X Ranch*. His lack of personal involvement in the stories he tells sets him apart from the artists— Joyce, Wilde, proponents of the 'stream of consciousness'—who interest the CRS stalwarts: he does not write what he knows, nor even from personal experience; never having visited the West that sustains his humble career, he merely reiterates generic conventions propagated by Zane Grey. If he is a professional, then he is one in the putative sense Q.D. Leavis used to describe Lytton—one who has discovered how to exploit the market. But the world Martins stumbles into reduces him to the status of a dilettante, and reveals in scene after scene the inadequacy of his romantic, genre-cultivated world view. For Martins, Calloway is a sheriff, who in the Western world he writes about is both the source of law and order and, invariably, the one who gets it wrong: 'You're the first [sheriff I've ever seen]. I guess there was some petty racket going on with gasoline and you couldn't pin it on anyone, so you picked a dead man. Just like a cop. You're a real cop, I suppose?'[11] (Of course, by the end of the story Martins learns that Calloway did not, in fact, have it wrong.) Moments into their first meeting Martins threatens to run Calloway out of Vienna in the style favored by his cowboy protagonists. In fact, he constantly reads the people he meets into a western narrative. Calloway's Lime becomes Martins's Harry, the mischievous trickster who 'never got caught' when they misbehaved at school. He molds Anna, the coldest fish in the Viennese pond, into his love interest, and from her cool evasions he manages to distil the hint of a tempestuous passion. His imagination works along wholly conventional lines that have never broken under the weight of reality or implausibility, so that his melodramatic perspective invests events in Vienna with an operatic plausibility whose logic (or lack thereof) the audience can grasp but whose content the audience can easily read ironically if it feels inclined to do so. At the CRS lecture, for instance, the audience's questions about literature stump Martins: for the audience watching a thriller, the CRS crowd seems ludicrously out of touch; for the audience watching an ironic deconstruction of Martins's western sensibilities, Martins seems ludicrously ignorant. The structure of the story reinforces the ambiguity when moments later Popescu questions him on his new novel, 'The Third Man':

> Tyler [renamed Popescu in the film]: Are you a slow writer, Mr. Martins?
> Martins: Pretty quick when I get interested.
> Tyler: I'd say you were doing something pretty dangerous this time.
> Martins: Yes?
> Tyler: Mixing fact and fiction, like oil and water.
> Martins: Should I write it as straight fact?
> Tyler: Why no, Mr. Martins. I'd say stick to fiction, straight fiction.
> Martins: I've gone too far with the book, Mr. Tyler.
> Tyler: Haven't you ever scrapped a book, Mr. Martins?
> Martins: Never.[12]

Martins's refusal to 'scrap the book' takes on a dark connotation when one considers that his investigation has already led to the death of the innocent porter at Lime's former residence. The reader moved by Martins's idealism may give the writer the benefit of the doubt and view Popescu's thinly veiled threats as confirmation that Martins is on the right track. For the reader cognizant of the blind alleys down which Martins's idealism has continually led him, Popescu's menacing tone illustrates how the writer's professionalism, his willingness to abide by the logic of stock responses, has once again placed himself and others in harm's way.

In contrast to Martins's muddle of romantic idealism and professionalism, the narrative presents two consummate professionals: Calloway and Lime. Like Anna, the narrative shows Calloway in an utterly pragmatic light. No question strikes the policeman as more trivial than the question of Lime's death: whodunit, and why, and how have all been answered to his satisfaction by Lime's death—'The best thing that ever happened to him', he informs a shell-shocked Martins.[13] Justice and abstractions do not concern him; only results catch his interest. As long as Lime is dead there will be no more penicillin racket. In a rare show of emotion Calloway chides Paine for loading the wrong slide in the projector as he prepares to assault Martins with the evidence against his friend. This breach in professional decorum—a crime against efficiency—touches him as the wholesale extermination of Vienna's criminal underclass (and quite possibly the Viennese who make it profitable) would not. If, as Q.D. Leavis had suggested, the machinery of contemporary, commerce-driven society had assumed a monstrous impersonality, then Calloway could in many ways serve as the embodiment of an idealized managerial class.

The battle between Calloway and Martins partially constitutes the tragic dimension of the story. In the end, Calloway's pragmatism and efficiency carry the day and drag Martins reluctantly (and quite literally) into the city's bowels, where the waste products of society go to be broken down and flushed out of the system. Here Calloway provokes Martins to pursue the western generic conventions through which he has attempted to organize his life to their logical conclusion. When Judith Hess describes the road Gary Cooper travels to redemption in the film *The Virginian*, she might almost be describing the one Martins travels as well. Having been forced to lynch his friend for rustling cattle, Cooper's eponymous Virginian sets about finding and destroying the villain, Trampas, the man responsible for luring his friend into the business:

Several acts of violence are condoned in the movie: traditionally sanctioned violence demanded by the group (note that Cooper never questions the lynching, he only suffers because he is forced to abandon his friend); violence which is brought about by repeated attacks on one's character (Trampas indicates that Cooper is a coward) and which redeems the violence Cooper has been forced to do to his friend.

... The westerner's code is at once personal and social—if a man lives by it he both conforms to social norms and retains his personal integrity. It is evident whence comes the satisfaction we get from the western. Momentarily we understand the peace which comes from acting in accord with a coherent moral and social code and forget our fragmented selves.[14]

At the end of *The Third Man*, Calloway experiences just such a moment when Martins kills Lime, a response underlined for the audience in the way the policeman shrugs off Paine's death: 'Poor old Paine'. For Martins the experience is more problematic: not only must he kill Lime in order to restore balance to the city that the gangster has outraged (traditionally sanctioned violence demanded by the group); in order to live up to the obligations of the social code he must compromise the moral code that has hitherto led him to pursue those he believes to be responsible for Lime's death. The western that Martins has written himself into thus denies him closure, the principal satisfaction of the genre as Hess imagines it. Having begun the story as an oddly inspired disaster wholly at odds with his environment, Martins ends as an automaton compelled by bureaucracy to offer his consent in a quasi-juridical murder. By the end of the story, it is Martins, not Lime, who accuses himself of cowardice, and his willingness to proceed in carrying out the execution against his better judgment marks his emergence into the 'real' world of the professional as opposed to the fictional world of the amateur he has hitherto inhabited.

The end of the story, like so many of Greene's earlier fictions, refuses to impose a definitive interpretation of the events it has related and instead prompts the viewer to assess the meaning of the story for himself. Martins hops off Calloway's jeep to meet Anna as she leaves the cemetery. As he does so, he utters the cryptic words, 'I can't just leave'. Does he wait for Anna in order to justify his behavior toward her former lover? To say that he is sorry for betraying Harry? Or perhaps to seize the opportunity to rekindle their aborted romance? When Anna walks straight past him, toward the camera, and then off-screen the question remains unanswered. The ambiguity of Martins's response—standing at the edge of the road, staring off into the middle distance—can confirm whatever suspicion the viewer has nurtured since the film's climax. In the novel, he walks away with the girl, an unreconstructed fool—but then Greene never claimed to have written the film's ending. (In fact, Reed's notes attribute the idea for the ending to Selznick.[15]) For one viewer Martins's silence in the closing moments conveys a quiet nobility quite in keeping with Selznick's conception of the charming hero—but for another it could just as easily convey yet another awkward moment suffered by a fool with literally nothing left to say.

The way the viewer responds to the sequence says more about the viewer's interpretive priorities than it does about the sequence itself. If he has watched the film with assumptions in keeping with Walter Wanger's vision of the infallibility of American good intentions, then Martins may retain some semblance of dignity. If he has watched the film with assumptions more in keeping the dim view of the Marshall Plan taken by Strout, then it seems unlikely that Martins will have earned the benefit of the doubt. The first reaction produced comments like Cyril Ray's in the pages of the *Spectator*:

> That [*The Third Man*] is nothing if not stylish may be as much criticism as compliment, for there is little in the story that would seem to matter. An American, as naïve as the cowboy tales he writes, arrives in Vienna to find his friend dead in an ambiguous accident, is moved to try and clear his name, is drawn into a black-market intrigue and a chase after a criminal.[16]

Ray treats the film as a text composed strictly according to a generic formula: Martins must try to clear his friend's name because that is what naïve Americans do in thrillers; the black market serves up intrigue as vague as the Vienna of Selznick's publicity trailer; and the relationship between Martins and Lime means little or nothing because the story 'is' a thriller and the hero is therefore obliged to chase the villain. Ray dismisses a good deal of the film in language that echoes Greene's own dismissal of Hitchcock's *Secret Agent* nearly 15 years earlier:

> [Hitchcock's] films consist of a series of small 'amusing' melodramatic situations: the murderer's buttons dropped on the baccarat board; the strangled organist's hands prolonging the notes in the empty church; the fugitives hiding in the bell-tower when the bell begins to swing. Very perfunctorily he builds up to these tricky situations (paying no attention on the way to inconsistencies, loose ends psychological

absurdities) and then drops them; they mean nothing: they lead to nothing.[17]

After *The Third Man*, of course, Greene ridiculed Selznick for making him forget 'the lesson which I had learned as a film critic—that to "establish" something is almost invariably wrong and that "continuity" is often the enemy of life'.[18] But Ray seems content with *The Third Man*'s moderate gaps in logic, primarily because he feels that the genre itself bridges them. Ray muses that 'Whether it was all worth doing with so much care and talent and wit (for there are some good jokes) can only be a minority's murmured query' before arriving at his unintended punch line: despite all of the reservations he has enumerated in his review he has also seen the film twice—precisely the sort of response Selznick and Korda desired.

The Guardian printed a review more in keeping with Strout's less optimistic perspective on the Marshall Plan:

> *The Third Man* is, typically, a thriller—a good one too—about black-marketeering, intrigue and murder. But, again typically, it is a thriller set in post-war Vienna, and what raises it right out of the ordinary is in the first place that, more perhaps than any other post-war film, it gives a convincing impression of life among the half-ruins under quadripartite control.[19]

The reviewer views the film's semantic and syntactic generic affinities as dynamic factors contributing to a realistic portrait of the city's strange mixture 'of terror, of beauty, and, not least, of humour'.[20] As the story gradually reveals Vienna it simultaneously reveals the ironies of Martins's misplaced idealism. William Whitebait had written that 'The worst that could be said of *The Third Man* is that at its weakest moments it is a thriller that enormously thrills', suggesting that the film tended to work on some higher level.[21] *The Guardian* elaborated this position; even during the reviewer's least enthusiastic moments he (or she) insists on considering the thrilling film as a work of literature:

> With this abundance of praise, there must, however, be one important reservation about the film. In Greene's best work the marriage between the bitter 'life-study' and the thriller is entirely successful. But in his second-best the marriage is sometimes less perfect—with the result, as a rule, that the serious literary element looks a bit awkward in its gangster company.[22]

Early critics of Greene's 'cinematic technique' had suggested that Greene had discovered a way to deploy literature toward cinematic ends; after *The Third Man* it became possible to publicly enunciate how, in Greene's work, the very category of the cinema served ends traditionally associated with literature.

By 1993 a critic like Glenn K.S. Man could even argue that while the final effect of the short novel *The Third Man* was that of a 'mere thriller', the effects of the film were far more complex: 'The film does not preserve the themes of the novel; rather it develops themes and concerns which the novel suggests and then sacrifices to generic demands.... [These themes] include the notion of society as a wasteland, the complexity of character ambiguity, and the play of self-reflexivity.'[23] Man's reading, like *The Guardian*'s, conceptualizes *The Third Man* as the work of an 'auteur', in the sense later articulated by the film critic Andrew Sarris:

> [The ultimate premise] of the *auteur* theory is concerned with interior meaning, the ultimate glory of cinema as an art. Interior meaning is extrapolated from the tension between a director's personality and his material ... It is ambiguous, in any literary sense, because part of it is embedded in the stuff of the cinema and cannot be rendered in non-cinematic terms.[24]

Sarris's thesis that the 'interior meaning' of auteurist cinema cannot be rendered in noncinematic terms is of course a redaction of the Leavisite and New Critical proposition that a work of literature necessarily 'means what it is': the interior meaning of literature would thus be ambiguous in any cinematic sense because part of it is embedded in the stuff of literature (i.e., language) and cannot be rendered in non-literary (i.e., visual) terms. Sarris's auteur theory, like I.A. Richards's theory of psychological value, excludes and ignores the audience—that is, the person or persons responsible for construing the director's personality *and* the material at the director's disposal *and* the relationship between these two entities.[25] Less a theory than a mode of rhetorical inflection, auteurism permits the critic to make definitive statements 'proven' through facts the critic assumes are self-evident (that is, without any *actual* evidence). Thus auteurism poses as a theory of production but functions as a set of reading practices that paradoxically imply the irrelevance of reading. Auteurism as a reading practice attempts to render the social aspects of meaning silent and/or invisible, and as such applies equally to criticism (or, more broadly, 'readings') produced in the fields of both film *and* literature (all the more so since individuals have been known on occasion to be both fiction readers *and* film viewers).[26]

Like the Leavisite genius, the auteur addresses an audience of one. In Man's reading of *The Third Man*, 'the film' develops its concerns autonomously and it sacrifices nothing to genre: 'it' communicates without hypothesizing an audience. Man suggests that *The Third Man* has no choice but to communicate 'the notion of society as a wasteland, the complexity of character ambiguity, and the play of self-reflexivity', as though these concerns were somehow the inescapable result of the viewing process, rather than the product of specific historical conditions influencing the sort of coherence Man himself desires the film to exhibit. His reading of *The Third Man* (a film he clearly respects) follows auteurism's circular logic to the conclusion that the film illustrates auteurist principles: the auteur's vision of society as a wasteland leads Greene to suspect others (particularly those who somehow succeed in the wasteland) and thus to formulate a mode of address that principally aimed at satisfying himself (self-reflexivity).

Jack Nolan took up the same theme (and methodology) in 'Graham Greene's Films':

> ... the character of Martins, the American writer who is summoned to Vienna by Harry Lime, is a mouthpiece for Greene himself. Martins is the Christian idealist adrift amid the flotsam of the twentieth century .... I also think it worthy of remark that though *The Third Man*'s philosophy is seemingly Christian, it is in fact existentialist. Not so much because of its use of Sartre's 'confrontations' ... as because almost no one can communicate with anyone else.[27]

On the contrary: everybody in the film communicates constantly with everyone else in the film—only they do not always communicate what they desire to communicate. Martins clearly communicates his displeasure with Calloway's insinuations by throwing a punch at him, and in doing so communicates his recklessness (or possibly his idealism) to both Calloway and the audience. The porter communicates the existence of 'the third man' to Martins despite the language barrier and his later recantation communicates to both Martins and the audience an insidious force at play in Vienna. Does any viewer doubt that Anna grasps both Martins's love for her *and* the hopeless inadequacy of that love? But since Nolan desires to communicate what *The Third Man* 'is' he must formulate what its author/auteur 'is' and, having done so, he must then apply a specific set of rules of coherence that bring the two together. By designating the allegedly uncommunicative Martins as Greene's 'mouthpiece' Nolan can argue that through *The Third Man* Greene speaks essentially (or perhaps 'existentially') to himself. In the Leavisite paradigm, the professional addresses the mass and so devalues himself; the genius, content to speak to himself (and also those clever enough to grasp what he says in isolation), is always something of an amateur. In *The Third Man* Greene crafted a fiction that could be read as the tragedy of professionalism: by the end of the story, Martins learns to speak Calloway's language—the language of social order, efficiency, and, by extension, commerce—at considerable cost to the idealism and integrity that initially draws the audience to him. Martins, however, only furnishes *The Third Man* with one of its tragic aspects: in the story of Harry Lime, Greene crafted a fiction that could be read as the tragedy of the amateur: the genuine artist, trampled underfoot by Philistines who fail to comprehend the majesty of his vision. Welles may have written the Wildean speech about the Borgias and the Renaissance versus Swiss democracy and the cuckoo clock (for which David Thomson censured him), but Greene's story relates the same sequence on the Prater Wheel. Martins has discovered the truth about Harry's criminal activities, has tracked him down to the Russian zone, and asked for a meeting with his old friend. They board the great wheel and it stops at the top. Martins can push Lime off if he chooses, and Lime can shoot Martins if he chooses. But Martins stays his hand, and Lime makes his fatal error: he trusts his friend.

> Again the car began to move, sailing slowly down, until the flies were midgets, were recognizable human beings. 'What fools we are, Rollo, talking like this, as if I'd do that to you—or you to me.' He turned his back and leaned his face against the glass. One thrust... 'How much do you earn a year with your Westerns, old man?'
>
> 'A thousand.'
>
> 'Taxed. I earn thirty thousand free. It's the fashion. In these days, old man, nobody thinks in terms of human beings. Governments don't, so why do we? They talk of the people and the proletariat, and I talk of the mugs. It's the same thing. They have their five year plans and so have I.'[28]

Lime holds nothing back from Martins, or at least delivers a truth so unpalatable that Martins—and most audiences—accept it as the outermost limit of Lime's self-awareness. He offers himself to Martins, and invites him to read the 'dots' swarming at the base of the Prater Wheel as he does: 'If I said you can have twenty thousand pounds for every dot that stops, would you really, old man, tell me to keep my money—without hesitation? Or would you calculate how many dots you could afford to spare?'[29] If, as Wyndham Lewis argued in *The Art of Being Ruled*, 'no artist can ever love democracy',[30] then Harry Lime—both Greene's and Welles's—appears well on his way to producing a modernist masterpiece by the time Martins, Calloway, and the forces of (bourgeois, philistine) law and order catch up with him and vanquish the individualist vision that threatens the safety and security of an unworthy society. Even contemporary critics felt moved by Lime's demise. Whitebait commented that the climax has the power to 'unpack a nightmare or two. The ten fingers coming up through a grating in a square and wavering helplessly I shan't ever forget.'[31]

Read as a 'conventional' thriller, the effectiveness of the climax depends on the audience's willingness to view Martins and Lime as opposing forces: idealism versus pragmatism, optimism versus pessimism, innocence versus experience, and so on—a perspective that the narrative's use of expectations certainly allows. But *The Third Man*'s strength as what intellectuals might call a work of art depends on the audience's willingness to view Martins and Lime as two sides of the same coin, as individuals gradually crushed by the vast, impersonal machinery of contemporary society. Prior to *The Third Man* Greene had written a dozen novels in various generic registers: the psychological novel, '*Grand Hotel* all over again', the chase thriller, the revenge thriller, the gangster story, and the 'Catholic novel'. Most had performed quite well in the literary marketplace, and film producers showed considerable interest in adapting his work—factors that weighed heavily against Greene's suitability for incorporation into contemporary scholarly discourse, which at the time busied itself decrying the same vast, impersonal machinery of contemporary society that consistently transformed Greene's words into hard currency. With *The Third Man* Greene produced a story that performed phenomenally well in the market (both in film and in novella form, as the various cases of continental piracy confirm) but which could also be read as both a condemnation of the market that sustained him and as an aesthetic manifesto declaring his indifference to prevailing tastes and his conviction in the autonomy of the artist. From this vantage it became possible for critics to look back at Greene's oeuvre and discern a unity and significance in his previous work that they had never before seen, or had insisted on attributing to 'the cinema' or to the various genres through which his fictions worked. To be certain, *The Third Man* did not change anything about the work

Greene had executed earlier; nor did it succeed in transforming scholarly perceptions of the popular; rather through its appeal to auteurist tastes and prejudices the film permitted scholars to incorporate the whole body of Greene's work more easily into a discourse that had hitherto been an uncomfortable fit.

Part III

From Author to Contested Authority

9
Auteurism and the Study of Greene

Various political and economic factors conspired to make auteurism a viable intellectual discursive strategy in the 1950s and also to render Greene a suitable candidate for consideration as a literary auteur.[1]

The vast, impersonal economic machinery Q.D. Leavis had warned against in 1932 had not disappeared as a result of the Second World War; on the contrary, commercial and political elites on both sides of the Atlantic had used the war as a convenient pretext for strengthening the relationship between the state and private industry. During the Depression and the Great Slump, business had seen socialism as a threat to its very existence; by the end of the war, however, the 'spectre' that had formerly haunted Europe and America had been welcomed— under different names, and in different disguises—as a kind of friendly ghost.[2] Only 3 years after the war, *Fortune*, a major organ of the business press, acknowledged that the technological demands of modern enterprise had in many ways rendered the 'free market' obsolete:

> [Only] the credit resources of the USA are sufficient to keep the aircraft industry going: to enable it to hire engineers, buy its materials, pay wages to its labor force, compensate its executives—and pay dividends to its stockholders. The fact seems to remain, then, that the aircraft industry today cannot satisfactorily exist in a pure, competitive, unsubsidized, 'free enterprise' economy. *It never has been able to*. Its huge customer has always been the United States Government, whether in war or in peace.[3]

Industry could no longer afford to pretend that it operated along the lines proposed by classical economists like Smith, Ricardo, and Malthus. Technological developments had begun to render the small firm obsolete save in the areas of retail sales and the provision of select services. As the firms engaged in manufacturing and heavy industry had grown so too had their ability to influence the market that theoretically determined what they produced and how they produced it, as well as how, when, and by whom their products could be consumed. As J.K. Galbraith demonstrated in *The New Industrial State*, technological change also demanded that businesses change the way they organized themselves: because no sole proprietor could hope to grasp the 'whole equation' of say, automobile manufacture, the prosperity of any given automotive firm depended on its ability to efficiently organize an army of specialists into an entity Galbraith termed the technostructure, which effectively replaced the entrepreneur with 'management':

> This is a collective and imperfectly defined entity; in the large corporation it embraces chairman, president, those vice presidents with important staff or departmental responsibility, occupants of other major staff positions and, perhaps, divisions or department heads not included above. It includes, however, only a small proportion of those who, as participants, contribute information to group decisions. This latter group is very large; it extends from the most senior officials of the corporation to where it meets, at the outer perimeter, the white- and blue-collar workers whose function is to conform more or less mechanically to instruction or routine. It embraces all who bring specialized knowledge, talent, or experience to group decision-making. This, not the management, is the guiding intelligence—the brain—of the enterprise.[4]

The emergence of the technostructure re-enacted across a broader range of society the adaptation of the press to the condition of mass literacy throughout the first decades of the twentieth century. By adopting economies of scale as an operational principle, the corporation lost its ability to react quickly to changing market conditions, but gained a larger measure of control over those conditions; in the Leavisite paradigm, the growth of the reading public and the popular press had initiated a decline in standards for the same reason: the prerogatives of the commercial apparatus left little room for the initiative of the talented individual.

As Alan Sinfield and Francis Mulhern have argued—following Forster to the logical end of his invective against the exam system—the

Leavisite program ironically helped create the conditions necessary for the evolution of the technostructure. Sinfield writes:

> ...the new professionals needed qualifications and, especially at the pivotal moment when leisure-class authority was still substantial, literature seemed suitable...By insisting that literary appreciation was not a class accomplishment but an individual attainment, Leavis rendered it suitable for teaching and examining. So literature was presented as a universal culture, detached from the class fraction that had produced and sponsored it, and then used as a criterion for entry to a different fraction.[5]

Analytical and writing skills served the new professional quite well in his capacity as an administrator of the technostructure, a designation that could be applied on the one hand to the modern corporation and, on the other, to the welfare state that continued to grow (particularly in Britain) after the war. Thus a movement designed to combat the commercial imperative found itself deeply implicated in the maintenance of the modern commercial apparatus.

From this perspective, the polemical appeal of the auteur theory becomes clear: if the Leavisite program had appealed to Newbolt-era educationalists partly on the grounds that close reading theoretically allowed for the existence of a classless classroom, then for the new generation of educationalists the auteur theory restored to the analysis of cultural artefacts the necessity for precisely that 'respectable store of literary, historical, and biographical information' whose absence Jonathan Culler cited as being among the Leavisite and New Critical dispensations' more democratizing characteristics. Because it ignored readers, however, practitioners failed to organize themselves around a coherent theory of reading and had little choice but to fall back on 'a common humanism' in order to show how texts produced 'a complex and ontologically privileged statement about human experience'.[6] Auteurism attempted to resolve this situation not by furnishing a theory of reading (or viewing) but rather by identifying the source of ontological certainty. This act of naming implied the development of a critical practice, usefully glossed by Andrew Sarris as follows: 'Only after thousands of films have been revaluated will any personal pantheon have a reasonably objective validity. The task of validating the *auteur* theory is an enormous one, and the end will never be in sight.'[7] Viewing *Notorious* and *Vertigo*, for instance, does not entitle a critic to call Hitchcock an auteur: one must view *all* of Hitchcock—and not Hitchcock only, but also *all* of the films that complement, complicate, contradict, and surround Hitchcock—before the critic may apply such a designation. In other words, the auteur theory restored genuine knowledge of art (i.e., an Althusserian ideology of art) to those classes who possessed the leisure and resources to experience it in bulk; in this sense, the theory itself was one of the academy's methods of adapting to an economy of scale necessitated on the one hand by industry's demand for an accredited managerial class and, on the other, by an increase in the number of people able to acquire some level of higher education thanks to higher wages, better working conditions, more scholarships, and so forth. Auteur theory did not necessarily impact directly on pedagogy, which Leavisism and the New Criticism continued (and continue) to dominate: its methods were too unwieldy and its interests too heterogeneous to provide a useful framework for classroom activity. However, as an inexhaustible field of study—that is, as a wholly subjective and utterly contentious one—it furnished intellectuals with a useful way of attaining the credentials required to secure a place in the academic firmament and also, perhaps, of investing the themes taught in the classroom with 'a reasonably objective validity'. Thus from the mid to late 1940s onward, the work performed by the institutional scholar began to qualitatively diverge from the work assigned to students: close reading of the text suited the classroom reasonably well, but the study of inter-textuality (and later of meta-textuality) furnished enough work to sustain a career indefinitely. Although the scholar—particularly the young scholar—would have to continue teaching students how to closely read texts (and thus do his part in maintaining the vast, impersonal economic machinery of contemporary commercial society) the advent of auteurism offered a kind of psychological—or even discursive—compensation: it reasserted the distinction between practical and higher knowledge that Leavisism, however unwittingly, had begun to erode. As a professional polemic, then, auteurism reinforced the superior position of the elite vis-à-vis a public taking advantage of improved access to education.

As an intellectual (rather than professional) polemic, the results of auteurism appear more democratic. No auteurist, after all, could have been satisfied with F.R. Leavis's declaration that 'the great English novelists are Austen, George Eliot, Henry James, and Joseph Conrad.'[8] On the surface, of course, this appears to be precisely the sort of argument that an auteurist like Sarris made when he wrote that 'At the moment, my list of *auteurs* runs something like this through the first twenty: Ophuls, Renoir, Mizoguchi, Hitchcock, Chaplin, Ford, Welles, Dreyer, Rossellini,

Murnau, Griffith, Sternberg, Eisenstein, von Stroheim, Buñuel, Bresson, Hawks, Lang, Flaherty, Vigo.'[9] Leavis's list ends at a 'comparatively safe point in history'—presumably the point at which intellectual opinions begin to diverge (e.g., Joyce versus Woolf), and certainly the point beyond which the popularity of the writers in question had ceased to be a cause for concern. By contrast, Sarris's list of film artists contains multitudes nearly as incommensurable as the lists that fill Jorge Luis Borges's stories: unabashedly popular directors (Chaplin, Hitchcock, Ford, Hawks), unabashedly unpopular directors (Buñuel, Welles, Mizoguchi), directors who worked without sound (Murnau, Griffith), directors who existed apart from the capitalist system of production (Eisenstein), and directors who purported to document reality rather than tell fictional stories (Flaherty). And like the literary critics of Borges's Tlön who 'take two dissimilar works—the *Tao Te Ching* and the *1001 Nights*, for instance—attribute them to a single author, and then in all good conscience determine the psychology of that most interesting *homme de lettres*',[10] Sarris projects 'the auteur' as a discursive field in which the personality of the director gradually breaks down and incorporates into itself all distinctions between levels of popularity, media, languages, modes of production, and genres in order to produce 'cinema', the common (albeit imaginary) language each manifestation shares with the others.

The largely self-appointed elite embraced the auteurist sensibility (if not Sarris's imprecise formulation) as it resigned itself to the encroachment of the public on the institutions responsible for producing and reproducing culture. Disgusted by mass civilization but also sustained by it, the postwar intellectual arrived at a neat solution: he turned the Leavisite fear of the popular on its head and became as all-devouring as the capitalism he suspected of innate Philistinism, save that he assiduously injected the products of mass culture into a discourse that denied the mass any role in the production of meaning. In theory a text's meaning belonged solely to its auteur, not to the audience who realized it; the intellectual therefore found himself on solid ground so long as he maintained the pretence that the auteur's personality could in some deep sense be grasped and understood. Sarris himself used the term 'mystical' to describe the relationship between auteur and text that produced 'interior meaning', although in light of the critical operations one needed to perform to grasp this interior meaning, he was also describing his own subtly privileged relationship to the text.

The auteurist sensibility could not exist, however, without a theory of genre—or, more accurately, without a theory of *fixed* genres: of generic conventions so inflexible that intellectuals could see and hear the strain of the auteur against them. The Leavisite project did not demand the elaboration of such a theory because the aim of the program was quite different: it furnished the means of organizing a holding action against the popularization of education, rather than of arriving at a comfortable accommodation with it. I.A. Richards could reduce all popular genres to a singular genre—'the popular'—and dismiss it as stock response; the auteurist had no such luxury since he needed to distil a distinct authorial voice from often heterogeneous texts. Thus throughout the 1950s, numerous critics began to produce semantic and syntactic definitions of genre.[11] Robert Warshow's oft-anthologized 1954 essay on 'The Westerner', for instance, began with a comparative taxonomy of 'the two most successful creations of American movies...the gangster and the Westerner: men with guns', thus identifying each genre with a semantic element: the presence of guns. He then addressed several syntactic affinities and differences:

> The Western hero...is a figure of repose. He resembles the gangster in being lonely and to some degree melancholy. But his melancholy comes from the 'simple' recognition that life is unavoidably serious, not from the disproportions of his own temperament. And his loneliness is organic, not imposed on him by his situation but belonging to him intimately and testifying to his completeness. The gangster must reject others violently or draw them violently to him. The Westerner is not thus compelled to seek love.[12]

For the auteurist, the average text deploys or reiterates these conventions (the only option for *any* generic text in the Leavisite paradigm); by contrast, the text of an auteur manipulates them, and mystically makes them his own. As David Thomson once remarked, 'the textual choice in cinema is what to do with the camera. This is not simply a functional decision; the camera in every shot is like the locus of God to a religion.'[13] By determining what the audience sees, the auteur theoretically imposes his own relationship to the genre upon the audience. A film like *Butch Cassidy and the Sundance Kid* works against the grain of the Western as defined by Warshow to the extent that its protagonist, Butch, appears garrulous and optimistic throughout. For Thomson, the film's director, George Roy Hill, achieves his finest moment as an artist in *Butch Cassidy and the Sundance Kid* precisely because the final shot expresses most fully Hill's ambiguity toward the western: '[The film] is unable to decide whether to parody or join in the Western legend. Its final frozen frame is the perfect expression of fissured purpose....'[14] In order to arrive at an interpretation like this the auteurist must imagine the personality of the auteur, decide what the auteur has attempted to communicate by comparing the actual shot with what the 'genre' suggests the shot *should have been*, and then evaluate the shot's success on the basis of how closely the execution approximates the auteur's intention. The audience need never enter the critic's calculations because, from the auteurist perspective, the audience never enters the auteur's calculations. Specifically, the auteurist substitutes the fixed rules of genre for actual or hypothetical audiences.

Butch Cassidy's screenwriter William Goldman observed that by valorizing the personality of the auteur at the expense of the audience, intellectuals effectively forced themselves to valorize all of a chosen auteur's work:

> Once an auteurist surrenders himself to an idol, for reasons passing understanding, said auteurist flies in the face of one of life's basic truths: People can have good days, and people can have bad days.
>
> *Any* movie by Chaplin, even shit Chaplin, is terrific. (I wish them all a very long life on a desert island with nothing but *The Countess From Hong Kong* for company.) *Any* John Ford, another of their favourites. And, of course, any Hitchcock.
>
> I think the last decades of Hitchcock's career were a great waste and sadness. He was technically as skilful as ever. But he had become encased in praise, inured to any criticism.
>
> Hitchcock himself had become The Man Who Knew Too Much.[15]

In other words, Hitchcock began to behave like a Leavisite genius: spinning out his fictions for a hypothetical audience of one (manifestly *not* Goldman), and incapable of taking on board the expectations, tastes, and biases of his actual audience. Although personal preferences undoubtedly color Goldman's anecdote, it helps illustrate the methodology of the auteurist critic who insists on evaluating all of a chosen auteur's work as though it had been composed for a hypothetical audience of one. Once a critic singles out a particular director (or writer) for the auteurist treatment, he must extrapolate the meaning of all of the auteur's work from the tension between the auteur's personality (which the critic has constructed) and his material (conceived as a fixed system of conventions).

* * *

Shortly after *The Third Man* critics began to treat Greene like an auteur. In many ways he was an ideal candidate for this type of valorization. *Stamboul Train* had transformed him into a 'popular' writer—even a 'cinematic' one—and thus, in the prevailing intellectual climate, an underappreciated one. His work had deployed generic conventions and character types that even by the early 1950s had been 'fixed' by intellectual observers: the spy thriller, the innocent on the run, the gangster, and so forth. He had written several novels with explicitly Catholic themes—*Brighton Rock*, *The Power and the Glory*, and *The Heart of the Matter*—that demonstrated the gravity of his interests, and even the novels he designated as entertainments (e.g., *A Gun for Sale*, *The Ministry of Fear*) tended to end in death or misery for all concerned. Pritchett and Waugh might have referred to Greene as a practitioner of the cinematic technique, but his novels clearly bore scant resemblance to the sort of popular genre fictions that the Hollywood studio system routinely produced—fictions influenced not only by the tastes and prejudices of producers and directors, but also by various censorship offices, which demanded, for instance, that criminals never be shown benefiting from their crimes.[16] *The Third Man* gave intellectuals ample opportunity to read the popular Hollywood film with which Greene had been most prominently and successfully associated as a disparaging critique of popular culture and as a lament for the difficulties that beset the visionary in a myopic world. Whether Greene intended it or not, his work did not offer much to deter the reader interested in assessing his work in auteurist terms, as the meaningful struggle between a strong personality and conventional material.

Greene's post-*Third Man* work likewise enabled critics and scholars to refocus their expectations along auteurist lines. Novels like *The End of the Affair* and *The Quiet American* helped furnish the scaffolding for auteurist readings: they employed first-person narrators (for the first time in Greene's career as a novelist) while addressing semantic territory similar to that ranged over by Greene's earlier third-person narrators. Brian Thomas has argued that with his turn to the first-person narrator in the 1950s Greene re-discovered 'the central structural principle of romance: the upward narrative turn from suspension and death to reanimation and rebirth' since the first-person narrative is almost by definition a survivor.[17] Whatever its thematic implications, the romance structure thus implied certain practical changes in the construction of narrative. The first-person protagonist could not die as Pinkie had, in a shower of vitriol, or as Raven had, shot to ribbons as he hangs out a window; instead he had simply to stop the novel at one more or less arbitrary point. Thus if Greene's work in the 1950s and afterward was more 'romantic' in Thomas's (and also Frye's) sense of the word, it was also more 'realistic' from the vantage of an interpretive community contemptuous of fiction that employed melodramatic or generic conventions (and particularly 'stock' endings) in order to achieve its effects.

These narratives' central 'I' also implied a particular worldview at work, and thus encouraged—even demanded—speculation about the narrator's personality, his point-of-view, his biases, his obsessions, etc. From this point it required no great imaginative leap to move from the personality of the narrator to the personality of the writer. Greene's authorized biographer makes precisely this unimaginative leap when he asserts that '*The End of the Affair*, despite its fictional cover, was a precise and intense account of the love life of Catherine Walston and Graham Greene, with Henry as Harry Walston.'[18] John Atkins writes from a very similar perspective, although thematic implications interest him more than reading the novel as Norman Sherry does, as a *roman a clef*: 'Greene, through the medium of his character Bendrix (also an author), writes out of bitterness.'[19]

Greene himself takes up this theme in several of the reviews he produced in the early 1950s. His 1951 analysis of Rider Haggard, for instance, foreshadows the critical perspective many scholars (including Atkins) would adopt toward his own work:

> [Haggard] was a public author and the private life remained the private life in so far as he could control it.
>
> The poetic element in Haggard's work breaks out where the control fails. Because the hidden man was so imprisoned, when he does emerge through the tomb, it is against enormous pressure, and the effect is often one of horror, a risen Lazarus—next time he must be buried deeper.[20]

Greene's portrait of Haggard is totally consistent with the auteurist perspective: writing in the genre of adventure stories imprisons the hidden Rider (but also makes him popular, a 'public author'); subsequently, the writer struggles against the pressure of 'the tomb' and impresses the reader more deeply for the visible struggle involved. Greene implies that the author who emerges from 'the tomb' is in a sense the 'real' Haggard, since the figure that emerges does so against the writer's conscious control and intention. Greene presents the power of Haggard's poetry as being intimately bound up in the writer's personality and therefore an innate quality more or less inadequately suppressed throughout the whole body of the writer's work.

The following year Greene reviewed a biography of A.E.W. Mason that led him to formulate a question to which his own career furnished a kind of answer. 'Why is it,' he pondered,

> one asks about certain authors, in a kind of envy of their talent and in the belief that, if one had been given so much, one could have progressed a little further, they have just stayed there? Why didn't they grow, with such a technical start—well, a little more worthy of consideration?[21]

This review followed shortly after publication of *The End of the Affair*, in which the protagonist, Maurice Bendrix, opens the novel by observing that he is 'a professional writer who—when he has been seriously noted at all—has been praised for his technical ability'.[22] In Greene's novel, however, the 'technical writer' had turned his attention to problems— the mystery of faith, the existence of God, the fragility of human relationships—that ranked quite highly on the lists of subjects intellectuals galvanized by existentialism found worthy. Greene concludes his portrait of Mason by comparing him to Conrad:

> [Mason's] task finished (and his manuscript [of *The Four Feathers*] was like a clean copy) there was mountaineering in the Alps, during the autumn a 2,000-acre shoot, a trip to South Africa. One remembers Conrad writing: 'It's late. I am tired after a day of uphill toil. Now it is always uphill with me. And the worst is one doesn't seem any nearer the top when the day is done.' One doubts whether Mason would have understood. They had set themselves different summits.[23]

Mason may not have understood, but Greene leaves little room to doubt that he himself did understand, and that he had set himself a summit comparable to Conrad's. As in the earlier review, Greene here attributes Mason's lack of understanding to the writer's unalterable, inescapable nature: if Mason did not grow more worthy of consideration, it was because Mason lacked the drive to create work that could be so considered. It is the writer as an auteur that interests Greene in this review—that is, the writer as the sole proprietor of the work, the source of its significance, the cause of its success or failure—and not the writer as 'mere technician' who produces texts that require mass audiences in order to become significant. In developing his argument,

Greene ignores the alternate meaning implied in his rhetorical opening gambit: that novels may grow worthier of consideration as the priorities of those audiences who read them change and not necessarily as a result of the author's 'growth'.

By quietly elaborating an auteurist conception of the writer's profession in these reviews—that is, a conception of the worthy artist as a non-professional ultimately motivated to produce art by some mysterious inner compulsion—Greene produced texts that scholars could easily appropriate as the grounds for an auteurist reading of Greene himself. Together with the films, stories, travel books, and novels he had produced between the beginning of his career and the 1950s, these articles formed the scaffolding of the proprietary (or auteurist) Greene genre, the ad-hoc experimental construct erected at different times, in different places, and for different reasons by various critics interested in Greene's work. Greene himself did not create the 'Greene genre', or establish himself as an auteur: both acts belong to the history of reading and its institutional corollary, criticism, rather than to the history of creative enterprise; rather, the way that Greene's work appealed to different audiences made possible various symbolic moves in the ongoing polemical battle between different classes of readers. If the auteurist Greene has in many ways superseded the other possibilities (the popular writer, the genre writer, the collaborator) the reason must rest with the aims and interests of the institution of criticism to an even greater extent than with the aims and interests of criticism's individual practitioners.

For a relatively brief period, from the early 1950s to the early 1960s, the 'Greene genre' helped produce a substantial body of criticism: the polemics it inspired among intellectuals sat easily between the interpretations the texts themselves appeared to sustain on the one side and, on the other, the aims and interests of the institutions that supported the intellectuals. Allott and Farris began the process of distilling Greene's personality from the various hints and traces scattered throughout the writer's work with the publication of *The Art of Graham Greene* in 1951:

> There is a sentence by Gaugin, quoted approvingly by Greene, that comes near to expressing his main obsessional outlook: 'Life being what it is, one dreams of revenge.' A terror of life, a terror of what experience can do to the individual, a terror at predetermined corruption, is the motive force that drives Greene as a novelist.[24]

In their introduction, Allott and Farris traced the lineage of this obsession from the various autobiographical sketches and reminiscences

Greene had published in the 1930s and 1940s, paying particular attention to 'The Revolver in the Cupboard' and 'The Lost Childhood'.
Having defined Greene's personality in these terms, it remained for the
scholars to examine the collected works and demonstrate how each constituted a manifestation of Greene's peculiar obsession: 'It would be
possible to illustrate both the reading of experience and the resultant
"terror of life" from any of the novels, but the terror is not everywhere
equally apparent.'[25] The novels in which Allott and Farris believe the
'terror of life' is most apparent turn out to be those that the scholars consider Greene's best, most accomplished works—particularly *The
Power and the Glory* and *The Heart of the Matter*. Those novels in which
they believe that the 'terror of life' is least apparent unsurprisingly turn
out to be his least successful novels. They dismiss *It's a Battlefield*, for
instance, as 'an immature book' that resonates with so many influences
that Greene's voice gets lost:

> At time successive influences can be traced as the style alters from
> section to section. Most of these influences—hints and half-hints
> of Woolf, Joyce, even Auden—are unimportant and can be ignored,
> but the irony is Conrad's irony and part of the book's pattern is
> owed to *The Secret Agent* . . . Conrad's technique of ironic presentation
> strengthened Greene's hand enormously in this first novel of his that
> needs to be taken seriously. But Greene's own tragic and ironic vision
> was not yet fully capable of integrating the various elements over
> which it is seen to play.[26]

Allott and Farris configure Greene's successes and failures in irreducibly
personal terms and repeatedly ask, 'How closely did the writer approach
the full realization of his personal vision in the novels?'

Frances Wyndham begins his study of Greene in the same fashion:
by quoting from Greene's non-fiction work in order to establish the
author's personality and personal vision. Wyndham quotes approvingly
from Greene's reviews of James and Mauriac, and from his memoir of
travelling through Liberia, *Journey Without Maps*, in order to show how
'the conflict between good and evil' characterize Greene's viewpoint:

> The struggle that [Greene] analyzes in his later book [*The End of the
> Affair*] between salvation and damnation is often unnecessarily tor-
> tuous; the final miracles explicitly treated in *The End of the Affair*, and
> hinted at in earlier novels, have been regarded as stretching things
> too far.

The answer is that Greene's view-point and the working-out of his themes demanded just such conclusions. He had to carry to their absolute ends both what he believes to be the human capacity for love, pity, fear, and, above all, despair, and God's capacity for mercy. Whether such conclusions are always technically and artistically successful is a different matter.[27]

Those novels in which Wyndham sees the struggle between good and evil most clearly become the most technically and artistically successful of Greene's novels. Thus, the ambiguities of *England Made Me*, in which neither protagonist nor antagonist is good or evil, make for a curiosity rather than a novel:

Artistically the book is a failure; it, [like *It's a Battlefield*], is too diffuse; moreover, somewhere [Greene] loses control of his raw material and the final effect is one of dissatisfaction. Nevertheless, in feeling the book is deeper than anything he had written hitherto, and the bitterness and irony here have a subtler edge; for all its imperfections, it has great interest for his admirers.[28]

As the judgment of a novel in which each of the characters grapples with the incommensurability of desire and ability, Wyndham's dismissal of the novel on the grounds that the final effect is one of dissatisfaction seems rather odd— unless one considers that dissatisfaction is not one of the effects a Greene novel (as hypothesized by Wyndham) should produce. He prefers *The Heart of the Matter*

because in it [Greene] has fully and finally developed the themes that have run through all his novels: the pity, fear, love, and despair; the search of a man for salvation. He has, too, carried to its conclusion the implications of his own faith—the love and mercy and mystery of God.[29]

In short, *The Heart of the Matter* satisfies Wyndham's expectations of the Greene novel in a fashion that *England Made Me* (and Greene's 'entertainments', save *Brighton Rock*) does not. Wyndham even dismisses *The Third Man* by paraphrasing Greene's introduction to the story: 'The earlier stories are sidelines to his work as a novelist, as is *The Third Man*, well known as a film, *which was never written to be read, but only to be seen*.'[30] As in Allott's and Farris's analysis, the success or failure of the work depends on how closely the scholar can force the text to conform to his or her vision of the author's personality and the expectations this vision engenders.

Greene received his first sustained critical attack in 1957 with the publication of Atkins's *Graham Greene*, an auteurist study executed in a contra-auteurist register. The auteur, after all, achieves a quasi-mystical unity between personality and the material at his disposal; for Atkins, however, Greene never ceases to reveal himself pulling the strings in his work, thereby devaluing most of the novels. He commences with what he believes is an apt metaphor for reading Greene:

> An onion is a vegetable peeled by housewives, and as the operation is frequently attended by tears it has served as a valuable image for generations of critics. One peels off layer after layer to get to the true, basic onion. But let us reverse this process and imagine the true, basic onion (which we can never know, it being the divine spark) being clothed and fattened.[31]

The auteurist always believes that he is peeling away the layers of the onion, whereas in fact he believes he knows—or has already divined—the true, basic onion, and his method is simply to pile layer upon layer on top of it so that nobody ever notices that there actually is no true, basic onion. On the one hand, Atkins reveals that there is no true, basic Greene, and that the collection of texts assembled under this heading is a rather heterogeneous, often contradictory lot; on the other hand, however, he tends to express this understanding in terms that reveal a distinct, rather negative conception of the true, basic Greene. For Atkins, Greene is first and foremost a writer who was not born great, and who has therefore had to undergo the rather ignominious process of developing his skills. Apropos of *The Quiet American*, for instance, he wrote:

> Greene's development tends to be a process of refining, and there is always the danger of its becoming pseudo-refining. At first only Catholics will pass muster, then American Catholics are excluded, and in time we are left with French Catholics alone. Later he will confine himself to French Catholics who have been purified by the pangs of adultery, and it will probably end with a select circle of adulterous French Catholics who know the Devil personally—only they won't live in France, they will cluster in Equatorial Africa.[32]

Here the auteurist sensibility appears to Atkins to run so deeply in Greene, and so over-determines his fictional representations, that it becomes visible, steps out into the open, announces its pretensions, and consequently holds its vessel, the writer, up to scorn. Atkins does not, however, deconstruct the auteur as such; he simply reveals that the true and basic onion is, in fact, a mercenary named Greene who produces his best fictions when he stops rationalizing and embraces the fact that he is a mercenary. 'In previous books Greene had often resorted to sensationalism, deliberate attempts to excite or horrify the reader. Here [in *The Heart of the Matter*] he does both, and there is not the slightest suggestion of strain.'[33] Atkins then goes on to buttress his argument by quoting liberally from a broadcast Greene had shared with Elizabeth Bowen and V.S. Pritchett:

> Disloyalty is our privilege. But it is a privilege you will never get society to recognize. All the more necessary that we who can be disloyal with impunity should keep that ideal alive... As a novelist, I must be allowed to write from the point of view of the black square as well as of a white.[34]

When Atkins published a second, updated edition of *Graham Greene* several years later he included a preface that related how his study had 'aroused the ire of the Greene claque'.[35] Particular exception was taken to two apostrophes Atkins addressed to Greene, which the scholar justified as follows:

> For the last dozen years I've lived in the land of apostrophe, and perhaps it's catching. Clearly, this is a form of mockery. Either there is something wrong with expressing mockery in this way, or you mustn't mock GG. Well, of course, so far as the acolytes are concerned it is the second interpretation.[36]

In this respect, the Atkins study drew a line in the sand between different, largely irreconcilable visions of Greene as an artist. When Elliott Malamet later observed the existence of 'a kind of cottage industry within Greene criticism pertaining to whether he is a "great" or even a "good" writer' he could have dated the birth of the industry to 1957 and Atkins's assertion that Greene was a 'good' writer some of the time, a 'bad' writer most of the time, and rarely, in those few moments that he did not try to hide his duplicity, a 'great' writer—which judgment, as Atkins himself notes, was not one that Greene scholars of the time were prepared to hear.[37] Suggesting, as Atkins had, that Catholicism was generally irrelevant to most of Greene's work and often a positive hindrance to its success proved too stark a contrast to the prevailing image of Greene that scholars had constructed partly by induction from the writer's non-fiction and partly from the interpretations that critics could reasonably require his work to sustain. Greene's next symbolic move, however, would help complicate the process of conceptualizing Greene as an auteur.

10
Our Man in Havana and Auteurism

Our Man in Havana, like all fiction, could be read by audiences in different circumstances in different ways, depending on the sort of expectations they brought to the text. The story deployed elements and processes associated with several genres, including the espionage thriller, the comedy of manners, and the romantic comedy. For those intent on appreciating the story specifically as a Greene novel, many of the semantic elements from his earlier work reappeared in this 1958 novel: a seedy atmosphere (this time Batista's Cuba), a protagonist with a checkered past and a seemingly dull future (here Jim Wormold, a British expatriate vacuum cleaner salesman), Catholicism (in the form of Wormold's daughter Milly, raised a Catholic in accordance with his ex-wife's wishes), and so forth. *The Third Man* was notable partly because it enabled intellectuals to read an explicitly anti-popular message in a film that 'mass' audiences made one of the most popular British films of all time; Greene's *Our Man in Havana*, by contrast, prompted intellectual readers to reconsider the legitimacy of the auteurist sensibility that scholars had brought to bear on his work in the intervening years. In short, it presented intellectuals with a Greene novel that refused to behave the way that they believed a Greene novel should have behaved.

Like *The Third Man*, *Our Man in Havana* places a creative writer at the heart of the story. Unlike Martins, however, Wormold does not count himself a member of the writer's profession: his creative writing consists of the confidential reports that he files for his MI6 superiors in London in his capacity as MI6's reluctant Havana operative. At first he derives most of these reports from real life, plucking a name from a Country Club directory, sometimes an occupation, and filling in the details he believes his superiors want to hear: installations in the middle of the jungle, weapons shipments, revolutionary stirrings, and economic information on the sugar and tobacco industries. In the beginning, his information comes primarily from newspapers: '... each day now he spent hours reading the local papers in order to mark any passages which could be suitably used by the professor or the engineer; it was unlikely that anyone in Kingston or London studied the daily papers of Havana.'[1] As the story progresses and Wormold's confidence grows, he begins to pay less attention to the papers and starts inventing characters and situations that later end in violence directed toward several innocent civilians. Thus, whereas *The Third Man* focuses on the romantic sensibility Martins cultivates through his professional activities, *Our Man in Havana* focuses on the professional activity itself: the story's development more or less mirrors Wormold's development *as* a writer.

In the early stages Wormold composes his fictions by placing simple facts about the business community in the mouths of his fictional characters. The novel's readers recognize these reports as fictions because they know that the reporters themselves do not exist as Wormold pretends they do; the reports' intended audience at MI6 headquarters accepts them as fact because they do not know that the reporters are fictitious; furthermore, the Chief in London valorizes the speakers because he does not realize that the information they communicate to him is actually available to anyone with the money to purchase a local newspaper and the time to read it. The narrative uses this discrepancy between the reader's understanding of Wormold's work and the Chief's to drive home the irony of the latter's complacency. On examining a set of blueprints, for instance, he remarks, 'Fiendish, isn't it? The ingenuity, the simplicity, the devilish imagination of the thing.... Like a gigantic spray....'[2] The reader, of course, knows that what the Chief is looking at *is* a spray, copied by Wormold from the schematics of one of his vacuum cleaners and attributed to Engineer Cifuentes.

From one perspective, then, the novel functions as a kind of allegory of writing. After Hawthorne, MI6's Caribbean operative, entices Wormold into the spy's trade with an offer of $300 a month tendered in the men's lavatory of the tourist dive, Sloppy Joe's, the vacuum cleaner salesman confronts the terror of the blank page:

> He thought: I must do something, give them some names to trace, recruit an agent, keep them happy. He remembered how Milly used to play at shops and give him her pocket money for imaginary purchases. One had to play the child's game, but sooner or later Milly always required her money back.[3]

Wormold understands that MI6 wants something from him, but has only a vague idea as to what something they might possibly want: he is a writer who knows he has an audience, but has little idea what that audience expects from him. He begins by cataloging his everyday surroundings, questioning the assistant of his shop (who mistakenly believes that Wormold desires a young prostitute), reading the local newspapers, and trying to inspire himself by recalling the circumstances under which Hawthorne managed to recruit him in the first place. In short, he attempts to write what he knows, and what he knows fortuitously finds favor with his audience. They even elect to supply their agent with a secretary. But as the admiration of his audience grows stronger and more particular, he finds himself increasingly thrown back on his own resources:

> The situation, whichever way he looked at it, was uncomfortable. Wormold was in the habit now of drawing occasional expenses for Engineer Cifuentes and the professor, and monthly salaries for himself, the Chief Engineer of the *Juan Belmonte*, and Teresa, the nude dancer. The drunken air-pilot was usually paid in whisky… Naturally to justify these payments he had to compose a regular supply of reports. With the help of a large map, the weekly number of *Time*, which gave generous space to Cuba in its section on the Western hemisphere, various economic publications issued by the government, *above all with the help of his imagination*, he had been able to arrange at least one report a week….[4]

Wormold's imagination only fails him when he needs to compose the 'spicy' reports from his nude dancer agent: instead he paraphrases these reports from a lurid celebrity magazine. This last detail paradoxically helps confirm for the reader that Wormold's reports are truly his own: it is the exception that demonstrates the felicity of his imagination in other, more pressing matters.

The situation grows uncomfortable for Wormold not only because he must juggle a wider assortment of characters but also because his 'readership' begins to grow. His secretary presses him to take over contact with his agents and develops a romantic longing for Raul, the drunken pilot whom Wormold believes he has crafted out of whole cloth.

> Raul Dominguez certainly had pathos. He had lost his wife in a massacre during the Spanish civil war and had become disillusioned with both sides, with his Communist friends in particular. The more

Beatrice asked Wormold about him, the more his character developed, and the more anxious she became to contact him. Sometimes Wormold felt a twinge of jealousy towards Raul and he tried to blacken the picture.[5]

As Wormold refines his storytelling skills, and as his audience expands, he begins to feel more keenly the pressure of meeting the expectations of that audience, and also to resent the conflicting demands that his profession places him under. Continuing to report 'the truth' in the terms laid out by his friend, the German expatriate Dr. Hasselbacher, no longer draws an altogether desirable reaction from his audience. He continues to draw his $300 per month—as well as the pay for his imaginary network of agents—but now begins to gauge success on a different, less commercial scale than the one which had prompted him to undertake the assignment in the first place. Unable to choose between professional and personal satisfaction, he persists in spinning out his fictions and attempts to alter Beatrice's perceptions of Raul through the medium of story.

If *The Third Man* was the story of a struggle between two authors for control of a narrative—Holly Martins and Colonel Calloway slugging it out over the interpretive rights to Lime's life—then *Our Man in Havana*'s first half seems to be the story of an author struggling to assert ownership of the rights to his own life. At first, of course, Wormold does not appear to possess a life worth claiming as his own: hemmed in by routine, counting paces to the Wonder Bar for his habitual drink with Dr. Hasselbacher, posting Christmas cards to the ex-wife who left him for an American professor, and allowing his daughter to mercilessly manipulate him, Wormold seems invisible even to the residents who watch him cross the street each day and who continue to treat him like a stranger. But the sudden blooming of Wormold's imagination at a rather advanced stage in his life does not particularly surprise the reader: the neophyte writer has merely encountered a fortuitous set of circumstances that conspire to permit him the luxury of expressing a talent that different circumstances had forced into dormancy. In other words, throughout the first half of the novel the narrative communicates Wormold's creative talent largely as a natural one—precisely the sort of talent valorized by the auteurist: one that stems from the indomitable force of personality.

But *Our Man in Havana* does not end half-way through the story: having presented a kind of allegory of writing (particularly of the writing of an 'author'), it continues by presenting an allegory of reading. At the beginning of his career, Wormold has only two readers to worry about: the agent who hired him, and the hypothetical reader in London to whom he must continue supplying persuasive reports. At several points in the story, however, the narrative abandons Wormold in Havana and transports the reader across the Atlantic to the offices of MI6.

Wormold's handler, Hawthorne, is a much cannier reader than the bureau chief, but he also lacks the power to apply the lessons he derives from his reading. It does not take very long for him to figure out that Wormold has filed bogus reports. When the Chief shows him the blueprints that Engineer Cifuentes has allegedly procured, he blanches.

> 'Could I take one more look at those drawings?'
> 'That one seems to interest you. What's your idea of it?'
> 'It looks,' Hawthorne said miserably, 'like a snap-action coupling.'[6]

In this moment Hawthorne becomes the only character in the novel to stand on the same footing as the reader and, significantly, he does not appear again until the climax of the novel, when he informs Wormold that the enemy plans to poison him. Had he returned immediately to Havana, of course, logic would have dictated he undertake some sort of remedial action. He might have blown Wormold's cover, fired him outright, or perhaps had him assassinated—all possibilities that would have either prevented the series of events that unfold throughout the second half of the novel or else cast the British government as the ultimate villain of the piece. But although Hawthorne's abrupt disappearance from the novel invites the sort of charge James M. Cain leveled against Greene for using the unlikely device of a dog drinking whiskey ('I never saw a dog drink hard liquor... but I do believe he had a look at the script, to know what he should do'[7]) his departure nonetheless plays a pivotal role in the novel. If Hawthorne's absence does not strain credulity to the same extent as the whiskey-sipping dog, it is because his disappearance transfers to the reader the responsibility for moderating the communications between Havana and London. It is, after all, Hawthorne's understanding of Wormold's pretence that illuminates the ignorance of the London office by contrast.

Before making his exit, Hawthorne comments on the Chief's preferred mode of understanding. When his superior suggests augmenting Wormold's staff, Hawthorne demurs and tells his superior that the premises are too small. The Chief replies:

'I know the type, Hawthorne. Small scrubby desk. Half a dozen men in an outer office meant to hold two. Out-of-date accounting machines. Woman-secretary who is completing forty years with the firm.'

Hawthorne now felt able to relax; the Chief had taken charge. Even if one day he read the secret file, the words would convey nothing to him. The small shop for vacuum cleaners had been drowned beyond recovery in the tide of the Chief's literary imagination. Agent 59200/5 was established.[8]

If Hawthorne's hints establish agent 59200/5 in the Chief's imagination, then the passage's hints establish the Chief's sensibility as an auteurist one in the reader's imagination. Once he clutches the idea that Wormold is some sort of 'merchant king', he believes that he knows everything that he believes it is possible to know about Wormold:

Our man in Havana belongs—you might say—to the Kipling age. Walking with kings—how does it go?—and keeping your virtue, crowds and the common touch. I expect somewhere in that ink-stained desk of his there's an old penny note-book of black wash-leather in which he kept his first accounts—a quarter gross of India-rubbers, six boxes of steel and nibs....[9]

The Chief reads Wormold the way Martins read Calloway, according to fixed generic conventions. In *The Third Man*, however, Lime's unwillingness to rest peacefully in the grave problematized the relationship between competing authors; here, the only character capable of mediating between the two (i.e., Hawthorne) conveniently drops out of the story. As far as the Chief is concerned, from this point onward Wormold can do nothing wrong, since he can attribute Wormold's flaws to the character type that has shaped him, while simultaneously attributing his strengths to the unique personality the Chief has (mistakenly) detected struggling to assert itself against the type. The relationship between the two men *does* remain problematic, of course, but in Hawthorne's absence the narrative prompts the reader to realize the significance of this difficulty, rather than any of the characters within the story.

Shortly after Hawthorne leaves the scene things begin to go badly awry for Wormold. The Cubana pilot Raul dies under mysterious circumstances. An unknown assassin attempts to murder Engineer Cifuentes. Wormold goes in search of his other fictional agents, notably Professor Sanchez (whose name he also appropriated from the Country Club list) and Teresa, the nude dancer and part-time prostitute whom Wormold does not even believe exists (but whom Beatrice demands be extracted from the field). After a menacing interview with Captain Segura, the chief of police, Wormold discovers that his old friend Dr. Hasselbacher has been blackmailed into decrypting the messages he has been sending on to London. At this moment in the story, the narrative abruptly switches viewpoints from Havana to the suburban home of the MI6 Chief, where over Granny Brown's Ipswich Roast and a Cockburn '27 he briefs the Permanent Undersecretary on the situation in Havana:

> They've become very active in Cuba... His best agent, as you know, was killed, accidentally of course, on his way to take aerial photographs of the constructions—a very great loss to us. But I would give much more than a man's life for those photographs. As it was, we had given fifteen hundred dollars.... Perhaps it was worth a few casualties to open his eyes. Cigar?[10]

The fine food and drink juxtaposed with the casual mention of slaughter in the streets of Cuba casts the Chief in an ominous light that grows darker the further one juxtaposes it: with the scenes of squalor at the Shanghai; with the image of Hasselbacher dressed up in his Uhlan uniform trying to stave off his guilt with recollections of faded glory and innocence; and with the corpse of the not-quite-anonymously-dead Raul. The scene reveals the underbelly of the Chief's auteurist reading of Wormold, less because he appears to know the value of a human life to the nearest dollar than because he invests his agent's fictional reports with unerring authority. The pilot's death, for instance, can hardly be counted as 'a very great loss' because the service has never actually 'had' Raul to lose. The Chief may believe that opening Wormold's eyes is worth a few casualties, but he can only believe it because he has blinkered his own eyes to Wormold's duplicity. If the Chief's words disturb the reader it is not simply because they reveal the Chief as a callous fool—for he has been that since Hawthorne's first rendezvous in London—but rather because he has constructed his attitude from the reports that Wormold has filed. The Chief's shortcomings as a reader insistently focus the reader's attention on the culpability that attends Wormold's naïve performance of his duties.

The dinner scene necessarily reveals the limitations of the auteurist perspective as a method of reading texts, since the narrative communicates nothing so clearly at this stage than Wormold's shame and disgust at the chain of events he knows he has to some extent set in motion. The scene reveals that the 'merchant-king' personality the Chief has insisted on attributing to 'his man in Havana', 59200/5's stubbornness and resourcefulness (for allegedly recruiting a double-agent whom the reader knows is the non-aligned Captain Segura) not only bears little resemblance to Wormold: its use as an interpretive principle has legitimized bloodshed that not even the 'author' in question believes justifiable. From the Chief's perspective, nothing that happens in the second half of the novel—neither Raul's death, nor Hasselbacher's—should have a negative impact on Wormold, since the authorial personality the Chief has constructed should in theory have little regard for ethics (or, in Peter Rabinowitz's term, 'extra-textual effects'). On the contrary: the deaths that follow in the wake of Wormold's reports should in the end make him a better agent (and also, of course, a better writer).

The Chief is not the only character who reads Wormold as an auteur: the unidentified 'enemy' reads Wormold's reports as well, aided by Dr. Hasselbacher's crossword-honed skill as a code-breaker. In the enemy's eyes, Wormold's institutional affiliation guarantees his veracity: they cannot conceive of somebody fabricating reports for the government. In this respect, the enemy shares the same assumption as the audience; after all, if people accepted as a matter of course that spies routinely lied to their superiors, then readers would have had a difficult time appreciating the novel's humor. And, like the reader, the enemy also knows that the reports are not, strictly speaking, accurate. Before he dies Hasselbacher even informs Wormold that they suspected his reports were invented. 'But then you changed your codes and your staff increased. The British Secret Service would not be so easily deceived, would it?'[11] Ironically, it is at this moment that Hawthorne returns and informs Wormold that he had also suspected the reports were invented until he learned that the enemy intended to murder him. Both sides read the same way. Like the Secret Service, the enemy desires certain propositions to become facts, and Wormold acts as a catalyst in the transformation. The less likely it appears to the enemy that Wormold's reports contain literal truth, the more they believe in their authenticity: 'Perhaps you wanted to disguise [Raul's] identity in case we broke your code. Perhaps if your friends had known he had private means and a plane of his own, they wouldn't have paid him so much.'[12] Lacking grounds for an assessment of the truths the reports contain, the enemy generally identifies Wormold's truths with their own objectives: 'They offered [Raul] a lot of money if he would work for them instead. They too want photographs, Mr. Wormold, of those platforms you discovered in the Oriente hills.'[13]

Both the enemy and the Chief believe they have privileged access to Wormold's personality, which they then apply to their reading of the material he produces. Although neither arrives at an accurate assessment of either Wormold or his reports, their readings clear the way for them both to perform actions capable of furthering their own interests. By making these reading strategies visible the novel encourages its readers to adopt a different, less auteur-centric strategy of configuring the significance of the events it narrates. As Henry Shapiro observed, '*Our Man in Havana* is not about "fiction-making" in the literary sense alone.... Fact and fiction, discovery and invention, are in both theory and practice ultimately indistinguishable from each other.'[14]

Our Man in Havana, however, does more than relate characters and situations capable of supporting an anti-auteurist reading of the novel. More significantly, perhaps, it takes some of the central tropes critics had isolated in Greene's work and uses them in a way that tends to drain the significance they enjoy as characteristic features of the Greene novel. In the novel, Wormold decides to accept Hawthorne's offer of a post with MI6 on the grounds that the extra money will help him to support his daughter Milly. During the course of the novel, Milly celebrates her seventeenth birthday. The narrative does not dwell abstractly on the sort of support a 17-year-old girl might require that she could not procure herself; instead, it presents the concrete problem of a horse that Milly desires, and that Wormold desires to give her. Milly addresses Wormold the same way that Orwell putatively imagined Greene addressing his readers, asserting that her father is an invincibly ignorant pagan, albeit a good one, and that his foolishness will probably earn him God's mercy when he arrives in Heaven. Elsewhere, however, the reader can scarcely distinguish between Milly's Catholicism and her rampant consumerism. When she prays to God, she prays for a pony—specifically, that He will somehow influence her father to come up with the money for the pony she desires. When Wormold tells her that he has decided to purchase the horse (simultaneously telling the reader that he will accept Hawthorne's offer) she contentedly responds 'It's wonderful, isn't it, how you always get what you pray for?'[15] The Catholic God had appeared in many guises in many of Greene's novels: as the task-master against whom Pinkie rebels in *Brighton Rock*; as the 'hound of heaven' chasing the Whisky Priest through purgatory in *The Power and the Glory*; as tempter and lover in *The End of the Affair*; never before, however, had God figured as the dispenser of consumer durables. After she receives the horse, Milly relates a dream in which she comes face-to-voice with an entity she believes was God: 'It said—only it sounded much more apocalyptic in the middle of the night—"You've bitten off more than you can chew, my girl. What about the Country Club?"'[16]

Wormold takes Milly's consumer-oriented faith quite seriously although he does not necessarily believe in it, as evidenced by his willingness to take on the work Hawthorne offers him despite his reservations. The specifics of Milly's faith are largely beside the point—as Cain observed, 'the Catholic Church has no monopoly on extravagant girls'—since the passage functions primarily to establish the dimensions of Wormold's character: the less sympathetic a reader finds Milly, the more unconditional Wormold's love for Milly will appear and the less unlikely his quick decision to join MI6 after all will seem. But for many intellectual readers the Catholic element should have been central, and so because the narrative did little to suggest the significance of the Catholic theme in the work as a whole—as Hawthorne did before her, Milly practically disappears from the narrative after God (i.e., MI6's Chief) grants her a membership at the Country Club—it left the novel open to charges that its Catholicism was a sham, or that Greene had simply used it as a prop, not qualitatively different than the edition of Lamb's *Tales from Shakespeare* that Wormold uses to encode his messages.

Depending on a given reader's sensibility, however, this possibility could have quite far-reaching repercussions. From the auteurist viewpoint in particular, *Our Man in Havana*, like the rest of the novels, should have been the expression of Greene's true personality. In John Atkins's terms, it should have been one more layer on the true, basic onion. Because all contradictions should have been reconciled in the personality of the author, the novel should not have been capable of contradicting the earlier work. Some readers did attempt to construct the novel's meaning along auteurist lines, identifying a thematic unity between *Our Man in Havana* and the earlier work, most notably Charles Rolo of the *Atlantic Monthly*.

> It has been said of Graham Greene that he reduces theology to melodrama and raises melodrama to theology. Wormold's lack of compunction about swindling the Secret Service—his derisive conviction that its activities are 'unreal'—reflects Greene's doctrine that human goals are irremediably sordid and pointless; that man is saved by grace alone. Milly is a symbol of grace, and Wormold, for all his 'invincible ignorance' of God, is touched by it.[17]

It is, of course, Wormold's conviction that the activities of the Secret Service are 'unreal' that results in the deaths of Raul and Hasselbacher, the assassination attempt on Engineer Cifuentes, and Wormold's own murder of the enemy agent Carter. And it is, of course, the protection of Milly's faith that grace is best embodied in a chestnut mare and membership at an exclusive country club that leads Wormold to undertake unreal activities for the Secret Service. Nonetheless, Rolo clearly believes that the novel must illustrate the author's personality, and since he has decided that the author truly believes that human goals are irremediably sordid and pointless, then the significance attached to the events related by the narrative must be made to match the predetermined meaning. Other critics later took the opposite approach (as Atkins had in 1957) and claimed that novels like *Our Man in Havana* demonstrated that '[Greene's] dedication to the ideas supposedly central to his own life is ultimately so cursory, so self-contentedly shallow, that he cannot possibly have anything of important to convey about such matters.'[18] This interpretive strategy embraces auteurism, but denies Greene auteur status; as such, however, it is a characteristic contribution to academic 'cottage industry' described by Elliott Malamet.

Robert Hatch objected to the film adaptation of *Our Man in Havana* because he could not decide whether the story called for laughter or tears: 'Three people (and a nice little dog) get killed in this yarn, and that is either too many or too few for burlesque. The plot is frivolously fantastic, but the bodies awkwardly real.'[19] One might have answered that illuminating the contrast between frivolity and the awkwardness of bodies constitutes one of the story's most prominent structural principles. Marc Silverstein observed that the heroes of Greene's thrillers were 'neither the supermen of Fleming nor the seasoned professionals of le Carré':

>... rather, as Arthur Rowe observes, they emerge from the ranks of 'dull and shabby human mediocrity'. Scarred by the painful consciousness of failure and the ubiquitous sense of guilt and corruption, they never passively resign themselves to chaos.... Dullness and shabbiness notwithstanding, their determination to confront their predicament with some conclusive action grants them a kind of heroic stature.[20]

Hatch's critique of *Our Man in Havana* (echoed by Cain and others) suggests the reviewer's desire to contain the chaos rather than to confront it. By figuring out where to fit the story in the generic schema that prevailed in 1960, and thus by ignoring the reader's role in both the problem and resolution of the story, Hatch hopes to postpone the moment that ultimately demands conclusive action.

James Yaffe sounded a similar note in his review of the novel, suggesting that in place of suspense Greene had

> filled the book with what its jacket calls 'undertones.' That is, a political philosophy, portentous in tone but easy to follow, is blatantly set forth at the end. It is expressed in a nutshell by one of the characters: 'Would the world be in the mess it is if we were loyal to love and not to countries?' Famous last words, to be murmured piously as the bomb falls.[21]

Beatrice murmurs the philosophy to which Yaffe objects in the novel's closing moments—but the reviewer seems to have forgotten the factor that weighed most heavily on Wormold's decision to join MI6 in the first place: love for his daughter, which he had hoped to communicate to the girl by earning the money to buy her the pony she desired. Divesting the novel's ending of irony paves the way for Yaffe's conclusion. He does not attempt to assign the significance of the text to a generic category, but rather to an auteurist one: 'It would seem that [Greene] considers the suspense thriller somewhat beneath him nowadays, that he must trick it up with "undertones" in order to remind us that it is being written not just by anybody but by Graham Greene.'[22] Where Hatch attempted to postpone the necessity of confrontation by trying to situate the novel in a fixed generic category, Yaffe attempts to deny the necessity of confrontation by attributing the novel's significance to Greene the auteur, whose personality and materials have somehow clashed in an unproductive way. For Yaffe, *Our Man in Havana* is a bad book because Greene calls attention to his status as the text's author, and because he believes that the authorial personality responsible for organizing the text succumbs to simplemindedness. In short, the reviewer chooses to read Greene, rather than the novel—an action the novel itself has dramatized through Wormold, whose decent intentions never quite compensate for the disastrous consequences of his actions.

Our Man in Havana did not change the work that Greene had executed earlier in his career and it did not transform intellectuals' perspectives on the auteurist sensibility; like *The Third Man*, his new novel merely furnished readers with a text that sustained a large (but not infinite) range of interpretations and that consequently enabled scholars to situate him at different points in the prevailing schema of intellectual discourse.

Greene had produced *The Third Man* at a fortuitous historical moment, when the academy's response to the professional challenges of the postwar settlement had gone some way toward breaking the Leavisite stranglehold on scholarly methodology. As we have seen, Greene's symbolic move thus dovetailed neatly with the symbolic move for which intellectuals desired to appropriate him and his work. Two of the novels that Greene produced after *The Third Man*, *The End of the Affair* and *The Quiet American*, enabled commentators to confirm their sense that they had accurately mapped 'Greeneland' despite the hackles the latter raised in the United States. (A.J. Liebling's review of *The Quiet American* clearly influenced the analysis offered by Atkins, who quoted liberally from the review.[23]) *Our Man in Havana*, however, offered intellectuals a very different range of symbolic moves, many of them less supportive of Greene's status as an author. But just because the novel made these negative moves possible did not imply that intellectuals necessarily had to make them; that many of them did so would seem to indicate that historical circumstances favored such a move.

Two years prior to the publication of *Our Man in Havana*, the Suez Crisis had embarrassed the British political class, and had driven home the extent to which postwar Britain depended on American consent to its policy objectives. Historian Diane Kunz observed that after Suez, neither Britain, its European neighbors, nor the United States could pretend that it remained a major power: 'A nation that was forced to recant an action, which it had labelled in its vital interest, at command of another country because it had run out of money was, at least temporarily, a client state, not a superpower.'[24] Contemporary intellectuals attempted to spin the inglorious defeat from a different angle, and concentrated on the aesthetic dimension of the crisis: how it had played out on the world stage. A front-page *New Statesman* editorial, for instance, denounced the invasion as a 'body-blow to the United Nations' and drew special attention to the plight of the British Ambassador whose nation had left him in the lurch:

> ...the pathetic figure of Sir Piers Dixon, fighting back his tears, and blocking successive Russian and American motions by employing a constitutional device [the absolute veto] whose use we had so often and so vehemently deplored, symbolized the dismay of all who had worked to weld the UN into an instrument of peace.[25]

Of course, in 1956 the largest single undertaking achieved through the UN had been the invasion of Korea (a project it had completed only because China had been removed from the Security Council when Mao took power and Russia was boycotting the Council when the United States tabled the resolution).[26] The *New Statesman* editorial thus communicates several myths: that the UN had been functioning perfectly well until Eden soured things, that international opinion carried a weight incommensurate with the power of nations to enforce it, and that a nation as dependent on US power and finance as Britain undoubtedly was could, through its own waywardness, somehow undermine the organization.[27] It projects an ethical dimension onto the UN that the organization never possessed, but does so in a fashion that pays a backhanded tribute to British exceptionalism. In debasing itself, the article suggests, Britain had in fact debased the entire internationalist project— a suggestion incommensurate with the political and economic weakness that had in fact brought the crisis to a boil in the first place.

Our Man in Havana could hardly help but frustrate or disappoint the reader who brought the sort of bias communicated by the *New Statesman* editorial to his experience of the novel. In his memoir *Ways of Escape* Greene wrote that he had abandoned the idea behind *Our Man in Havana* in 1938, when he decided that:

> [the shadows of] the war to come had been too dark for comedy; the reader could feel no sympathy for a man who was cheating his country in Hitler's day for the sake of an extravagant wife. But in fantastic Havana, among the absurdities of the Cold War (for who can accept the survival of Western capitalism as a great cause?) there was a situation allowably comic, all the more if I changed my wife into a daughter.[28]

In one sense, this passage describes the novel's authorial audience quite accurately. Somebody who understood how vehemently the political classes desired the Cold War to be taken seriously, but who also acknowledged how spurious so many of the actions sanctioned by Cold War ideology were, could hope to grasp most fully the comedy and pathos of Wormold's situation. The problem, of course, was that so few intellectual readers were quite as agnostic about the Cold War as this ideal reader.

The left understood that the survival of western capitalism implied the survival (indeed the flourishing) of inequality, exploitation, and military aggression; as such, the Cold War did not necessarily appear absurd. Sartre, for instance, analyzed how US policy toward Cuba had created a colony characterized not by political oversight but by economic dependence. After the Spanish–American War, American industry had offered to buy Cuba's unrefined sugar at the cost of American beetroot sugar, a much higher price than it was worth, but one that effectively dis-incentivized Cuban industrialization. Sartre writes:

[The] arrangement worked so well that the whole island was inundated with [American] merchandise, from bulldozers and mechanical cranes to cigarettes and washing machines. As for agriculture, things came to the point where the most fertile country of the Americas had to procure from the U.S.A. a third, and in some sections a half, of the foodstuffs necessary for its nourishment... [The Americans] continued to furnish autos and frigidaires. They gave credit to everyone and the country crept along, weighed down with skyscrapers and machinery; and each new government, on taking power, discovered a debt-ridden financial system, a deteriorating economy, and obligations which, though discreetly referred to, were unrelenting.[29]

For Sartre (and other left-leaning readers), the 'fantastic Havana' of the Batista regime, subsidized by the United States and maintained as a leisure spot for the wealthy at the expense of the native population, may not have provided a suitable setting for a comedy. Nor would he necessarily have found the main character, a middle-class European expatriate with a profligate daughter, a suitable vehicle for their sympathy. Nor would he necessarily have appreciated the comic uses made of Captain Segura, the chief of police who confides to Wormold the niceties involved in distinguishing the non-torturable class from the torturable class, who include 'the poor in my own country, in any Latin American country':

The poor of Central Europe and the Orient. Of course in your welfare states you have no poor, so you are untorturable. In Cuba the police can deal as harshly as they like with émigrés from Latin America and the Baltic States, but not with visitors from your country or Scandinavia. It is an instinctive matter on both sides. Catholics are more torturable than Protestants, just as they are more criminal.[30]

At the end, Segura receives a potentially humanizing touch: everyone in Havana knows that he carries a cigarette case made from human skin, and at the end he reveals that it was made from the skin of the man who had tortured and killed his father. For the left reader, the detail could easily be interpreted as a nod to bourgeois individualist values.

For intellectuals on the right, the Cold War was an absolute necessity both as a defence of the right to private property against public ownership, and as a defence of private property's corollary, liberal-humanist individualism. The political class conceptualized the state as the means of defending the perpetuation of these values: firstly, by deploying its coercive power against regimes that ostensibly posed some sort of threat to them; and secondly, by using the vast apparatus that maintained this coercive power (namely, the military–industrial complex) to ensure that internal threats to the established order did not evolve as a result of the state spending that, even by the late 1940s, nearly *all* intellectuals had recognized as necessary to political and economic stability. As *Business Week* put it:

> Military spending doesn't really alter the structure of the economy.... As far as business is concerned, a munitions order from the government is much like an order from a private customer. [Welfare and public works spending] does alter the economy. It makes channels of its own. It shifts demand from one industry to another.[31]

In other words, both the United States and, to a lesser but still quite large extent, the United Kingdom had settled into an economic and political pattern that enabled the wealthy to retain their privileges: private property and the sort of individualism one could not purchase from Woolworth's. It merely needed defending, and intellectuals on the right briskly rose to the challenge.

The American statesman George Kennan delivered a typical defence of the status quo during his talks for the Charles R. Walgreen Foundation lecture series at the University of Chicago in 1949. When confronted by the intractable ignorance of the world community the American had only to fall back on his 'attitude of detachment and soberness and readiness to reserve judgment'. Then, he continued:

> ...we will have the modesty to admit our own national interest is all that we are really capable of knowing and understanding—and the courage to recognize that if our own purposes and undertakings here at home are honest ones, unsullied by arrogance or hostility toward other people or delusions of superiority, then the pursuit of our national interest can never fail to be conducive to a better world.[32]

The assumptions of Kennan's argument mirror the assumptions of the *New Statesman* editorial on the Suez Crisis: American and British purposes and undertakings are by their nature virtuous because the American and British people are by their nature virtuous. When bad things happen and the world becomes a worse place (as it does in *Our Man in Havana*), it is because a few 'bad apples' have had their way. Wormold, however, is precisely an honest man 'unsullied by arrogance or hostility toward other people or delusions of superiority' and it is precisely these qualities that lead him to swindle the British Secret Service, which he correctly detects privileges results above honesty. This juxtaposition of characteristics makes him a sort of 'heroic bad apple' who does the wrong things for the right reasons, as unthinkable (or at least unspeakable) a proposition on the right as the idea that the pursuit of the national interest could actually fail to be conducive to a better world.

Our Man in Havana could conceivably lay claim to the status of Greene's most 'popular' novel, not necessarily because of the number of copies it sold, or because the film adaptation, also directed by Carol Reed, performed reasonably well for Columbia Pictures, but because in playing the Cold War for laughs it made light of an issue that consumed a massive amount of intellectual energy and effort, but that only rarely intruded directly into the lives of private citizens until the Vietnam War. A belief in the value of ideas is not one that *Our Man in Havana* particularly privileges or demands of its readers, and for this reason numerous critics found levelling the charge of anti-intellectualism against Greene quite painless; one suspects, for instance, that the novel began the process by which David Pryce-Jones moved from tentative approval of Greene's work in 1963 to the rabid assessment he offered in 1989:

> No writer outside the Communist Party has led such a campaign against the West... Greene is sincere. His projection of the cold war years is pure melodrama, but he has come to believe it absolutely... Written with the added authority of someone once on the inside, *Our Man in Havana* and *The Human Factor* are novels celebrating the bankruptcy of British intelligence in its efforts at defence. Such efforts were a waste of energy, evidence only that the innocent were persecuted and the upper crust unscrupulous.[33]

Twenty-six years earlier, Pryce-Jones had simply dismissed *Our Man in Havana* as a minor effort; he had not found it deeply offensive.

During those 26 years Greene's novels had not changed, but his place in the pantheon of twentieth-century letters certainly had. Prior to *The Third Man* it had been possible for critics to discuss Greene as a good-but-popular writer. Only rarely did critics offer a negative assessment of Greene's work. At worst, reviewers couched their praise in generic terms (cinema, thriller, etc.) designed to distance the quality of their approbation from institutional standards. After *The Third Man* it became possible for critics to discuss his achievement in auteurist terms within intellectual institutions. The Greene criticism of the 1950s helped lay the groundwork for his future reputation among scholars by presenting him as a strong personality who worked with materials that were, for a literary artist, quite unconventional on account of their popularity, but which the author deployed to explicitly intellectual ends. Ironically, when read from the auteurist perspective applied to Greene throughout the 1950s, intellectuals could construe *Our Man in Havana* as an attack both on themselves and on the auteurist sensibility. Furthermore, the specific narrative strategies, tropes, and characters deployed by the novel made it difficult for the auteurist reader to avoid sensing that the author had in some profound way betrayed his own personality. If as Fredric Jameson suggests, genre is always an ad-hoc construct devised for a specific textual occasion which is abandoned like so much scaffolding once the analysis is done, then with *Our Man in Havana* the author abruptly pulled the 'Greene' scaffolding out from under the legs of his critics. Thus Greene's reputation gradually arrived at the strange impasse where it continues to stagnate: the scholars who most vehemently attack him produce readings that assume he is—to use the phrase splashed across the *New York Times Book Review* on 9 September 1973— 'England's largest living novelist';[34] the scholars who most respect him continue to produce readings that barely pass muster by contemporary academic standards; and the generation of intellectuals responsible for maintaining those standards, who came of age after structuralism and post-structuralism had supplanted auteurism as the academy's ruling paradigm, largely ignore him.

Part IV
The Polemical Battlefield

11
Greene and the Polemics of Canonical Reading

When Robert Murray Davis argued in 1973 that 'unless a better case can be made for [Greene], the Collected Edition may have to be the slab over his reputation instead of a monument to it' he did not imply that Greene would simply disappear, or that the public would stop reading his novels, or even that Hollywood would stop acquiring the rights to adapt those novels for the cinema.[1] On the contrary, public acclaim and demand for Greene's work had rarely been as high.[2] Davis's concern was limited to a more specific institutional context. Unless scholars began assessing Greene from different perspectives than had hitherto been brought to bear on the writer's work, his significance within the academy would likely wane. Specifically, he suggested the need for scholars to move away from emphasis on the 'incredibly dated' dogmatic issues that had virtually monopolized Greene criticism throughout the 1950s and 1960s. Davis reflected: 'One wonders what college-age readers make of [Greene] behind the polite, bland, note-taking façade....'[3] As Davis conceived it, the problem stemmed less from Greene's texts than from teachers and scholars who continued to insist that understanding the dogmatic issues in the texts was tantamount to understanding the texts themselves. Nothing, of course, was more understandable than the parochialism of critical interest: two decades of criticism had struggled to assert that an obsession with matters of faith was the factor that distinguished Greene from other popular novelists and that made his work stand apart from more conventional material. These assertions in turn implied a biographically oriented criticism, for where did the dogmatic issues come from if not the author's strong personality? Without Greene's strong personality, how could one distinguish *Brighton Rock* from the latest *Scarface* clone? The answers to questions like these, however, did not constitute a better case.

Davis clearly believed that Greene criticism had reached a dead end of sorts: it no longer furnished a persuasive rationale for studying the novels. Twenty years later Alan Warren Friedman observed that the situation had not actually improved. Citing Greene's 'obsessions' with religion and politics (rather than with, say, 'language, aesthetics, literary structures, narrative unreliability, or self-reflexivity') Friedman observed that:

> ...the critical response to his work has been primarily thematic and biographical, and, as Jeffrey Meyers puts it, it 'has not been particularly perceptive'. Unlike the slightly younger Samuel Beckett, for example, Greene has inspired few major critical thinkers to significant theoretical speculation. One looks in vain among Greene critics for Freudians, deconstructionists, new historicists, reader-response theorists, or feminists; and one finds only the beginnings of Marxist, post-colonial, and cultural critiques.[4]

Critics and scholars had clearly not lost interest in Greene; they had simply continued to read Greene in terms of the 'dogmatic issues' that had seemed so dated to Davis 20 years earlier and which had hardly become more contemporary in the intervening years. Like Davis, Friedman assumed that Greene was, for one reason or another, worth studying. Furthermore, he appeared to believe that Greene's reputation would only be vouchsafed if and when major critical thinkers began using Greene's texts in order to make 'significant theoretical speculations'. Until that happened, Greene's status within intellectual discourse would remain problematic—even illegitimate.

Neither Friedman nor Davis suggests that Greene's work had become irrelevant; on the contrary, if they had believed that it had, then there would have been no point arguing that a better case needed to be made for his work. Rather, each responds—quite strongly—to the specifically institutional use that had been made of Greene and his work. They grasp the tradition of Greene criticism less as a body of knowledge that scholars had carefully cobbled together than as a patchwork of scholarly polemics seeking to situate Greene somewhere within intellectual discourse. However, by rather successfully fetishizing biography and theme—that is, by pursuing the methodology this study identifies as auteurist—the scholars Davis and Friedman address had gradually managed to marginalize Greene in the context of evolving intellectual discourses. What had arguably constituted the bleeding edge of intellectual inquiry circa 1950 had healed by 1973, and virtually no trace of the scar remained visible 20 years later. Thus Davis's and Friedman's articles themselves constitute scholarly polemics aimed at persuading critics to make better use of Greene by working to reach some sort of accommodation between the work and the intellectual methodologies valued by their respective institutions (broadly speaking, structuralism and post-structuralism).

The status of these arguments as institutional polemic has an interesting consequence: they not only attempt to persuade scholars to assess Greene's work using contemporary methodologies, but also affirm (or reaffirm) Greene's entitlement to such treatment. Like the auteurist critiques Davis and Friedman clearly find unconvincing, their own analyses communicate Greene's uniqueness, and suggest that some quality in his work distinguishes him from other writers who presumably would not benefit from analysis by deconstructionists, new historicists, feminists, etc. In the context of the academy, this sort of polemic has a very specific function: canonization, in the sense formulated by Harold Bloom: 'The Canon ... has become a choice among texts struggling with one another for survival, whether you interpret this choice as being made by dominant social groups, institutions of education, traditions of criticism, or, as I do, by late-coming authors who feel themselves chosen by particular ancestral figures.'[5] Davis's and Friedman's arguments, like those of Allott and Farris, Frances Wyndham, and early David Pryce-Jones, assert that in the competition for survival among texts, Greene's deserve whatever assistance intellectuals can muster in their defence.

At no point, however, does Greene (or anybody else) definitively 'enter' the canon; after all, the canon as such does not exist in any binding or physical sense. Critics may produce readings of work that function more or less as canonical readings: that is, as readings that on one level aim at securing canonical status for a particular writer, text, collection of texts, or even movement (particularly in non-literary disciplines). To the extent that a portion of the critic's audience agrees with the polemic, that author may be considered canonical. Thus a writer like Shakespeare is considered 'canonical' because a huge portion of those responsible for teaching Shakespeare believe that he is in some way essential. Among scholars of hard-boiled fiction, by contrast, there is some question as to whether Mickey Spillane should be accorded canonical status.[6] Greene's status is even more problematic: when a scholar like Mary Warner argues that *The End of the Affair* can be read 'like a sacred text', she clearly imagines and presents Greene as a canonical figure; but she also couches her argument in language that necessarily limits the audience who will in all likelihood agree with her.[7]

Bloom has observed that the canon itself has come under threat by what he refers to as the 'six branches of the School of Resentment: Feminists, Marxists, Lacanians, New Historicists, Deconstructionists, Semioticians'.[8] Bloom argues that since the members of these critical schools do not approach the problems of literature from the perspective of aesthetic value, there can be no real grounds for preferring Shakespeare to Greene (or, for that matter, to Spillane). In a sense he is correct. Because a feminist scholar, for instance, is less interested in literature *as* literature than in literature as the documentary crystallization of social phenomena, there is no reason that she should learn more about the oppression of women in the early twentieth century from F. Scott Fitzgerald than from Margaret Barnes. This in turn reveals an irresolvable contradiction in Friedman's polemic. When, for instance, Peter Rabinowitz chooses to use Fitzgerald's and Barnes's novels in order to make 'a significant theoretical speculation' concerning the politics of canon formation, the use he makes of the novels illustrates that the special status accorded to one and not the other stems from institutional reading norms, rather than from any innate quality.[9] In other words, Rabinowitz's reading reinforces not only how arbitrarily Fitzgerald has been valorized, but also how arbitrary it would be to valorize Barnes. In singling Greene out for special treatment, Friedman's polemic seems to ignore the priorities embedded in the methodologies he recommends be applied to Greene's writing.

From this vantage point, the strength of the auteurist sensibility as a vehicle for canonical reading becomes clear. By situating the strength of a text or collection of texts squarely within the bounds of an author's strong personality, the polemicist leaves his addressee no choice but to either take heed or reject the argument out of hand. For example, saying that *The End of the Affair* can be read like a sacred text implies two possible answers: 'Yes, it can' or 'No, it cannot'.[10] Within the parameters the statement establishes an addressee may not respond, for instance, that 'The sacred is not a legitimate category of textual understanding.' One may assent to the text's unique strength, or one may deny it; but however one answers, one confers legitimacy upon the notion that the text in fact possesses a unique strength, that it partakes of the quality Bloom has described as 'canonical strangeness':

> The answer [to what makes the author and the works canonical], more often than not, has turned out to be strangeness, a mode of originality that either cannot be assimilated, or that so assimilates us that we cease to see it as strange. Walter Pater defined Romanticism as adding strangeness to beauty, but I think he characterized all

canonical writing rather than the Romantics as such. The cycle of achievement goes from *The Divine Comedy* to *Endgame*, from strangeness to strangeness. When you read a canonical work for the first time you encounter a stranger, an uncanny startlement rather than a fulfilment of expectations.[11]

The auteurist goes slightly further and isolates the principle of uncanniness in the figure of the author, since it is only through an entity as obscure and subject to mystification as the strong personality that one may communicate the possibility of originality in a medium as defined by limitation and expectation as language without necessarily inviting skepticism. As a mode of canonical reading, therefore, auteurism never needs to confront the contradictions courted by readings like Davis's and Friedman's: its object may be vague, and its methods vaguer still, but they are at least consistent with one another and with the valorizing project of canonization.

Because the vast majority of Greene critics have attempted to read the writer himself as an auteur and the texts as manifestations of canonical strangeness—that is, as texts produced by an author who set out to startle by some Herculean effort at originality, rather than by engaging with the expectations of a hypothetical audience—their criticism has operated at the institutional level as canonical reading. But as Bloom's analysis of canonical strangeness makes clear (perhaps unwittingly), the canonical reader always knows in advance the sort of originality he will experience. By the early 1970s Greene's reviewers had abandoned reviewing the novels he produced and had taken instead to canonical reading, offering accounts of Greene's canonical strangeness and calculating the writer's place among the avatars of twentieth-century letters. George Steiner, for instance, began his review of *Lord Rochester's Monkey* with the following auteurist reading:

> Like an ice-skater cutting an intricate figure, a major writer may often be tracing patterns, seemingly random or eccentric, around a single, unwavering point. His divagations have in fact been a constant return. The strength of Graham Greene has been a compulsive amazement at the pendulum motion of sin and redemption, at the interwoven closeness of human disgrace and divine repair. Various are their locations and style—novels, entertainments, books of travel, thrillers, plays—the works of Graham Greene have their obsessive focus in the mystery of man's fall and in the mystery of spiritual, psychological resurrection that could not come to pass without the fall.[12]

Here, Greene is both utterly consistent and ultimately unfathomable—save, of course, by Steiner himself, who alone has located the single, unwavering point around which Greene's work has orbited. The mysteries to which Steiner has been privy are timeless, and the case for Greene's interest nearly irrefutable. V.S. Pritchett communicated a similar portrait of Greene through his analysis of Rochester:

> For Greene particularly, Rochester had the attraction of the gifted, tormented sinner, the man of split nature, divided between lust and love, familiar with remorse in his self-sought ruin, and unable to apply the salve of hypocrisy to a raw conscience. 'Half devil, half angel,' a handsome dissipated charmer and fine poet, Rochester was a character of great complexity who offers dramatic guesses to any biographer.[13]

Pritchett hardly bothers to hide the fact that he is asking his readers to draw a parallel between the poet and his biographer. These reviews communicate Greene as a model canonical author: spiritually consistent (if only in the tortured paradoxes that obsessed him), relentless in his pursuit of new forms in which to embed the truths to which he was privy, and possessed of a sensibility ostensibly as universal as the fall of man. Together, they label Greene 'of permanent interest'.

Grahame Smith identified the source of Greene's canonical strangeness in his attitude toward anguish. For Greene 'anguish is inseparable from the daily experience of human life; like the act of breathing it amounts almost to an involuntary accompaniment to existence'.[14] Anguish becomes the single, unwavering point around which Greene traces his patterns—an observation that in turn implies a method of analysis: close reading to find the underlying order of the seemingly random patterns Greene has traced, and the vigorous application of what Rabinowitz has termed 'rules of coherence', conventions of critical analysis designed to cement various blocks of a narrative into a sound structure capable of producing meaning for a particular reader.[15] Smith's analysis, however, not only implies Greene's canonical significance but also suggests that his technique needs to be situated specifically in the tradition of high modernist poetics. Because '[i]t is frankly incredible to expect complete agreement between an uncommitted reader and a work of fiction to which a detailed system of belief is essential', Greene's narratives produce through their themes the same ironic distance achieved through formal experimentation by his modernist contemporaries. On the one hand, Smith's is one of the few critiques of Greene to take account of how the texts position the reader; on the other, however, the role he allocates to the reader consists in fathoming how Greene conceives of anguish—that is, of tracing the pattern Greene has already cut in the ice.

Smith's view of Greene's obsession was hardly a novel one. Wilfrid Sheed, for instance, seems to have read *Travels With My Aunt* as though its central theme *should have been* that 'anguish is inseparable from the daily experience of human life':

> To be sure, [the protagonist Henry Pulling] represents the respectable world (which Greene detests, but which will love his book). But Henry's main characteristic, his refusal of life, relates him also to Pinkie and to the boy in *This Gun For Hire*—young Englishmen with undeveloped hearts, terrified to nausea by the Flesh. Except that the prig is now a joke and not a theological problem...But Greene is unlikely to leave it at that. Auntie is also a flagrant sentimentalization, a schoolboy's dream of the 'super' relative who talks bawdy and gives you a sip of her drink. It is bad fantasy to suppose she can wave away guilt and anguish for long. Worse yet, she is not even allowed to look old but must, like a crone being flattered, have the skin of a girl. Think young, as we say in Miami, and you will stay young forever. Americanism triumphant. It *has* to be a joke.[16]

Sheed's review anticipates the tautological marriage of Sheed's insights and Pritchett's method: all of Greene's novels are filled with anguish because Greene himself is full of anguish. Greene wrote *Travels With My Aunt*, therefore since it does not appear to be full of anguish, it must be a joke—a particularly rancid one—that demonstrates nothing less than Greene's anguish.

The frustration of expectations no longer forces these readers to revise those expectations (as, say, the formal experimentation in *Stamboul Train* forced readers to revise theirs). Instead, the canonical Greene outweighs their experience of the text and clears the way for the imposition of an extra-textual standard of interpretation. Instead they hammer the hermeneutic circle into a straight line leading directly from one's prior knowledge of the canonical Greene to a valid interpretation of both the whole *and* its constituent parts.

The educational theorist Paulo Freire accurately terms the institutional practice associated with canonical reading 'the banking concept
of education':

> ... knowledge is a gift bestowed by those who consider themselves
> knowledgeable upon those whom they consider to know nothing.
> Projecting an absolute ignorance onto others, a characteristic of the
> ideology of oppression, negates education and knowledge as a process
> of inquiry. The teacher presents himself to his students as their nec-
> essary opposite; by considering their ignorance absolute, he justifies
> his own existence. The students, alienated like the slave in Hegelian
> dialectic, accept their ignorance as justifying the teacher's existence—
> but, unlike the slave, they never discover that they educate the
> teacher.[17]

The critic who offers a canonical reading of Greene similarly negates
knowledge as a process of inquiry—that is, of reading. What has already
been read becomes paramount: how else does one discover that *Travels
With My Aunt* is in fact a rancid joke demonstrating Greene's anguish—
an argument whose relationship to the text seems highly tenuous—
unless one knows prior to reading that the novel *should* demonstrate
anguish somehow? The reading proposes 'the critic as banker'. On
the one hand, he becomes the master who knows Greene and may
lead others to a knowledge of Greene, while on the other, he is the
one whose superior knowledge confirms others' ignorance. Thus Frank
McConnell writes of *Dr. Fischer of Geneva* that 'Greene has achieved the
stature where his quotations from and allusions to his own earlier books
are a central part of his meaning.'[18] He might also have written that
because professional readers can detect quotations from and allusions
to Greene's earlier work, and because they can use these quotations
and illusions to construct a narrative of the work's meaning, they may
endeavor to thrust a certain stature upon Greene. McConnell concludes
that while 'it would be reductive, even silly, to call [*Dr. Fischer*] a "great
book"' it is still 'in a deep sense, essential'.[19] How does a book that is not
'great' become essential? If Greene's significance stems from the way he
quotes from and alludes to his earlier work, then nothing that Greene
ever wrote (or ever would write) is inessential—although this reading
tells us nothing about why anything Greene wrote should matter to
anybody. McConnell's reading is the canonical polemic *par excellence*:
it asserts Greene's value as a pure tautology while subtly reserving the
right to signify—to interpret, to read—for the initiate.

Even canonical reading, however, requires texts; and if, as this study has argued, *The Third Man* set the stage for a re-evaluation of Greene along auteurist lines, it seems unlikely that such a re-evaluation would have occurred had Greene failed to produce texts that invited such analysis. Between *The Third Man* and *Our Man in Havana* Greene produced two such texts, *The End of the Affair* and *The Quiet American*. Both used first-person narrators which, as Greene remarked in his dedication to *Loser Takes All*, could easily lead readers to 'mistake "I" for me'[20]— particularly since the novels' protagonists were respectively a novelist ('who—when he has been seriously noted at all—has been praised for his technical ability'[21]) and a journalist as conspicuously well-traveled as the writer who produced him. If *The Third Man* marked the beginning of a brief period characterized by broad consensus concerning the means and ends of Greene's fictions, then *The End of the Affair* and *The Quiet American* gave shape to the critical understanding of Greene's canonical strangeness, and furnished interested scholars with the ammunition they would hurl at one another over the polemical battlefield of Greene's reputation after *Our Man in Havana*.

For the student of Greene's reputation, however, these novels have a dual interest. In addition to the considerable body of canonical reading they have occasioned, they have also occasioned readings in the vernacular languages of the cinema, the television, and even the newspaper travel supplement in recent years. Both *The End of the Affair* and *The Quiet American* were adapted into films during the 1950s; neither won Greene's approbation or proved particularly tempting to the viewing public and both films had implemented major changes to the source material. On the one hand, this point suggests that Greene had not yet established a reputation strong enough to warrant a 'literal adaptation'. On the other, however, it seems a remarkable testament to Greene's status and popularity that a Hollywood producer would choose to film a novel by a writer with a well-publicized Communist past at a time when the blacklist remained in full effect.[22] This is particularly true of *The Quiet American*, which (with the exception of the 'treacherous' ending) followed the novel's plot and dialogue rather closely. By the time Columbia released Neil Jordan's adaptation of *The End of the Affair* in 1999, Greene had come to cast an even longer shadow over the adaptations from his work: the film's faithfulness to 'the spirit' of the novel received considerable notice *despite* major revision: namely, the prolongation of Sarah Miles's life and the inclusion of a 'dirty weekend' in Brighton with her lover, Maurice Bendrix. Philip Noyce's version of *The Quiet American* was similarly 'faithful', particularly in contrast to

Joseph Mankiewicz's earlier adaptation, which had seen the central role of Alden Pyle transformed from CIA operative responsible for killing scores of civilians in the Place Garnier into the blameless victim of the British journalist Thomas Fowler, whose murderous jealousy plays into the hands of the scheming Communists. Noyce follows the plot laid out in Greene's novel much more closely than Mankiewicz but naturally comes no closer to reproducing the effects of the novel than Jordan, Edward Dmytryk (who directed the earlier adaptation of *The End of the Affair*), or Mankiewicz; rather, Noyce, like each of these filmmakers, produces a text that comments on Greene's novel through what it retains from the book, what it cuts, how its montage is assembled, and where it places its accents via close-ups, sound effects, musical accompaniment, and so forth.

These films contest the fundamental assumptions of canonical reading to the extent that they openly, emphatically solicit the participation of the audience in the construction of meaning. There is, of course, infinitely more money at stake in a film than in a scholarly article, and any given film's status as a financial investment is bound to influence the demands it places upon its viewers; unlike canonical reading, the criticism embodied in a film adaptation does not have the luxury of wishing that society did not exist.[23] Commercially successful producers like David Selznick, Alexander Korda, or *The Quiet American*'s Harvey Weinstein rarely allow their films to turn a blind eye to their status as historically determined objects subject to prevailing social mores and aesthetic vocabularies which only a fiscally irresponsible film producer or financier might characterize as 'universal'.[24]

Chapter 12 will therefore consider the various ways that Greene's 'autobiographical' novels solicit the participation of their readers in socially constituted narrative strategies. It will then examine the fashion in which canonical readings have attempted to both limit the participation of readers in Greene's texts and impose the sort of tautological scheme of value which is broadly consistent with Freire's 'banking concept of education'. Finally, it will consider a different sort of criticism, embodied in recent film adaptations and journalistic appropriations of Greene's work, that comments on the novels not through *ex cathedra* pronouncements fixing canonical value but by inviting readers to participate in the realization of readings of Greene's novels. Throughout, the chapter will investigate how the ongoing processes of canonization and popular (re)appropriation affect what it has been possible or desirable to say about Greene and about literature at large.

12
Depopulating the Common: Reading *The End of the Affair*

Critics have often supported their canonical readings of *The End of the Affair* by suggesting that Greene and the novel's narrator, the popular writer Maurice Bendrix, are doppelgangers. Michael Shelden, for instance, describes Bendrix as a 'lonely man who shares his creator's dedication to writing':

> Regardless of what is happening in his personal life, he can turn out 500 words a day and finish a novel in a year or two. When he is not writing, he is tortured by emotions that he cannot control, and is driven to hurt others for no logical reason. He broods about the past and is amazed by Sarah's ability to live completely in the present. Her beauty and candour fascinate him, but he also feels intimidated by her.... His sexual feelings are usually aroused by the sense that he is somehow superior to the other person.[1]

Shelden makes use of the novel in a very particular way: for him, its mysteries are transparent, and the narrative little more than a pretext for Greene to produce a laundry list of his own personal faults and moral failures—precisely the *same* faults and failings that Shelden takes pains to underline in the archival sections of his study. He concludes that 'In life, [Greene] was never sure when the affair [with Catherine Walston] would end; in art, he could end it at will and imagine all sorts of exciting repercussions.'[2] For Shelden, *The End of the Affair*'s coherence has become contingent upon the reader's ability to extrapolate meaning from the circumstances that conditioned the creation of the text: here, Greene's professional habits, and the impact of his psychological 'flaws' on his conduct of the affair with Walston. Reading the novel becomes a purely voyeuristic exercise in which pleasure is derived from watching Greene's wish fulfilment unfold.

Reading from this perspective, the narrative no longer constitutes an invitation to read as the author intends, but rather becomes a puzzle with only one correct solution. By leaning too heavily on the equation 'Greene=Bendrix', Shelden avoids developing the most interesting— certainly the least orthodox—claim in his analysis of the novel:

> ... a Catholic organization in New York gave Greene a literary award for his work. It is a shame—for truth's sake—that an anti-God organization was not available to present him with an outstanding achievement award. No major novelist has shown as much ingenuity in abusing the God of Christianity. It is a dubious distinction, but one that Greene fully deserves.[3]

Claiming that *The End of the Affair* can be read as an assault on the God of Christianity suggests a radical break with a tradition of Greene criticism that has vigorously disagreed on the novel's aesthetic merits but has rarely questioned the ends to which its devices were deployed. The self-imposed parameters of Shelden's stridently anti-Greene polemic, however, prevent him from investigating the problem his line of argument raises—namely, that readers (Catholic or secular) play at least as prominent a role in determining a novel's 'meaning' as its author. He implies that the Catholic organization in New York engages in a wilful 'misreading' based primarily upon popular misconceptions propagated by the media. But rather than consider the group's misreading as evidence of the social character of the reading process, he seeks only to furnish a 'corrected version' of Greene that, when properly digested by the public and applied to its understanding of Bendrix's hate, will ultimately restore the true meaning of the work, which may then be definitively judged. In short, he argues for Greene's exclusion from the canon on grounds that should logically provoke a re-evaluation of the aesthetic (or even metaphysical) priorities enshrined in the canon; but here he draws up short, perhaps sensing that to engage in such an analysis might undermine the value of his own profession.

By locating the figure of Bendrix at the center of the novel, however, Shelden follows a rather different path than many commentators who found it far easier to marginalize the figure of the obtuse writer in order to arrive at the 'real meaning' of the novel. In a contemporary review of *The End of the Affair*, Anne Fremantle observes that 'Graham Greene is one of the most eschatological of our living writers:

always his concern is with the last things—death, resurrection, immortality, and judgment; and he pre-eminently builds his stories with ends not means.'[4] She moves almost imperceptibly from what she presumes to be Greene's philosophical posture to the method he employs in the construction of the novel. For Fremantle, Sarah Miles must be the novel's central figure because she is the only character in whom one detects 'last things', and who actually arrives at some sort of an end. '*The End of the Affair* is about a woman who dies, is judged, and goes emphatically—perhaps a little too emphatically—straight to heaven.'[5] The novel is *not* about Bendrix, the writer who provides the bulk of the narrative's voice (and who even edits Sarah's journal by choosing what passages to disclose to the audience); it is not even about the relationship between the narrator and Sarah; to Fremantle, Bendrix is merely a 'poor chap' who is bodily dragged 'into the everlasting arms',[6] a reading that seems slightly reductive in light of the novel's final words, uttered by Bendrix in a moment of utter exhaustion: 'I found the one prayer that seemed to serve the winter mood: O God, You've done enough, You've robbed me of enough. I'm too tired and old to learn to love. Leave me alone forever.'[7] Armed with a sense of how she feels Greene ought to understand God, Fremantle makes a prodigious (though superficial) effort to keep Bendrix's unsettling influence in check, and lists all of the 'twentieth-century devices' Greene 'brilliantly' employs 'to get around the first narrator's suspect authority': 'the flashback, the stream-of-consciousness, the interior monologue, the dialogue carrying the action forward à la Hemingway...diaries, letters, detectives emptying wastepaper baskets....'[8] Like Shelden, Fremantle invokes history—and even suggests a model of reading determined at least in part by social convention—but backs away from examining it too closely when it appears to threaten the underlying assumptions of her argument. The novel's loose temporal organization, for instance, involves the reader in interpretive strategies that simply cannot be understood purely in terms of eschatology (particularly of the Catholic variety). The desire to read eschatologically, of course, can be understood historically, but not without rather embarrassing consequences for the eschatologist.

A.A. DeVitis remarked that '[o]ne of the flaws of the novel is quite simply the fact, sexual matters excluded, that it is difficult to understand why Sarah loves [Bendrix].'[9] Presumably DeVitis managed the formidable task of distinguishing between intellectual love and its physical manifestations; even allowing for this possibility, however, brings one no closer to understanding DeVitis's objection. Following Fremantle, he enumerates the various devices with which Greene divorced himself from 'the allegorical and melodramatic contrivances' of his earlier 'Catholic' novels: 'the emotionally involved and therefore unreliable narrator, stream-of-consciousness, the flashback or time shift, the diary, the letter, the inner reverie, the use of dream for symbolical as well as foreshadowing purposes, and the spiritual debate'.[10] DeVitis specifically characterizes Bendrix as an unreliable (and unpleasant) narrator who is too emotionally involved in the story he is relating to accept at face value, but the critic relies entirely on the narrator's own testimony to establish what *should* have been his repugnance in Sarah's eyes, an interpretive strategy that sits uneasily with his conclusion that '[c]apable of great hatred, Bendrix is equally capable of great love; and the reader cannot believe that he is too old to learn [to love God]'.[11] By the end of his analysis, DeVitis even manages to claim that the techniques Greene borrows from Henry James and Ford Madox Ford (having become aware of 'the artistic demands of the novel form') in fact confer a 'symbolic unity' on the novel—although presumably it only holds true if one possesses the sort of Jamesian will to primness necessary to imagine the novel without sex (i.e., without Bendrix and, hence, without the narrative). *The End of the Affair* ceases to function as a novel and becomes instead a personal fantasia of Sarah Miles as an illustration of the dogmas DeVitis evidently holds dear.

Reviewing the novel in 1951, Charles Rolo declared 'the sinful part of the proceedings ... vastly more satisfying than the journey into the Light'.[12] By the end of the novel, Rolo argues, Greene has begun 'stage-managing his characters and his action in order to put across his theological message'.[13] He inverts DeVitis's critique, suggesting that Sarah's personality is too 'blurred' to sustain the reader's interest: it is not Sarah's passion that appears unfounded, but Bendrix's—a conclusion which paradoxically aligns Rolo with DeVitis, eschewing the novel's sexual dynamic and therefore the narrative itself, whose 'mystery' (in the sense generally associated with detective fiction) he praises. Seven years after *The End of the Affair* Rolo would eccentrically praise *Our Man in Havana* for its theological coherence, suggesting that 'Greene reduces theology to melodrama and raises melodrama to theology' and applying a standard of coherence only vaguely supported by the text.[14] Here, however, he appears to fault Greene for reducing melodrama to theology and for unsuccessfully attempting to raise theology to melodrama. To be certain, Rolo reads against the grain—few critics reviewing *The End of the Affair* used their first paragraph to remark upon its 'matchless comedy'—but he nonetheless ends up producing a reading of the novel as inscrutably tautological as DeVitis's.[15]

In each critique cited above, the critic treats the text of the novel as a tool for elucidating the figure of Greene: his convictions, his prejudices and biases, and perhaps to some lesser extent the choices he makes as an artist. Fremantle and DeVitis, for instance, remark upon the modern techniques he employs in order to communicate his theological concerns; they do not, however, offer any analysis of how these various devices—stream-of-consciousness, the unreliable narrator, etc.—inform their own readings. The status of these devices in their criticism performs a different, less analytical function: they signal the seriousness of Greene's endeavor and locate it within a matrix of socially conditioned, institutionally valorized writing practices that had, by the 1950s, been accepted as *de rigueur* for the consideration of fictional work in the context of the cultural establishment. What they studiously ignore, of course, is the fact that these writing practices necessarily imply the existence of parallel reading practices which can never be reduced to expressions of individual genius.

In a sense, of course, these critics were only repeating what had emerged as the critical orthodoxy on Greene following the publication of *Stamboul Train* in 1932—save that the 'modern' devices which critics had formerly associated with the popular medium of the cinema had now been absorbed into Leavisite and New Critical methodology and thus could safely imply a very different sort of readership.[16] Terry Eagleton notes that this methodology implied a discrete set of priorities for the individual reader:

> Reading poetry in the New Critical way meant committing yourself to nothing: all that poetry taught you was 'disinterestedness', a serene, speculative, impeccably even-handed rejection of anything in particular. It drove you less to oppose McCarthyism or further civil rights than to experience such pressures as merely partial, no doubt harmoniously balanced somewhere else in the world by their complementary opposites.[17]

Unsurprisingly, the expansion of Leavisite and New Critical hegemony in the liberal arts coincided roughly with the rise of an 'art-house' cinema. The latter was less an autonomous branch or mode of cinematic production than a set of viewing and interpretive strategies sanctioned by academe—particularly those associated with the auteur theory, which would prove essential in laying the foundation for the construction of a cinematic canon. In the 1930s, Greene's troublesome 'good but popular' work could be effectively dismissed as 'cinematic' because on the one hand his own public persona had yet to crystallize sufficiently to sustain the dominant, specifically literary mode of canonical reading, while on the other hand, the cinema itself had yet to give rise to a coherent body of interpretive practices.

By the early 1950s, however, this situation had changed. The Italian neo-realists and other European avant-garde movements had helped split the hitherto populist cinema into the conventional 'high' and 'low' camps of intellectual discourse. Simon Harcourt-Smith even went so far as to identify Rossellini's techniques with *The Third Man*'s in the pages of *Sight and Sound*.[18] Cultural institutions naturally scrambled to exploit the latent cultural capital of the previously neglected medium by forcibly adapting the cinema's alien vocabulary into its own critical grammar. Thus, by the time *The End of the Affair* was published, the 'cinematic' interpretive strategy, first invoked as a defence against Greene's manifest popularity, had become one of the writer's strongest selling points. Greene's style and technique may not have substantially changed since *Stamboul Train*, but the standards and methodologies brought to bear upon them certainly had. Where earlier critics had shied away from the meaning of the work in order to marvel at its technical virtuosity, modern critics focused on the meaning of the work without generally considering the techniques by which it was produced—a tactic whose privileging of the moment of conception rather than the moment of reception tended to localize textual meaning in the figure of Greene. With two volumes of autobiography already in publication by 1939 there was little doubt as to the shape this figure would assume. One passage from *The Lawless Roads* would become particularly shop-worn:

> And so faith came to me—shapelessly, without dogma, a presence above a croquet lawn, something associated with violence, cruelty, evil across the way. I began to believe in heaven because I believed in hell, but for a long while it was only hell I could picture with a certain intimacy....[19]

By reading *The End of the Affair* as an elucidation of this figure—that is, by reading canonically—Fremantle, DeVitis, and the rest followed a norm with a long pedigree in the institutional humanities, producing interpretations that validated canonical reading within the framework of the text by drastically curtailing the role played by readers in its realization.

Canonical readings of *The End of the Affair* have focused on what popular perceptions of Greene's life suggest should be the religious theme of the novel. Shelden, for instance, seems less irritated by the novel's alleged defamation of the Christian God than by the public's insistence on mistaking the novel's libellous tone (and thus Greene's 'true' allegiance) for piety. God, he suggests, will somehow manage to survive Greene's assault; the faithful, however, may fall into error through exposure to persuasive but ultimately false doctrine: in this back-handed fashion Shelden posits an ultra-orthodox deity at the center of the novel, one who battles not only the narrator but also the author and his audience for supreme interpretive authority. Regardless of the biographer's spiritual convictions, the existence of an omnipotent, specifically Catholic God is implicitly postulated as the keystone that keeps Shelden's argument from crumbling. DeVitis, Rolo, and Fremantle take fewer pains to disguise their theological allegiance, but the result is the same: *The End of the Affair* re-imagined as a sort of sacred text, demanding the sort of strictly literal interpretation championed by fundamentalists of all faiths as a defence against the mutability of language and the utter dependence of all interpretive processes on shifting social codes.

Approaching the novel from this perspective makes it difficult to consider the fashion in which the narrative problematizes the very idea of supreme interpretive authority. In contrast to DeVitis and Shelden, John Atkins noted that his opinion of the novel changed half a dozen times over the course of his reading:

> I find that while reading the book I marked a passage on page ninety-nine and made this comment: 'At this point the book turns rotten—the nastiness is too much. From now on Bendrix can only be a person worth listening to by accident....' But a few pages later I find this note: 'On the other hand we must remember the effects of hate and suspicion and envy.' In other words I had been wrong, too hasty. I had been condemning the novel on the basis of a character. No-one dreams of condemning *Othello* because of Iago, but that is because Shakespeare is by now sacrosanct.[20]

DeVitis happily takes Greene's sanctity for granted, while Shelden reads as though it has been conferred on dubious authority; Atkins, approaching the novel as a successful instance of Greene's mercenary proclivities, at least remains open to the text and recognizes sanctity's categorical inapplicability to the twin processes of writing and reading. The difference between Atkins and, say, DeVitis is *not* that they approach fundamentally different texts—the former an open text, the latter a closed one—but that each approaches the same text with different interpretive priorities: Atkins demonstrates an 'opening' orientation to the text, DeVitis a 'closing' one. Although Atkins never rejects the possibility that Bendrix is in some way a surrogate for Greene, he makes it clear that the definitive establishment of such an identity would do little to influence his reading. 'Bendrix may well be Greene, but the point I wish to make is that Greene can see Bendrix whole. Here is a man, he says, who has been nearly destroyed by frustrated desire, and a very nasty specimen he is.'[21] When Atkins suggests that in *The End of the Affair* 'Greene has achieved the rare feat of depicting a man in process, rather than in a series of disconnected states' he admits (perhaps unwittingly) his own willingness to view the narrative *as* process, rather than as one of those puzzles in which a player may, by shifting pieces around a frame, finally produce a picture placed there by the manufacturer.[22]

The role of God in *The End of the Affair* merits special attention, given the extent to which it has dominated criticism of the novel. Once one abandons the pretence of Greene's sanctity, and concedes that the novel's claim to the status of sacred text is insupportable, one may perhaps better understand the position of God in the matrix of generic and readerly conventions deployed throughout the novel. In short, however one chooses to regard the existence or nature of God outside the text, his position within the text is subject to historically determined, politically significant, socially constituted interpretive codes.

The *New York Times*'s George Mayberry made the link between *The End of the Affair* and the detective novel explicit in his synopsis through his choice of terms: 'After several suspects have been eliminated, [the lady's current favourite] turns out to be God.'[23] Michael Gorra addressed the issue with greater incisiveness and less tact when he wrote that the novel 'made a nemesis of God himself'.[24] The first two chapters of the novel explicitly invoke semantic and syntactic features generally associated with the genre: an adulterous affair that the narrator assures the reader has gone sour, a suspicious but ineffectual husband, and the clean, grim office of Mr. Savage, the 'specialist who dealt in only one disease, of which he knew every symptom'.[25] The 'case' to be solved is a relatively straightforward one: Henry suspects that his wife Sarah is having an affair, and Bendrix, her former lover, takes it upon himself to discover the identity of the man with whom she has become involved. The reader is never encouraged to believe that Sarah is *not* having another sexual affair; on the contrary, the narrative shores up this possibility in a number of ways. When Bendrix and Henry first meet on the Common, Bendrix establishes Henry's credibility by suggesting that although 'the world would have said [Henry] had the reason for hate, not I', Henry himself does not appear disposed to the sort of violent passions that animate and to some extent undermine Bendrix's own narrative.[26] Henry's suspicions concerning Sarah's fidelity therefore carry a weight with the reader that they would not have carried had they been voiced solely by Bendrix. When Mr. Savage smugly confides to the narrator that 'the fact that a man feels the need of our services almost invariably means that there is something to report', it is Henry's suspicion rather than Bendrix's that inclines the reader to accept the validity of the detective's truism.[27] This early passage helps readers to configure their expectations throughout the novel, particularly where the question of Bendrix's jealousy is concerned.

What some critics have described as Bendrix's 'nastiness' is communicated to the reader largely through his response to the casual affairs that checker Sarah's past, and which continuously intrude throughout the period of their own affair, from 1939 to 1944. In a representative scene, Sarah telephones Bendrix to inform him that Henry's illness will keep her tied to the house, although she makes it clear that she wants to see Bendrix anyway:

> There was silence for a moment on the phone, and I thought we had been cut off. I said, 'Hullo. Hullo.' But she had been thinking, that was all, carefully, collectedly, quickly, so that she could give me straight away the correct answer. 'I'm giving Henry a tray in bed at one. We could have sandwiches ourselves in the living room. I'll tell him you want to talk over the film—or that story of yours.' And immediately she rang off the sense of trust was disconnected, and I thought, how many times before has she planned in just this way.[28]

On the one hand, the reader's suspicion that Sarah is probably involved in another affair makes it difficult, as Atkins noted, to definitively condemn Bendrix for his jealousy, while on the other hand, the increasingly virulent manifestations of Bendrix's jealousy make it difficult to definitively condemn Sarah for turning elsewhere in the pursuit of love. The use of the first-person narrator throughout the novel does little to assist the reader in finding a point of equilibrium between the two characters, but this imbalance itself becomes a means of configuring the novel's detective story: one major expectation is that once the 'culprit' is revealed, some sort of order will be restored, as Holmes and Poirot so often restored the order and stability of upper middle-class society by revealing 'whodunit'.

But the revelation of God's culpability in bringing the affair to a premature end does not restore order to the world of the Common; on the contrary, the solution to the novel's mystery has more in common with the hard-boiled fiction of Raymond Chandler, whose *Big Sleep* ended less with the identification of a guilty party than with Philip Marlowe's selection of a relatively arbitrary point at which to cease cataloging the various crimes that together comprised the operation of power in Los Angeles society.[29] In *The End of the Affair*, of course, there is no Carmen Sternwood and so there cannot be even an inadequate 'unmasking' scene; instead, the mystery plot is wrapped up simply with Parkis's presentation of Sarah's journal to Bendrix. In the journal, selections from which occupy the bulk of the third part of the novel, Sarah presents the events leading from the night during the war that V-1 attacks occasioned her abandonment of Bendrix to approximately two weeks before her death. Bendrix has already related these events in passages of narrative punctuated with his own interpretation, thus forcing the reader to mediate between two distinct versions of the affair's demise. The factual errors of Bendrix's account—particularly his insistence that Sarah abandoned him in order to engage in a sexual affair with another man ('Is there no end to this? Have I now got to discover Y?'[30])—tempt the reader to view Sarah's account as somehow more objective, as capable of transcending the limitations of first person narration and hence, for some readers, of illuminating the meta-textual truth of God's love. But Sarah's journal becomes capable of resolving (rather than undermining) the expectations that the novel's use of detective fiction conventions has helped to configure only to the extent that one accepts an extra-textual order as an adequate resolution of textual tensions—that is, to the extent that one can accept *The End of the Affair* as a sacred text. For DeVitis and Fremantle, for instance, Sarah's becomes the 'true' voice of the novel because she presumably speaks with God's voice, a role Shelden allocates (for strikingly similar reasons) to Bendrix's more cynical voice, which he views as belonging properly to Greene. Each perspective implies the subordination of the various voices in the novel to one particular voice (i.e., Sarah's or Bendrix's), which critics may then interpret as signaling the immanence of an authorial figure, be it God or Greene.

Valorizing Sarah's narrative (the more common critical procedure) requires a pronounced willingness to wholly disregard Bendrix, as a late entry in her journal suggests:

But was it me [Bendrix] loved, or You? For he hated in me the things You hate. He was on Your side all the time without knowing it. You willed our separation, but he willed it too. He worked for it with his anger and his jealousy, and he worked for it with his love. For he gave me so much love and I gave him so much love that soon there wasn't anything left when we'd finished but You. For either of us.[31]

What Bendrix primarily appears to hate at this point in the novel is Sarah's willingness to stay with Henry. Although Bendrix has spoken of his desire to end the affair quickly, 'as though our love were a small creature caught in a trap and bleeding to death; I had to shut my eyes and wring its neck', he has also made it quite clear that he feels this way because of his awareness that 'love' in Henry's shadow will eventually become a 'love affair', with both a beginning and an end toward which he feels drawn by a jealousy that he fears will cheapen their love.[32] Although Sarah insists that Bendrix hates in her all of the things God hates in her, there are few facets of her character that having once prompted Bendrix's unqualified scorn are not, in a different light, shown to elicit his equally unqualified admiration. This situation reveals to the reader not only the chasm between Bendrix's awareness of both changing circumstances and the different perspectives offered by them on one side, and on the other, Sarah's efforts to furnish herself and her actions with an unchanging, eternal rationale; it also reveals the extent to which Sarah's pursuit of God is itself a response to the same historical and psychological forces from which she hopes to extricate herself.

Sarah's alleged 'sainthood' poses a number of problems for readers who do not approach the text as a somewhat lurid manifestation of idealist philosophy. The vow she makes to God, that she will give Bendrix up forever if only He will let her lover be alive, causes Bendrix considerable pain, particularly in light of the fact, unexplained by the narrative, that she chooses not to disclose the terms of the bargain to her lover— although she feels little compunction about sharing them with the atheist preacher Richard Smythe. She remains with Henry and, after a brief attempt at filling the Bendrix-shaped abscess in her life with 'Dunstan' from the Ministry of Home Security, even remains faithful to him despite her cognizance of the fact that for Henry losing her would be no more traumatic then changing his daily newspaper. 'It will be inconvenient, but you can [do without me].'[33] By so doing she allows Henry to believe that their love means more to her in both quantitative and qualitative terms than in fact it does—a tactic that certainly soothes Sarah's own conscience but which does precious little to assist Henry in feeling the sort of divine pain that she insists has been essential to her spiritual growth. She even manages to alienate Smythe when she kisses him on the cheek because he quite accurately senses her repugnance and construes the gesture as a pitying one. A critical imagination capable of integrating Sarah's actions and their ramifications into the story of a saint's progress necessarily betrays a strong distaste for human life and love in any but that latter term's most scholastic sense: a love divorced from the fashion in which it is enacted and manifested in the world, and which ironically dovetails with the concept of God put forward by Bendrix at the beginning of the novel when he suggests that he finds it 'hard to conceive of any God who is not as simple as a perfect equation, as clear as air'.[34] And also, one presumes, as indifferent to the suffering He causes as a quadratic equation is to its variables.

The grotesque qualities of Sarah's elevation to the company of saints are deeply felt by Bendrix throughout the novel. But they are also felt keenly by readers, who of course have no access to the afterlife Sarah ostensibly enjoys among the departed great and good. Instead they witness Bendrix sitting down for dinner with Sarah's mother:

> Mrs. Bertram and I had dinner at the Isola Bella. I didn't want to go anywhere I had ever been with Sarah, and of course I began to compare this restaurant with all the others we had visited together. Sarah and I never drank Chianti, and now the act of drinking it reminded me of that fact. I might as well have had our favourite claret, I couldn't have thought of her more. Even vacancy was crowded with her.[35]

For Bendrix, Sarah's love may be more than the sum of its manifestations in a glass of claret, her back propped up on a pillow, or an oddly shaped pebble that causes them both to laugh, but it is also inseparable from those manifestations: it is Bendrix's awareness of the fundamentally social character of meaning that leads him to reflect that in dying, Sarah 'had lost all our memories forever, and it was as though by dying she had robbed me of part of myself. I was losing my individuality. It was the first stage of my own death, the memories dropping off like gangrened limbs.'[36] A glass of claret has little significance in and of itself, save perhaps that Bendrix enjoys its taste: its meaning, however, is intimately bound up with its status as a physical point of mediation in his relationship with Sarah, much as the word 'onions' becomes charged with romantic and sexual meaning because both lovers consent to its power of signification.

Sarah's behavior in the wake of her vow becomes deeply self-defeating, a quixotic quest to restrain society from encroaching upon the life she seeks to invest with a purely ontological meaning. As Gorra has observed, her efforts in this direction seem strikingly Protestant as they are presented in her journals, since one might argue that while she turns her back on society 'in the world', she also cultivates the society of a very personal God, through whom her actions become personally meaningful, whatever their cost in pain and despair for others.[37] Hers becomes a variety of the American religion described by Harold Bloom, which since about 1800 'has found ... its own freedom—from the world, from time, from other selves. But this freedom is a very expensive torso, because of what it is obliged to leave out: society, temporality, the other. What remains, for it, is solitude and the abyss.'[38] Sarah repeatedly describes the abyss as 'the desert', but seems happily ignorant of the fact that by entering the desert she has dragged others along with her. When one substitutes 'God' for 'others' in one's discourse, then there is no reason to presume that one's actions have ramifications beyond the self, save to a god or gods who have historically been rather reluctant to make their opinions known.

The End of the Affair constantly undermines the reader's understanding of Sarah's sense of God. Its temporal structure, flitting back and forth from the present (in which the book is being written by Bendrix), the past of the affair, and the present of the affair (in Sarah's journal, for instance), suggests that while time may be flexible, intruding uncomfortably on the present and helping to mould both the future and one's understanding of the past, it can hardly be evaded—nor would such a response be desirable even if one could somehow extricate oneself from its continuum. If Sarah's death has any meaning for the reader, it is because her efforts to extricate herself from time have been so passionately (and hence vainly) *of* their time, and have involved her in negotiations with a society in which God is only one of many potential interlocutors—and not necessarily the most desirable one.

Likewise it is difficult for readers to sympathize with efforts to deny the existence of a social 'other' when the narrative has, from the very first page, focused their attention on the identity of 'that other, in whom in those days we were lucky enough not to believe'.[39] Until Bendrix reads the diary, the reader is given little reason to suspect that this 'other' is not a human male (and thus one subject to the same socially constituted norms as the protagonists). It is not only Sarah, therefore, who approaches God as a personal interlocutor, but also the reader who has been prepared throughout the first half of the novel to consider God in explicitly social terms, as a potential rival to Bendrix for Sarah's love. It is in this sense that Greene might legitimately be accused of 'abusing

the God of Christianity': the structure of the novel strips God of his transcendence and prompts the reader to consider His value entirely in terms
of His immanence—that is, in terms of the fashion in which believers
relate to Him, what sorts of behavior and decisions one's relation to
Him makes possible, and, most damningly, what sort of ramifications
this belief can have on less exalted 'others'. While Sarah may try to convince herself of the tautological nature of God, the reader is confronted
with a God mired in contingency, and whose ethics come under fire
not merely from Bendrix's savage pen (as, when contemplating Sarah's
cremation, he challenges God to 'resurrect that'[40]) but from the subtly
radical suggestion that, perhaps, in the scale of quotidian human values readers bring to the novel, He may periodically be found somewhat
lacking.

Nor does society disappear from the novel, despite Bendrix's often-
voiced desire that it should: his one moment of near-perfect happiness
comes after he has been 'killed' in the V-1 raid:

> My mind for a few moments was clear of everything except a sense
> of tiredness as though I had been on a long journey. I had no mem-
> ory at all of Sarah and I was completely free from anxiety, jealousy,
> insecurity, hate; my mind was a blank sheet on which somebody had
> just been on the point of writing a message of happiness. I felt sure
> that when my memory came back the writing would continue, and
> that I should be happy.
>
> But when memory did return it was not in that way. I realized first
> that I was lying on my back and that what was balanced over me,
> shutting out the light, was the front door.... After that, of course,
> I remembered Sarah and Henry and the dread of love ending.[41]

Bendrix approaches happiness when the handle of the front door, the
threshold between the public Common and the privacy of his flat,
knocks him unconscious. The distinction between the public and private continues, but the necessity of making this distinction is removed,
just as the difference between past and future collapses into a prolonged
present. When Bendrix wistfully describes imagining eternity as the
'endless prolongation of the moment of death' he seems to go some
way toward aligning himself philosophically with the post-conversion
Sarah, although he never manages to desire the disappearance of memory. Even in the passage cited above, the return of memory figures as a
condition of the happiness somebody seems on the point of inscribing
on his blank mind. He never desires happiness *qua* happiness, but rather

a happiness in which he is an active participant and which is necessarily shared. He rejects the masochistic hunger for the desert Sarah manages to develop, and considers the dread of love ending an insufficient reason for withdrawing from the struggle to prolong it.

In his article 'The End of the Catholic Cycle: The Writer Versus the Saint', Herbert Haber suggests that while Bendrix himself 'will not, or so he flaggingly insists, become a saint', still 'the scar on his leg [received while saving a man during an air raid], his growing tenderness toward Henry, and the weariness of his last prayer [to be left alone forever] seem to belie him'.[42] Haber implies that Bendrix is moving toward an accommodation with God of the same order and magnitude as Sarah's, although he never provides a convincing reason that these events should constitute a turning toward God rather than to the humanity from which Sarah struggled to emancipate herself. He accurately observes that 'the novel finds Bendrix increasingly dissatisfied with his own novelist's heightened sense of transience and the way in which it has robbed him of Sarah's love' but deploys this observation in an effort to suggest that for Bendrix escaping from the tyranny of time (and thus also of memory) has become paramount by the end of the novel.[43] Of course, one might just as easily argue that the end of the novel finds Bendrix resigned to his own transience and, subsequently, more open to the realization of time's potential through participation in society.

The rationale of Haber's interpretive choices, however, becomes clear when one considers the general slant of his argument: that by propagating what Rayner Heppenstal termed 'a lie put out by an author to test the credulity of the world around him' Greene has in fact been 'testing [his] personal morality against what he may continue to feel is the spongier morality of the civilized world'.[44] For Haber, *The End of the Affair* constitutes an effort on Greene's part to subject the novelist's profession to this sort of moral scrutiny, and to illustrate how '... even the coercion of the language the novelist feels called upon to use and his lost hope of death, leads Bendrix back to Sarah and the desperate alternative she and her remaining diary represent, offering as they do proof that one may escape, albeit painfully, from time and self.'[45] This is, however, a difficult argument to reconcile with a protagonist who chooses neither death nor Sarah's faith as a means of escape, but rather the medium of language, the ultimately contingent arbiter of time and self through which one escapes not from the world but from isolation, that abyss or desert to which Sarah was drawn and from which Bendrix recoils. Haber is able to speak of Bendrix's (and Greene's) need to maintain a 'detached existence' in order to make 'the thousand or so technical choices the novelist makes in the process of creation' only by failing to grasp the extent to which the choices a writer makes in the 'process of creation' are not pulled readymade from the abyss but instead arise from an awareness of the conventions that govern both reading processes and the conduct of life.[46] One retains a sense of Bendrix's capacity for transcending time and the self (as well as of Greene's ability to transcend the political nature of literary history) only by turning a blind eye to the social norms which may valorize such a project but which ultimately render it untenable.

13
Liberal Commitment: Reading
The Quiet American

Critics have paid nearly as much attention to the question of Fowler's 'radical' commitment in *The Quiet American* as they have to Bendrix's faith in *The End of the Affair*, an interpretive strategy that owes a considerable debt to two contentious premises: first, the popular view of Marxism as a kind of mad faith in which the inevitability of the dictatorship of the proletariat takes the place of Christ's thousand-year reign before the Last Judgment; and second, the equally popular view that Greene fancied himself a Marxist.[1] In the west during the Cold War, the former view demanded no justification and brooked no contradiction. Justification for the latter came not from *The Lawless Roads*, but from Greene's brief flirtation with the Communist Party of Great Britain (CPGB) in the 1920s, his subsequent expulsion from McCarthy-era America, and his statement, issued in 1967, that 'If I had to choose between life in the Soviet Union and life in the United States, I would certainly choose the Soviet Union.'[2] Some critics, like A.A. DeVitis, scarcely register any distinction between Greene's post-1951 commitment and his earlier Catholic faith:

> Fowler is trapped by his pity for suffering, first when he sees the dead guard at the outpost, then when he sees the dead child on his mother's knees after Pyle's diolacton bomb explodes in the square. Fowler realizes that uninformed innocence in a ravaged world amounts to pain and suffering that can be counted as dead bodies and mutilated children.... Fowler has taken sides, and the realization of his compassionate spirit overwhelms him.[3]

DeVitis's is an admirably economic method for understanding *The Quiet American*, since it permits the orthodox conception of Greene's beliefs and values to remain firmly in place while quietly conceding that the old concerns have been mapped onto new rhetorical territory. Philip Stratford finds himself on adjacent ground when he argues that: '*The Quiet American* must be seen as the story of how Fowler is forced out of his initial position of non-commitment, and in this sense the novel closely parallels Bendrix's story in *The End of the Affair*, though the terms of the narrative are political and not explicitly religious.'[4] For neither DeVitis nor Stratford is the relationship between political commitment and religious faith a problematic one: they are two sides of the same coin—that is, they are both methods of realizing one's potential as an individual, and perhaps of healing the psychic wounds inflicted by original sin or the post-Reformation alienation of man from his social existence.[5] Here the Communist party becomes a sort of Proletarians Anonymous, where, after recognizing the existence of a higher power (perhaps the Dialectic), one may work one's way through the suffering and various insults to one's dignity propagated by the class system and eventually transcend the class system altogether.

Miriam Allott takes the superficially more nuanced view that Fowler 'acts as he does because he has never, in any real sense, managed to remain uninvolved'.[6] She places particular emphasis on Fowler's relationship with Phuong, which she feels helps communicate the 'tenderness, selfishness, compassion, pain, respect for human dignity, and...bitter sense of the limitations of human faith and love' that Fowler ostensibly shares with his creator.[7] Allott argues against the grain of existentialist readings that had privileged commitment as such by suggesting that commitment is in a sense superfluous, since everybody is already so entangled in human relationships that the sort of Olympian detachment a person would require in order to 'choose' commitment is simply inconceivable. Her view anticipates the popular slogan 'the personal is political' insofar as it suggests that commitment can be realized somewhere other than the social sphere. Why any particular action should be preferable to any other is less clear, since any and all actions would seemingly speak of one's involvement; nonetheless, she concludes:

> ...what has mattered in Fowler's story is that he is capable of feeling...pity and sorrow for the lost young man [Alden Pyle]; that as an ordinary, nonpolitical, moderately selfish, but intelligent human being he is moved to act against violence and stupidity; and that he is impelled toward such action above all by his insight into human suffering, especially the suffering caused by war and political conflict.[8]

Allott gathers evidence of Fowler's pity from the last line of the novel: 'Everything had gone right with me since [Pyle] had died, but how I wished there existed someone to whom I could say that I was sorry.'[9] Of course, this line may also be read (as Wm. Thomas Hill has recently read it) as an 'almost laughable twinge of guilt', since the text is positively littered with people to whom Fowler could say that he was sorry if he was so inclined: Vigot (the French police chief), Phuong (Pyle's former fiancée), the Economic Attaché, or even Pyle's mother, whose existence the reader may plausibly deduce from the packages of Vit-Health sandwiches she sends to her son.[10] But here one begins to understand that Allott's reading is not as different from DeVitis's or Stratford's as it seemed at first, since Fowler's secular pity (in Allott's phrase, the pity of an *homme moyen sensual*) has what appears to be an irreducibly spiritual effect: it mitigates the guilt that he has personally incurred by acting against violence and stupidity through an exploit that promises to assist those with an interest in escalating the very violence (i.e., that of the Communists, the US State Department, and even General Thé) to which he is ostensibly opposed. Allott's Vietnam undoubtedly furnishes the would-be actor with a much larger stage than those afforded by DeVitis's Catholic Church or Stratford's Communist Party, and the range of actions personal remorse may legitimize is far larger than the range of actions sanctioned by institutional or otherwise dogmatic faith or commitment. Still, Allott's Vietnam operates according to a strikingly similar logic: the community as a medium for the realization of individual personality, which extracts no obligations in return for the services it renders.

It is difficult to read Thomas Fowler as a portrait of political commitment without doing serious violence either to the text or to a rational conception of political commitment. Fowler is a journalist who works for the *Times*. He has been stationed in Vietnam for 8 years, has a wife in London and a local mistress, and prides himself on being uninvolved in the conflict that perpetually threatens to engulf him. 'The human condition being what it was, let them fight, let them love, let them murder, I would not be involved... I took no action—even an opinion is a kind of action.'[11] His antagonist, Alden Pyle, hails from the United States, where he has recently 'taken a good degree in—well, one of those subjects Americans take degrees in: perhaps public relations or theatrecraft, perhaps even Far Eastern studies'.[12] When Pyle arrives in Indochina, his work outwardly involves 'electrical sewing machines for starving seamstresses' and 'that kind of thing', although his ability to negotiate the demilitarized zone (DMZ) and other off-limits areas quickly leads Fowler

and his colleagues to make a few unsavoury and wholly accurate speculations concerning the former Office of Strategic Services (OSS).[13] Pyle
sets about organizing an indigenous army to fight the Communists with
the assistance of General Thé. After the General's forces bomb a crowded
square in Saigon with Pyle's connivance, and after Pyle himself has successfully seduced Fowler's mistress with the promise of a respectable life,
Fowler helps the Communists plan an ambush in which Pyle is stabbed
and drowned. The action that signals Fowler's new-found commitment
occupies slightly less than one page. He speaks with Monsieur Heng, a
leader of the Communists, who suggests that Fowler could help the situation by publishing a story on General Thé; Fowler rejects this proposal
on the grounds that his newspaper is only interested in stories about
the Communists. Heng then proposes that 'If you would invite [Pyle]
to dinner tonight at the Vieux Moulin ... we would talk to him on the
way.'[14] Fowler leaves a note asking Pyle to come for dinner; Pyle comes,
the Communists ambush and murder him while Fowler has dinner and
takes in a film (*Scaramouche*). As noted, the reporter feels a slight twinge
of guilt at the end.

One can only nod in agreement when Allott argues that through
the relationship between Pyle and Fowler '[Greene] takes us a long
distance ... from the moral position implied in a good deal of modern
existentialist thought', although it might have been more accurate for
her to suggest that in the terms she lays out, Greene takes his readers
a long distance from any moral positions whatsoever.[15] Fowler's actions
do not stop the war, or contribute in any way to the mitigation of the
suffering that haunts him and ostensibly prevents him from taking pleasure in life: 'I cannot be at ease (and to be at ease is my chief wish)
if someone else is in pain, visibly or audibly or tactually.'[16] This line
lies at the heart of arguments concerning Fowler's 'commitment'. But
has pain stopped by the end of the novel, when Phuong has returned
to him and he can comfortably retreat into three or four opium pipes
each evening? Optimists like DeVitis suggest that the recollection of his
betrayal ('Am I the only one who really cared for Pyle?'[17]) will henceforth prevent him from being truly at ease, although the pain of this
recollection is not so different than it might have been had Fowler accidentally knocked down his rival with a lorry: it is a purely personal
pain that may admit of no easy reconciliation but that likewise does
not call for further action. (Significantly, Fowler proclaims his neutrality
to the police chief *after* Pyle's death as a defence when Vigot insinuates that the reporter was involved in the killing, thus incurring only a
private penalty for an action with social ramifications.) Pessimists like

Allott suggest that Pyle will probably be forgotten, and Fowler's pain with it, but that all has been worthwhile since it has created an environment capable of nurturing what she describes as Fowler's nascent 'moral intelligence'.

Both orientations, however, seem to view suffering as something abnormal: as bad luck visited upon the unfortunate by chance, rather than as the inevitable product of a particular form of social organization ('old' colonialism in the novel). One cannot, of course, 'commit' to fighting bad luck; one may only hope that it passes oneself *en route* to afflicting another. Moral intelligence in this formula would seem, from Fowler's perspective, to entail knowing when to close one's eyes, shut up one's ears, and refrain from touching anybody insofar as circumstances allow. Pyle's courage, which Allott also commends, would appear similarly useless since it would appear to lack an object against which it might test itself. One is left with a sort of knowing Stoicism, which John Atkins identifies as a position shared by *both* Pyle and Fowler. The latter, he notes, 'begins to waver when he realizes that the logical end of non-involvement, the Third Force, is impracticable. It has nothing to fight for. It is an idea from a book.'[18] Unlike Allott, DeVitis, or Stratford, however, Atkins does not proceed to suggest that Fowler's wavering results in commitment or involvement, much less in faith. 'Neither Bendrix nor Fowler are pleasant chaps, but perhaps Bendrix is truer than Fowler. His unpleasantness is partly the result of injured decency, whereas Fowler's is entirely natural to him. He is a split character who never acts a whole piece.'[19] Fowler may act in handing Pyle to Heng and the Communists, but he does so for reasons that do him little credit where they may be surmised at all.

The degree to which apprehending Fowler's commitment must be considered central to an understanding of *The Quiet American* is itself far more open to debate than has been chronicled in the scholarly record. Any political significance one may attach to the novel is necessarily distilled from a complex interplay of generic conventions: an inversion—perhaps even a parody—of the romantic comedy and the comedy of manners, war reportage, and, as in *The End of the Affair*, the detective novel. This last gives the novel its central structure, so that reading *The Quiet American* is like reading a whodunit where a romantic comedy performs the narrative work that might otherwise have fallen to police procedure or private investigation. The narrative outlines the basic situation quite rapidly: an American who had been working for the Economic Aid Mission (and quite probably the CIA) turns up dead in a ditch. This 'very quiet' American was shortly due to marry Phuong, an Indochinese girl who had been cohabiting with the narrator (Fowler) 6 months before the novel opens. Fowler appears rather incensed by the girl's defection and conceals his distaste for Pyle from Vigot largely through asides to the reader which problematize the possibility of Fowler's non-involvement as a valid hypothesis for configuring the shape of the novel. Charles Rolo noted in his review of *The Quiet American* that the narrator does not quite 'play fair' with his reader since he in fact knows the answer all along, although the generic reasons for the narrator's deception are quite revealing.[20]

The whodunit's political dimension is invoked by Fowler early on, after Vigot asks him who he thinks might have been responsible for killing Pyle.

> Well, he might have been murdered by the Vietminh. They have murdered plenty of people in Saigon. His body was found in the river by the bridge to Dakow—Vietminh territory when your police withdraw at night. Or he might have been killed by the Vietnamese Sureté— it's been known. Perhaps they didn't like his friends. Perhaps he was killed by Cadaoists because he knew General Thé... Perhaps he was killed by General Thé because he knew the Cadaoists. Perhaps he was killed by the Hoa-Hoas for making passes at the General's concubines. Perhaps he was just killed by someone who wanted his money.[21]

The sheer number of likely candidates makes it difficult to believe that any one of these—or a combination of them—will ultimately yield the genuine culprit. But the passage does more than this: it suggests that if the killing was politically motivated it was also, in all likelihood, meaningless. Each party—Thé's faction, the Cadaoists, the Vietminh, and so forth—is already so steeped in blood as to render the question of culpability null and void (a point Vigot reinforces moments later when he confesses that he is not even pursuing a culprit). One possibility, however, does stand out, principally because Fowler does not include it in his list of possibilities; instead, just as the narrator has nearly reached the end of his speculations the police chief abruptly interjects, 'Or [perhaps it was] a simple case of jealousy.'[22] Fowler's immediate response is to deflect Vigot's insinuation by suggesting the French Sureté as a possible candidate. Fowler struggles to situate the murder in a political context whose potential for leading the reader to a satisfactory resolution of the novel's mystery the narrator himself has already liquidated. The emphatically personal motive offered by Vigot is more persuasive not only because it might reasonably yield a genuine culprit (and hence a resolution to the mystery) but also because it conforms to a pattern of expectations current at the time *The Quiet American* was published.[23]

Less than one fifth of the way through the novel the possibility of implementing a conventional detective fiction structure has closed: there is no point in an 'investigation' into the various political groups cited by Fowler since they are all already guilty, just as it is impossible to pursue the line of inquiry Vigot suggests because it leads directly to the narrator himself. In fact, the narrative *does* pursue Vigot's line of inquiry, although not through the conventions of detective fiction. Instead *The Quiet American* begins deploying semantic and syntactic features associated with the romantic comedy: mismatched lovers, an interloper, and a bittersweet parting, all capped off with an unexpected reunion between people who have (possibly) matured in the interval and who now face the equally unexpected prospect of marriage.

The scene in which Pyle requests Fowler's help in translating his proposal of marriage to the reporter's mistress, for instance, strongly resembles a scene from screwball comedy or a Noel Coward play:

'You don't want me to add a little fire to it, do you?'
'Oh, no,' [Pyle] said, 'just translate. I don't want to sway her emotionally.'
'I see.'
'Tell her I want to marry her.'
I told her.
'What was that she said?'
'She asked me if you were serious. I told her you were the serious type.'
'I suppose this is an odd situation,' he said. 'Me asking you to translate.'
'Rather odd.'
'And yet it seems so natural. After all you are my best friend.'
'It's kind of you to say so.'
'There's nobody I'd go to in trouble sooner than you,' he said.
'And I suppose being in love with my girl is a kind of trouble?'[24]

But if *The Quiet American* is in part structured as a romantic comedy, then the laughter it provokes has rather more in common with the 'comedy' of Shakespeare's sour problem plays than with *The Philadelphia Story* or *Bringing Up Baby*. Fowler can offer Phuong no reason to stay with him, since his means are modest and his London wife is in any case not inclined to grant him a divorce. Pyle, on the other hand, comes from a prosperous bourgeois family, has prospects for advancement in his chosen career, and is single. Readers, of course, are privy to information that neither Fowler nor Phuong possesses when the scene takes place: they have seen the books on Pyle's bookshelf and have listened to Fowler's withering commentary.

> *The Advance of Red China, The Challenge to Democracy, The Rôle of the West*—these, I suppose, were the complete works of York Harding... On what did he relax? I found his light reading on another shelf: a portable Thomas Wolfe and a mysterious anthology called *The Triumph of Life* and a selection of American poetry. There was also a book of chess problems. It didn't seem much for the end of the working day, but, after all, he had Phuong. Tucked away behind the anthology there was a paper-backed book called *The Physiology of Marriage.* Perhaps he was studying sex, as he had studied the East, on paper. And the keyword was marriage. Pyle believed in being involved.[25]

The passage gives the reader a sense of Pyle's sexual inadequacy and suggests that Fowler is (or at least considers himself to be) rather more virile than his rival. During the wooing scene, the reader is cognizant of Pyle's inexperience and the likelihood that he will prove disappointing as a sexual partner. Penned in by his own liberal indifference, Fowler can only answer the threat Pyle's bourgeois respectability poses with an appeal to tradition and inertia: 'Well Phuong... Are you going to leave me for him? He'll marry you. I can't. You know why... Marriages break. Often they break quicker than an affair like ours.'[26] While Fowler is on solid ground when he suggests that a change in circumstances by no means implies progress, the vacuity of his position is underlined when he later writes to his wife that '[i]f I leave her, she'll be a little unhappy I think, but there won't be any tragedy. She'll marry someone else and have a family.'[27] If losing Phuong will be, for Fowler, 'the beginning of death', it nonetheless remains difficult for the reader to believe that death has not already embarked on its march to the Rue Catinat.

In order to read the scene as comically as Fowler's sarcasm and (more importantly) Pyle's *gravitas* suggest that it must be read, one must take seriously the desirability—indeed, the social necessity—of marriage as the form into which love inexorably coagulates. Although he seems unhappy with this convention, and although he continually ridicules Pyle for his bourgeois willingness to abide by social norms, Fowler also accepts its inevitability when, shortly after the wooing scene, he informs Phuong that '[i]t would be very uncomfortable for you [in London] if we were not married.'[28] The subtext, of course, is that it would also be rather uncomfortable for *him* to flout the very laws of propriety for which he feels an unbridled contempt when he detects them embodied in his American rival. In other words, Fowler's attitudes are subject to the same sort of bourgeois prejudices as Pyle's are; as a result, the distinction between the two men emerges as a predominately formal one. The 'anti-American' attitude which has so often elicited comment stems largely from Fowler's nostalgia for the specific tropes of British bourgeois life, rather than from the (rather frail) critique of liberal pluralism critics have eagerly grafted onto the novel. In his remarkable, outrageous review of the novel, A.J. Liebling implicitly noted this tendency (albeit from the equally chauvinistic stance of American exceptionalism) when he suggested that he was 'impressed by the *toupet* of Mr. Greene, sneering down at Pyle [and his Vit-Health sandwiches] from the gastronomic eminence of a soggy crumpet'.[29]

The object of Pyle and Fowler's rivalry, Phuong, is herself no Katherine Hepburn. She keeps her opinions to herself and, like Isabella in *Measure for Measure*, seems quite detached from the situation in which she finds herself—or, more accurately, in which Pyle and Fowler conspire to place her. Neither rival seems to pique her interest in any way, save perhaps as a means of keeping her predatory sister at bay: a tactical aim which Pyle's influence at the Economic Aid Mission seems likelier to help her achieve than Fowler's caustic wit and social penury. Coming from a character so singularly ill-equipped to play the role of romantic protagonist, Phuong's silence has an interesting interpretive effect: it prompts the reader to apprehend quite clearly that what is at issue between Pyle and Fowler is not a woman but what one must presume are opposed (or at least competing) world views—a position that the text does precious little to corroborate. She is not, after all, being asked to choose between Fowler (or Pyle) and one of the scared, hungry Vietnamese watchmen.

Presuming, however, that a reader accepts that the difference between Fowler's preference for *Chapon duc Charles* and Pyle's taste for bland sandwich spreads constitutes a genuine philosophical or ideological impasse, then the function of the comic sub-structure becomes clear: it prompts the reader to assume a classical liberal posture vis-à-vis the politicized detective or 'whodunit' plot. In short, it becomes impossible to say precisely who or what is responsible for Pyle's death. In one sense, he has signed his own death warrant by assisting General Thé to plant the bomb in the square. In turn, Thé plants the bomb in order to lash out against the communists and the French administration, whose respective powers are reinforced by the representation of the war in the newspapers. As an agent of these newspapers who consents to editorial biases, Fowler assumes a measure of responsibility. Vigot himself notes that the French Sureté has reason to be glad that Pyle is dead, and so the French Sureté is in a sense responsible for not taking steps to safeguard the ambush site. The Communists are obviously glad that Pyle is dead, since the forces he was helping to build were not yet strong enough to challenge the French authorities directly and so passed the time by fighting the Reds. By the end of the novel, then, the narrative has come full circle: as Fowler suggested earlier everybody is responsible and so nobody is responsible. What has changed is the reader's orientation to the problem set out by Fowler during his interview with Vigot. The comic structure that occupies the central sections of the novel encourages the reader—particularly the liberal reader—to view the diffusion of responsibility as a satisfactory resolution to the political tensions the narrative dramatizes.

By rather eccentrically placing Phuong at the center of the novel, Allott earnestly attempts to transform the novel's comic structure into a tragic one. She consequently views the differences between Pyle and Fowler as very grave and eventually formulates the theory of liberal commitment (i.e., primarily to oneself) outlined above. DeVitis follows this method to its *reductio ad absurdum* when he describes the same Phuong who gazes adoringly at picture magazines and dreams of one day seeing an actual skyscraper as 'the enigma of the East and the desire of Vietnam for political status'.[30] By valorizing Phuong, both critics attempt to valorize by proxy the perspective they share: that of the engaged observer, 'committed', quite literally, to disinterestedness. If, however, one reads the comic scenes in the spirit in which the narrative appears to offer them, a very different narrative emerges: one that gradually makes the reader cognizant of the extent to which both Pyle and Fowler have involved themselves in a situation that demands a kind of commitment which neither appears disposed to provide. As Barry Hillenbrand recently noted, the novel 'misses some important elements. Like the Vietnamese . . . .'[31] The one Vietnamese character Greene arguably does portray is Phuong, and her priority throughout the entire novel clearly seems to involve catching the earliest available flight out of Vietnam—a flight that neither Pyle's nostalgic ardor for bourgeois revolution nor Fowler's idyllic vision of Pascal-quoting colonial decadence would incline either of her lovers to make. Reading *The Quiet American* according to the conventions Greene uses rather than according to the conventions received wisdom dictated he should have used reveals to the non-canonical reader the grotesque assumptions underlying both protagonists' actions, and provokes the very real question, 'What is to be done?'

That so many scholars have claimed that Fowler's life as it is related in *The Quiet American* constitutes a contribution to the literature of commitment (including, of course, those scholars who see it as a profoundly *undesirable* contribution) is perhaps less surprising than it might seem on the surface. The narrative deploys images and tropes that would seem to require a political response of some sort, as only befits a narrator whose business it is to report on a war. One of the most striking instances occurs when Fowler relates a journey with a company of soldiers in the vicinity of Phat Diem: 'The canal was full of bodies: I am reminded now of an Irish stew containing too much meat.'[32] Or again: 'Six of us got in [the punt] and he began to pole towards the other bank. He pushed away with his pole, sinking it into the human clay, and one body was released and floated up all its length beside the boat.'[33] A little later, the soldiers open fire and accidentally kill two civilians: 'They were very clearly dead: a small neat clot of blood on the woman's forehead, and the child might have been sleeping. He was about six years old and he lay like an embryo in the womb with his little bony knees drawn up.'[34] Punctuating the stillness of these moments with the dead comes Fowler's leitmotif, 'I hate war.'[35] A consoling conclusion is not difficult to draw: the images the war spits up are nauseating; Fowler says he hates the war; therefore by killing Pyle he hopes to end the war and put a stop to the carnage. But does the reader necessarily hate the war?

Anthony Swofford's recent memoir of military life during the first Gulf War demonstrates how readers can violently appropriate texts for uses that may at first seem alien to them. When his US Marine division desires to steel itself for combat on the eve of deployment to Kuwait they rent 'all of the war movies they can get their hands on', many of them ostensibly 'anti-war':

> But, actually, Vietnam war films are all pro-war, no matter what Kubrick or Coppola or Stone intended...Corporal Johnson at Camp Pendleton and Sergeant Johnson at Travis Air Force Base and Lance Corporal Swofford at Twenty-nine Palms Marine Corps Base watch the same films and are excited by them, because they celebrate the terrible and despicable beauty of their fighting skills.[36]

It would, of course, be difficult to imagine a soldier reading *The Quiet American* in order to get riled up about the terrible and despicable beauty of their fighting skills; nonetheless, Greene's novel *does* arguably have a related effect, particularly on his more conventionally liberal readers. DeVitis, Stratford, Allott, and most rational critics would, in all likelihood, agree that war is as 'terrible and inhumane' as Swofford suggests Kubrick and Stone believe it to be. Logically it should be avoided at all costs; still, it is Fowler's deepening involvement in the war that draws their admiration, which in DeVitis's commentary even becomes symbolic of 'the realization of his compassionate spirit'.[37] However, the mitigating factor of Fowler's guilt is at best a personal solution to what is irreducibly a social problem. To insist on regarding it as symbolic of commitment is to recognize the individual as the outermost limit of ethical action: war begins to appear 'inhumane' on the odd grounds that it interferes with individual choice. Fowler's great act of commitment thus consists *not* of betraying Pyle to the communists, but of vigorously holding onto the illusion of individual autonomy despite the unwelcome intrusion of society in the form of mortars, grenades, and bombs.

Fowler manifests his autonomy in a number of ways that *under different circumstances* would probably lose him the hearts and minds of most of his readers. He treats Phuong with indifference, his professional colleagues with contempt, and his romantic rival with undisguised scorn that evolves into homicidal rage when Pyle fails to grasp the extent of the destruction and carnage he has helped cause in the Place Garnier, instead distractedly taking note of the blood on his shoes: 'I must get them cleaned before I see the Minister.'[38] The reader is prompted to pass judgment against Pyle in much the same fashion as *The Stranger's* anonymous jurors condemn Mersault for murder on the grounds that he did not love his mother. The charges against Pyle include criminal naiveté and callousness, but not mass murder. Once again, the reader is prompted to adopt a perspective on the character that Fowler has already subjected to withering commentary. After sneaking into Phat Diem, Pyle informs Fowler of his intention to ask for Phuong's hand in marriage; this accomplished, he confesses that he doesn't 'feel half as mean as I did, now that I've told you'. Fowler writes:

> Was he the only one that mattered? I wondered angrily, and yet I knew that he didn't intend it that way. To him the whole affair would be happier as soon as he didn't feel mean—I would be happier, Phuong would be happier, the whole world would be happier,

even the Economic Attaché and the Minister. Spring had come to Indochina now that Pyle was mean no longer.[39]

When Pyle fails to feel mean at the appropriate time, Fowler decides that the time has arrived to liquidate him. By contrast, Fowler's strangely impersonal act of violence demands no retribution because he *does* feel adequately mean at the appropriate time. He himself does not need to be liquidated in turn because the meaning of his act has already been liquidated as far as the liberal reader is concerned, his jealousy and hatred more than balanced by the 'laughable twinge of guilt at the end'.

Saigon during the war, like London during the Blitz (or Mexico during the purges, or Brighton during one of its intermittent racecourse gang wars), furnishes the narrative that produces it with a setting in which society does not merely haunt the margins as it does in screwball comedy or the 'classical' detective story; it intrudes, its bombs and mortars demonstrate its physical existence, and it constantly threatens to expose the paradox of liberal ideology: 'For to claim that the state should be neutral in respect of the good seems inevitably to assert a certain conception of the good, and thus not to be neutral at all.'[40] The interplay of popular generic conventions makes it difficult for any save the most liberally 'committed' reader to fail to grasp the fact that commitment is born in specific social circumstances and demands a response that fits the time and place rather than one that fits the psychological demands of a universal human nature. Both Pyle and Fowler invert A.J.P. Taylor's famous quip that he held extreme views but held them moderately: they hold appallingly modest views, but hold them extremely. The tendency of scholars to valorize Fowler's 'commitment' betrays an intellectual's nostalgia for war, an arena in which the terrible and despicable beauty of one's interpretive skills may be celebrated without a thought for the inhumane consequences of one's neutrality.

14
Appropriating Greene: Re-Reading *The Quiet American* and *The End of the Affair*

In 1973, when the Collected Edition of Greene's work was in the early stages of publication, Robert Murray Davis offered the following assessment of the writer's transition 'from standard to classic':

> The continued respectful attitude towards Greene's works stems from his contemporaneity, a journalistic virtue much admired by Peter Wolfe in his study of the entertainments and by reviewers more capable of dealing with newsworthiness than with art. This has been true of Greene's reputation ever since he began to acquire one in the 1940s. The mixture of melodrama, theology, and what some called existentialism in novels like *The Power and the Glory* was one especially appealing to the readers and characteristic of the literature of the post-war decade.[1]

Davis's article serves as a useful reminder that writers exert only a modest influence on the shape their reputations assume. History, politics, economics, and institutions all weigh heavily on the 'classic' or 'canonical' writer, despite the protestations of canonical readers. Fortunately for Greene, the postwar economic boom had served him both well (in the financial sense) and obliquely. It had contributed to the development of a particular set of attitudes—an exhausted redaction of the ideological tenets of classical liberalism which had yet to suppress its rhetorical concern with social values—that enabled intellectuals to appropriate his work for use in those institutions responsible for producing and reproducing social relations in the postwar West: colleges and universities, the entertainment industry, religious organizations, and others. The development of the welfare state in the Anglophone world, the provision of wider access to higher education, and, consequently, the growth of the professoriate all helped mitigate the taint of Greene's undoubted popularity. Developments in academe required professional critics to reorient themselves toward a canon now called upon to absorb work that might otherwise have remained marginalized. Greene's use of theological tropes in his early work and political tropes in his later work opened his ambiguously literary novels to a mode of inquiry consistent with Leavisite and New Critical prejudice (if not practice): the investigation of how a writer's personality gave shape to his work and invested a given text with meaning.

But the fault-lines along which Greene's reputation would split were already beginning to appear. The growth of the humanities had begun to expose both the myopia of Leavisite and New Critical prejudice and the severe quantitative limitations of their methodologies—particularly the close reading of canonical texts. Reservations prompted numerous scholars to subject both the body of material with which they had traditionally worked and the methods they had traditionally employed to protracted scrutiny.[2] While the most significant result of this self-critique, structuralism, was by no means a revolutionary discourse in and of itself, its apex nonetheless coincided with a historical moment when an unhealthily large proportion of liberal thinking occupied itself with the business of furnishing a rationale for stuffing its students into the meat-grinder of the Vietnam War and the smaller-scale battles of the Cold War. The contrast between what was being learned and the uses to which this learning was to be put strained credulity too far, and the student movement began taking its learning rather more seriously than the ruling classes were prepared to allow. It was one thing to suggest, as Herbert Marcuse suggested in 1964, that 'coming to life as classics, [artistic classics] come to life as other than themselves; they are deprived of their antagonistic force, of the estrangement which was their very dimension of truth'; it was quite another to occupy the streets of Paris 4 years later in an effort to seize the powers of transgression and indictment from the remnants of 'feudal-aristocratic culture'.[3] The student movement's failure to create a functional alternative to the liberal orthodoxy on either side of the Atlantic, however, had been accepted by most observers by 1973.

It was during the period bracketed by the Second World War and by the disillusion with and retreat from post-1968 political life that a generation of liberal scholars—Kenneth Allott, Miriam Farris, John Atkins, David Lodge, David Pryce-Jones, etc.—laid the groundwork for Greene's future critical fortunes. Davis's article in some ways constituted a challenge to the reigning orthodoxies. For him, the grip of 'the fallen world' on the readerly imagination attributed to Greene by Francis and Allott had decidedly slackened.

> Since the middle fifties, Greene has grown more secular, more revolutionary, more equivocal, and at times more frivolous, and so have many of his readers. To those of us raised in the fifties, the explicitly dogmatic issues of his 'Catholic' novels now seem incredibly dated. One wonders what college-age readers make of him behind the polite, bland, note-taking façade; perhaps those beliefs and practices seem as ludicrous as Shakespeare does to the inhabitants of *Brave New World*. Thus, because Greene's novels were 'contemporary' twenty-five years ago, they no longer seem so, and in any case contemporaneity is a shaky standard.[4]

Greene's texts had not changed, but what it was possible or desirable to say about them had. The novels that had made his reputation had aged poorly; there was no longer any reason to press the question of Fowler's commitment—or that of Bendrix's faith—because those concepts found themselves devalued in intellectual discourse in the wake of 1968, and increasingly subject to suspicion (sometimes amounting to scorn) in emergent post-structuralist discourses.

The interest Greene's novels retained for the modern reader rapidly assumed an antiquarian aspect: by reading them one could attempt to excavate and reconstruct an epistemology that had vanished from the earth in the time that had elapsed since the novels could lay a legitimate claim to contemporaneity. Davis illustrated this point with a blunt précis of Peter Wolfe's book *Graham Greene: The Entertainer*: '...the book is not *about* anything; its only real reasons for being are the undeniable facts that Wolfe likes Greene's thrillers and that no one had previously devoted an entire critical book to them.'[5] A book that extended the scope of knowledge to which the academy could reasonably lay claim without fundamentally altering the conditions of that knowledge was, of course, the ideal product of the postindustrial cultural establishment: one that might have contested the forms in which liberal orthodoxies had been embodied in the past, but that politely refrained from contesting liberalism itself.

* * *

The fate of *The Quiet American* serves as one indication of the direction Greene's reputation has taken since the appearance of the Collected

Edition. When Davis quipped that 'unless a better case can be made for him, the Collected Edition may have to be the slab over [Greene's] reputation instead of a monument to it' he nonetheless held firm to the belief that 'writers have a way of surviving weak support and unintelligent blame and even their own worst work.'[6] *The Quiet American* endured a rather long exile from the thoughts of scholars concerned with Greene—one that recently received a brief reprieve thanks mostly to renewed US involvement in Iraq and the scandal of a film adaptation that received its first screening on 10 September 2001.

If modern readers were no longer moved by Fowler's rather shabby act of resistance (or even amused by Bendrix's sardonic profession of 'faith'), nor were they particularly enthusiastic about taking heed of a reminder to act courageously and morally in a society that had born witness to the seeming triumph of a revanchist pluralism. As Terry Eagleton notes, 'In its post-imperialist phase, and in a supposedly multicultural society, the system can no longer plausibly claim that its values are superior to those of others, simply—key postmodern term—different.'[7] If one has internalized the non-value structure of this morally relativist system, then it is Fowler's indecision which must be celebrated, since it suggests a self that remains in play, and Pyle's ignorance which must be forgiven since it is impossible for him to know anything anyway. The dramatic irony of *The Quiet American* becomes invisible, and pragmatically ceases to exist. The text remains the same, but the biases privileged by the norms of contemporary scholarship prevent one from engaging the text in a way that allows the irony to be realized. That the novel has been roundly ignored by even those scholars who profess an interest in Greene suggests that postmodernity is perhaps less at ease with its assumptions than it often pretends.

One use to which the novel *has* been pressed, however, is a strange and perhaps unexpected one that makes few concessions to intellectual rigor, postmodern or otherwise: *The Quiet American* has surfaced, repeatedly, in the travel supplements of national newspapers, particularly in Britain. In 'From Greene to red and back', Robbie Millen asks the readers of the London *Times*:

> What would Greene recognize of Saigon? What would he make of a country which after he and the French left endured 20 years of civil war, Agent Orange, the impoverishing Puritanism and isolationism of a triumphant Communist Party, then doi moi, Vietnam's attempt at perestroika and transforming itself into an Asian Tiger?[8]

The question is in many ways rhetorical. It suggests that Greene would not recognize much of Saigon, but also strangely hints that Greene would not have been particularly interested in the 20 years of civil war and Agent Orange since they eventually gave rise to the Asian Tiger—which Millen soon reveals has not been kind:

> The Metropole is still there, now rather too 'international hotel, any-where' .... But what of Le Club, where officers of the Sureté met to play Quatre Cent Vingt-et-un? Le Vieux Moulin, the restaurant where Fowler waited for Pyle to meet his grisly end? The Pavilion, where European and American women met for coffee? All gone.... Unsurprisingly, in a nation whose people are so young, no one remembers the French street names.... [9]

The autumnal, elegiac tone is unmistakable—'*Mais ou sont Le Vieux Moulin d'antan?*'—but seems wholly fatuous in light of the fact that the article describes a society no longer torn by civil war or policed by its totalitarian apparatchiks as heartily as in former times. The atmosphere of comely decadence evoked by Greene in his novel has dissipated, and with it, the vaguely transgressive pleasure of taking coffee at the Pavilion as an outsider, one who ostensibly exists both beyond and above political conflict. Much to Millen's regret, Saigon (as denizens of South Vietnam continue to call their city) no longer occupies a place on 'the dangerous edge of things'; in becoming 'anywhere' it has lost the sordid specificity that had once made it possible for someone like Fowler to confuse radical commitment with a nostalgic longing for the bourgeois Britain wrecked by Attlee.

Millen's breezy prose masks a subtly postmodern ambiguity. The city has not become depoliticized; if anything, in becoming international it has become so politicized that politics itself has been reduced to gesture:

> You know that you can [cross the road] when you watch a woman ... back-beetle across the swarm of trick-cyclists to emerge unscathed on the other side of the road. She will have dodged families, four-to-a-bike; Del Boys, their motorbikes loaded high with toilets to flog; or a gaggle of fashion-conscious girls wearing arm length gloves and face masks to ward off the sunlight and keep their skin pale and beautiful. [10]

In the absence of what Millen refers to as 'democracy' (perhaps taking his cue from York Harding), to be fashion-conscious is a quiet act of rebellion—but one that no longer sets the pulse racing since it is a trait shared by the anonymous international clientele of the Metropole. In this fashion Millen's article parrots Fowler at his most bitter and least persuasive: 'Even [the Americans'] lavatories were air-conditioned, and presently the temperate tempered air dried my tears as it dries the spit in your mouth and the seed in your body.'[11] Rank and stifling lavatories, of course, are principally extolled by people who do not have to regularly shit in one, a point even Fowler concedes during the long night he spends with Pyle in the watchtower: 'With a return ticket courage becomes an intellectual exercise, like a monk's flagellation. How much can I stick?'[12]

For Millen, *The Quiet American* has become a sort of Baedeker describing a world that no longer exists for Britons: Saigon as a latter-day Atlantis, where, once, playing a game of Quatre-vingt-et-un could have been construed as a statement of principle, like the colonialists of old who dressed to dine in the midst of the jungle. Millen was not alone guilty of this nostalgic fallacy. *The Quiet American* has perhaps resurfaced most often in the pages of the *Financial Times*, where the novel has consistently occupied pride of place in the reading lists recommended to 'the hardier expatriate' who aspires to exploit 'the sense of new opportunities, to be won by hard work and enterprise in difficult conditions' by setting up shop in Vietnam.[13] Alexander Nicoll presumably recommends *The Quiet American* for its evocation of Saigon's 'frontier atmosphere', rather than for any practical light it might shed on the 'rapidly growing' number of foreign companies with offices in Vietnam: 'Oil companies such as Shell, BP Enterprise and Total have been well established for some time. Seven foreign banks (Standard Chartered, five French banks and Thai Military Bank) have representative offices, and an Indonesian bank has a joint venture. Branch licenses are expected to be awarded soon....'[14] Nicoll's selection of *The Quiet American* as suitable reading material for corporate frontiersmen seems at best an eccentric one and, at worst, demonstrative of a peculiar strain of masochism, softened somewhat solely by the propensity of entrepreneurs and executives to think of themselves in martial terms, a fiction that John Kenneth Galbraith observes may do something for the executive's self-esteem 'and possibly for his domestic life'.[15] For Millen, the end of the war signaled the start of Saigon's decline; for Nicoll, by contrast, the war has fortunately never actually ended; it has merely been cleaned up a bit and relocated from the jungle to the boardroom. Both writers share their propensity for morbid nostalgia with the reporters described by J.D.F. Jones (also in the *Financial Times*), who reminisce interminably, and for whom 'a dismal whiskey in dreary London or New York reminds them of those dangerous, appalling, happy years in Da Nang, Phnom Penh, or Vientiane' evoked with such felicity by Greene 'with his weary, enchanted *Telegraph* man [*sic*] in *The Quiet American*'.[16]

Sandy Gall was one such reporter who returned to Vietnam in 1997 and produced an article for the *Financial Times* outlining his impressions of modern Saigon. Gall opens his article with an allusion to Greene, as a child tries to sell him a pirated edition of *The Quiet American* for two dollars. He stands in front of the Continental 'where everyone used to gather for a drink in the evening: prostitutes, pimps, politicians, journalists, French colonels, American contractors, Vietcong agents and little girls selling necklaces of sweet-smelling jasmine'.[17] Gall leaves blurry the line separating his own recollections from the events recounted in Greene's novel, perhaps sensing that *Financial Times* readers had more likely perused the book than spent time on the front lines of the war. This short portrait of a journalist 'waylaid by the past' (as the article's sub-heading reads) does not suggest why Gall's particular memories are poignant so much as it communicates the idea that memories as such are poignant. The reader learns that the main thoroughfare was called 'Rue Catinat by the French, then Tu Do by the South Vietnamese, and now Dong Khoi by the Communists' and that the road 'used to hum with girlie bars selling an insipid but costly concoction called Saigon tea'.[18] Working girls would ask customers at the bars to buy them Saigon tea in order to 'work out how many dollars you were good for'. This last memory waylays the journalist during dinner:

> The Liberty ... reminded me of the girlie bars, although there was no Saigon tea, only Black Label and Napa Valley Red, and two mini-skirted chanteuses belting out old 1960s favorites. We drank a rather good Robert Mondavi Cabernet Sauvignon called Stockbridge, and ate delicious prawns and crab; the seafood in Vietnam is still excellent.[19]

Why the Liberty, delicious prawns, and a rather good Robert Mondavi Cabernet Sauvignon should have reminded Gall of the girlie bars on the Rue Catinat is left entirely to the reader's imagination. The names of people and, particularly, of places like the Liberty or the Majestic (from which spot he watched the evacuation of Saigon in 1975) possess a strange incantatory power for Gall, suggestive of a continuum between past and present which he alone commands, and which alone is capable of investing the present with meaning. Gall clearly shares

Fowler's distaste for those who believe they can somehow grasp a country by *reading* about it; both, however, are compromised and frustrated by the professional necessity of grasping a country by *writing* about it, a process which necessarily entails finding common ground with precisely those less informed readers whom they hold in contempt. Thus while *The Quiet American* is a novel that at its best constitutes a critique of journalistic shibboleths (impartiality, objectivity, and the possibility of transparent reportage, for instance), it has by virtue of its popularity ironically become a staple of journalistic rhetoric insofar as it provides reporters and readers with a common set of assumptions for understanding Vietnamese society and the war. Because intellectual readings of the novel insist on the value of Fowler's commitment, their deployment in the context of war reportage excuses—or even exorcises—the partiality of the reporters themselves.

In a United Press International release occasioned by the tardy appearance of Philip Noyce's film, the former Vietnam correspondent Uwe Siemon-Netto praised Greene's 'masterpiece' for 'reflect[ing] the sleazy sensuousness of its venue' but objected to both the novel and the film on the grounds that 'It is perfidious by what it insinuates—that the U.S. has always been the culprit and can be counted on to be a culprit again in the war to come.'[20] For Siemon-Netto, war crimes like the My Lai massacre were 'aberrations, not part of stated United States policy', a verdict that betrays a staggering naivety. What Siemon-Netto shares with writers like Millen and Nicoll is a willingness to concede *The Quiet American*'s 'greatness' when doing so poses no threat to the sacrosanct narrative of American good intentions in Vietnam. As Chomsky and Herman point out in *Manufacturing Consent*:

> ...from the point of view of the media...there is no such event in history as the U.S. attack against South Vietnam and the rest of Indochina. One would be hard put to find even a single reference within the mainstream to any such event, or any recognition that history could possibly be viewed from this perspective—just as *Pravda*, presumably, records no such event as the Soviet invasion of Afghanistan, only the defense of Afghanistan against 'bandits' supported by the CIA. Even at the peak period of peace-movement activism there was virtually no opposition to the war within the intellectual culture on the grounds that aggression is wrong—the grounds universally adopted in the case of the Soviet invasion of Czechoslovakia in 1968—for a very simple reason: the fact of U.S. aggression was unrecognized.[21]

Millen, Siemon-Netto, Nicoll, and others attempt to fit *The Quiet American* into the framework of mainstream understanding of the Vietnam War by dismissing its political implications, both for societies and for the individuals who compose them; in no other way can the veteran journalists square their undisputed affection for the novel with 'the fact of U.S. aggression' and the disconcerting questions this fact would raise if the idea did not continue to seem to their readers 'as ludicrous as Shakespeare does to the inhabitants of *Brave New World*'.

Since these questions fall outside the arena of responsible debate, Greene's novel can only serve as a barometer for contemporaneity, as it does in Graham Lord's article for the *Times*:

> If [Greene's] ghost returned today it would recognize a great deal. The brothels and opium dives that Greene frequented have been swept away by years of communist Puritanism, along with the casino and the Chinese gambling dens of Cholon, but the city is still a whirling mass of suicidal cyclists and rickshaws.[22]

Lord discovers that while 'the constant whiff of danger' that attracted Greene to Saigon has mostly dissipated, interested parties can recapture some sense of menace if they search out the Dakow Bridge where Pyle was murdered by venturing into the 'savage areas of Districts 4 and 8, where the anticommunists who were dispossessed when they lost the war 20 years ago still suffer brutal discrimination and poverty, along with their ostracized children and grandchildren'.[23] After this entertainment—best enjoyed by taxi, rather than on foot—Lord advises his readers to retire to the New World Hotel, where rooms cost £192 with suites up to £652.

It was perhaps articles like those cited above that provoked Colin Donald to beg publishers to impose 'an immediate ban on quoting from Graham Greene's *The Quiet American*' on senior correspondents preparing their memoirs of Vietnam.[24] The novel, he feared, was 'in danger of being pecked to death by lazy writers in search of an easy resonance'.[25] His own use of the novel had been slightly more nuanced when 2 months earlier he had begun a piece on Vietnam's collective descent into drug addition with an image drawn from Greene.

> Graham Greene, that connoisseur of picturesque decay, described it best in his Vietnam novel *The Quiet American*: the dingy opium den in Haiphong with the wizened figures sliding into oblivion on hard boards and wooden pillows. The combination of asceticism and

decadence symbolized to him the melancholy glamour of French Indochina.[26]

Like Lord, Donald believes that Greene would probably recognize a considerable amount of present-day Vietnam; but where Lord sees continuity in such superficial features as the *ao dai* worn by the 'prettiest schoolgirls in the world', Donald's vision of continuity is deeper and darker, a matter of syntactic structures rather than semantic features. The opium dens remarked upon by Greene might have disappeared, but they have been replaced by back-alley shooting galleries where young Vietnamese addicts flock in search of cheap heroin fixes. The melancholy glamor of French Indochina, Donald suggests, was as much a wilful delusion as 'Vietnam's glittering promise as the new place for foreign investors', which has already begun to fade thanks to the growth industries of 'corruption and serpentine bureaucracy'.[27] The conflicts Donald describes demand morally intelligent, courageous participation, rather than the detached observation through which lazier writers had filched their easy resonances, perhaps assisting business executives with their 'domestic lives' along the way. What, for instance, would readers of Mark Hodson's piece for the *Financial Times* be prepared to recognize of Donald's Vietnam? Hodson writes: 'Ironically, it is the very lack of western involvement that has made Saigon such a delight for tourists fed up with the pollution and filth of many Asian cities.'[28] The US trade embargo did not, apparently, count as 'involvement' for Hodson, who praised the pastoral splendor of a city where 'young girls wash dishes in the gutters while their mothers sell Russian vodka and American cigarettes under the shade of old parachutes.'[29] These images, he argued, suggested that 'the elegance and vigour described in Greene's 1950s novel' remained intact—a far simpler idea to incorporate into the orthodox narrative of the Vietnam War and its aftermath than Donald's insistence that a neutral posture is already a kind of involvement.[30]

When *The Quiet American* has appeared in the press, it has often been treated as a plotless portrait of Saigon that exists apart from politics and makes few demands on its readership, like a well-executed but bland still-life. The narrative the novel relates is simply no longer relevant in the context of the mainstream media: if, as most of the Western press insists, capitalism has triumphed and all alternatives to the neoliberal outlook have been discredited, then there no longer exists a language in which the question of commitment—like the question of US aggression—can be posed. Like the 'Catholic dogma' that made Greene's most critically acclaimed novels seem 'incredibly dated' to Davis in

1973, the idea of political engagement no longer sets intellectuals' pulses racing since it implies a set of values that ignores, even negates difference as grounds for individual or collective identity. Commentators in the mainstream media are of course less constrained by intellectual orthodoxies, but they nonetheless remain rather embarrassed by a novel whose popularity may provide common ground for spouting platitudes to the reading public but whose narrative defies the very usage to which it is pressed.

Noyce's film adaptation was barred from the theatres after the September 11 attacks by Miramax chief Harvey Weinstein until its star, Michael Caine, allegedly threatened to abandon his contractual obligation to do public relations work for another upcoming release.[31] *Cineaste* quoted Weinstein proposing that 'In light of everything that happened, you needed to have your head examined if you thought this was a time for questioning America.'[32] Whether or not the question was a valid one did not enter into Weinstein's calculations: ideological expediency, rather than intellectual honesty or even commercial acumen, determined the film's chances of reaching the public. Anthony Lane of the *New Yorker* compounded the irony of the executive producer re-enacting the role of Fowler on the public stage when he suggested that the film was actually quite innocuous, that it lacked the 'vehement sourness' of the novel, and that 'a film that precisely reproduced the Greene tone—an old man's sin-sated weariness, blended with an anguish almost adolescent in its attraction to death—would be close to unwatchable.'[33] Weinstein's reluctant decision to release the film 2 years after it was scheduled to appear mirrored Fowler's own act of 'commitment': too little substance, and far too late to provoke the sort of public questioning and debate it might have. By the time the film was released, the orthodox narrative of shattered American innocence had already been rehashed by the American media and had assumed a largely uncontested position in the public consciousness, while news outlets abroad were left to grapple with the divide between American good intentions and reality. The antiwar movement peaked on 15 February 2003 and resignation set in; in the face of a fait accompli like 'the war on terror', it seemed, *The Quiet American* had very little to say.

Prior to the release of Noyce's film, a large proportion of *Quiet American* criticism had appeared in the travel sections of newspapers like the *Times* and in newspapers geared toward investors, like the *Financial Times*. Greene's popularity and reputation meant that he could usefully serve as a means for communicating information to the readers of these and other, similar organs. The novel's central preoccupation—the value of commitment—was less suited to the message these organs were in the business of communicating. The solution of writers like Millen, Hodson, and Nicoll was simple and elegant, and consisted of divorcing the evocative descriptive passages from the narrative that both propels them forward and is in turn shaped by them. They then employed these passages to nostalgically conceptualize a historical moment (now relegated to the Bakhtinian epic past) when commitment *did* mean something, and to construct a present space in which the political mystique Greene had so ably communicated in his novel could be purchased through the relatively painless and commitment-free activities of international tourism and venture capitalism. The biases and prejudices of these organs' readerships provided a surety that the implications of Greene's narrative would not be taken altogether seriously, since the worldview the papers cultivated rendered many of these implications as unrecognizable as the fact of US aggression during the Vietnam War.

When *The Quiet American* once again emerged in a medium, the cinema, that made its appeal to a much broader cross-section of biases and prejudices, the narrative's potential for galvanizing public opinion was naturally far greater, as was the reluctance of those with a large stake in maintaining the status quo to permit it to come before the public. Criticism of the film naturally focused on Greene's 'anti-Americanism' and the dubious wisdom of releasing a movie like *The Quiet American* at a time when the United States was healing itself by bombing Afghanistan back into primordial slush—decades of civil war having already returned the country to the Stone Age—and by preparing to invade Iraq. Lamenting Greene's myopia (in the United States) or praising his foresight (in the rest of the world) while universally voicing contempt for Weinstein's spineless handling of the film offered a safe alternative to posing the serious 'what is to be done' question the film raised. By June 2004, *The Quiet American* had been returned intact to the travel pages, and had even trickled down to the petty bourgeois pages of the *Daily Mail* as the portrait of a city in which the street-hawkers peddling Greene's novel have 'so much charm . . . it's hard to turn them away' and where doubles at the Majestic start at just £45.[34]

Noyce's version of *The Quiet American* led reviewers to question Greene's alleged 'anti-Americanism' rather than Fowler's indisputable distaste for all things of American provenance—a somewhat strange choice, since it was with Michael Caine playing Thomas Fowler and not Graham Greene playing himself that the reviewers had passed a few hours. Although critics in the United States (and also at the *Daily Telegraph*[35]) were stridently outraged by Greene's anti-Americanism, they were almost universally impressed by Caine's performance of this unspeakable bigotry—so much so that the Academy honored Caine with an Oscar nomination for the role. That this display of aesthetic detachment and impartial judgment was perhaps out of place in reference to a film whose central themes were the inadvisability of impartial postures and the impossibility of detachment was not widely remarked upon.

* * *

Released nearly 4 years prior to *The Quiet American* (and nearly 2 years prior to 11 September 2001), Neil Jordan's film adaptation of *The End of the Affair* occasioned far less overtly polemical commentary than Noyce's film. History, after all, had not yet thrown up events that would help smooth the transformation of Greene's suspect ties to communism (an irrelevance in the media since the collapse of the Soviet Union) into an implicit support for terrorism to be derided at every opportunity in respectable news outlets. Instead, nearly all the reviewers concentrated their efforts on answering the question of whether Jordan had managed to be 'faithful' to Greene.

Contemporary reviewers had not contemplated whether or not Hitchcock had been 'faithful' to Robert Bloch's *Psycho*. And when modern reviewers question whether or not filmmakers have been faithful to a novel by, say, John Grisham or Stephen King, they do not necessarily imply that departure from the words on the page is a flaw. Popular fiction is as susceptible to tautological readings as its literary counterpart, save that intellectuals tend to read popular fiction as the expression of a socially constituted but standardized genre that 'speaks' itself, and literary fiction as the expression of a unique talent or genius that speaks to himself or herself. A popular work can therefore be transformed in a way that enables the adaptation to more closely approximate the conventions associated with the genre, while the adaptation of a work of literature runs a far greater risk of travestying the genius who created it and therefore requires a more subtle handling and as few changes as possible. Joseph Mankiewicz, as noted in Chapter 11, had crossed this line with his adaptation of *The Quiet American* (1958), certainly to Greene's profound irritation but also greatly to the relief of the reviewing establishment, which was not called upon to risk being unpatriotic in due deference to Greene's talent.

Jordan made substantial changes in his presentation of the material— so many, in fact, that some reviewers questioned whether or not the film was even entitled to be called *The End of the Affair*. Stanley Kauffmann's verdict in *The New Republic* was among the most venomous:

> Aside from ravaging the spiritual elements in the novel, aside from other sorts of subtleties that are trashed, Jordan has vulgarized the book's very structure.... Jordan's screenplay is not an adaptation, it is a devastation. It's so drastic that we are left puzzled as to why Jordan, who also directed, wanted to adapt the novel at all if he was going to violate it this way.[36]

For Kauffmann, Jordan has profaned a sacred object and meddled with matters too deep for him to plumb. The reviewer aligns himself with the earlier generation of Greene scholars when he writes that:

> Greene, except for one mention of Sarah's experience of orgasm with Bendrix—none with her husband—keeps the emphasis on the specificity of these individuals, not the universals of copulation. Sarah's rites of religious passage, Bendrix's love-hate relationship with God as his rival for Sarah's love, are smothered in the way of all this flesh.[37]

Kauffmann wisely declines to explore how a director might have gone about filming the specificity of an individual whose lover remarks that 'only when he is there, with me, in me, does he feel safe' *without* running the risk of simultaneously filming the 'universals of copulation'.[38] His view clearly reflects A.A. DeVitis's for whom *The End of the Affair* works best when it echoes most thoroughly the theological position DeVitis attributes to Greene. For Kauffmann, viewers have only understood the story if and when they can consider it as something other than a story about people who passionately enjoy having sex with one another. For both commentators, sex and the spirit are mutually exclusive concerns—a proposition that it is difficult to imagine winning the agreement of either the story's protagonists or its author (whom Michael Shelden mischievously alleges passionately enjoyed having sex with his American mistress in the churches of Italy[39]).

Commonweal's Richard Alleva concurred with Kauffmann, but generously estimated that Jordan had successfully translated three quarters of the novel into celluloid. The film, which he dubs 'Son of *The English Patient*' ('Conference of the [Columbia Pictures] Suits: Ralph Fiennes, adultery, World War II, British accents, and one hundred and ten minutes of guilty sex and emotional misery. Academy Awards, here we come!'), achieves 'cinematic flow, convincing characterizations, and wonderful atmosphere'. The problem, he writes, is that in the last act the director chooses to 'cut the heart out of the movie'.[40] Alleva strenuously objects to the most drastic of Jordan's changes to the novel: reuniting Bendrix and Sarah and whisking them away for a dirty weekend in Brighton before Sarah's pulmonary infection kills her.

> Whatever the moral and theological implications of this, it is a dramatic, artistic mistake. The force of Sarah's character, her fate (and that of two men in her life), and the central irony and piteousness of the story, all flow from Sarah's determination to keep her promise. Jordan dumps all this and opts instead for simple domestic pathos as husband and lover unite to nurse the dying woman they both love, later becoming a sort of poignant 'odd couple' after her death.

> I was touched but couldn't help seeing that this made Sarah's promise over Bendrix's (seeming) corpse nothing but a temporary stumbling block to the affair and not, as Greene intended, a transformation of it into a crucible.[41]

Numerous critics agreed that the dirty weekend undermined Sarah's character, though many were less restrained in drawing attention to the moral and theological implications. Owen Gleiberman of *Entertainment Weekly* remarked that '[t]he affair itself, in its genteel way, does catch fire, but it's the end of the affair that needs to move us to rapture, and the movie, instead, just drifts away.' In its place he recommended *Breaking the Waves* as 'the rare man/woman/God triangle that's as transporting as it is far-fetched'.[42] In the pages of the *Guardian*, Peter Bradshaw observed that the film conveyed the secular aspects of the story but that Jordan conceded too much by 'giving [the] affair its Second Act' since without the spiritual intensity of Sarah's struggle to keep her bargain '*The End of the Affair* is, really, a little banal.'[43]

Each of these reviewers treats Jordan's *The End of the Affair* as a translation of the novel from the printed word to the screen, rather than as an interpretation of the material. If the film does not meet with the critic's approbation it is because Greene's vision has not been adequately realized—a standard that clearly would not be applied to adaptations assembled from fiction whose authors were held in less esteem. If, on the other hand, the film does meet with approbation, it is because Jordan has effectively forged Greene's style in an alien medium—a standard that clearly would reflect poorly on the director's judgment had the adaptation been assembled from the work of a lesser talent. (This may be why successful Hitchcock films are rarely discussed in terms of their literary origins.) In either case, the viewer is excluded from the process of realizing Greene's work, which is instead parcelled out to the assorted geniuses at work on the project: author, director, stars, cinematographers, producers, and so on. Nobody speaks of a genius for watching films (or even for reading fiction), but this is precisely what these reviews imply. After all, it is their own vision of the film that they celebrate or denigrate as though it was Greene's.

Neil McDonald offered another example of this critical tendency when he wrote that because both directors 'have striven to be faithful to the original novel...the reason [Neil Jordan's] *The End of the Affair* is a far better film than [Scott Hicks's] *Snow Falling on Cedars* is that Graham Greene is a better writer than David Guterson'.[44] This formula implies an unfettered pluralism in suggesting that it is possible to produce identical aesthetic effects in different media. (As usual, readers and viewers are absent from his analysis.) The narratives of both Greene's *The End of the Affair* and Jordan's make use of this convention when Bendrix and Sarah attend a film adapted from one of his novels. Bendrix insists that what they see on the screen is not what he wrote, but Sarah manages to pick out the one scene that *is* what he wrote. This sequence comes at the very beginning of their relationship, before they have spoken at length with one another, much less slept together. The narrative uses the sheer unlikelihood of the incident to economically invest the relationship with an uncanny depth in the eyes of the audience. But this convention works only if the audience agrees that the aesthetic pluralism it invokes is implausible. Kauffmann objected to Jordan's inclusion of this sequence in the film as 'sheer gall' since he believed the film was manifestly *not* what Greene wrote—an accurate enough observation that ironically seems to fail to take into account the fact that Greene did *not* write Jordan's film.[45]

Admirers of Jordan's adaptation celebrated the film for many of the same reasons its detractors derided it. Fr. Robert E. Lauder's praise was perhaps the most effusive, and so serves as a fitting counterpart to Kauffmann's acerbic reading: 'Blessings on Neil Jordan! For various reasons, distinguished directors such as Fritz Lang, Carol Reed and Otto Preminger could not pull off what Jordan has now accomplished: He's made an exciting film from a Graham Greene novel that captures not only its setting but its substance.'[46] Lauder argues that Jordan has at last 'put Greeneland and God together on the screen' by following Greene's lead and 'depict[ing] sexual love as a movement toward divine love'.[47] For him, there is no question of too much flesh transforming the specificity of individuals into the universals of copulation; in fact, he even goes so far as to suggest that Greene's prior mixed fortunes on the screen stemmed from over-rigorous censorship laws, rather than incompetent directors. Although Lauder deplores the rarity of God's guest appearances on the cinema screens of 'our secular age', his argument implies that the secularization of cinematic mores has given Jordan the latitude to give God His cameo in the film. Lauder unsurprisingly draws the same conclusion from the film that many critics drew from the novel, that 'Bendrix will not escape, no matter down what labyrinthine ways he flees, that even his hatred of God will open up space for grace.'[48] Philip French concurred despite minor reservations about Jordan's changes, suggesting that '*The End of the Affair* is about the novelist as God, and God as a novelist who gives his characters free will. It's about faith, transcendence and the possibility of sainthood in the modern world.'[49]

All of these readings help illustrate the extent to which—and the direction in which—intellectual priorities and reading practices have diverged from the public's. The Brighton interlude in Jordan's film is a primary example. Although the sequence does not appear in the novel, and although it suggests the implausibility of some of the interpretations critics have offered of the novel, it also helps draw to the reader's attention aspects of the novel which have hitherto been neglected. One insists that the Brighton interlude is a travesty—or worse, a heresy—not only because it shows Sarah reneging on her promise to God, but also because it allows Jordan to show the viewer the unlikely spectacle of a happy Bendrix, thus reinforcing for the viewer the extra-personal costs Sarah's vow has extracted from those she ostensibly loves over the years that she has managed to preserve it intact. It forces the nonintellectual viewer to consider God from a pragmatic perspective: what is the 'cash value' of a belief in God? What effect does such a belief have on the possibility of human happiness? The intellectual viewer has difficulty apprehending this interpretive crux because Jordan presents Bendrix's happiness in highly conventional images: Sarah sleeping beside Bendrix on the train to Brighton, the lovers arm-in-arm on a carnival ride, and walking together beneath the boardwalk. Whether he follows the Leavises or Derrida, the modern intellectual generally looks upon convention with suspicion, and elects to view conventional material as signifying nothing rather than as an invitation to participate in the social construction of textual meaning. This bias prompts Kauffmann to suggest that the 'place that Greene gave ... spiritual elements ... is simply left empty' in Jordan's film.[50] The pursuit of human relationships does not provide, for Kauffmann as for DeVitis, Allott, and others, an adequate alternative to Sarah's fundamentally anti-social beatification—an interpretation he insists on attributing to Greene despite the glaring ambiguity of Bendrix's final 'conversion'.

French, by contrast, defends the film on the grounds that Jordan simply continues the process of rewriting that Greene undertook for the Collected Edition. Jordan 'makes things easier for rationalists in the audience', he argues: '...by conflating the characters of Smythe and the fearsome Father Crompton into a single, benevolent priest (though retaining the name Smythe), and transferring the birthmark from the atheist to the private detective's schoolboy son, thus reducing the number of miracles...'[51] It seems likely that Greene began amending his work for the Collected Edition on the very grounds outlined by Davis above: miracles had simply ceased to work their magic on popular audiences. It seems quite likely that Jordan would have also recognized the alienating effect a plethora of miracles would have had on his own audience. And it seems almost certain that the Columbia Pictures 'suits' would have vetoed a film that did not appeal in some way to the rationalists in the audience—particularly prior to the box office phenomenon of Mel Gibson's *The Passion of the Christ* (2004). Nonetheless, French, like Kauffmann, insists on viewing the film as a translation (albeit a more successful one) rather than as an interpretation.

Few reviewers of the film expressed reservations about its literary source—a striking fact, given the ambiguity of the response that greeted *The End of the Affair* when it was first published. In 1973, Davis might have felt that the novel's Catholic tropes 'dated' the novel; by 1999, however, contemporaneity had ceased to be the measure by which Greene's novels were judged, and the Catholic tropes he employed had been pressed into service by his critics as the imprimatur by which the work of the master could be recognized. As the response to Jordan's film demonstrates, recognition—rather than, say, analysis—was the foremost critical operation performed on Greene's work. Postmodernity's celebration of popular art made it difficult to ignore Greene's fiction, but its liberal outlook and tendency to pursue pluralism to the point of paralysis rendered engagement with the work nearly impossible. As a result, Greene's work has tended to attract particular types of critics: those who reject postmodernity and post-structuralist discourse (often on religious or quasi-religious grounds), those who belong in one way or another to the cult of the auteur, and, of course, people like Jordan, for whom the experience of reading Greene is not tantamount to an exercise in intellectual orthodoxy.

The End of the Affair and *The Quiet American* were challenging works when they were published in the early 1950s. They remain so today, although the themes they address and the engagement they demand of their readers have rendered them unpalatable to the discourses presently favored by the cultural establishment. The texts force their readers to confront difficult, often unpalatable truths about humanity's potential and shortcomings—but such truths are no longer in vogue. Despite a brief resurgence after September 11's forceful reminder that society is ignored only at one's peril, *The Quiet American* has returned to its former status as a Baedeker for the hardier type of investment banker. *The End of the Affair* continues to be read by scholars who have an interest in orthodox Catholic theology, despite the challenge the novel poses to metaphysicians of all stripes. The work's brief reappearance on the public stage served mostly to remind people that geniuses are not to be taken lightly—an exhortation that serves admirably as a summary of the idea most contemporary Greene criticism communicates. Thirty years after the Collected Edition it seems that 'a better case' remains to be made for Greene's work.

Conclusion: The Problem of a 'Better Case'

Graham Greene is hardly the only author for whom a better case could be made. As Mary McCarthy noted in the mid-1940s, he is the sort of writer whose books intellectuals keep on their nightstand and read before going to bed and in this respect he is hardly alone.[1] Hammett, Chandler, James Hadley Chase, Elmore Leonard, Mickey Spillane, John le Carré, Len Deighton, Joseph Wambaugh, and James Ellroy (to name just a few of the more prominent writers who have languished at greater or lesser lengths in the same generic ghettos as Greene) would all benefit from closer inspection—less because scholarly analysis would assist readers to understand the significance of these authors' novels as for the light such analyses might shed on the tastes, biases, and prejudices readers bring to their experience of texts.

Several of the small number of scholarly analyses of le Carré begin with the same sort of qualification encountered again and again in Greene criticism—save that the touchstone testifying to le Carré's purity of purpose *is* Greene:

> ... le Carré has developed as a writer much the same way Graham Greene did in the 1930s and 1940s. Like Greene in his thrillers, le Carré in his novels has, within the limits of the genre, increasingly attempted to use the spy story to say something about larger human and social issues.[2]

The scholar still conceives of genre as a straightjacket that invariably prevents the writer from producing genuine 'art', or as a checklist of conventions that must be relentlessly ticked off one by one and which invariably prevents the writer from producing genuine 'art'. To the intellectual, the good spy novelist (and Richard Nolan, like Ben Ray Redman

213

discussing Greene 50 years before him, does not deny that le Carré is in fact a *very good* spy novelist) 'uses' the genre in order to say something about larger human issues—but why is this the case when spy novels clearly do say something about larger human and social issues? When every page, every passage, and every event related in a 'spy' novel depends for its success on appealing to readers' fears and desires (and not simply those they learn by reading Shakespeare) how is it possible to maintain the pretence that 'the need...for technical detail and mystery-suspense [detracts] from the exploration of character'?[3]

Spy novels—and particularly popular spy novels—clearly explore character as deeply as *Hamlet*, *Ulysses*, or *To The Lighthouse*. But they do not necessarily do so explicitly on the page, through the naturalistic treatment of the physical world, or by representing the tortured syntax of the contemporary psyche. Although they may do any of these (and although an 'artistic' text may do none of them), they are not obliged to because the characters they most consistently probe are their readers'. What will the readers believe, what do they desire, to what will they consent or object, what will make them recoil, what will engage their curiosity and make them want to turn the page are just a few of the problems to which writers who manage to produce popular fiction have furnished adequate solutions. They are also problems that many writers of so-called literature have failed to solve successfully, or else have wilfully declined to address. They write (or believe they write) for an audience of one. In Harold Bloom's words (and also Milton's) 'They know no time when they were not as they are now; self-created, self-begot, their puissance is their own.'[4]

But, Bloom continues, 'As assertions by poets, playwrights, and prose fiction-writers, these are healthy and understandable, however self-deluded. But as declarations by supposed literary critics, such optimistic pronouncements go against both human nature and the nature of imaginative literature.'[5] The vicissitudes of the literary profession in the 1950s arguably rendered such declarations necessary for those critics interested in facilitating Greene's entry into intellectual discourse, just as the vicissitudes of the profession circa 1980 apparently continued to make such declarations necessary in order to discuss le Carré. Both writers had clearly solved the problem of what the public feared and desired, but their manifest popularity has made it difficult to maintain the pretence that they were self-begotten without doing violence to the texts they each produced. This has nonetheless been the substance of the case that has been made for Greene and other so-called 'popular writers' so far: in making his symbolic move the intellectual uses his rhetorical skill to transform the popular writer into an unpopular one—that is, an author or *auteur*.

It remains to be seen whether a better case will be made for Greene because it remains to be seen whether the institutional conditions will arise that might enable a better case to be made. For how precisely should a scholar interpret 'a better case'? Will a better case have been made for Greene if his work can be made to support deconstruction- ist, new historicist, feminist, and Lacanian psychoanalytic readings? The problem here is that the work can already sustain these readings. Will a better case for Greene be the argument that finally encourages deconstructionists, new historicists, feminists, and Lacanians to offer readings of Greene's work? The problem here is that such an argu- ment, aimed at changing opinions, would necessarily fall outside the customary limitations of academic discourse.

In fact, any case made explicitly 'for' Greene would necessarily involve valorizing some particular aspect of his work—its contemporaneity, its use of thriller conventions, its existential engagement, and so forth— in order to make visible Greene's unique personality and the fashion in which he brought it to bear on the manipulation of conventional material. Such a case would reinforce an ideology of Greene (to para- phrase Louis Althusser) rather than a knowledge of his work.[6] A rupture with the language of 'ideological spontaneity' that has hitherto char- acterized both pronouncements on Greene and approaches to his work seems necessary.

A rigorous course of historicization could help produce such a rupture. By treating Greene as a producer rather than as a 'creator' it becomes possible 'to conceive of the artist as a worker rooted in a particular his- tory with particular materials at his disposal'.[7] With several exceptions, psycho-biographical criticism has tended to produce and reproduce figures of Greene the creator (or, in the terminology used here, the auteur) that sit easily within the dominant scheme of canonical dis- courses; it has demonstrated little inclination to assess this figure—or rather, the plethora of such figures that exist in different interpretive communities—as a functional component of the reading process (as in Peter Rabinowitz's formulation of the authorial audience).[8] By sit- uating these authorial figures in their historical contexts the scholar may better apprehend the raw materials Greene worked with (language, genre, assumptions, expectations, biases, and so on), the products he produced (i.e., books and texts), and the dialectical relationship between the processes of production and the processes of consumption. Only then may the critic 'seek out the conflict of meanings' at work in a text and 'show how this conflict is produced by the work's relation to ideology'.[9]

In theory, these measures could lead out from the texts into the lived relations between texts, readers, and ideologies rather than inward toward the ultimately inscrutable mind of the auteur; in practice, they could lead to a reassessment of different aspects of Greene's work, as well as consideration of works that have eluded scholarly attention. *The Heart of the Matter*, for instance, has often been read in light of its explicitly theological content to the exclusion of its form or other considerations. Is Scobie—or Greene—damned or saved? Of course it is impossible to say; this has not, however, prevented several generations of critics from attempting to do so, although their efforts tend to cast more light on their own peccadilloes than on the narrative, its characters, or its writer—much less its readers. But by historicizing the dialectical relationship between textual production and reception scholars can estrange and re-interrogate even the most shop-worn tropes in Greene criticism. What, for instance, does a writer's ability to successfully situate a theological problem in the middle of a domestic farce tell one about the status of faith in the postwar world for which he wrote? How has the changing status of faith in the second half of the twentieth century influenced the reading strategies brought to bear on the text since its publication? How do these reading strategies embody, reflect, or contest deeper ideological trends in society at large?

The gravitational pull exerted by Greene's explicitly Catholic novels has prevented many critics from entering the orbit of the comedies (or at least of the comic sensibility that circulates through many of the novels), possibly because these novels sit uneasily beside the easy assumptions Greene's 'serious' novels have been made to reinforce. Readers, however, appear to have had an easier time assimilating their expectations to the comedy—often quite black—of novels like *Our Man in Havana* and *Travels With My Aunt*. Rare is the London or New York bookshop that lacks for a copy of either; rarer still, however, is the scholar who poses the question, 'Why did people find them funny (or mildly amusing, or entertaining, or persuasive) and why do they continue to do so?' To what sorts of attitudes do the characters, situations, and narratives in these novels appeal? Is the laughter they help produce nostalgic, subversive, both, or neither? Has the quality or quantity of this laughter altered over time? If it has, then to what shifts in attitudes or relationships to the dominant ideology can this alteration be attributed? If it has not, then is it possible to draw conclusions concerning the relationship between comedy and the status quo? The deeper one delves into how readers realize the effects of the novels through historically contingent reading strategies, the closer one gets to precisely the sort of 'theoretical speculation' that Alan Warren Friedman found conspicuously lacking in the critical record.[10]

Realistically, however, the prospect of contemporary scholars spontaneously beginning to use Greene's work in order to problematize the mechanics of literature, gender regimes, psychology, and ideology seems an unlikely one. Having acquired a reputation, that reputation now weighs heavily on the uses to which Greene's work may be put. When, for instance, Gerard Genette wanted to produce a study of narrative discourse he chose to focus his analysis on a writer, Proust, who had taken the act of narrating for his subject and who—more importantly—was widely recognized as having taken the act of narrating as his subject by the sort of readers who might have been interested in the discursivity of narrative.[11] One of the few studies that specifically attempted to use Greene's work in a vaguely theoretical way was Bruce Merry's *Anatomy of the Spy Thriller*, which (as its title suggests) furnished precisely the sort of taxonomy of semantic and syntactic elements that enabled a critic like Nolan to ultimately dismiss le Carré on the grounds that 'In even the most meaningfully charged spy novel, I suspect, plot and fable will always dominate the mimetic exploration of character' despite the writer's success 'within the built-in limitations of that genre'.[12] The intellectual 'case for le Carré', of course, is that he may be better than the spy novel—a strange argument, given that he writes novels about spies; naturally, then, the ultimate criterion for le Carré's value (as an author) would have to come from somewhere other than the writer's work—presumably from his personality.

The research undertaken for this study suggests that most popular contemporary writers who manage to find their way into the intellectual discourse tend to proceed through an auteurist stage in which the public's understanding of the writer in question is shown to be lacking in some substantial way: it has failed to appreciate the strength of the author's personality, or the way that the work undermines 'stock responses'. The auteurist scholar then demonstrates how the work in question communicates difficulties, subtleties, and complexities of which 'the masses' had remained blissfully ignorant. As this study has argued, the difficulties revealed in Greene's work during this stage in the evolution of his reputation do not continue to excite the intellectual avant-garde. It tends to prefer work that wears its difficulty more openly: Proust, Joyce, Beckett, and, more recently, Thomas Pynchon, Salman Rushdie, and Jonathan Franzen (at least in his own self-estimation) are its avatars. Why, one wonders, do writers like these so rarely stand accused of allowing 'technical detail' to detract from 'the exploration of character'? Presumably because the character intellectuals feel most comfortable discussing is the author's, and the writer whose work stands apart from the crowd through its use of an idiosyncratic style or technique seems to confirm that he is 'self-begotten'. As Rabinowitz has persuasively argued, intellectuals tend to prefer texts that are not quite closed (as they presume popular texts to be) but which require the application of institutionally ordained rules of coherence in order to make them meaningful.[13] For them, the popular novel seems overdetermined, its meaning too obvious; they prefer the sort of work that manifests an ambiguity that their special skills as professional readers can help clarify. In a sense this is only natural—an expedient response to professional demands. It is far easier to 'do things' (i.e., deconstruct, historicize, and so on) to a text that 'asserts that its puissance is its own' (in other words, by being recognizably irregular) than it is to do those same things to a text that does little to declare its independence from conventional understanding.

The best case that can be made for Greene, then, is that no case needs to be made for him—or for le Carré or for any of the other authors mentioned above. If anything, a better case needs to be made for literature and the fetishization of the individual talent implied by the concept of literature that has prevailed in the academy since the Leavises helped professionalize the study of vernacular fiction and legitimize the discipline's claim to institutional status. Dan Brown's quasi-theologial conspiracy thriller, *The Da Vinci Code*, sold 2,893,284 copies within 14 months of publication in the United Kingdom.[14] One out of every 20 people in the country owned the book within 14 months of its debut. Many of those copies—particularly those acquired by public libraries— have been read by more than one person. If a scholar wanted to know something about 'human and social issues' in the United Kingdom in the twenty-first century, would he be better off reading and analyzing *The Da Vinci Code* or the complex work of a self-begotten author with a limited readership? Likewise, if a scholar wanted to know something about human and social issues in 1932, would he better off watching *Grand Hotel* or reading Q.D. Leavis? Ideally he should do both, but in the contemporary, post-Birmingham academy he may well face censure for reading *The Da Vinci Code* or watching *Grand Hotel* unless he makes it clear that these works have somehow been misunderstood by the publics that made them popular phenomena, or unless, at the very least, he communicates a sense of how these texts truly belong to 'the margins'. In other words, unless he rejects *a priori* the very qualities that could make such a reading profitable he may well encounter difficulty in reaching an intellectual audience.

Unless a better case can be made for literature, the study of English will continue to privilege the individual, the exception, the exaggeration, the marginal, the ignored, the eccentric, and the antiquated to the exclusion of fiction to which the public actually responds. Whether the public will continue to support such an institution in a political and economic climate that favors pragmatism is, of course, an open question. Nostalgia may sustain it indefinitely, or else the gaping divide between what it is possible and desirable to say in academic discourse and what it is possible and desirable to say in public discourse may prompt a serious contraction (as Bloom has predicted, for rather different reasons than those proposed here). Should the former happen, there is no reason to make a better case for Greene than the auteurists have already made: the valorization of Greene's personality, however delusional, will at least not be at odds with the discipline's valorization of the individual talent, and will in no way hamper the discipline's institutional role in reproducing the relations of production under late capitalism. Should the latter happen, of course, the discipline's discourse will become irrelevant and no better case will have to be made for Greene or for any other putatively popular writer. I.A. Richards's psychological theory of value might have helped ensconce the study of fiction in the academy, but it now appears that only by realizing the 'sinister potentialities' of Richards's nightmare ('the transvaluation by which popular taste replaces trained discrimination') can the contemporary intellectual hope to make the case for literature on which its survival depends.[15] Reading Greene's work (as well as the work of le Carré, Brown, Cecilia Ahern, and, indeed, Pynchon and Rushdie) as a communicative act realized between parties that share a language—rather than as the expression of a unique personality, or as the more or less explicit attempt to join some elite artistic or intellectual cartel—might serve as a useful starting point.

Notes

Introduction: The politics of reading Greene

1. David Lodge, *Graham Greene* (New York: Columbia University Press, 1966) 3.
2. Ibid. 5.
3. Whenever possible I have used the plural 'readers'; where clarity has favored the use of the singular 'reader', I have referred to this entity with the masculine pronoun 'he', principally because the reader I know best is also—perhaps unfortunately—a 'he'.
4. Roger Sharrock, *Saints, Sinners and Comedians* (Tunbridge Wells: Burns & Oates, 1984) 11.
5. Dan Cryer, 'Graham Greene at 100', *New York Newsday* (2 November 2004) B2.
6. Robert Hoskins, *Graham Greene: An Approach to the Novels* (New York: Garland Publishing, Inc., 1999) 139.
7. Peter Mudford, *Graham Greene* (Plymouth: Northcote House in association with the British Council, 1996) 7.
8. See Heyward Brock and James M. Welsh, 'Graham Greene and the structure of salvation', *Renascence* (Autumn 1974) 32–39; A.A. DeVitis, 'Religious aspects in the novels of Graham Greene', *The Shapeless God*, edited by Harry J. Mooney, Jr. and Thomas F. Staley (Pittsburgh: University of Pittsburgh Press, 1968) 41–65; Wm. Thomas Hill, *Perceptions of Religious Faith in the Work of Graham Greene* (Oxford: Peter Lang, 2002).
9. See John A. Stotesbury, 'Metropolitan space in Graham Greene's *The End of the Affair*', *London in Literature: Visionary Mappings of the Metropolis*, edited by Susana Onega and John A. Stotesbury (Heidelberg: Universitätsverlag, 2002) 118; Henry Shapiro, 'The infidel Greene: Radical ambiguity in *Our Man in Havana*', *Essays in Greene*, edited by Peter Wolfe (Greenwood: Penkevill Publishing, 1987) 83–98; Martin Turnell, 'Graham Greene: The man within', *Ramparts* (June 1965) 54–64.
10. See Cates Baldridge, *Graham Greene: The Virtues of Extremity* (Columbia: University of Missouri Press, 2000); Satnam Kaur, *Graham Greene: An Existentialist Investigation* (Amritsar: Guru Nanak Dev University Press, 1988); Anne T. Salvatore, 'Graham Greene, Soren Kierkegaard, and the discourse of belief', dissertation, Temple University, *DAI* 46 (1985) 699.
11. See Judith Adamson, *Graham Greene: The Dangerous Edge* (London: Macmillan, 1990); Bruce Bawer, 'Baseless dreaming: The novels of Graham Greene', *New Criterion* (September 1989) 17–33.
12. See Amporn Amaracheewa, 'Graham Greene's paradoxical views of morality: The nature of sin', dissertation, Bowling Greene State University, *DAI* 43 (1983) 2343; Doreen D'Cruz, 'The pursuit of selfhood in the novels of Graham Greene', dissertation, University of Michigan, *DAI* 41 (1980) 2093; Kathleen Behrenbruch Hindman, 'The ambiance of Graham Greene's fiction: The functions of milieu in his novels', dissertation, Pennsylvania

State University, *DAI* 41 (1980) 2122; William Thomas Hill, 'The search for dwelling and its relationship to journeying and wandering in the novels of Graham Greene', dissertation, University of Nebraska, *DAI* 54 (1994) 4101; Adam John Schwartz, 'The third spring: Roman Catholic conversion and rebellion against modernity', dissertation, Northwestern University, *DAI* 57 (1997) 4890; Valerie Frances Sedlak, 'From the religious dimension to the spiritual vision in the novels of Graham Greene', dissertation, University of Pennsylvania, *DAI* 53 (1993) 2384; Richard Stephen Vogel, 'Avenues to faith: Encountering God in the fiction of Graham Greene and Walker Percy', dissertation, St. John's University, *DAI* 57 (1996) 223.

13. See Brian Diemert, *Graham Greene's Thrillers and the 1930s* (Montreal: McGill-Queens University, 1996); and Elliott Malamet, *The World Remade* (New York: Peter Lang, 1998).
14. Wayne Booth, *The Rhetoric of Fiction* (Chicago: University of Chicago Press, 1961) 90.
15. Diemert, *Graham Greene's Thrillers and the 1930s* 181.
16. Damon Marcel DeCoste, 'Modernism's shell-shocked history', *Twentieth Century Literature* (Winter 1999) 430.
17. John Coates, 'Experimenting with genre: Greene and The Confidential Agent', *Renascence* (Fall 2002) 46–64.
18. Brian Thomas, *An Underground Fate: The Idiom of Romance in the Later Novels of Graham Greene* (Athens: University of Georgia Press, 1988).
19. See Thomas Wendorf, 'Greene, Tolkien and the mysterious relations of realism and fantasy', *Renascence* (Fall 2002) 78–100.
20. John Kenneth Galbraith, *The Affluent Society* (Middlesex: Penguin, 1958) 107–20.
21. Norman Sherry, *The Life of Graham Greene, Volume Three* (London: Jonathan Cape, 2004) 804. See also: Andrew Gumbel, 'The end of the affair', *The Independent* (22 September 2004) Review, 2–3.
22. See Miranda France, 'A burnt-out case', *Guardian* (9 October 2004); Gumbel, 'The end of the affair' 2–3; Paul Theroux, 'Damned old Graham Greene', *New York Times Book Review* (17 October 2004) 1.
23. Janice Radway, *Reading the Romance* (Chapel Hill: University of North Carolina Press, 1984) 190. [Emphases in the original]
24. John Spurling, *Graham Greene* (London: Methuen, 1983) 53.
25. Ibid. 50.
26. See Booth, *The Rhetoric of Fiction* 89–116.
27. Michel Foucault, 'What is an author?', *The Critical Tradition*, 2nd Edition, edited by David Richter (Boston: Bedford, 1998) 895.
28. For a full discussion of the ideological ramifications of this practice, see Mary-Louise Pratt, 'Ideology and speech-act theory', *The Stylistics Reader*, edited by Jean-Jacques Weber (London: Arnold, 1996) 181–93.
29. V.V.B. Rama Rao, *Graham Greene's Comic Vision* (New Delhi: Reliance Publishing House, 1990) 96–99.
30. Miriam Allott, 'Graham Greene and the way we live now', *Critical Quarterly* (Autumn 1978) 9.
31. See John Atkins, *Graham Greene* (London: Calder and Boyars, 1966); and Michael Shelden, *Graham Greene: The Man Within* (London: Minerva, 1994).

32. Neil Sinyard, *Graham Greene: A Literary Life* (Hampshire: Palgrave Macmillan, 2003) 11.
33. Fredric Jameson, *The Political Unconscious* (London: Routledge, 2002) 70–71.
34. Malamet, *The World Remade* 1.
35. Peter Rabinowitz, *Before Reading* (Ithaca: Cornell University Press, 1987) 20–29.
36. Ibid. 32.
37. See Eric Hobsbawm, *Age of Extremes* (London: Abacus, 1994) 257–86.
38. See E.M. Forster, *Aspects of the Novel* (London: Penguin, 2000) 28–30.
39. Terry Eagleton, *Literary Theory: An Introduction* (Minneapolis: University of Minnesota Press, 1983) 31.
40. See I.A. Richards, *Principles of Literary Criticism* (London: Routledge, 2001) 39–51.
41. Reynolds Price, Review of *The Honorary Consul*, by Graham Greene, *New York Times Book Review* (9 September 1973) 1.
42. See David Pryce-Jones, *Graham Greene* (Edinburgh: Oliver and Boyd, 1963); and David Pryce-Jones, 'Graham Cracker', *New Republic* (23 January 1989) 28–31.
43. Louis Althusser, 'Ideology and the state', *Lenin and Philosophy*, translated by Ben Brewster (New York: Monthly Review Press, 1971) 148–59.
44. See Robert Murray Davis, 'From standard to classic: Graham Greene in transition', *Studies in the Novel* (Winter 1973) 530–46; Alan Warren Friedman, 'The status of Greene studies', *Library Chronicle of the University of Texas at Austin* (1991) 36–67.
45. 'Third Man tops British film charts', *BBC News* (23 September 1999) http://news.bbc.co.uk/1/hi/entertainment/454744.stm.
46. See Bruce Bawer, 'Graham Greene: The Catholic novels', *New Criterion* (2 October 1989) 24–32; and Pryce-Jones, 'Graham Cracker' 28–31.
47. Stuart Hall, 'The rediscovery of ideology', *Literary Theory: An Anthology* (Oxford: Blackwell, 1998) 1050.
48. Robert Young, 'The idea of a Chrestomatic University', quoted in *The Rise and Fall of English*, by Robert Scholes (New Haven: Yale University Press, 1998) 45.

1. Institutional and critical priorities at the beginning of Graham Greene's career

1. Stanley Unwin, *The Truth About Publishing*, 8th Edition (London: George Allen and Unwin, 1976) 114.
2. Q.D. Leavis, *Fiction and the Reading Public* (London: Bellew, 1990).
3. Richards, *Principles* 55.
4. John Carey, *The Intellectuals and the Masses* (London: Faber and Faber, 1992) 218.
5. Noam Chomsky and Edward Herman, *Manufacturing Consent* (London: Vintage, 1994) 4.
6. See James Curran, 'Advertising and the press', *The British Press*, edited by James Curran (London: Macmillan, 1978) 229–67.

7. Leavis, *Fiction* 163.
8. Ibid. 161.
9. F.R. Mumby and Ian Norrie, *Publishing and Bookselling*, 5th Edition (London: Jonathan Cape, 1974) 274.
10. Ibid. 406.
11. Robert Graves and Alan Hodge, *The Long Week-end* (London: Faber and Faber, 1941) 58–59.
12. Leavis, *Fiction* 202.
13. A.J.P. Taylor, *English History: 1914–1945* (Oxford: Oxford University Press, 1965) 308.
14. Graves and Hodge, *Week-end* 212.
15. Forster, *Aspects of the Novel* 28–29.
16. Taylor, *English History* 2.
17. Ibid. 286.
18. J.M. Keynes, 'The Great Slump of 1930 Part II', *Nation and Athenaeum* (27 December 1930) 427.
19. Leavis, *Fiction* 270.
20. F.R. Leavis, *Mass Civilization and Minority Culture* (Cambridge: Minority Press, 1930) 3.
21. F.R. Leavis, 'From *The Great Tradition*', *The Critical Tradition*, 2nd Edition, edited by David Richter (Boston: Bedford, 1932) 263.
22. Leavis, *Fiction* 272.
23. Richards, *Principles* 32.
24. Eagleton, *Literary Theory* 31.
25. Jonathan Culler, *The Pursuit of Signs* (Ithaca: Cornell University Press, 1981) 3.
26. Ibid. 4.
27. Leavis, *Fiction* 185.
28. Sir Henry Newbolt, Board of Education of Great Britain, and the Committee on English in the Educational System of England, *The Teaching of English in England* (London: HM Stationery Office, 1921) 21.
29. Ibid. 21–22.
30. Ibid. 259.
31. John Guillory, *Cultural Capital* (Chicago: University of Chicago Press, 1993) 13.
32. Raymond Williams, *Culture and Society* (London: Hogarth Press, 1993) 257–58.
33. Newbolt 205. Newbolt writes: 'Great literature is only partly the reflection of a particular year or generation: it is also a timeless thing, which can never become old-fashioned or out of date, or depend for its importance upon historical considerations.'
34. Rabinowitz, *Before Reading* 7.
35. Richards, *Principles* 189.
36. Leavis, *Mass Civilization* 9.
37. Leavis, 'From *The Great Tradition*' in Richter 606.
38. T.S. Eliot, 'Tradition and the individual talent', *The Critical Tradition*, 2nd Edition, edited by David Richter (Boston: Bedford, 1998) 500.
39. Rabinowitz, *Before Reading* 146.

2. The failed novelist

1. Sharrock, *Saints* 11.
2. Bartlet Brebner, 'Promise almost fulfilled', review of *The Man Within*, by Graham Greene, *Saturday Review of Literature* (19 October 1929) 287.
3. Florence Codman, review of *The Man Within*, by Graham Greene, *The Nation* (23 October 1929) 468.
4. 'Doubleday, Doran Discoveries!', advertisement for *The Man Within*, by Graham Greene, *New York Herald Tribune Books* (20 October 1929) 23.
5. Norman Sherry, *The Life of Graham Greene, Volume One* (London: Jonathan Cape, 1989) 366.
6. Review of *The Man Within*, by Graham Greene, *Times Literary Supplement* (20 June 1929) 492.
7. *TLS* (20 June 1929) 492.
8. Graham Greene, *The Name of Action* (London: William Heinemann, 1930) 328.
9. Katherine Tomlinson, review of *The Name of Action*, by Graham Greene, *The Nation and Athenaeum* (15 November 1930) 242.
10. Ibid. 242.
11. Edith H. Walton, 'An unusual tale by Graham Greene', review of *The Name of Action*, by Graham Greene, *New York Times* (8 March 1931) 7.
12. Sherry, *Volume One* 384.
13. Graham Greene, *Rumour at Nightfall* (London: William Heinemann, 1931) 30, 31.
14. Review of *Rumour at Nightfall*, by Graham Greene, *Spectator* (26 December 1931) 892.
15. Review of *Rumour at Nightfall*, by Graham Greene, *The New Republic* (27 April 1932) 308.
16. Greene, *Rumour* 203.
17. Graham Greene, *A Sort of Life* (London: Vintage, 1999) 150.
18. Kenneth Allott and Miriam Farris, *The Art of Graham Greene* (New York: Russell and Russell, 1951) 74.
19. Greene, *A Sort of Life* 151.
20. Review of *Rumour at Nightfall*, by Graham Greene, *The Nation* (18 May 1932) 578.
21. F.R. Leavis, *Mass Civilization* 19.
22. Review of *Rumour at Nightfall*, by Graham Greene, *Times Literary Supplement* (3 December 1931) 978.
23. Leavis, *Fiction* 156.
24. Forster 87.
25. Ibid. 86–87.
26. Richards, *Principles* 55.
27. Graham Greene, *Ways of Escape* (London: Vintage, 1999) 26.
28. Graham Greene, 'Servants of the novel', review of *The Popular Novel in England*, by J.M.S. Tomkins, *Collected Essays* (London: Vintage, 1999) 76–77.
29. See Allott and Farris, *The Art of Graham Greene*.
30. Atkins, *Graham Greene* 30.

31. See Hans Robert Jauss, 'From *Literary History as a Challenge to Literary Theory*', *The Critical Tradition*, 2nd Edition, edited by David Richter (Boston: Bedford, 1998) 942–45.
32. Rabinowitz, *Before Reading* 21.
33. Jameson, *Political Unconscious* 70–71.
34. Walter Lippmann, *Public Opinion* (New York: Free Press, 1922) 147.
35. Carey, *Intellectuals and the Masses* 20.
36. Rabinowitz, *Before Reading* 16.
37. Umberto Eco, 'Narrative structures in Fleming', *The Role of the Reader* (Bloomington: Indiana University Press, 1984) 162.
38. Jameson, *Political Unconscious* 131–32.
39. See Greene, *Ways of Escape* 26. 'Before I had completed the book, Marlene Dietrich had appeared in *Shanghai Express*, the English had made *Rome Express*, and even the Russians had produced their railway film, *Turksib*.'

3. Readers and generic processes in *Stamboul Train*

1. John Buchan, *The Thirty-Nine Steps* (London: Penguin, 1994) 5–15.
2. Graham Greene, *Stamboul Train* (Middlesex: Penguin, 1979) 37.
3. Ibid. 35.
4. Ibid. 64.
5. Ibid. 69.
6. Ibid. 95.
7. Richards, *Principles* 47.
8. Greene, *Stamboul Train* 9.
9. Ibid. 11.
10. Ibid. 12.
11. Ibid. 30.
12. Ibid. 24.
13. Ibid. 32.
14. Ibid. 47.
15. Ibid. 134–35.
16. Ibid. 161–62.

4. Cinema as a strategy of containment

1. Ben Ray Redman, 'Chance acquaintances', review of *Stamboul Train*, by Graham Greene, *Saturday Review of Literature* (18 March 1933) 489.
2. Anne Armstrong, review of *Stamboul Train*, by Graham Greene, *Saturday Review* (24 December 1932) 673.
3. Ibid.
4. Redman, 'Chance acquaintances' 489.
5. Review of *Orient Express*, by Graham Greene, *New York Times* (12 March 1933) 21.
6. Redman, 'Chance acquaintances' 489.
7. Robert McKee, *Story* (New York: HarperCollins, 1997) 367.
8. Atkins, *Graham Greene* 30.
9. Allott and Farris, *The Art of Graham Greene* 84.

10. Ibid.
11. Diemert, *Graham Greene's Thrillers and the 1930s* 54.
12. V.S. Pritchett, 'A modern mind', review of *It's a Battlefield*, by Graham Greene, *Spectator* (9 February 1934) 206.
13. Ibid.
14. Seymour Chatman, 'What novels can do that films can't (and vice versa)', *Film Theory and Criticism*, 5th edition, edited by Leo Braudy and Marshall Co-en (Oxford: Oxford University Press, 1999) 440.
15. Pritchett, 'Modern mind' 206.

5. Cinematic evasions after *Stamboul Train*

1. For example, see review of *It's a Battlefield*, by Graham Greene, *New York Times* (8 April 1934) 7; N.L. Rothman, 'Greene atmosphere', review of *The Ministry of Fear*, by Graham Greene, *Saturday Review of Literature* (26 June 1943) 11; Anne Fremantle, 'In pursuit of peace', review of *The End of the Affair*, by Graham Greene, *Saturday Review* (27 October 1951) 11. For more contemporary takes on Greene's association with the 'cinematic technique', see Bernard Bergonzi, *Reading the Thirties* (London: Macmillan, 1978) 145; Richard Kelly, *Graham Greene* (New York: Frederick Ungar Publishing, 1984) 11; Sinyard, *Graham Greene* 42–57; Thomas, *Underground xiv*.
2. Atkins, *Graham Greene* 78.
3. Ibid.74.
4. Ibid.
5. For example, see Christine De Vinne, 'Truth and falsehoods in the metaphors of Graham Greene', *English Studies* (5 October 1993) 445–50; Gene Kellogg, *The Vital Tradition: The Catholic Novel in a Period of Convergence* (Chicago: Loyola University Press, 1970) 111–36; and Kelly, *Graham Greene* 113–44.
6. Virginia Woolf, *To The Lighthouse* (Hertfordshire: Wordsworth, 2002) 3.
7. Graham Greene, *It's a Battlefield* (London: Vintage, 2002) 18.
8. Ibid. 28.
9. Allott and Farris, *The Art of Graham Greene* 84.
10. Sherry, *Volume One* 461.
11. See Stephen Moss, 'Ouch', *The Guardian* (11 October 2004) G2, 7.
12. See Marshall McLuhan, *Understanding Media* (London: Routledge, 2001), for a discussion of the difference between hot and cool media.
13. Graham Greene, *Brighton Rock* (Middlesex: Penguin, 1970) 165.
14. Review of *Brighton Rock*, by Graham Greene, *Times Literary Supplement* (16 July 1938) 477.
15. Judith W. Hess, 'Genre films and the status quo', *Film Genre: Theory and Criticism*, edited by Barry K. Grant (London: Scarecrow Press, 1977) 61.
16. Louis Kronenberger, review of *Brighton Rock*, by Graham Greene, *New Yorker* (25 June 1938) 94.
17. Ibid.
18. Basil Davenport, 'Religious melodrama', review of *Brighton Rock*, by Graham Greene, *Saturday Review of Literature* (25 June 1938) 6.

19. Review of *Brighton Rock*, by Graham Greene, *New Republic* (6 July 1938) 260.
20. William Plomer, 'Pinkie and Rose', review of *Brighton Rock*, by Graham Greene, *The Spectator* (15 July 1938) 116.
21. Jane Spence Southron, 'The career of a gangster studied by Graham Greene', review of *Brighton Rock*, by Graham Greene, *New York Times Book Review* (26 June 1938) 6.
22. The year 1992 saw the publication of two essays that bucked this trend, one by investigating how *Brighton Rock* dismantles the generic structures it invokes, the other by historicizing the novel in light of the collapse of British power. See Brian Diemert, 'Ida Arnold and the detective story', *Twentieth Century Literature* (Winter 1992) 386–404; and Trevor L. Williams, 'History over theology: The case for Pinkie in Greene's *Brighton Rock*', *Studies in the Novel* (Spring 1992) 67–77.
23. Greene, *Brighton Rock* 243.
24. Evelyn Waugh, 'Felix Culpa?' review of *The Heart of the Matter*, by Graham Greene, *Commonweal* (16 July 1948) 322.
25. Sister Sheila Houle, 'The subjective theological vision of Graham Greene', *Renascence*, 23:1 (Autumn 1970) 12–13.
26. George Orwell, 'The sanctified sinner', review of *The Heart of the Matter*, by Graham Greene, *New Yorker* (17 July 1948) 68.
27. Quentin Falk, *Travels in Greeneland*, Revised and Updated 3rd Edition (London: Reynolds & Hearn, 2000) 47.
28. Ibid. 29. Falk gives the figure £10,000 for the film rights, although this is almost certainly wrong, perhaps a dollar denomination. Sherry gives the figure £3250. The Paramount contract in the Ransom Center at the University of Texas in Austin gives the sum as £2250, and it seems highly unlikely that the contract would have failed to stipulate a payment of £1000 for other services to be executed by Greene and/or additional rights to the property.
29. Catherine de la Roche, 'Cannes', *Sight and Sound* (December 1949) 25.

6. Greene and genre

1. Rabinowitz, *Before Reading* 35.
2. Falk, *Travels in Greeneland* 20–21.
3. Greene himself observed that the reason he attracted large audiences was that he did not write for a hypothetical audience composed solely of Catholics. 'Any author writing strictly for a Catholic audience would not reach a large public.' See Gene D. Philips, 'Graham Greene on the screen', *Conversations with Graham Greene*, edited by Henry J. Donaghy (Jackson: University Press of Mississippi, 1992) 78.
4. Rick Altman, 'A semantic/syntactic approach to film genre', *Film/Genre*, edited by Rick Altman (London: BFI Publishing, 1999) 218.
5. Ibid. 214.
6. Leavis, *Mass Civilization* 17.
7. Antonin Artaud, *The Theater and Its Double*, translated by Mary Caroline Richards (New York: Grove Press, 1958) 74.
8. Hess, *Film Genre* 60.

7. Strategic moves: genres, brands, authors and *The Third Man*

1. See Theodor Adorno, *The Culture Industry*, edited by J.M. Bernstein (London: Routledge, 2001) 185–86.
2. William Whitebait, review of *The Third Man*, directed by Carol Reed, *New Statesman and Nation* (10 September 1949) 272.
3. David O. Selznick, 'Notes from DOS on The Third Man', 5 October 1948, *David O. Selznick Collection*, Harry Ransom Center, University of Texas, Austin, 2733.7.
4. Rabinowitz, *Before Reading* 23–24.
5. Woodrow Wyatt, 'Parliament and film monopolists', *New Statesman and Nation* (10 January 1948) 24.
6. Ibid.
7. Selznick, 'Notes from DOS'.
8. See Letter from Yu Yung-His (Guozi Shudian Secretary) to Pearn, Pollinger & Higham, 11 April 1958, Laurence Pollinger General Files, Harry Ransom Center, University of Texas, Austin.
9. Woodrow Wyatt, 'Champagne for Hollywood', *New Statesman and Nation* (20 March 1948) 231.
10. Ibid.
11. Alexander Korda, 'Reply to Paul Rotha', *World Review* (December 1948) 56.
12. Graham Greene, review of *The Marriage of Corbal*, directed by Karl Grune and F. Brunn, *Mornings in the Dark*, edited by David Parkinson (Manchester: Carcanet, 1993) 107–08.
13. Graham Greene, 'Memories of a film critic', *Mornings in the Dark*, edited by David Parkinson (Manchester: Carcanet, 1993) 454–55.
14. Ibid. 454.
15. See Charles Ramirez Berg, 'The Third Man's Third Man: David O. Selznick's Contribution to *The Third Man*', *Library Chronicle of the University of Texas at Austin* (1986) 92–113.
16. This does not imply, of course, that critics writing after the fact have not attempted to transform the film into *Blood of a Poet*. Jim Gribble, for instance, has recently argued that the film attempts, in high modernist fashion, to allow 'the characters and events to speak for themselves, without mediation'. His argument would perhaps have been more convincing if Reed had decided to never move the camera, make a cut, use music, light his actors and sets and so on. See Jim Gribble, '*The Third Man*: Graham Greene and Carol Reed', *Literature/Film Quarterly* (1998) 235–39.
17. United States v. Paramount Pictures Inc., et al., 334 US 131 (3 May 1948).
18. See Patrick McGilligan, *Alfred Hitchcock: A Life in Darkness and Light* (West Sussex: John Wiley, 2003) 219–20.
19. See Thomas Schatz, 'The genius of the system', *Film Theory and Criticism*, 5th Edition, edited by Leo Braudy and Marshall Co-en (Oxford: Oxford University Press, 1999) 602–06.
20. See John Kenneth Galbraith, *Economics and the Public Purpose* (Middlesex: Penguin, 1973) 108–15.
21. Altman, *Film/Genre* 57.
22. Ibid. 78, 105.

23. See Richard Griffith, 'Where are the dollars? Part Two', *Sight and Sound* (December 1949) 33.
24. Original US trailer, *The Third Man*, directed by Carol Reed, DVD supplement (Criterion Collection, 2000).
25. Whitebait, review of *The Third Man* 42.
26. Cyril Ray, review of *The Third Man*, directed by Carol Reed, *Spectator* (9 September 1949) 272.
27. Anthony Hopkins, review of *The Third Man*, directed by Carol Reed, *Sight and Sound* (December 1949) 23.
28. Charles Drazin, *In Search of The Third Man* (London: Methuen, 2000) 107.
29. Ibid. 101.
30. David O. Selznick, *Memo From David O. Selznick*, edited by Rudy Behlmer (New York: Macmillan, 1973) 391.
31. Drazin, *In Search of The Third Man* 106.
32. Altman, *Film/Genre* 120.
33. *The Third Man*, produced by Lux Radio Theater, *The Third Man*, directed by Carol Reed, DVD supplement (Criterion Collection, 2000).
34. Drazin, *In Search of The Third Man* 138. Laurence Pollinger's files at the Ransom Center in Austin show that Harry Alan Towers produced the programs for the BBC, which means that the idea for the series probably did not originate with the BBC as Drazin's account suggests.
35. Orson Welles, 'A ticket to Tangier', *The Third Man*, directed by Carol Reed, DVD Supplement (Criterion Collection, 2000).
36. Drazin, *In Search of The Third Man* 142.
37. David Thomson, *New Biographical Dictionary of Film*, 4th Edition (London: Little, Brown, 2003) 722. For a more sympathetic account of Welles's charisma, see Gribble, *Literature/Film Quarterly* 238–39.
38. Foucault, *The Critical Tradition* 897.
39. For a wealth of Greene/Hitchcock correspondences see Neil Sinyard, *Filming Literature* (London: Croom Helm, 1986) 109–10.
40. Francois Truffaut, *Hitchcock* (New York: Simon and Schuster, 1984) 20.
41. Drazin, *In Search of The Third Man* 141.
42. Letter from Graham Greene to David Higham, 15 February 1951, Laurence Pollinger General Files, Harry Ransom Center, University of Texas, Austin.
43. Letter from Harry Alan Towers to Graham Greene, 19 April 1951, Laurence Pollinger General Files, Harry Ransom Center, University of Texas, Austin.
44. Letter from David Higham to Graham Greene, 12 February 1953, Laurence Pollinger General Files, Harry Ransom Center, University of Texas, Austin.
45. Letter from Jean Leroy to Graham Greene, 11 July 1958, Laurence Pollinger General Files, Harry Ransom Center, University of Texas, Austin.
46. Letter from B. Torbica to David Higham, 11 August 1952, Laurence Pollinger General Files, Harry Ransom Center, University of Texas, Austin.
47. Letter from Jean M. Tsamados to David Higham, 4 July 1953, Laurence Pollinger General Files, Harry Ransom Center, University of Texas, Austin.
48. Letter from Graham Greene to David Higham, 10 July 1953, Laurence Pollinger General Files, Harry Ransom Center, University of Texas, Austin.
49. Letter from David Higham to Graham Greene, 5 January 1955, Laurence Pollinger General Files, Harry Ransom Center, University of Texas, Austin.

50. See Kenneth O. Morgan, *The People's Peace* (Oxford: Oxford University Press, 1992) 124. The average weekly earning for an adult male was £8.30 in 1951, the year Greene sold his permission to use the character Lime to Harry Alan Towers for £2000 and a percentage of the profits.
51. Graham Greene, preface, 'The Third Man', *The Third Man and The Fallen Idol* (Middlesex: Penguin, 1977) 10.
52. Norman Sherry, *The Life of Graham Greene Volume Two* (London: Jonathan Cape, 1994) 241.
53. Graham Greene, preface, 'The Fallen Idol', *The Third Man and The Fallen Idol* (Middlesex: Penguin, 1977) 123.

8. Amateurs and professionals, auteurs and intellectuals

1. See W.J. West, *The Quest for Graham Greene* (London: Phoenix, 1997) 133, 142.
2. Walter Wanger, 'Donald Duck and diplomacy', *Public Opinion Quarterly* (Fall 1950) 451.
3. Ibid. 444.
4. Richard Strout, 'Marshall Plan Report', *New Statesman and Nation* (31 January 1948) 90.
5. Selznick, 'Notes from DOS'.
6. Mary McCarthy, 'Graham Greene and the intelligentsia', *Partisan Review* (Spring 1944) 228–29.
7. See Wilson Harris, 'Tainted histories', *Sight and Sound* (February 1992) 31.
8. Graham Greene, *The Third Man* (London: Faber and Faber, 1988) 34.
9. Ibid. 39.
10. Transcribed in Drazin, *In Search of The Third Man* 123.
11. Greene, *The Third Man* 26.
12. Ibid. 74.
13. Ibid. 26.
14. Hess, *Film Genre* 57.
15. Drazin, *In Search of The Third Man* 23.
16. Ray, review of *The Third Man* 326.
17. Graham Greene, review of *Secret Agent*, directed by Alfred Hitchcock, *Mornings in the Dark*, edited by David Parkinson (Manchester: Carcanet, 1998) 102.
18. Greene, 'Memories' 454.
19. Review of *The Third Man*, directed by Carol Reed, *The Guardian* (3 September 1949).
20. Ibid.
21. Whitebait, review of *The Third Man* 272.
22. *The Guardian* (3 September 1949).
23. Glenn K.S. Man, '*The Third Man*: Pulp fiction and art film', *Literature/Film Quarterly*, 21:3 (1993) 171.
24. Andrew Sarris, 'Notes on the auteur theory in 1962', *Film Theory and Criticism*, 5th Edition, edited by Leo Braudy and Marshall Cohen (Oxford: Oxford University Press, 1999) 516–17.

25. See Susan Hayward, *Cinema Studies: The Key Concepts*, 2nd Edition (London: Routledge, 2000) 19–27.
26. From a practical standpoint the terms 'author' and 'auteur' are used synonymously. When I refer to Greene as an auteur (rather than as an author) I do so in order to draw attention both to auteurism's status as a historical discourse and to the historical factors underpinning its application to Greene's work.
27. Jack Edmund Nolan, 'Graham Greene's films', *Literature/Film Quarterly* (Fall 1974) 306–07.
28. Greene, *The Third Man/The Fallen Idol* 106.
29. Ibid. 104.
30. Quoted in Carey, *Intellectuals and the Masses* 185.
31. Whitebait, review of *The Third Man* 272.

9. Auteurism and the study of Greene

1. For an overview of British auteurism see Eric Hedling, 'Lindsay Anderson: *Sequence* and the rise of auteurism in Britain', *British Cinema of the 1950s: A Celebration*, edited by Ian MacKillop and Neil Sinyard (Manchester: Manchester University Press, 2003) 23–31.
2. See Galbraith, *Economics and the Public Purpose* 292–303.
3. 'Shall we have airplanes?', *Fortune* (January 1948) 77. [Emphasis in original]
4. John Kenneth Galbraith, *The New Industrial State* (Middlesex: Penguin, 1967) 85–86.
5. Alan Sinfield, *Literature, Politics and Culture in Postwar Britain* (Oxford: Blackwell, 1989) 54–55. See also: Francis Mulhern, *The Moment of Scrutiny* (London: New Left Books, 1979).
6. Culler, *The Pursuit of Signs* 147.
7. Sarris, *Film Theory and Criticism* 517.
8. F.R. Leavis, 'From *The Great Tradition*' in Richter 601.
9. Sarris, *Film Theory and Criticism* 517.
10. Jorge Luis Borges, 'Tlön, Uqbar, Orbius Tertius', *Collected Fictions*, translated by Andrew Hurley (New York: Penguin, 1998) 77.
11. See Henri Bergson, 'Laughter', *Comedy*, edited by Wylie Sypher (New York: Doubleday, 1956) 161–90; Robert Brustein, 'Reflections on horror movies', *Partisan Review* (Spring 1958) 288–96; Edward Connor, 'The mystery film', *Films in Review* (March 1954) 120–23; David Fisher, 'The angel, the devil, and the space traveler', *Sight and Sound* (January–March 1954) 155–57; Harry A. Grace, 'A taxonomy of American crime film themes', *Journal of Social Psychology* (August 1955) 129–36; Richard Hodgens, 'A brief and tragical history of the science fiction film', *Film Quarterly* (Winter 1959) 30–39; Siegfried Kracauer, 'Silent film comedy', *Sight and Sound* (August–September 1951) 31–32; David Robinson, 'Spectacle', *Sight and Sound* (Summer 1955) 22–27, 55–56.
12. Robert Warshow, 'Movie chronicle: *The Westerner*', *Film Theory and Criticism*, 5th Edition, edited by Leo Braudy and Marshall Co-en (Oxford: Oxford University Press, 1999) 654.
13. David Thomson, *America in the Dark* (London: Hutchinson, 1977) 89.

232   *Notes*

14. Thomson, *New Biographical Dictionary* 400.
15. William Goldman, *Adventures in the Screen Trade* (London: Abacus, 1983) 105.
16. See Selznick, 'Notes from DOS'. Selznick includes a letter from Joseph Breen in his memo to Korda and Reed. Breen specifically objects to the script's treatment of Paine's death and impresses upon Selznick the necessity of making sure that 'At no time must be there any showing of scenes of law-enforcing officers dying at the hands of criminals.'
17. Thomas, *Underground* xiv, 3.
18. Norman Sherry, *The Life of Graham Greene, Volume Three* 382.
19. Atkins, *Graham Greene* 194.
20. Graham Greene, 'Rider Haggard's secret', review of *The Cloak that I Left*, by Lilias Rider Haggard, *Collected Essays* (London: Vintage, 1999) 158.
21. Graham Greene, 'Journey into success', review of *A.E.W. Mason*, by Roger Lancelyn Green, *Collected Essays* (London: Vintage, 1999)161.
22. Graham Greene, *The End of the Affair* (New York: Viking, 1951) 3.
23. Greene, 'Journey' 164–65.
24. Allott and Farris, *The Art of Graham Greene* 15.
25. Ibid. 19.
26. Ibid. 100.
27. Frances Wyndham, *Graham Greene* (London: Longmans, 1955) 7.
28. Ibid. 10.
29. Ibid. 21.
30. Ibid. 28. [Emphasis mine]
31. Atkins, *Graham Greene* 11.
32. Ibid. 235.
33. Ibid. 166.
34. Quoted in Atkins, *Graham Greene* 168.
35. Atkins, *Graham Greene* vii.
36. Ibid. viii.
37. Malamet, *World Remade* 1.

10. *Our Man in Havana* and auteurism

1. Graham Greene, *Our Man in Havana* (London: Penguin, 1958) 59.
2. Ibid. 79.
3. Ibid. 55.
4. Ibid. 101. [Emphasis mine]
5. Greene, *Our Man* 102.
6. Ibid. 80–81.
7. James M. Cain, 'Out of a need for money', review of *Our Man in Havana*, by Graham Greene, *New York Times* (26 October 1958) 5.
8. Greene, *Our Man* 47.
9. Ibid. 48.
10. Ibid. 146.
11. Ibid. 142.
12. Ibid. 141.
13. Ibid. 142.
14. Shapiro, *Essays in Greene* 92.

15. Greene, *Our Man* 33.
16. Ibid. 44.
17. Charles Rolo, review of *Our Man in Havana*, by Graham Greene, *The Atlantic Monthly* (November 1958) 175.
18. Bruce Bawer, 'Graham Greene: The politics', *The New Criterion* (November 1989) 41.
19. Robert Hatch, review of *Our Man in Havana*, directed by Carol Reed, *The Nation* (13 February 1960) 156.
20. Marc Silverstein, 'After the fall: The world of Graham Greene's thrillers', *Novel: A Forum on Fiction* (Fall 1988) 44.
21. James Yaffe, 'Of spies and lies', review of *Our Man in Havana*, by Graham Greene, *Saturday Review* (15 November 1958) 19.
22. Ibid.
23. See A.J. Liebling, 'A talkative something-or-other', review of *The Quiet American*, by Graham Greene, *New Yorker* (7 April 1956) 148–54.
24. Diane Kunz, *The Economic Diplomacy of the Suez Crisis* (London: University of North Carolina Press, 1991) 189.
25. 'Back to anarchy', *New Statesman* (10 November 1956) 576.
26. During the Formosa standoff the *New Statesman* offered a sound analysis of the fallout from Mao's takeover in 'The Civil War in Washington' (13 September 1958) 340–41.
27. See Gabriel Kolko, *The Politics of War* (New York: Pantheon, 1990) 275–79, 361–64.
28. Greene, *Ways of Escape* 241.
29. Jean-Paul Sartre, *On Cuba* (New York: Ballantine, 1961) 27–29.
30. Greene, *Ways of Escape* 151.
31. 'From Cold War to Cold Peace', *Business Week* (12 February 1949) 19.
32. George Kennan, *American Diplomacy, 1900–1950* (Chicago: University of Chicago Press, 1951) 102–03.
33. Pryce-Jones, 'Graham Cracker' 29–30.
34. Price, review of *The Honorary Consul* 1.

11. Greene and the polemics of canonical reading

1. Davis, *Studies in the Novel* 546.
2. See Denis Donoghue, 'A visit to Greeneland', review of *The Honorary Consul*, by Graham Greene, *Commonweal* (30 November 1973) 241. Donoghue remarks: 'Surely we cannot be reading anything but the new Graham Greene, already a Book-of-the-Month-Club selection and a godsend for possessors of a Christmas book-token.'
3. Davis, *Studies in the Novel* 531.
4. Friedman, 'The status of Greene studies' 37.
5. Harold Bloom, *The Western Canon* (London: Macmillan, 1995) 20.
6. See Max Allan Collins, 'Introduction', *The Mickey Spillane Collection Volume One*, by Mickey Spillane (New York: New American Library, 2001) vii–xii.
7. Mary Warner, 'Faith born of anguish', *Perceptions of Religious Faith in the Work of Graham Greene*, edited by Wm. Thomas Hill (Oxford: Peter Lang) 312.

8. Bloom, *The Western Canon* 527. Ironically, of course, these are also the six branches of contemporary thought that show little or no interest in Greene.
9. See Rabinowitz, *Before Reading* 209–31.
10. For a discussion of the political uses of this strategy, see Lippmann, *Public Opinion*.
11. Bloom, *The Western Canon* 3.
12. George Steiner, 'Burnt-out case', review of *Lord Rochester's Monkey*, by Graham Greene, *New Yorker* (28 October 1974) 185.
13. V.S. Pritchett, 'Rogue poet', review of *Lord Rochester's Monkey*, by Graham Greene, *New York Review of Books* (3 October 1974) 17.
14. Grahame Smith, *The Achievement of Graham Greene* (Sussex: Harvester Press, 1986) 76.
15. See Rabinowitz, *Before Reading* 141–69.
16. Wilfrid Sheed, 'Racing the clock with Greene and Pritchett', review of *Travels With My Aunt*, by Graham Greene, *Atlantic* (April 1970) 111.
17. Paulo Freire, *Pedagogy of the Oppressed* (New York: Continuum, 1996) 53.
18. Frank McConnell, 'Everything banished but love', review of *Dr. Fischer of Geneva*, by Graham Greene, *Commonweal* (20 June 1980) 376.
19. Ibid.
20. Graham Greene, *Loser Takes All* (Middlesex: Penguin, 1977) v.
21. Greene, *Affair* 3.
22. See 'Trials and tribulations', *Time* (12 February 1952). http://www.time.com.
23. See Bloom, *The Western Canon* 16.
24. Peter Biskind documents Weinstein's reluctance to release Noyce's film in the wake of the 9/11 attack in his study *Down and Dirty Pictures* (London: Bloomsbury, 2004) 463–64.

12. Depopulating the common: reading *The End of the Affair*

1. Michael Shelden, *Graham Greene: The Man Within* (London: Minerva, 1994) 374.
2. Ibid. 380.
3. Ibid. 377.
4. Fremantle, 'Pursuit' 11.
5. Ibid.
6. Ibid.
7. Greene, *Affair* 240.
8. Fremantle, 'Pursuit' 11.
9. A.A. DeVitis, *Graham Greene*, Revised Edition (Boston: Twayne Publishers, 1986) 95.
10. Ibid. 96.
11. Ibid. 105.
12. Charles Rolo, review of *The End of the Affair*, by Graham Greene, *Atlantic* (November 1951) 88.
13. Ibid.
14. Rolo, review of *Our Man in Havana* 176.
15. Ibid.
16. See Armstrong, review of *Stamboul Train* 673.
17. Eagleton, *Literary Theory* 50.

18. Simon Harcourt-Smith, 'The stature of Rossellini', *Sight and Sound* (April 1950) 86.
19. Graham Greene, *The Lawless Roads* (London: Vintage, 2002) 14.
20. Atkins, *Graham Greene* 195.
21. Ibid. 196.
22. Ibid.
23. George Mayberry, 'Mr. Greene's intense art', review of *The End of the Affair*, by Graham Greene, *New York Times* (28 October 1951) 5.
24. Michael Gorra, 'On *The End of the Affair*', *Southwest Review* (Winter 2004) 112.
25. Greene, *Affair* 22.
26. Ibid. 5.
27. Ibid. 24.
28. Ibid. 57.
29. See Rabinowitz, *Before Reading* 195–208.
30. Greene, *Affair* 102.
31. Ibid. 151.
32. Ibid. 39.
33. Ibid. 144.
34. Ibid. 8.
35. Ibid. 201.
36. Ibid. 171.
37. Gorra, 'On *The End of the Affair*' 121.
38. Harold Bloom, *The American Religion* (New York: Simon and Schuster, 1992) 37.
39. Greene, *Affair* 3.
40. Ibid. 170.
41. Ibid. 85.
42. Herbert Haber, 'The end of the Catholic cycle', *Graham Greene: Some Critical Considerations*, edited by Robert O. Evans (Louisville: University Kentucky Press, 1963) 148.
43. Ibid. 138.
44. Ibid. 149.
45. Ibid. 140–41.
46. Ibid. 129.

13. Liberal commitment: reading *The Quiet American*

1. See Cryer, 'Greene at 100' B2.
2. Sherry, *Volume Three* 746.
3. DeVitis, 'Religious Aspects' 114.
4. Philip Stratford, *Faith and Fiction* (London: University of Notre Dame Press, 1967) 310.
5. For a comprehensive analysis of the psychological ramifications of the Reformation, see Erich Fromm, *The Fear of Freedom* (London: Routledge, 2001) 33–88.
6. Miriam Allott, 'The moral situation in *The Quiet American*', *Graham Greene: Some Critical Considerations*, edited by Robert O. Evans (Louisville: University of Kentucky Press, 1963) 196.

7. Ibid.
8. Ibid. 205.
9. Graham Greene, *The Quiet American* (London: Vintage, 2001) 189.
10. Wm. Thomas Hill, 'Introduction', *Perceptions of Religious Faith in the Work of Graham Greene*, edited by Wm. Thomas Hill (Oxford: Peter Lang, 2002) 17.
11. Greene, *Quiet American* 28.
12. Ibid. 21.
13. Ibid. 41.
14. Ibid. 174.
15. Allott, 'Moral situation' 206.
16. Greene, *Quiet American* 114.
17. Ibid. 22.
18. Atkins, *Graham Greene* 229.
19. Ibid. 236.
20. Charles Rolo, review of *The Quiet American*, by Graham Greene, *Atlantic* (April 1956) 83.
21. Greene, *Quiet American* 27.
22. Ibid.
23. For examples of the use of jealousy as a reasonable justification for murder, see Ian Fleming, *Casino Royale* (London: Penguin, 2002) or Mickey Spillane, *The Mike Hammer Collection, Volume One* (New York: Penguin, 2001).
24. Greene, *Quiet American* 77.
25. Ibid. 29.
26. Ibid. 77.
27. Ibid. 80.
28. Ibid. 81.
29. Liebling, 'A talkative something-or-other' 148.
30. DeVitis, 'Religious Aspects' 112.
31. Barry Hillenbrand, 'What's missing in this picture?' review of *The Quiet American*, directed by Philip Noyce, *Commonweal* (28 February 2003) 21.
32. Greene, *Quiet American* 51.
33. Ibid. 52.
34. Ibid. 53.
35. Ibid.
36. Anthony Swofford, 'The sniper's tale', *Guardian Unlimited* (15 March 2003) 27 October 2004. http://books.guardian.co.uk/print/0,3858,4624222-101750,00.html.
37. DeVitis, 'Religious Aspects' 114.
38. Greene, *Quiet American* 162.
39. Ibid. 63.
40. Terry Eagleton, *The Illusions of Postmodernism* (Oxford: Blackwell, 1996) 77.

14. Appropriating Greene: re-reading *The Quiet American* and *The End of the Affair*

1. Davis, *Studies in the Novel* 530.
2. See Terry Eagleton, *After Theory* (London: Penguin, 2004) 80.
3. Herbert Marcuse, *One Dimensional Man* (London: Abacus, 1972) 63.

4. Davis, *Studies in the Novel* 531.
5. Ibid. 545.
6. Ibid.
7. Eagleton, *Illusions* 40.
8. Robbie Millen, 'From Greene to red and back', *Times* (31 May 2003) Weekend, 2.
9. Ibid.
10. Ibid.
11. Greene, *Quiet American* 147.
12. Ibid. 95.
13. Alexander Nicoll, 'Vietnam: Guide for hardy business people', *Financial Times* (14 November 1991) Vietnam supplement: 4.
14. Ibid.
15. Galbraith, *Industrial State* 106.
16. J.D.F. Jones, 'The romance of war', *Financial Times* (23 September 1995) Books Section: vii.
17. Sandy Gall, 'Back to Vietnam and its poignant memories', *Financial Times* (17 May 1997) Travel Section: 10.
18. Ibid.
19. Ibid.
20. Uwe Siemon-Netto, 'Troubling *Quiet American*', *United Press International* (25 February 2003) 1008055w5494.
21. Chomsky and Herman, *Manufacturing Consent* 184.
22. Graham Lord, 'The return of the quiet American', *Times* (20 August 1995) 12.
23. Ibid.
24. Colin Donald, 'Fighting a way through Vietnam's peace', review of *A Wavering Grace*, by Gavin Young, *The Scotsman* (26 April 1997) 15.
25. Ibid.
26. Colin Donald, 'Vietnam's revolution goes up in smoke', *The Scotsman* (12 February 1997) 7.
27. Ibid.
28. Mark Hodson, 'Old description still fit Saigon', *Financial Times* (18 July 1992) Travel: vii.
29. Ibid.
30. Ibid.
31. David Gritten, 'The film that scared a studio', *Daily Telegraph* (26 November 2002) 23.
32. Geoffrey Jacques, review of *The Quiet American*, directed by Philip Noyce, *Cineaste* (Summer 2003) 45.
33. Anthony Lane, 'Love and war', review of *The Quiet American*, directed by Philip Noyce, *New Yorker* (2 December 2002) 117.
34. Ray Connolly, 'How I'll miss Saigon', *Daily Mail* (19 June 2004) First Edition: 54.
35. See Mark Steyn, 'They'll have to think again about *The Quiet American*', review of *The Quiet American*, directed by Philip Noyce, *Daily Telegraph* (1 December 2002) 23.
36. Stanley Kauffmann, 'This side of paradise', review of *The End of the Affair*, directed by Neil Jordan, *New Republic* (27 December 1999) 24.
37. Ibid.

38. Greene, *Affair* 111.
39. See Shelden, *Man Within* 513.
40. Richard Alleva, 'Graham Greene lite', review of *The End of the Affair*, directed by Neil Jordan, *Commonweal* (28 January 2000) 18.
41. Ibid.
42. Owen Gleiberman, 'Adulterated romance', review of *The End of the Affair*, directed by Neil Jordan, *Entertainment Weekly* (10 December 1999) 80.
43. Peter Bradshaw, 'An unholy communion', review of *The End of the Affair*, directed by Neil Jordan, *Guardian* (11 February 2000) 18 August 2004. http://film.guardian.co.uk/print/0,3858,3961933-3718,00.html.
44. Neil McDonald, 'Book to film', *Quadrant* (May 2000) 45.
45. Kauffmann, 'This side' 24.
46. Fr. Robert E. Lauder, 'A film at last does justice to Graham Greene's vision', review of *The End of the Affair*, directed by Neil Jordan, *National Catholic Reporter* (14 April 2000) 21.
47. Ibid.
48. Ibid.
49. Philip French, 'Bitter and twisting', review of *The End of the Affair*, directed by Neil Jordan, *Observer* (13 February 2000) 10.
50. Kauffmann, 'This side' 24.
51. French, 'Bitter' 10.

Conclusion: The problem of a 'better case'

1. McCarthy, 'Graham Greene and the intelligentsia' 229.
2. Richard W. Nolan, 'The spy fiction of John le Carré', *Clues* (Fall/Winter 1980) 54. See also John Nelson, 'International relations', review of *The Spy Novels of John Le Carré*, by Myron J. Aronoff, *The American Political Science Review* (March 2001) 249–50; and William M. Chace, 'Spies and God's spies: Greene's espionage fiction', *Graham Greene: A Revaluation*, edited by Jeffrey Myers (New York: St Martin's Press, 1990) 156–80. The former refers to Le Carré as Greene's 'heir', the latter as 'Greene's most successful beneficiary'.
3. Nolan, *Clues* 68.
4. Bloom, *The Western Canon* 7.
5. Ibid. 7–8.
6. See Althusser, *Lenin and Philosophy* 226.
7. Terry Eagleton, *Marxism and Literary Criticism* (Berkeley: University of California Press, 1976) 68–69.
8. See Rabinowitz, *Before Reading* 22–32.
9. Eagleton, *Marxism* 35.
10. Friedman, 'The status of Greene studies' 37. It is worth remarking, however, that while Greene's novels have failed to attract much historicist comment, the short stories—particularly 'The Destructors'—fared slightly better, particularly during the 1970s and early 1980s as the cultural studies project crystallized in Birmingham and elsewhere. See A.R. Coulthard, 'Graham Greene's "The hint of an explanation": A reinterpretation', *Studies in Short Fiction* (Fall 1971) 601–05; Hans Feldmann, 'The idea of history in Graham Greene's "The Destructors"', *Studies in Short Fiction* (Summer 1982) 241–45;

Jesse F. McCartney, 'Politics in Graham Greene's "The Destructors"', *Southern Humanities Review* (Winter 1978) 31–41.

11. See Gerard Genette, *Narrative Discourse*, translated by Jane E. Lewin (Ithaca: Cornell University Press, 1980).
12. Nolan, *Clues* 69. See also: Bruce Merry, *Anatomy of the Spy Thriller* (Dublin: Gill and Macmillan, 1977).
13. See Rabinowitz, *Before Reading* 141–69.
14. 'The Guardian Top 40', *Guardian Review* (25 June 2005) 38.
15. Richards, *Principles* 31.

Index